Epic Urban Adventure by a New Star of Fantasy

DRAW ONE IN THE DARK

by Sarah A. Hoyt

Every one of us has a beast inside. But for Kyrie Smith, the beast is no metaphor. Thrust into an ever-changing world of shifters, where shape-shifting dragons, giant cats and other beasts wage a secret war behind humanity's back, Kyrie tries to control her inner animal and remain human as best she can....

"Analytically, it's a tour de force: logical, built from assumptions, with no contradictions, which is astonishing given the subject matter. It's also gripping enough that I finished it in one day."

Jerry Pournelle

1-4165-2092-9 • $25.00

Available in boo
Or order online at our s
www.b

D0009885

DID YOU KNOW YOU CAN DO ALL THESE THINGS AT THE

BAEN BOOKS WEBSITE ?

* Read free sample chapters of books

* See what new books are upcoming

* Read entire Baen Books for free

* Check out your favorite author's titles

* Catch up on the latest Baen news & author events

* Buy any Baen book

* Read interviews with authors and artists

* Buy almost any Baen book as an e-book individually or an entire month at a time

* Find a list of titles suitable for young adults

* Communicate with some of the coolest fans in science fiction & some of the best minds on the planet

Visit us at www.baen.com

O YE OF LITTLE FAITH

The shuttle was decelerating at four hundred gravities, headed for the narrow slot left at the opening. The plug had been moved into position to close while they were gone and there was only a two hundred meter gap left.

"Tell me you can hit that," Hartwell said.

"I can hit that," Dana said.

"And by hit I mean miss the big chunks of metal," Hartwell said.

"I'm going to miss the big chunks of metal," Dana said.

"Thirty-Three," Paris said. *"Abort, abort, abort. Horvath emergence. Door is closing."*

"Oh, bloody hell," Hartwell said.

"Paris," Dana said, coolly. "I don't have enough burn to abort." The door was visibly closing as the tugs went to full power. "It's either shoot the gap or impact."

"Roger," Paris said, voice turning metallic. *"Understood. Insufficient time to make the gap."*

"Do I have permission to try?" Dana asked.

"Permission . . . granted," the metallic voice said.

"We've got incoming Horvath missiles," Hartwell said, cool again. "They're not going to hold the door open for us."

"Not a problem," Dana said, cutting power.

"What are you doing?" Hartwell asked, too calmly.

"I've got seven kilometers to brake on the inside," Dana said. "And about thirty seconds to make it through the gap. Which is a kilometer and a half *long. You* do the math. I'm doing this by the seat of my pants."

"My math brain just went to bed and pulled the cover over his head," Hartwell said. "I don't think we're going to make it."

"O ye of little faith," Dana said.

CITADEL

※

JOHN RINGO

CITADEL

Copyright © 2011 by John Ringo

A Baen Book

Baen Publishing Enterprises
P.O. Box 1403
Riverdale, NY 10471
www.baen.com

ISBN: 978-1-4516-3757-1

Cover art by Kurt Miller

First Baen paperback printing, November 2011

Library of Congress Control Number: 2010042091

Distributed by Simon & Schuster
1230 Avenue of the Americas
New York, NY 10020

Pages by Joy Freeman (www.pagesbyjoy.com)
Printed in the United States of America

ACKNOWLEDGEMENTS

I am NOT a physicist. Nor an astronomer nor a mathematician nor, indeed, much of a biologist. Assuredly not a rocket scientist. I'm one of those people who uses the word "integral" only and always to mean "central to some subject." You can get me to cringe by saying the word "polynomial."

I took physics, I took calculus, I took astronomy. (And, yes, passed all three.) That's not the same thing. Like Barack Obama on the subject of economics (which I can talk about much better than physics) the information was stored just long enough to pass the course and then forgotten.

Obviously, this has been something of a trial while writing this series. In the Vorpal Blade series I have the luxury of simply tossing that on my coauthor, Dr. Travis Taylor. Alas, Travis got a real job and he's been busy. So I had to find other people to help.

As with *Live Free or Die*, I'd like to thank Bullet and Belinda (Gibby) Gibson for their assistance not only with the math but also with general proofreading. However, the task being somewhat more complex this time others got involved. I'd like to thank Stephanie

Osborn, who *is* an astronomer, as well as "The Croatian Mafia," Ivan Knezevic and Robert Bosnjak. The three of them have gotten me back to the point I could get C– in college-level Newtonian physics.

In addition, when it got *really* complicated, I'd like to thank Dr. Les Johnson, Deputy Manager NASA Advanced Concepts Office, Dr. Larry Kos, also of NASA and Dr. Charles L. John, ditto. I often poke fun at NASA but the reality is that the recent decisions of the Administration in that area have me fuming.

Thank you all for your help and support.

My eyes are closed I feel you're far away
Far beyond that shining star
I know you'll find what you've been fighting for
Far beyond that shining star

"Glory to the Brave"
—Hammerfall

ONE

"ARRIVING ASSIGNED PERSONNEL FOLLOW THE YELLOW LINE!" the M1C blared. "UNAS-SIGNED PERSONNEL FOLLOW THE GREEN LINE TO ASSIGNMENT. PERMANENT PARTY FOLLOW THE BLUE LINE! ARRIVING ASSIGNED PERSONNEL FOLLOW THE YELLOW LINE...!"

"Are we assigned or unassigned?" Spaceman Apprentice Jack Yin said, looking around the echoing shuttle bay. The *Columbia II* shuttles held sixty people, mixed about equally between military and civilian. But if any of them were willing to give directions to some newbie recruits it wasn't evident and none of the threesome was about to ask.

"Do I *look* like I know?" SA Sarin Chap said, shrugging his A bag up on his shoulder.

"The lowest of the low have to be unassigned," Engineering Apprentice Dana Parker said. "And since we are the lowest of the low, we will go to unassigned."

"And if we're wrong?" Sarin asked, gulping.

"Then we will get chewed out," Dana said. "And told where to go."

1

"Heh," Jack said, grinning. "You know, there's more than one way to—"

"Just walk, Jack," Dana said.

Her earliest clear memory was walking. Walking and fire.

She sort of had a vague memory of being somewhere with her mom and dad. She was pretty sure, thinking about it later, that it was a mall. And that was about the only real memory she had of her dad. The first *clear* memory was the walking. And the fire. And the smell of things that weren't made to burn. And a sky that was a strange red. Like it should be dark but it was red like a banked fire. And ash. Thin. Light. Constant.

She sort of remembered the buses. And staying places she wasn't used to. Hotels. Tents. She remembered telling her mom it was okay to cry. Which didn't make any sense 'cause her mom was *always* crying.

Then they were at Uncle Don and Aunt Marge's farm.

And then her mom "went away" too. That was how they phrased it to a three-year-old orphan from the L.A. bombing. That they went away, like they were taking a trip to Maui for a while or something. They had three nearly grown kids of their own and a sister who had carefully hung herself where only her sister would find her, and a new three-year-old to raise and they just said "Your mom had to go away. You're going to be staying with us for a while."

The door had a big sign that read "Unassigned Receiving." Dana pushed it open and negotiated her seabag through the door. Jack didn't even think about trying to give her a hand. He knew better by now.

"Engineering Apprentice Parker," Dana said. "With a party of two, I guess."

The woman behind the desk was a civilian, blond and, unsurprisingly, pregnant. Dana was even more blond, had had full-blown Johannsen's until she got gene-scrubbed by the Navy doctors, and managed to keep from getting belly-full in high school by determination and a lot of cold showers.

"Transmit your orders," the civvie said, nibbling on a cracker. She considered her screen and sighed. "You're *assigned*."

"Told you," Sarin said.

"Go down the corridor to the hatch that says Assigned Personnel," the woman said, pointing to the door.

"Thank you," Dana said.

Jack, by dint of being barely able to squeeze into the small compartment, was by the door. He yanked it open and squeezed more so Sarin and Dana could get out.

"If this thing is so huge," Sarin said. "Why the hell is everything so squeezed?"

The corridors were narrow. They had to hug the bulkhead so a harassed looking PO could sidle by.

"Do I look like I know?" Dana said, opening the door to Assigned Personnel.

This compartment was larger and included nicely uncomfortable looking chairs for those unfortunate enough to have to wait.

There was no line.

"Engineering Apprentice Parker," Dana repeated. "With a party of two."

"Orders?" the PO behind the desk said, then contemplated his screen. "One-Forty-Second Boat Squadron.

Take the purple line. That leads to the One-Forty-Second offices."

"Aye, aye, PO," Dana said, turning around. "Jack? You're in my way."

"Sorry," Jack said, stepping aside.

They called him "Gentle Ben" from the old TV show. As blond as Dana, and therefore a carrier for Johannsen's before he got scrubbed, he was about as big as a grizzly and, except when you got enough beer in him, about as gentle as a lamb. Unfortunately, when you *did* get enough beer in him, it turned out he had a mean streak a mile wide. That also showed up, fortunately, when friends needed a hand. Dana could generally hold her own with difficulties, but Jack was useful to have around.

The three had been at separate A schools that were co-located at McKinley Base. They had run into each other from time to time, mostly in the EM club and the combined mess. They weren't the only guys who got to following the short blond engineering apprentice around sniffing like bloodhounds. But they were a couple of the nicer ones, so Dana was just as glad they'd been scheduled to ship out together.

McKinley was just about the largest Navy base in the U.S. after the loss of Diego, Jax and Norfolk. A collection of rapidly growing prefabricated, prestressed, dug-in concrete buildings, it was located about fifty miles outside Wichita, Kansas, in what had once been a dense-pack nuclear missile base. The *second* largest Navy base in the U.S. was outside of Minot, North Dakota. Every base anywhere *close* to a city, including Kings Bay, Bremerton, Pearl and Great Lakes, was either closed or in the process. The "wet" navy had squeezed down to a collection of fast frigates, most of which were based either overseas or at Key West. There was talk of calling it the "Sea Guard" or something.

Dana didn't really care. The only Navy that mattered to her was the one that kept more rocks from falling. The one that might, someday, get her some payback for a mom and dad who had to go away.

The purple line seemed to go on for freaking *ever*. She didn't have trouble with carrying her A bag—it wasn't much heavier than a bale of hay—but it seemed like a mile of up and down and sideways until they finally got to a corridor with a big sign over the hatch reading *"Welcome to Myrmidon Country."*

"Finally," Sarin said, shifting his A bag.

Sarin was not much taller than Dana, with black hair and a fading but clearly once severe case of acne. The way that he drove a plant, Dana had asked him why he wasn't in IT or something.

"I deliberately failed the exam," he'd said. *"I spent five years working for my brother running cable. I'm about sick of it."*

The line continued on for a while but you could tell they were finally in Myrmidon country. Most of the personnel were Navy, for one thing, and most of them were wearing flight suits.

Finally the line terminated in a hatch, and it was a *real* hatch, that read "142nd Receiving." Someone had taped up a hand-lettered sign under it that read *"Abandon All Hope, ye who enter here."*

"Cheery," Sarin said.

"Yeah," Dana said, cycling the hatch. It didn't open.

"Who dares approach the gates?" The voice was a "com" in her plants. The caller ID was blocked.

The first time she got a plant com it was unnerving. The voice sounded like it was in your head but a "real" voice at the same time. Sort of like telepathy. On the other hand, it made communication over distance easier than radio since hyperwave was faster than light.

Glatun implant technology was still rare and expensive. Mostly it was being used by the U.S. and other "advanced" militaries. There was more to the implants than just a super-radio. The plants acted as a sort of PDA that could record video, drawn from vision, and audio, recall notes, act as a cell phone and last but not least, could connect to other computer systems and the Internet or hypernet. And there were physical aspects. There were various upgrades and improvements that could be installed with the plants. In Dana's case that included a "spaceman's package" that permitted up to six hours in an airless condition, resistance to toxins and radiation, elimination of motion sickness and resistance to vacuum and various smoke inhalation issues. It didn't mean you could breathe vacuum for very long, but you could survive longer than an unaugmented person.

"EA Parker with a party of two, reporting?" Dana commed.

"You may enter, EA Parker," the voice said. *"One at a time."*

The outer hatch undogged and Dana entered an air lock. She cycled the hatch, then checked the telltales.

"Uh . . ." she said. "The other side of this is vacuum?"

There was a banging on the bulkhead and the light cycled to green.

"Try it now."

The hatch opened outward. If it was *really* vacuum, she was about to do a Dutchman without a *space suit*.

She thought about that for a second. This was just another test. She was good at tests.

Beneath the main air lock control panel is the manual testing system. Manual tests of atmosphere integrity may be obtained...

Thank God she hadn't slept through that class. She opened up the access panel and twisted the knob. Air immediately started sucking out. She quickly closed the test knob.

Asking another question was out. There was *no way* they were just going to *kill* an arriving noob. Somebody was playing silly buggers.

She put her ear to the steel bulkhead. Faintly, she could hear something that sounded very much like a small motor.

"Tell you what," she said. "I'll open the hatch if the joker with the vacuum cleaner will shut it off."

The hatch cycled from the other side and a tall coxswain's mate first class grinned at her.

"Welcome, junior space eagle," the CM1 said. "Come in! Come in!"

There were three people in the compartment, a bosun's mate second and a spaceman first behind desks and the CM1. The CM waved with both hands, like he was directing a taxiing shuttle.

"Come, come, we don't bite!"

"Much," the BM2 sitting behind a desk said. He was bent over some paperwork and clearly not enjoying his reading.

"Uh..." Dana said. She'd gotten it right the first two times but the vacuum indicator had sort of thrown her. "Engineering Apprentice Parker with party of two?"

"Welcome, EA Parker," the CM1 said. "You are a

sight for sore eyes. A FUN that actually can figure out that red means stop. Stand by." He got the distant look of someone using a plant and set up a small hand vac on the manual indicator. "Hold this, will you?" he said, handing it to Dana.

A moment later, Jack stepped through the inner hatch and looked around.

"Hey, Dana! Is this where we're supposed to report or not?"

"It becomes clear why EA Parker was placed in charge of this group," CM1 Keith Glass said, considering their orders. "*Two* of you just failed the single most important test of being *useful* junior space eagles. You will hear this not once, but again and again and again. This is not Earth. This is the *Troy*. Around Earth there is a protective sheath of, fortunately breathable, gases called an *at*-mo-sphere. Around *Troy* there is this thing called *va*-cuum. It smarts rather severely when one attempts to breathe it. *Two* of you just attempted to test that fact. Had you done so in other than controlled conditions you would now be swelling up like freeze-drying grapes and I'd probably have to do the body recovery.

"Since there are still far too few mighty master space eagles with much time in this thing we call space, I have been chosen to deliver your inbrief. You just got the first and second part. The first part was the test, the second part was the lecture. I repeat. Always. Check. Air lock. Integrity. Can I get a repeat back?"

"Always check air lock integrity, aye," the three newbies parroted.

"That sounded very rote," Glass said. "But if you

don't check air lock integrity you will not live to be mighty *master* space eagles such as myself. So it's up to you. I don't even have to write the next of kin.

"The third part of the in-brief. You have joined the mighty One-Forty-Second Tactical Assault Squadron, part of the First *Troy* Boat Wing. I might add that since there is no second, third or fourth squadron, we *are* the First Boat Wing. Our job is very simple and oh so complex at the same time. We deliver the mail. The mail may be food, supplies, scrap metal, equipment, *actual* mail, or, if we are very unlucky, Marines express service. Whatever we are delivering, our job is to ensure timely delivery. Neither snow, nor asteroids, nor laser fire shall stay us from our appointed rounds. Please be very clear on that. Whether your mission is to ensure that the boats remain functional or to drive them, your first, last and only job is to *ensure* delivery.

"The fourth part is like unto the first three. Most of the things we do, there is only one way to do them and survive. There is no third option. Do it right or someone dies. There is no 'good enough.' There is no 'close enough for government work.' If you cannot get your head around everything you do, every moment, every day, being a *very big deal*, please see BM2 Grumwalter for paperwork to transfer to the Army or something where it's not. Please do so before you kill me or someone I like. You do not yet fall into that category but you're unlikely to just kill yourself. Are there any viable and intelligent questions?"

He looked at the three and nodded.

"Good. I wasn't going to answer them anyway. That is what your division petty officers are for. Who are on the way to collect their little lambs. Go in violence to deliver the mail."

"This is your rack."

Engineer First Class Sean Sumstine clearly was enjoying showing the new Engineer Recruit around. That might have been because it got him out of his normal duties but Dana figured it was the way he was looking at her with calf-eyes.

Being in quarters, alone, with a guy had some rather unpleasant memories associated, but Dana decided to take Sean on first impression. He was a nice guy. Unlike certain EM1s she'd met in A School.

The quarters were much better than she'd expected, a two-person room with its own head. And, apparently, otherwise unoccupied. There were two racks and wall-lockers but both racks were unmade, indeed the mattresses were still in plastic, and the wall lockers were empty. And, as Sean had briefed her, they were also capable of supporting two people for up to six days without external support. She *really* didn't want to test that.

"You get to pick your side," Sean said. He was short, five-six or so, with sandy brown hair. She didn't even have to ask if he'd had Johannsen's. Not that it was any problem for *guys*. They were *all* born with Johannsen's. They called it being male. "We, uh..."

"Don't have many chicks," Dana said, setting down her A bag. Sean had made a motion when he picked her up at Squadron to help her with it. She'd just glared.

"I, uh, wouldn't have said 'chicks,'" Sean said. "But, yeah. Just leave your A bag. Next step is getting your suit. Then you're off until next watch."

"When do I start..." Dana said, then shrugged. For all the classes she'd had, she wasn't sure what her job actually *was*. "When do I start working?"

"I'll come get you next watch," Sean said. "Thermal's off-watch at the moment so I don't even know your assignment."

"Thermal?" Dana said.

"Sorry," Sean said. "That's Engineering Mate First Class David *P.* Hartwell. Also known as Thermal, behind his back, because he managed to get one of our first *Myrmidons* drifted right in the way of a SAPL. It was on dispersed beam and the *Myrm* just sort of... melted."

"Oh my God," Dana said. "Was the..."

"There was no crew," Sean said. "And it was written off as an accident after about a zillion Incident Evaluation Reviews. It really *wasn't* his fault. But he doesn't expect to make chief any time soon. Anyway, he's the division engineering mate who's in charge of us lowly wrench turners. And since he's off-watch, I get to show you around."

"So... where do I get my suit?" Dana asked.

"Prepare for a looong walk," Sean said.

"There's no way I'm ever going to be able to find my way around," Dana said.

They must have walked a mile but she figured it wasn't in anything like a straight line. There had been about four elevators, two escalators, several sets of stairs, more corridors than she could count and two grav walks. Those were new but they weren't that much different from the sliding walkways in airports. She'd just followed Sean and tried not to seem like a noob.

"You'd be surprised," Sean said. "I felt the same way when I first got here. You figure it out. If you get totally lost, and there's not a priority, you can ask Paris where the hell you are."

"Paris?" Dana asked as they walked through a large, already open hatch that read "Environmental Fittings Department."

"*Troy's* AI," Sean said, walking up to the counter. The guy manning it was older, probably in his thirties, with a bit of a paunch. And clearly a civilian. "New arrival."

"Got it," the man said, looking at his screen. "Engineer Apprentice Dana Parker?"

"Here," Dana said.

"Helmet," he said, reaching and pulling down one from a rack. "Boots, gloves and suits down the end."

Sean gestured to three slots on the bulkhead marked, remarkably, "Boots, Gloves, Suits." She opened them up and pulled out the space-suit parts.

"And we're done," Sean said. "Thank you."

"No problem," the man said, finally looking up. "Mind you keep the seals checked and if you want some personal advice, *always* keep the catheter lubed."

"Yes, sir," Dana said, coloring slightly.

"They run air-breach drills about every two days," the civilian said. "If you maintain lubrication on the catheter, you're not scrambling for the gel when you're in a hurry."

"Yes, sir," Dana said, again. "Thank you, sir."

"I tell the guys, too, miss," the man said, nodding. "Good day."

"Boots and gloves go in the helmet," Sean said, stuffing the gloves in. "The helmet goes, neck-ring up, under your left arm. The suit," he continued, tossing it over her right shoulder, "is prescribed to be carried in a jaunty manner over the right shoulder. That shows you're a real junior space eagle."

"Yes, Engineer," Dana said, trying not to smile. But once she got the leopard suit adjusted so it wasn't sliding, it *did* feel rather jaunty.

"Suity has a point," Sean said as they exited into the corridor. "But we're in and out of suits so much, you just sort of do it anyway. If you want my advi—" He stopped and blushed.

"Sean," Dana said, frowning. He was an engineer, she was just an apprentice. But getting it out of the way was a good idea. "I know that Johannsen's means there's not many women in the military these days. With the Horvath hitting us over and over, there's no time for mommy-track. And if you've got Johannsen's, and I *did*, you practically have to wear a chastity belt to *not* get belly-full. But I'm gene scrubbed, I *didn't* have four kids by the time I was out of high school and I'm here to do a job. I've got different parts but that's all it means. I don't get offended when somebody says something racy. I grew up on a farm with four male cousins. If they couldn't get me to choke up at the jokes they tell, *you're* not going to. Or what they talk about. You'll know you've crossed a line when I start talking about what having Johannsen's PMS is like."

"Ouch," Sean said. "Message received."

"So you were about to impart some wisdom about suits to a fricking useless noob," Dana said. "Yes, I even know what a FUN is. And I know I'm a fricking useless noob. So you said...If I want your advice about wearing suits."

"Yeah," Sean said. "Thing is, we spend about half our watch time in suits. We don't have bays for the *Myrmidons*, yet. We're on an external spine system."

"Outside the *Troy*?" Dana said, her eyes widening.

"No, no," Sean said. "We're in the main bay. It's a sort of... Well, from the entrance to the bay it looks like a fricking hypodermic needle with warts. It's a tube of steel they welded on the wall. There are fifty shuttles, as of this morning's roster, locked on. So when we have to do an exterior inspection..."

"Which by standard is once a day," Dana said.

"Yeah," Sean said. "Well, you have to do it in a suit. So we're in and out of suits pretty much all the time. You're not fully suit qualed, so you're going to have to qual for that before you get really put to work. But when you're qualed, you'll be in and out all the time. So... Always, always, *always* take a dump before watch. You *can* dump in a suit, but it sucks. And so does doing the maintenance on the fecal matter repository. And getting out of it sucks, especially if you're in a hurry. So take a dump. If you get an inflammation from the catheter, don't hardcore it. See the corpsman. Check your seals. Check your, check your, *check* your *fricking* seals. Check 'em for any FOD every day, every time before you put it on, every time you just happen to be going by. When you put it on, do a buddy check if you can. If not, do the best single check you can. And, can I repeat, check your fricking *seals*?"

"I take it you've been having noobs not checking their seals?" Dana said, chuckling.

"Define noobs," Sean said, hitting the 32 button on an elevator. "We had a chief get assigned to us.

Straight out of 'we're going to make you a master *space* chief' school."

"They've got one of those?" Dana asked.

"They've got one of those," Sean said. "Where do you think we're getting all our chiefs? And you'd think that a chief petty officer with twenty years in the Navy would have learned something called attention to de-*tail*. By which I am not making a sexual innuendo."

"I take it he didn't?" Dana said. "I mean, a *chief*?"

"Decided to make an inspection walk to ensure that 'maintenance tasks were performing to standard,'" Sean said. "Which means 'people aren't screwing off.' Let me point out that *nobody* screws off in vacuum, Engineer Apprentice. I am the *master* of screwing off and even *I* don't go ghosting in the main bay. But I guess on carriers or something they go hiding out in the escape boats. I dunno, I've never been in what the old timers call the 'real' Navy. But he knew that somebody, somewhere, was going to be ghosting and the obvious place was clearly hiding in vacuum in the main bay to, I dunno, play null g cards or something!"

"And he didn't check his *seals*?" Dana said.

"We know that this was his intention because," Sean said, pausing as they exited the elevator, "and I do not lie, he left a voice log." His voice deepened and assumed a pompous tone. "'Sixteen-thirty, port watch, performing inspection to ensure maintenance tasks performing to standard.'"

"Uh..." Dana said, blinking. "And the point of leaving a voice log? Aren't we supposed to log actions?"

"Nobody but utter geeks or noobs leaves a *personal* log," Sean said. "I mean, do you *regularly* narrate your way through the day? '2230, arrived *Troy*. 2243, assigned 142nd Shuttle Wing. 2247, took dump . . .' I mean, I mean, what is this? *Star Trek*?"

"Uh," Dana said, as they got on a grav walk.

"No, to answer my own question," Sean said. "This is the *Troy*. Which exists not to go where no man has gone before and as a vehicle for narration by ham actors, but to sit on the door and pound the ever-living *crap* out of anybody who comes through the gate we don't like. And as a further word of advice, we do *not* leave personal voice logs. But fortunately, in this case, we didn't have to have a major Article Thirty-Two investigation when Chief Buckley was found a-Dutchman in the main bay. The point of this anecdote is check your seals. Check your navopak . . ."

"Navigation and atmosphere support system?" Dana guessed.

"Right," Sean said. "Which everybody calls the navo. Make sure your capacitors are charged, make sure you got dio . . ."

"Di . . . oh?"

"Sorry," Sean said, sighing. "I think the Navy is so addicted to slang we're trying to catch up. Di-oxygen molecules. O2."

"Oh," Dana said, starting to feel totally out of her depth.

"Two," Sean said, grinning. "Get it? Oh-Two? Mono is not good stuff nor is trio. Dio makes you bright. Not too few atoms, not too many. Juuuust right."

"Okay," Dana said, grinning. "Monatomic oxygen *is* pretty nasty stuff. And trio is . . . ozone."

"Nio is for fun," Sean sang, taking a little skip. "Sio makes you sad. And Suo is so very very bad."

"I won't even try to catch up on those," Dana said, adjusting her suit on her shoulder.

"We occasionally carry some very scary stuff," Sean said. "There's just not enough transport and all the loading bays aren't done yet. So we do a lot of what the oldies call 'lighter' work. Picking up cargo on freighters and bringing it into bays. The coxswain and engineer have to sign off on the cargo, which means at least having a clue about the MSDS."

"Material Safety Data Sheet," Dana said.

"Roger," Sean said. "Nio: Nitrogen dioxide. Nitrous in other words. You can huff it if you're a druggie type but this stuff is liquid so doing it straight is a baaad idea. We've never actually carried silica dioxide. It's a waste material from grav-well steel production but it rhymes. Suo is sulfur trioxide which we *have* carried and it's beyond nasty stuff. If you get a fire in it you can open up the ports and watch it burn in vacuum. Which I suppose would be cool... And speaking of screwing off," he continued as they exited another hatch.

The air was filled with the buzz of people and the smell of food. Dana's mouth started to water and she looked around in surprise. It looked pretty much like...

"The food court," Sean said, waving expansively. "Courtesy of Apollo Mining and LFD Mall Division."

The food court looked huge at first, rising six stories above the bottom level where they were standing. But then Dana noticed that only the ground floor was in business. There was an angle around a corner she couldn't see into that seemed to stretch into more space.

"There's a mall?" she asked.

"And her eyes lit with the passionless passion of shopping," Sean said, grinning. "Not as such, no. Not yet. It's planned for Phase Two. There are currently three thousand something military and about an equal number of civvies living on the *Troy*. That's not enough to support a real mall. When section one is at full capacity... it'll support a mall. They're talking about getting a Wal-Mart first but I'll believe it when I see it. For now, there's just the food court and a couple of independent stores that sell civvy clothes and stuff and a little-bitty Publix. But I, hereby, by the authority invested in me by BM2 Johnson, under orders to 'go get the noob a suit and show her around and stuff,' declare it to be lunch time at the food court. I'm going to get a gyro. Meet me over by the purple caterpillar."

The "purple caterpillar" turned out to be an orientation poster on the Ogutorjatedocifazhidujon... The name was two lines long. After a bit it just seemed to be a stream of random letters. They were, according to the poster, "a peaceful race dedicated to hospitality in all its forms."

According to one of the briefings they'd gotten in A School, the Ogut civilians did tend to fill positions like hospitality, gardening, personal care, and such in other polities. If for no other reason than to get the hell out of the Ogut Empire. The Ogut government was anything *but* hospitable. It was a hereditary empire run mostly by its aristocracy and during the Multilateral Talks that had ceded the E Eridani system to the Horvath, the Ogut had bitten off a good bit of the Ormatur worlds as "protectorates." And the instructor had made clear that meant pretty much the same as the "protection" the Horvath had once afforded Earth. "That's a right nice planet you've got there, shame if a rock fell on it."

Dana had admitted she was hungry and had gotten a double meat teriyaki special at the Sushi House. Which made her wonder where the gym was. She was pretty sure it wasn't going to be on Sean's version of "showing her around."

Then there was the question raised by the Ogut poster.

"So..." she said as Sean sat down. "Say there's a pressure drop. *I've* got my suit. What are *you* going to do?"

"See the red exit signs?" Sean said. "They go to emergency survival centers. They're the heads, mostly. Sealed against pressure breach and there are boxes that open in the event of a loss that have emergency survival packs. We just call 'em body-bags 'cause if you're down to those you're probably a carbonite sculpture waiting to happen. However, at the moment we're about four hundred meters in from the main bay and about a kilometer and a bit from the exterior. Somehow I'm not worried about pressure loss. Now when we're at the *quarters*, I'm pretty careful."

"*Troy* isn't even officially commissioned yet, is it?" Dana asked.

"Nope," Sean said. "They've only got one laser tube cut and one missile tube. They're still in test phase. Commissioning ceremony is in about three months and everybody is already freaking out. Expect a lot of brass. Military *and* civilian."

"I guess that's going to be kind of an issue," Dana said. "And I'd expect you're probably going to figure out a way to...ghost it?"

"Already working on it...." Sean said, then a flash

of annoyance crossed his face. "Roger, Bosun's Mate. Still getting her suit, BM. Roger. Will do. Aye, aye. Frack."

"Problem?" Dana asked.

"Bosun Mate Johnson has just queried the time I am expending 'showing you around and stuff,'" Sean said, picking up his tray. "Especially since, apparently, nobody has seen either of us in a while. I hope you can gobble."

"I'm done," Dana said. "Am I in trouble?"

"You were just following orders," Sean said, dumping the contents of his tray in the trash. "And if nobody mentions going to the food court that would be a good thing."

TWO

"Forty-seven, door four!" the speaker announced. "Forty-seven, door four!"

James F. "Butch" Allen gulped and got out of the hard plastic chair. He suddenly wished he'd dressed better.

Butch had graduated from high school in June at which point his dad had, politely but firmly, reminded him that he was now a legal adult. Kids didn't stick around in the Allen household. Home was always where, if you had to go there, they had to take you in. But with Mama Allen having Johannsen's and Papa Allen having no great liking for condoms, there was always another bed being taken up. Eighteen and out was The Rule.

The same month that Butch and his dad had The Talk, he'd gotten his draft notice. But Butch was pretty sure he wasn't suited for military life. That meant college, which was still deferred for the moment, or finding a "qualified civilian occupation" that meant he was exempt·from conscription. He wasn't the college type, either.

The Allens had a long and illustrious history of

working with their hands. His dad had worked at the GE plant in Springfield since he graduated from high school and was a fixture of the maintenance department. Butch had taken the vocational track at school. He wasn't bad at math and he liked tinkering and was even in the physics club. But he wasn't real big on the "language arts" stuff and his SATs had shown that. College was pretty much out.

So he'd hitched a ride down to the Labor Office to look at the list of jobs he was qualified for that were "qualified civilian occupations." The list was depressingly short. He wasn't *qualified* for any of them. Most of them were defense tech related jobs that he couldn't even start to figure out. He could apply to be trained as a clean-room technician, for example. But when he checked, there were zero spots available.

That left space. Just about *any* space slot was exempt. There were two problems, though. The first was that Apollo, which was the big name in space industries, mostly wanted older, more experienced people. Most of the slots called for things like "three or more years commercial diving experience." And even if you got accepted, it was a five year contract. Working in space took advanced training and high-tech implants.

But Apollo was the only company that accepted "untrained, entry-level" space technicians. Again, Butch had looked at the list of positions and his brain had sort of shut down. He didn't know what an "Optical Welding Technician" was except it had something to do with welding. He could weld. He'd learned from his dad way before taking it in shop.

So he took a deep breath and walked in door four of the Springfield Apollo Mining Employment Office.

The room was small. The ceiling was low and it wasn't much wider than the narrow desk of the pregnant lady manning it. How she got in and out was a question.

"Good afternoon, Mr. Allen," the lady said, smiling. She was pretty old, probably thirty or so, but not bad looking. And the pregnancy had clearly done some development on her knockers.

"Hey," Butch said, smiling and sitting down.

"I've reviewed your record," the lady said, smiling thinly. "You're not very experienced."

"I just got out of high school, ma'am," Butch pointed out. "And there's stuff isn't on there. My dad's been teaching me to do stuff since I was a kid. I can rebuild a car, even one with computer ignition. And I can weld. Better than the B I got in shop makes it look like. I'm good with stuff with my hands, ma'am. I'm good at turning a wrench."

"Things are a little different in space, Mr. Allen," she said, tapping on her computer. "It's a very dangerous, very hostile environment. And you can't do things quite like you can on Earth. Turning a wrench is a very *complicated* job in space. Why do you want to work at Apollo?"

"It seems like a good job, ma'am," Butch said. "Lots of opportunities."

"And it's draft exempt," the lady said, looking up.

"I don't think I'm really set out to be in the Navy, ma'am," Butch said. "I do what I'm told but I'm not all up on that 'Yes, sir, three bags full' thing. I work good. I'm just not all up on . . ." He paused and shrugged. "I don't think I'd do good in the Navy, ma'am."

"Describe . . ." the lady said, clearly reading off her

screen. "Describe the procedure for assembling a four barrel injection system."

"On a car?" Butch asked. "Diesel?"

"Car," the lady said, looking puzzled. "I think."

Butch ran through the usual way that you'd assemble a four barrel injection system as she tapped on her keyboard.

"You are using an electric arc welder to join a plate of stainless steel to a plate of conventional steel..."

There were about nine questions related to various mechanical processes. They were mostly the sort of thing Butch could answer in his sleep. If his gay teacher hadn't been a bastard he'd have made an easy A in shop.

"When would you be available to start?" the lady asked at the end.

"Am I hired?" Butch asked, surprised.

"Hiring decisions are made at a later time," she said. "You will be informed by a phone call or e-mail if you are hired. But I need to know when you are available."

"I can start today," Butch said. "If I don't get an exempt job I gotta report to the draft board in three weeks."

"Very well," she said, tapping some more. "Thank you for your time. You will be informed of our decision by phone or e-mail within two weeks."

"Okay," Butch said.

"Have a nice day."

"How'd it go?" Mama Allen asked when Butch walked in.

The Allen house was part of a block of two-story

"mill" houses built in the 1920s. The mill had closed back in the '50s, but the houses remained. With brick walls and solid construction, they'd been up and down over the years. Currently, the neighborhood was back on the "up" cycle as more and more people moved into Springfield and crowded out the families like the Allens that had been there for decades.

"Don't know," Butch said, picking up Clarissa. She was one of three sisters, all younger. She wriggled for a second in his grip then subsided, sticking her thumb in her mouth. "That's gonna make you get bucktooth, kid. The lady didn't seem to think there was much chance but she asked me a bunch of shop stuff. Said I'd find out in two weeks or less."

"Well," Mama Allen said, wiping her hands. She was preparing meatloaf, heavy on the bread. "You gotta go to the Board in three weeks. I told your father that it's only three weeks." She stopped and wiped at her eyes. "Onions. I told him you should have that much time at least."

"Yes, Mama," Butch said. "Thank you, Mama."

"Go make sure Charlie and Susie're doing their homework," Mama Allen said, sticking the meatloaf in the oven.

"Yes, Mama."

"Good Lord, thank you for this food that you put on the table . . ." Papa Allen prayed.

Butch sat between Clarissa and Susie, holding their hands, as his father said grace. Clarissa kept trying to pull away but that was just Clarissa.

At a certain level it all seemed sort of distant. He'd been raised in this house. He didn't know anything other than Springfield, his friends from school and the neighborhood. But in two or three weeks, he was going away. He might be going to the Board and then into the Navy or the Army. The way things were going, they were talking about a big war with the Horvath and some guys named the Rangora.

The people already in the Navy, including some kids from the last class, were in "for the duration of hostilities." If he got drafted, he'd be in "for the duration of hostilities." And nobody knew how long "hostilities" might last. If you went by the Horvath, until their planet was a smoking ball of craters. The Horvath just didn't seem to get what a "truce" meant.

In a few weeks he'd be leaving this house. And he might never be coming back. That was kind of . . . It wasn't scary so much as confusing.

"Amen," his dad said and reached for the bowl of mashed potatoes.

Butch's cell phone rang and he looked guiltily at his dad.

"No phones at the table," his dad said. "You know the rules."

"It might be something about a job," Butch said.

"Check," his dad said. "If it's one of your girl-friends . . ."

Butch checked the phone and didn't recognize the number. It was an 800 number, though.

"Hello?"

"Mr. . . . Allen . . ." a robotic voice said. "This is a recording. You have been accepted by the . . . Apollo Mining Corporation as a . . . probationary optical welding technician. The contractual commitment is . . . five years. Starting salary is . . . eighteen dollars per hour with off-planet bonuses if the work occurs outside terrestrial atmosphere. If you conditionally accept this position, press one."

Butch carefully pressed one.

"You are required to present yourself at the ... Springfield, Missouri ... Apollo Mining Employment office where you applied for this position within three days. Your confirmation code is six-one-seven-three-five-two. Thank you. Goodbye."

"What was that?" Maricela asked.

"I've got a job with Apollo," Butch said, blinking in surprise. "A probationary ... optical welding technician? I don't even know what it is."

"Laser welding," Papa Allen said, nodding. "It's the new thing. Apollo's pretty much the only people teach it right now. That's a good job. See you don't mess it up."

"Yes, sir," Butch said.

"Now eat your food 'fore it gets cold."

"Good afternoon and welcome to the Probationary Optical Welding Technician course," the instructor said. He was a big guy with fair hair and a beer gut. Butch figured he probably carried Johannsen's. He also had a really raspy voice. "My name is Mr. Joseph Monaghan. I am one of the instructors of the space based OWT course here at the Apollo Melbourne Facility and, as such, I was chosen to welcome this new class. You will refer to me as Mr. Monaghan, not Joe or Joseph, just as you will address all of your instructors as Mr. or Ms. and their last name.

"Some people wonder why Apollo based its training course in a place like Melbourne, Florida," Mr.

Monaghan continued. "Since the Mercury program in the 1950's, Melbourne has been the primary support city for the Cape Canaveral Kennedy Space Center. Other smaller local cities include Palm Bay, Cocoa, Cocoa Beach and Titusville. From experience I know that some of you will become more enamored of Cocoa Beach than will be good for you.

"Brevard Community College is one of the few community colleges in the world to offer a vo-tech course in space technology. Apollo based its training here shortly after the launch of its first SAPL mirror. Over the last ten years we have graduated thousands of young men and women to fill the burgeoning space industry, where they work in thousands of fields from robotic management technician to food services. Yes, we train people on space-based food services because everyone who goes into space has to know, at a minimum, how to survive if the worst happens and you find yourself trying to suck vacuum.

"Some people have also asked why I have a voice like a fifty-year smoker when I don't smoke. The answer, boys and girls, is that *I* tried to breathe vacuum. I am one of, at this point, four people who have been exposed to full death pressure and survived. I only survived because of quick action on the part of a co-worker, who was trained in this facility, a nearby air lock and good doctors, also trained here."

"So you understand that I have a personal interest in ensuring that the training here at Melbourne remains top-notch. I may, hope to some day, go back to space. In that case, should I again be, God forbid, in the position of sucking on nothing, it may be up to one of *you* to save my life. God, again, forbid.

"This course is very, *very* expensive. Were you to find another such school, the course would cost in excess of half a million dollars. There are still very few qualified instructors and we don't work cheap. It requires, of course, high-power lasers, which are also not cheap. At least in breathable. That, for those who are wondering, is the slang for atmosphere with breathable air.

"There is, rarely, a second chance in space. Space is an absolutely unforgiving *bitch*. The Company only wants very good people in space. They want people who are going to make them money, not cost them money by paying for medical and death benefits. Therefore, figure that about half of you are going to wash out. Some, most, will wash out in the first few weeks. Others, despite the pre-tests, will not be able to handle the conditions in space. Boost has gotten relatively cheap but it still costs money to move people around. There's also the cost of your suits and implants. Again, at least a half a million dollars for the course, another half a million for the equipment. We are going to do our level best to find the weak links and eliminate them on the ground before they become a danger to themselves and others in space.

"So be prepared to work harder than you ever have in your miserable lives."

"Hey," Butch said, hitching up his backpack and looking around his dorm room.

The dormitory building looked sort of like a three-story hotel but he'd noticed it was different. There weren't any windows except on the ground floor. And it had looked bunched up.

The reason became obvious when he saw his room. It was about half the size of most bedrooms with a low ceiling and no windows. It had a set of bunk beds that had about half the normal head room. There weren't any lockers or anything, just a sort of box welded to the base of the bed. He was going to have a hard time fitting. For that matter, there wasn't much space in the room, period. He could barely get into the room for the bunks, the desk and the guy sitting at it. They had managed to squeeze in a little fridge, though.

"Hey," the guy sitting at the desk said, not bothering to look up. He was hunched over a book, reading by the single light, and had papers scattered all over the desk.

"Uh, I think I'm your roommate," Butch said.

"Frack," the guy said, finally looking around. "I knew it was too good to last. Well, you get top bunk."

"Okay," Butch said, tossing his bag on the bunk. Part of the briefing before he got his tickets to Melbourne was that he was only supposed to carry one bag capable of being used as a carry-on for all his gear. "I'm James Allen. Call me Butch."

"I'm Nathan Papke," the guy said, spinning the chair around and standing up.

If Butch thought he was going to have a hard time fitting in the bed, Nathan must hate it. The guy was a ten-foot string-bean with a shock of unruly black hair on top. Okay, maybe six-seven. *Really* fracking tall and just skinny as hell. "I'm mostly called Nate."

"'Kay," Butch said. He'd been given the rest of the afternoon to "get acquainted with the area." Courses started in the morning.

"What are you here for?" Nate asked, shaking his hand.

"Optical welding," Butch said. "You?"

"I'm here for the robotics course," Nate said. "It's not as much EVA and I'm pretty good with computers. I'm not an In the Black kinda guy."

"How long've you been here?" Butch said, sitting on the lower bunk. He had to hunch forward because the top bunk was shorter than he was when sitting down.

"Two weeks," Nate said. "And it's been a ball buster, let me tell you. All it's been is more psych tests and robotic theory. We haven't even seen a schematic of a bot yet, much less what we're going to be working on. And we've already lost about half the class."

"Dang," Nate said. "Why?"

"This," Nate said, waving at the papers on his desk. "The academic portion is absolutely killer. I was a geek in high school and I'm having a hard time keeping up."

"Oh," Butch said, rethinking his decision to take the course.

"It's not as bad as all that," Nate said, seeing the expression on his face. "All you got to do is keep your nose to the grindstone. And clean. We had two people get tossed out for popping on a piss test and one got a DUI. They don't want anybody that's got a substance abuse problem in space. Most of the rest quit 'cause of the academics."

"There any papers we gotta write?" Butch asked.

"No," Nate said. "Not so far. Most of the stuff is fill in the blank and short answer. No essays or anything. They just want to see you're learning the stuff, not how well you can write."

"Math?" Butch asked.

"Lots of math," Nate said, nodding. "At least in my course. I don't know about yours."

"I can do math," Butch said. "What's there to do around here?"

"There's the beach," Nate said, grinning. "Cocoa Beach is pretty nice and the view's pretty good if you get my drift."

"Got it," Butch said, grinning back.

"Lots of beaches," Nate said. "Cocoa Beach is also the party spot. But unless you're a lot smarter than, sorry, you look, don't figure on doing a lot of partying. The homework is killer and they even load you down on the weekends."

"That sucks," Butch said, scratching behind his ear. "But if it's just math, I figure I can handle it."

"Other than that, there's the mall," Nate said, shrugging. "It's just up the road. Some pretty good restaurants if you've got the squeeze. But the food in the cafeteria is good so I've been saving my money."

"Food's good?"

"Food's great," Nathan said. "It's buffet style, but it's got stuff like Mongolian barbeque and crab legs. Big buffet. They feed us right. I guess so we don't keep going out for food and keep up with studying. From what the instructors who have been out say, it's pretty much the same if you're on a big installation like *Troy*. Not as good on the ships."

"We work on the *Troy*?" Butch said, confused. "I thought that was a defense station."

"From what I hear, it's a work in progress," Nathan said, grinning. "There are nearly as many Apollo employees on *Troy* as military. Then there's the Wolf stuff. Most of that is ship based, but there's room for about five hundred people on Granadica."

"The *fabber*?" The Granadica fabber had been all

over the news when it came through the Sol system on the way to Wolf. The mobile factory was the largest and most expensive piece of Glatun technology ever purchased and even though it was nearly a thousand years old, the most high tech. But he'd never heard that people could live on it.

"The fabber," Nathan said, nodding. "There's a research and design team on it and guys who work on the space dock and gas mine Apollo's building. You got your afternoon to get your shit straight?"

"Yeah," Butch said.

"Go buy some pop and stuff," Nate said, gesturing at the fridge. "You're going to want to have something in the room. There's times I don't want to take time to go to the vending machine. And speaking of which... I've got homework to do."

Shit, Butch thought. *High school never ends.*

"What you're looking at is the Mark Four Grosson optical welder," Mr. Methvin said, holding up what looked a lot like an oxyacetylene welder head. "And you're all thinking, 'That thing ain't nothin' but a fancy OA rig.' And you're all wrong. If you keep thinkin' that you're gonna be *dead* wrong."

The first time Butch saw his gay shop teacher in school he'd been bothered by the fact that Mr. Tews was missing about half the fingers on his left hand. But he'd learned that was pretty much where you got shop teachers. If they weren't missing bits, they'd still be working in the field, not teaching shop.

Mr. Methvin had run into the same press or welding rig or jack or whatever that every other shop teacher ran into at one point or another. Except it had taken off half his left hand and he had some sort of funny stubs on that hand for fingers. They looked a hell of a lot like toes.

"Tell you one thing's different right off," Mr. Methvin continued. "You, Allen, what's the maximum distance of an efficient flame on an oxy torch?"

The course had started with fifty-three guys and two chicks. After the first three weeks, it was a six-week course, they were down to thirty-seven guys and both chicks. And it was just getting harder.

Hand laser welding was done almost exclusively in space. There was a good bit of it in robotics on Earth but most of it was in space. So a good bit of the eight hour a day course was about how to work in space. Which, it turned out, meant a good bit of math and a lot of attention to detail.

Then there were the lasers themselves. Optics was a whole branch of physics, one that Butch's high school teacher had barely touched on.

The course was a lot of skull sweat. But fortunately it was the sort of skull sweat that Butch was good at. He'd stuck with it. He'd avoided going to the titty bars and pick-up joints along the Cocoa Strip to do homework. He'd read optical laser manuals until his eyes bled. He'd worked harder than he ever had in school. There were two big reasons. The first was that he really didn't want to join the Navy. The second was that he just didn't want to tell Papa Allen that he'd failed.

There were some little reasons, too. The training he was getting worked just about as well on the robots being used in every part of industry. When he was done with his five year hitch with Apollo, he could just about set his salary. Laser robotic technicians, which was a short course in robotics from what he was learning, earned over a hundred grand a year groundside. More in space.

That was the other part. He was currently being paid twelve bucks an hour and the course had dormitories for "probationary" technician trainees. When he passed the course, that jumped to eighteen bucks an hour, which wasn't chump change.

The rate for space work was time and a half when you were in atmosphere and *double* time in EVA. Overtime was time and a half up to forty-eight and double time after that. If he was working EVA on overtime over forty-eight hours, he'd be making seventy-two bucks an hour. As a *probationary* tech. And there was a bump in pay each year he stayed rated during his first hitch.

Rate for full tech, base, was *twenty-four* bucks an hour. A fully qualified technician made nearly a hundred bucks an hour on OT in EVA, *and* they provided room and board so you weren't even out that.

Butch wasn't planning on getting hooked to a wagon any time soon, but like most guys he figured he'd get married someday. Even if his wife had full blown Johannsen's, he'd have an easier time supporting a family on a hundred bucks an hour than his dad did working in the mill.

Then, hell, it was *space*. Butch had enjoyed the astronomy portion of his physics classes and he'd even gotten into reading science fiction, partially because all the geeks in the class read it and he couldn't get most of their jokes without some basis. There were hardly any new books out but the old guys were still pretty popular. He'd gotten hooked on the vision of space as the next frontier. He wasn't old enough to remember Grandpa Allen, who had been a kid when his parents moved to the Missouri frontier. But he'd heard the stories. There might not be red Indians, but there were Horvath and Glatun and more and more star systems getting opened up all the time. Truth was, space was the place.

And this question was dead easy for once.

"Depending on the system," Butch said, "inch and a half to two and a half inches, Mr. Methvin."

"Right," Mr. Methvin said, walking over to a sheet of steel he had propped up. Butch noted that there was another, much thicker, piece of steel behind it. "Behold," Mr. Methvin said, holding the optical welder about a yard away from the plate. He fiddled with the controls for a second then held it out. "Goggles."

Even with the goggles, Butch could see the beam from the optical welder. And it cut through the steel faster than any oxy rig he'd ever used.

"Whoa," one of the guys in the class said.

"A Mark Four has a maximum range of about six meters," Mr. Methvin said, cutting off the beam. "Which is just a *stupid* design. There's a way to set the beam for any length you want, from either a tiny little beam that's not much thicker than a hair to one thick as a finger and six meters long. Which you monkeys are probably going to cut each other up with once you get in space. But I don't get to tell the people that design these things they're idiots. So I'm telling *you*. They're idiots. *You're* idiots. And if you ever use a long beam on one of these things, you're probably gonna *kill* some *other* idiot..."

✳ ✳ ✳

"Welcome to your final exam," Mr. Monaghan said. He'd been Butch's instructor for "theory and practice of space movement," and he'd been an absolute bastard. Now he was the "faculty advisor" for the "extreme confinement environment test."

They'd been warned that the test wasn't just "can you handle an extreme environment?" It was "can you handle an extreme environment under enormous stress?" Stress wasn't just cumulative, it was multiplicative. General stress, is everything okay at home, got multiplied by other stress, am I going to make my car payment, got multiplied by other stress, is my air working, until just about anyone had a break point.

The ECET wasn't designed to find that break point. Everyone has a break point and if you hit it what you have afterwards is what's called PTSD and generally you were busted for space work. It was designed to find people whose break point was too *low*.

Nate had flunked out on the ECET. The ECET was the last major test before you went to the "space environment" portion of the training, going out in the Black. Because they weren't going to spend the money on boosting and planting you if you couldn't pass the ECET.

"The first thing I want to stress," Mr. Monaghan said, "is that this test is perfectly safe. The reality is that you will never be in danger. Since the grabber material does not allow for movement, you can't even get the mask off. And if you can't get the mask off, you—probably—can't die."

The ECET was simple. You got loaded in a steel tube, put on a mask, a bunch of gunk got poured in on you that prevented you from moving, at all, and you got asked questions. For hours.

Most of the answers were less important than how you handled them. The point was that you had to be hard, not impossible, to get upset in the test. The ones that were important were the ones that related to your field. There were two hundred of those alone and you had to have the answers at the tip of your tongue.

"In the likely event that you totally freak out," Mr. Monaghan said, "you will be sedated, decanted and wake up in recovery. You will then be given your final check and a ticket back to whatever miserable hole you crawled out of. There is no appeal. You pass the ECET or you don't. Period. We will be taking four at a time. I would suggest that those of you who are not called at first study your test question booklets. Allen, Armstead, Ashline and Beckett."

Damn.

"Good morning, Mr. Allen. Are you comfortable?"

Just my luck I get fracking Monaghan. As to the question, the grab-goo was pressing on his chest so he could barely breathe. But since he *liked* confined spaces . . .

"Just fine, thanks, Mr. Monaghan," Butch said. "It's sort of comfy."

One of Butch's favorite games growing up was hide and seek. As the runt of three brothers, it gave him some time when he wasn't getting pounded on. It was amazing the spaces you could squeeze into with a little will.

"List all the major parts of the navopak of a Mark Fourteen Space suit," Mr. Monaghan said.

"Recycler . . ."

"In *alphabetical order*. Take your time . . ."

❋   ❋   ❋

Butch wasn't sure how long he'd been in the tank but he was sure the recyclers were messing up. He wasn't getting enough breathable and he was getting a carb panic. The CO2 was up.

"I've got a picture of your sister here," Mr. Monaghan said. "Cute. Clarissa, is it?"

"I've got a sister named Clarissa, Mr. Monaghan."

"So why'd you have a *naked* picture of her on your iPod, Butch? Don't you know that's child pornography."

"I don't *have* one, Mr. Monaghan," Butch said.

"Well, I'm looking at one," Mr. Monaghan said. "Cute. Nice little picture. Nice girl. You think she's hot?"

"She's *six,* you sick bastard!" Butch said.

"She's six, Mr. Monaghan," Mr. Monaghan said.

"Anybody that talks about a guy's six-year-old sister like that don't deserve the title *Mister*, Mister."

"Do you want to pass the course, Butch?" Mr. Monaghan said mildly.

"Yes," Butch said.

"So, repeat after me. You are a sick bastard, Mr. Monaghan."

"You are a sick bastard, Mr. Monaghan," Butch snarled.

"And then there's...Susie. Beautiful hair. Both ends."

Butch snarled and ground his teeth but didn't say anything.

"She's really blossoming, don't you think, Butch? I require a response, Butch."

"I have a sister named Susie," Butch said. "And you don't have a naked picture of her. Or Clarissa."

"Susie, I note, has a mole on her butt," Mr. Monaghan said. "So, yes, I am currently looking at a picture of your naked sister. Your naked, twelve-year-old..."

"I still don't think you've got a picture," Butch said.

"She's probably got Johannsen's with hair like that," Monaghan said. "If you catch them at just the right time, girls like that are just putty in your hands..."

"When I get out of here I'm going to rip your head off and shit in your neck," Butch said. "*Mister* Monaghan."

"That would cause you to fail the course, Butch," Mr. Monaghan said, in that same mild tone.

"Screw the course," Butch said. "You don't go around looking at pictures of a guy's sister. You don't talk about popping 'em. And you sure as *hell* don't tell him about it."

"How's he doing?" Monaghan asked, looking over at the vitals tech.

"Angry, that's for sure," the tech said. "But his heart rate and BP aren't up all that much. He's balancing as well as he can. Or he's just a natural."

"You're not going to top him on this track," the psychologist said. She was monitoring all four tests and making suggestions.

"It's his main hot-point," Monaghan said. "He's *very* protective of his sisters."

"It will require counseling," the psych said. "He's marginal. He's very wrapped up in that emotional attachment. I'd say you've gone about as far as you can. I'd also say that with some training he's a pass. That's my professional opinion."

"Concur," Monaghan said.

"Okay, Butch, we're letting you out, now," Monaghan said. "We're also going to up your O2 and get rid of some of that carb. When you come out, you can take a swing at me or we can talk. Your call. Take the swing and you're going home to see your sisters."

"Sit, Butch," Monaghan said, tossing the probationary trainee a half-full pack of Marlboros. "As long as you were in the tank you could probably use a smoke."

"Thought there was no smoking in the building," Butch said, still glaring.

"There are rules and rules," Mr. Monaghan said, shrugging. "They're waived under certain conditions. Get the nic fit under control so we can talk. To start, no, I never had a picture of your sisters. I am, in fact, a *very* sick bastard. But not on duty.

"The next question at the top of your head is did you pass. The answer is . . . sort of. You got all the fixed answers solid. You did your homework, that's obvious."

"Thank you, sir," Butch said, his jaw working.

"But you need to get that temper under control," Mr. Monaghan said. "There's a time and a place for it. But if you get put on a crew they're going to test you. They won't have all the information we have, but they'll wiggle it out of you. And they'll find your hot points. And they'll poke. They test the *hell* out of the FNGs that come up there, much harder than we can here. The best I could do was talk dirty about your sisters. They'll find a picture of one of them, Photoshop it onto a real piece of child porn and stick it in your locker just before you go on shift. Then call the nosies to tell them you've got child porn in your locker."

"That's sick," Butch said.

"They are, *we* are, a very sick crew," Mr. Monaghan said, still in that same mild tone. "There's actually a reason for it. The same reason we do it here. You know about the ninety-day probationary period and the penalties for failure if you don't pass it?"

For the first ninety days of actual work, the trainee was on "hard probation." They could be dismissed with or without cause. And they owed the *full* cost of their training, preparation and suit, nearly three quarters of a million dollars. It was more money than Butch could *ever* repay and one of the tiny little codicils in the contract he'd barely read.

You could quit at any point in training and not owe a dime. But once you got implants and a suit, the company *owned* you.

"What is not mentioned in the contract," Mr. Monaghan said, "is that every crew has the right of refusal over a new member. Oh, they don't abuse it. There's just too much damned work. But if two crews refuse to work with you, you get dismissed. And then you owe more money than you're ever going to see in your life.

"They are, in fact, the final test. They don't want to work with anybody that can't hack it. Their lives depend on you being able to keep your cool, no matter *what*. So they're going to push and push and push and push, looking for a weak point. Your protectiveness of your sisters is admirable. I did have pictures of them, but only fully clothed. They are lovely young ladies and you are blessed to have them in your life. The crews are going to take that admirable emotion and rip it to shreds. That is why you are still considered marginal. You can probably hack the actual physical aspects of space work. The emotional part is your weak point."

"So what do I do?" Butch said. The smoke was helping and he was smart enough to see what Mr. Monaghan was driving at. It made sense in a sick sort of way. He figured once he was a full tech, he was probably going to do the same thing. You didn't want somebody who was a hothead holding a laser that could cut through the suit of the guy next to him.

"There are various techniques," Mr. Monaghan said. "Deflection: 'Yep, she's hot.' One-upmanship: 'Yeah, Susie's a nice piece. Unlike your wife.' Rolling with it. That, however, can make you look like a wuss and they'll be wondering when you're going to crack and go SAPL. Practice responses in a mirror. Come up with a list of good one-liners. You can often stop something like that with a good joke at the right time. There are books of practical jokes and that is another thing that will be practiced on you. Be *prepared*. And prepared to retaliate. The crews much prefer a smart come-back or a good counter to a joke over somebody who just smiles and takes it. They tend to keep upping the ante to see what will work. But mostly you need to find your hot buttons and get them under control. You with me?"

"Yes, Mr. Monaghan," Butch said.

"Good," Monaghan said, nodding. "I still think the best part of you dripped down your momma's leg."

"At least I *had* a momma, Mr. Monaghan," Butch said, smiling pleasantly.

"Ah, it *can* learn."

THREE

"I take it Sean showed you around?" Engineering Mate First Class David P. Hartwell was tall, 6' 4", and heavy-set. Dana realized she looked like a china-doll next to him but it didn't bother her. Her cousins were all about the same size or bigger.

"Yes, EM," Dana said.

The engineering office of 142/C/1, First Division, Charlie Flight, 142nd Boat Squadron, was already cluttered. There were manuals stacked on every horizontal surface that didn't have bits and pieces of *Myrmidons* already there. A mug of coffee barely fit on the corner of the 142/C/1 ENCOIC's desk.

"So he showed you the docking bays?" the EM asked.

"We didn't quite get to that, EM," Dana said.

"Knowing Sean, I can figure where he headed," Hartwell said. "During your next three months, you have certain specified duties. Until you get fully qualed on EVA, you're of limited use as an engineering tech, you understand that?"

"Roger, EM," Dana said, glad that Hartwell hadn't pressed the question.

"So in addition to your other duties, you need

to get EVA qualed as rapidly as possible," Hartwell said. "Until you get full EVA qualed you can't even *start* on getting Eng qualed. As long as you meet the standard rate of qualification, you are more or less on your own on that. But I'll be keeping an eye on your qual rate. If you fall behind in qual rate, I will then have to become involved in your retraining. You do not want me involved in your retraining."

"Yes, EM," Dana said.

"The qualifications for EVA full standard are knowledge of the parts and functions of your suit," Hartwell said. "To be capable of donning your suit in a prescribed time to task and standard. To be capable of handling first and second level faults while suited to task and standard. And the last, and surprisingly the most tricky, to be capable of maneuvering your suit in microgravity to task and standard. I need a readback."

"Knowledge of the parts and functions, aye," Dana said. "Capable of donning suit in a prescribed time to task and standard, aye. Capable of handling first and second level faults while suited to task and standard, aye. Capable of maneuvering suit in microgravity to task and standard, aye."

"The way that you train is to get experience," Hartwell said. "You need to be working on donning and undonning in any free time you have. You also need to be studying not only the parts and functions of the boats but the parts and functions of your suit. *You have to qual on your implants,*" he commed without actually opening his mouth, *"which is mostly a matter of just using them.* Last but not least," he continued, speaking normally, "you need to get familiar with micrograv. That's where personnel are falling down in qual. Where they're falling down *after* qual is forgetting the basics. Like checking their seals."

"Yes, EM," Dana said.

"I'm getting *really* tired of training reviews," EM1 Hartwell said. "They cut into things like actually making sure the *Myrms* start. Or don't screw up in mid-space. They're straight from the fabber in Wolf but they've *still* got problems. So I need you EVA qualed. Fast."

"Roger, EM."

"But EVA qual is in *addition* to other duties," Hartwell continued. "Your *primary* mission is to make sure, to the extent you are currently capable, that Boat Twenty-Nine is up and running. So where you had better be when I come looking for you on duty hours is in the boat."

"In the boat, aye, EM."

"You'll also be on the watch schedule, of course," Hartwell said. "But we don't run watch and watch so you don't have to worry about that for a week or so. From here we are going to go to Twenty-Nine and you get to see your new home away from home."

"Roger, EM," Dana said, trying not to smile.

"You are glad to finally see your boat?" Hartwell said, standing up.

"It's why I'm here, EM," Dana said.

"You will come to be less enthusiastic," Hartwell said. "Among other things, Twenty-Nine is the command boat. Until you are fully qualed, it will not be 'your' boat. The current engineer is EN Andrew Jablonski. AJ will be overseeing your quals and overseeing your maintenance of the boat because CM1 Glass and the skipper, Lieutenant Commander Martin, aren't about to climb in a boat that has been rated by an EA. But keep that motivation as long as you can. To reduce it somewhat, among other things, we don't climb into those cockleshells without our suits on. Come back here with your suit. We'll start on basic quals now."

"Roger, EM," Dana said, just a trace nervously.

"Which, I just realized, is a problem," Hartwell said, clearly trying not to curse. "Because while donning suits is normally no problem..."

"I don't have issues, EM," Dana lied.

"The *Navy* has issues with naked people of opposite sexes in the same room alone," Hartwell said. "I'll figure something out by the time you get back."

"This didn't used to be a problem," Chief Petty Officer Elizabeth Barnett said bitterly. "We had nearly twelve percent female personnel and if a gal had to disrobe for duty's sake she damned well could do it in a room *full* of guys if she had to. God *damned* Horvath."

Chief Barnett was tall and generally slender. The "not slender" part had Dana wondering what her handle was. "Elizabreasts" came to mind. Dana wasn't flat but she also wasn't stacked. She harbored a touch of jealousy about chests like the chief's.

"Roger, Chief," Dana said. She picked up the parts of her suit and began carefully checking the seals.

"Do you want a checklist?"

"I'd prefer to do this myself, Chief," Dana said, *pretty* sure she'd done a good inspection of her glove seals. "The only person I'm going to kill screwing it up is me."

"Not necessarily," the chief said, taking a seat at the desk. The "evolution" had been moved from the

Division Bay to Dana's quarters. And it had required calling in the coxswain chief of Flight A and getting a navopak out of stores. "If you're performing a critical evolution when you have a failure, it cascades. You're going to hear this over and over: there is no *small* mistake in space. I'm spending half my time performing training and incident reviews. *More* than half. Suit failures. Boat failures. Bad driving. More bad driving. Half the damned drivers are down groundside right now testifying at an incident review because we lost *another Myrm* to what looks like bad driving. Just flew right into a SAPL beam. Called a mayday then *zap*!

"I used to think the *sea* was merciless. And now I'm having to fill in on suit quals because we've finally got another split in the squadron."

"Roger, Chief," Dana said. "Sorry, Chief."

"Not your fault," Chief Barnett said. "Like I said, blame it on the damned Horvath and their damned Johannsen virus."

"Roger, Chief," Dana said, paying even more attention to her boot seals than they were really worth.

"And *that* caused a penny for your thoughts moment," Chief Barnett said, looking up.

"Chief?" Dana said.

"Big girls in this man's Navy don't cry," Chief Barnett said. "And I see you're managing not to. Barely. Who?"

"I'm from Anaheim, Chief," Dana said, setting down the boots. She took a deep breath and picked up the suit to check the seals on it. "Dad in L.A. Mom committed suicide right after."

"Brother and sister-in-law," the chief said. "Two nieces and a nephew. Mother. Father was already dead. Chicago."

"Yes, Chief," Dana said.

"How old?" the chief said. "Never mind, I can count. Where'd you grow up?"

"Indiana, Chief," Dana said. "Middle of *no-where* Indiana. Place called Tangier."

"Best place to be," the chief said. "You handling it?"

"Haven't you heard?" Dana said, as lightly as she could. "PTSD is the new normal. Something like eighty percent of the U.S. has lost someone close to them. Fifty-three percent have had direct experience of a Horvath attack. And that doesn't begin to touch the whole Johannsen thing. The strange part about being in Tangier was that I *was* weird. I was the only person in my school who had been in a target city. They... didn't get it."

"Bitter much?" the chief said.

"Sorry, Chief," Dana said.

"I actually understand what you're talking about," the chief said. "You're not old enough to know ancient history like the *Cole* bombing. So I won't go into it, and compared to what's happened since, it's a minor blip. But I know about being the only person around who has nightmares."

"Roger, Chief," Dana said, setting the suit down. Now for the neck ring seals on the helmet.

"These are brand new," the chief said, picking up the gloves and inspecting them. "And the fabber here doesn't seem to have the problems of the ship fabber in Wolf. They're generally perfect right off the line. But you need to make sure the seal material is on solidly."

"Roger, Chief," Dana said, suddenly panicking. She was pretty sure she'd checked the seal material.

"You checked," the chief said, looking up. "I watched. And I'm double-checking."

"Thank you, Chief," Dana said.

"That was a pretty good job," Chief Barnett said when Dana was done with her inspection. "You know the parts and functions. You did a good, quality, detailed inspection. Technically, I could sign you off on parts and functions and inspection right here. Which is amazing considering most of the nitwits we've been getting. But I expect that, 'cause you're a split. Especially since this Johannsen's shit, we've got *twice* as much to prove as ever."

"Yes, Chief," Dana said, not sure what else to say.

"And I'm not going to sign you off," the chief said, picking up the gloves again. "Because what I'm about to teach you ain't in the book. Yet. It's how to *really* inspect your suit. By the numbers, to the task and standard we ought to be requiring. Pick up the other glove."

"Yes, Chief," Dana said.

"Place glove in left hand, palm up," the chief said, demonstrating.

"Glove in left hand, palm up, aye," Dana said.

"Run the index finger of your right hand down the inner thumb of the glove, checking for any burrs, irregularities or cuts," the chief said.

"Run index finger of right hand down inner thumb of glove, checking for burrs, irregularities or cuts, aye . . ."

The standard for donning a full suit was thirty-five seconds, about the maximum time a person could hold out in absolute vacuum. The initial "evolution" took nearly thirty minutes and by the end Dana was sweating in her suit and wondering if she really wanted to be in the Navy.

The new chief who had gone Dutchman in the main bay may have had some issues with attention to detail. Chief Barnett did *not*. Chief Barnett probably had a task, condition and standard for going to the *head*.

"And now you're a *fine* junior space eagle," Chief Barnett said. "As soon as you learn to do that in thirty seconds."

"Roger, Chief," Dana said, her voice muffled by the bubble helmet.

"I've placed the inspection document in your mail-box," the chief said. "Use it. If you can demonstrate that you can perform the task, condition and standard I'll check you off on inspection and parts. Check back with me in a week."

"Check back in a week, aye, Chief."

"And now you're ready to see your boat."

"I am going to do this with gloves and helmet off," Hartwell said, cycling the lock marked 142/C Bay. "Because I'm qualed to get them on if there's a problem. You're going to have to stay in the suit, buttoned up."

"Roger, EM," Dana said.

The "leopard" suits were not the Michelin-man suits of yore but a marvel of modern technology impossible without Glatun support.

Made of extremely thin layers, they wore like a wet-skin rather than a puffy NASA suit. Normally that would mean that, due to vacuum dilation, the user would be stuck in a starfish configuration. Vacuum "sucked" on a person in a space suit and they tended to end up in a spread-eagle. The suits got around that by being, in effect, very low-powered armor. The inner layer was an Earth-tech material that was used in high-end wetsuits. It was slick enough to slide on easily over bare skin, making it possible to don the suits rapidly. The next layer was a complex of heat transfer tubes that looked not unlike the human capillary system. That permitted the wearer to maintain temperature control in the varied conditions of space. It also absorbed transpired CO_2 and other gases from the skin and carried back O_2 to prevent degradation.

The next layer was a thin layer of woven carbon nanotube. Beyond that was the Glatun "autoflex" material. Essentially, it magnified the movements of the user just enough to overcome the suction aspects of vacuum. It couldn't be powered up, much, but it was enough to overcome the problem of moving in space.

Over that were two more layers of carbon nanotube to prevent damage to the suit. They also were so finely woven, no volatiles like, say, blood and oxygen, escaped.

A wonder of modern technology and Dana was already starting to loathe it.

"Oh, yeah," Hartwell said as the inner door cycled. "Micrograv."

"Roger, EM," Dana said as the yellow micrograv light started flashing.

The lock was in gravity. Hartwell reached into the corridor and grabbed a bar, pulling himself up and into micrograv.

"Be careful," Hartwell said, going slowly hand-over-hand down the corridor. "Don't overexert. The shuttles are in grav but they're configured all over the place so they left the corridor in micro."

"Roger," Dana said, reaching up and, barely, getting a hand on the bar. But by just pulling forward out of the lock she was able to enter micrograv without much effort. And immediately found herself going out-of-control as the momentum more or less threw her into the corridor. She bounced off the bulkhead and had to make a quick snatch for another bar. Fortunately, all the bulkheads were lined with them like four sets of monkeybars. She still bruised the heck out of her thigh.

"Like I said, don't overexert," Hartwell said. "You okay?"

"All good, EM," Dana said, slowly moving around so she could orient in the direction of travel. She had had one familiarization flight in a shuttle in micro.

"Follow me," Hartwell said, pulling himself down the corridor.

He stopped at an air lock marked 40.

"Flight C, Division One, Twenty-Nine," Hartwell said, checking the air lock then cycling it.

"Roger, EM," Dana said, following him through the double hatches.

She'd spent dozens of hours in the *Myrmidon* mock-up at A School but to be in *her Myrm* was a shock. It was another of several shocks she'd had since signing up. The creeping realization that she was *in the Navy*. It wasn't just some strange dream or daydream. This was *her* shuttle. Well, hers and AJ's. She was responsible for the six hundred and eighty-seven *thousand* moving parts, electrical parts or electronic boxes that required checks and maintenance.

It was enough of a shock she nearly floated out into gravity.

"Whoa, space eagle," Hartwell said, pushing her back into micro. "*Grab* the *bar*."

Dana grabbed the safety bar and swung herself down into gravity with much more grace than she'd demonstrated going *into* micro. Her earlier screw-up was humiliating on several levels since she considered herself something of a gymnast.

The interior of the cargo bay of the *Myrm* wasn't much to look at. Six gray steel bulkheads—two point three meters high, four wide—most of them covered in access patches and latch points. At the rear was a hatch to the guidance section. In flight, that was her normal station, manning the engineering and EW position.

"What do you think?" Hartwell asked.

"It looks brand new," Dana said.

"It is," Hartwell said. "It's straight from the Granadica Yard in Wolf 359. You have permission to temporarily undog your helmet. Because it also *smells* brand new. And it's never going to smell quite the same again."

Dana carefully undogged her helmet and took a sniff. The EM was right, it did smell brand new. Not like a new car, just...new. Steel and oils with a touch of ozone. But...new.

"Don't get used to that smell," Hartwell said. "Because in short order it's going to smell like stinky jarheads. And all the other crap we haul. There's no way to fully turn over the atmosphere and it just... builds up. The recyclers never quite clean it out. I thought about stiefing it, but I'm just getting all the crap that's wrong with Thirty-Three done and I didn't want to do *that* again."

"EM?" Dana said.

"It's like a new car, isn't it?" Hartwell said. "A new car from an entirely new *line*. There's stuff that's just not right. So far, none of it has been absolutely critical, but most of our birds are deadlined about half the time. Most of it's warranty work, but Apollo is so backed up, we're handling it. And none of it's consistent. No, I take that back. Watch your port, lower, grav grapnel. For some reason those seem to be about half bad. AJ! Yo! Jablonski! *Jablonski*."

"*I heard you*," a voice commed back. "*Micro in three . . . two . . . one . . .*"

A couple of seconds after the power cut off, a suited but unhelmeted engineer came floating out of the flight compartment towing a large capacitor.

"The Six-One-Eight is out," Jablonski said, lifting his chin to point at Dana. "What's up?"

"This is your new EA," Hartwell said.

"You're sticking me with a FUN?" Jablonski said sourly. The EN was as tall as Hartwell but seemed to be slender from what she could tell in the suit. "What the hell did I do to you?"

"I'm not," Hartwell said. "The Old Man stuck you with a FUN. Which brings me to the FUN's first mission."

"Yes, EM?" Dana said.

"*You* need to do the thirty day, ninety day and six month PM on this bird," Hartwell said. "That catches most of the major faults. Jablonski will supervise your checks and sign off on your quals on this analysis."

"Thirty day, ninety day and six month PM, aye, EM," Dana said, trying not to curse. That was going to take *forever*. But it sure would get her used to the bird.

"*I'm* going to have to be checking on Jablonski's sign-off," Hartwell said. "I'll be either in the Division Bay or Thirty-Three or . . . well, *here*. You have the manuals on your plant?"

"Yes, EM," Dana said.

"Dog your helmet and get to work."

FOUR

"Yo, Behanchod, you got the cut done, yet?" BFM commed.

Butch figured the company got the name of his job wrong. He wasn't an optical welding technician. That implied he occasionally joined two pieces of metal together. So far all he'd been was an optical *cutting* technician.

Robots did most of the actual welding. Putting things together, the way Apollo did it, was dead simple. Most of the parts were pre-fabbed on Earth and generally went together like Legos. He hadn't been part of the crew that did the life-station on *Troy* but he'd heard enough about it. There were sixty different massive pieces that had fit in the plug cut out of the *Troy* like a three dimensional puzzle. But it was a puzzle the robots had in their guts and so no problem.

Almost no problem. The plans were never perfect and when it got to putting stuff together there were *always* problems. Sometimes a part needed to be joined that wasn't on the plans. More often, some joker on Earth had left a bit too much steel here or there. The stuff on Earth was supposed to be all robots, too. But Butch had seen enough of how dumb ass robots could be to not be too impressed.

Point was, when something like that happened and it wasn't too big, it was generally easier to get a "sophont" with a laser rig to come over and cut the bit off. Chop here, chop there, stuff fit together.

When it was too big for a human to cut, they brought in the SAPL and everybody ran for cover.

"Just done, Mr. Price," Butch said. He could ignore his handle at this point. Despite the fact that that bastard Monaghan had been right and the crews had zeroed in on his sisters the first week. Then Gursy found the perfect handle to piss him off.

And they pushed. He'd had little mutilated Barbie dolls left in his locker, his personal stuff messed with. They'd found pictures of his sisters on the Internet, Susie and Maricela had both ended up in the hometown newspaper a couple of times, and done really ugly things with them. Just about everything but his suit messed with. The rules on that one were absolute. It was an automatic, do not pass go, firing offense to "molest, disturb, change, modify, add to or in any other way bother the personal safety system of another employee."

Gursy was the worst. The rest of the guys seemed to do it for the reasons Mr. Monaghan had talked about. But Gursy was just a bully. Butch was pretty sure it was Gursy who had put the girls' pictures in his locker with . . . stuff on 'em.

Well, Gursy had his "issues," too. And the rules said you couldn't futz with a guy's suit. They never said *nothing* about a sled. Butch had checked real carefully.

Most of the welding wasn't done in suits. Butch had been on the *Troy* for a month and he'd spent maybe four hours, other than "familiarization," in his suit. Most of the time he worked in a laser sled. The lasers they used were powered by an annie plant and an emitter, not the SAPL. So they had to have something to tow the laser around with. The laser sled was like a little mini space ship with arms, called waldoes for some reason, that you controlled from the inside. Some of the control you did with your plants. Most of it was using your hands to manipulate the waldoes.

Two of the waldoes were laser heads, one a low-power and the other high. There were four more "grip arms" that could go in just about any direction and amplify the strength of the user. Overall, the sleds looked sort of like an octopus. With, and this was important, a crystal porthole on the front.

"Move down to lever Two," Price said. "They're putting in a power plant and figure it's going to have something needs done the fracking bots can't figure out."

"Right away, Mr. Price," Butch said, turning his sled around and heading towards the big "lever" horns that punched up into the main bay of the *Troy*.

"Who the frack?" a voice screamed over the open channel. "God damn joking bastards! This is a safety violation! Get it off! Get it OFF!"

Butch tried not to giggle as he headed down to lever Two and somebody else had to pull off the plastic spider taped to Gursy's porthole.

"Somebody has been a *bad* boy," Dracula said, rolling into his bunk and turning on the TV.

"Really?" Butch said, trying not to sound too interested. "What happened?"

Dracula, AKA Drac, AKA Vladimir Anthony DeRosa

was also a probie but he'd made it past the "hard" probation period. He only had a couple more months and he'd make full tech. He was also Butch's roommate and a ready source of the sort of gossip that wasn't shared with an absolute FNG.

"Somebody, and Gursy is steaming mad to try to find out who, taped a spider to his porthole," Drac said. "He's also filed an official safety complaint."

"I'm so sorry to hear that," Butch said.

"What I can't figure out is how they did it," Drac said. "Somebody would have to go out in a suit, or a sled, and tape it there."

"Unless, and this is just a guess," Butch said. "Somebody noticed that Gursy always uses the sled parked at slot Three. Then, if somebody was an evil bastard, all they had to do was put the spider on *their* sled and park it at Three."

"In which case, when Gursy finds out the last guy to use the sled, he's going to be making a formal complaint," Drac said.

"That assumes that the last guy to use the sled *knew* the spider was there," Butch said.

"How could you miss a spider on your porthole?" Drac asked.

"Well if, and this is just *thinking* you understand," Butch said. "If you knew that the guy using the sled was going to go back to three because Gursy was out and three is the closest to the entrance that didn't have a sled and you knew that he was only going to be gone for less time than Gursy, somebody, and I've got no idea who, could tape the spider in place above the porthole on a bit of monofilament and space tape and hold it in *place* with regular scotch tape. The

scotch tape was going to last long enough for somebody like, oh, BFM, to go out and back and never
notice the spider 'cause it was way up over where he
could see without doing a full exterior. And it might
be particularly hard to spot sin... if it was up under
the Number Four Arm. Just a guess."

"Damn," Drac said. "That's... complicated. Whoever
thought that one up was a genius. But... BFM?" He
chuckled at that and then guffawed.

The team lead was a regular and serious practical
joker. But whereas Gursy's jokes were never very funny,
BFM's were hilarious. It had just the right touch to
be a Price. Complicated, hard to prove...

"Gursy is going to try to pin this on Price," Drac
said. "Which means making an official safety complaint."

"Read the regs," Butch said. "Strangely enough,
futzing with a suit is covered but not a sled. The
spider could have been *in* the sled, and it wouldn't
have been a safety violation. Not officially."

"I see a new reg being written," Drac said. "And
since you're a temp probie..."

"I had nothing to do with it," Butch said. "What
temp probie could possibly have come up with something *that* crazy?"

"First, I didn't do it," Ben "BFM" Price said, holding up his hands. "Second, it's not a safety violation."

The team lead was simply huge, six-eight with a big
bear gut, a beard that hung to his chest and a mass
of shaggy hair. He looked like a black-haired Bigfoot.

"It was messing with my *suit*," Carter Gursy said.
Gursy was much shorter but with the same general
shape and just about as hairy. Except on top where

he was pretty much bald. "That's a firing offense. And you were the last person to use it, Price!"

"Calm down," Doug Purcell said. The welding crew manager had been working for Apollo since the days when all they had was the *Monkey Business* and a couple of BDAs. Before that he'd worked in the drilling industry so he'd seen his fair share, and more, of dust-ups like this one. "I do have to admit this seems like a violation of Six-Three-Eight-Four-Nine-Delta."

He also had an elephant's memory for regulations.

"Nope," Price said. "Checked just before I come up here. Niner-Delta refers only to personal suits. Nothing about sleds. Doesn't mean I did it. But it does mean it's not a violation."

"I see a new reg being written," Mr. Purcell said, sighing. "And you insist that you did *not* do this?"

"I'd admit it if I did," Price said. "It was a *sweet* set-up and since it's not covered by regs I'd be in the clear. Who was the last guy before me to use the sled?"

"Uh . . ." Mr. Purcell said, accessing his plant. "Allen."

"The FNG?" Price said, chuckling. "No *way* an FNG did this. And Allen's Mister Pure. His big problem is he isn't tough enough. But he's been putting up with Gursy's crap so I guess he might slide."

"I want somebody's *hide* for this," Gursy said. "I don't care if it's covered by regs or not, it's a safety violation!"

"You're one to talk with all the crap you pull," Price said. "Gursy, here's the lowdown. I don't know how you made it through probe. Because *nobody* on the crew likes you one damned bit, nobody trusts you and if you were probe we'd have voted you off the island. I joke. Everybody jokes. Some of them get rough. You're just a buddy-screwer. I don't like that on my crew.

Joking's one thing. Being a buddy-screwer's another. So you want to bitch about this hard enough, we can put in an official request for transfer as incompatible. I noticed you come to us in the middle of a placement zone. Which told me you'd already got one transfer. But I decided to let it slide. Some crews you got to be one kind of guy to work with them. Quick enough, I figured out why you were kicked off a crew."

"I think we need to break up this little pow-wow," Mr. Purcell said, raising his hands. "Mr. Gursy, you're off shift. I'm not going to have anyone as agitated as you in the Black with a laser in your hand. Mr. Price, if you could stay a moment."

"You try to kick me off the crew, I'll appeal," Gursy said, standing up.

"You just do that," Price said, not looking up. Of course, he didn't really need to since he was Gursy's height sitting down.

Mr. Purcell leaned back in his chair and crossed his arms, looking at the team lead.

"I didn't do it," Price said, holding up his hand with three fingers extended. "Honest."

"Then who did?" Purcell asked.

"Allen," Price said instantly.

"Really?" the manager said, looking amused. He'd been around this game long enough to enjoy a really good joke. You either developed a sense of humor about such things or you got out.

"Yeah," Price said. "He stuck it up with a piece of scotch tape. He didn't know who was going to use the sled but he figured it was going to go back to Three, which Gursy always uses 'cause he's a buddy-screwer."

One and Two were reserved for Mr. Purcell and

other construction managers. Three was the next closest to the door.

"You're sure of this?" Mr. Purcell said.

"Why do you think I made sure I parked it at Three?" Price said. "I said I didn't do it. I didn't say I didn't *help*."

"Mr. Allen seems to be doing well..." Mr. Purcell said.

"If you're asking if I think he needs to be transferred, the answer is no," Price said. "I'd take three of Allen over Gursy. In fact, if it's a choice of Gursy or Allen, I'd take Allen, even though he's a probie. Usually when a guy's been on a crew and he knows what he's doing, even if he's an asshole guys'd rather work with him than a probie. But Gursy's an asshole and a buddy-screwer and everybody knows it. He does what he has to to get by. Allen works his tail off."

Mr. Purcell leaned back and closed his eyes, his lips working from side to side. After a few moments he opened them and regarded the team lead.

"You ever want to sit in this seat?" Purcell asked.

"Sure," BFM said. "Some day."

"What's your primary motivation going to be?" Purcell asked.

"The good of the guys," Price said.

"Wrong," Purcell said. "Dead wrong. Depends on which seat you're sitting in what, exactly, your motivation is. But in this seat, working for Apollo, the answer is: The best long-term interest of the company. Allen is a probationary tech, still not very good at his job and not yet a net asset to the company. Gursy is a trained tech and while I could wish he was more motivated in his position, he is a net asset."

"So you're saying get rid of Allen, who's a damned good kid, for a jackass like Gursy?"

"Not saying that," the manager said. "If I was at BAE, and God save me from another such assignment, the answer would be yes. If I was still at Shell the answer would be yes. But there's a reason I work for Apollo. Here's the thing. When you sit at this desk, there are two things you have to think about: What's going to make the company money and what's going to do it in the future. That's *all*."

"Then I don't want to sit at that desk," Price said.

"Don't be so quick to judge," Purcell said, smiling. "The work is physically much easier than spending all your time in the Black and the pay is generally better and always steadier. And it's not quite the selling your soul you're thinking. You ever met Tyler Vernon?"

"No," Price said, furrowing his brow. "And hell no. I don't got nothing against him, seems like a straight up guy and I think he runs a good company. Seems to care about his people. But I never come near meeting him. I mean, I see his ship in the bay from time to time, but . . ."

"He, rarely, teaches a class on business ethics for Apollo managers," Purcell said. "Fascinating guy. I mean, you know the history. But I mean *personally* he's a fascinating guy. The course is titled 'Capitalism Clothed' and it's a mandatory class for management at Apollo. The title's a take on Naked Capitalism. You get it?"

"Got it," Price said, smiling a bit.

"You think you get it," Purcell said, crossing his arms. "The first point of the class is to point out that every economy is at some level naked capitalism.

We just put various clothes on it. Unions are naked capitalism clothed in the rhetoric of organized labor."

"You said the U word," Price said.

"I know," Purcell said, grinning. Apollo was *death* on organized labor. "I'm pretty sure only Paris is listening and he doesn't talk. But one of the things Vernon talks about, once he's gotten everyone understanding the lingo, is Apollo clothing."

"Heard that," Price said, frowning. "I thought it was those shirts you all wear."

"He's . . . *inspirational* when he talks," the manager said, rubbing the Apollo symbol on his golf shirt. "'Apollo was the Greek god of the sun, of philosophy and art and as his burning chariot was the light that brought philosophy and art to the barbarian West, Apollo's *first* mission is to carry the light of civilization into the Black. The light of the sun is the clothing of Apollo and it is the clothing of this corporation.' I can't do it. He's got the knack, I don't."

"That's our boss?" the team lead said, chuckling. "Huh."

"The thing is, he's got a different vision from most other corporate heads," Purcell said. "He even admits it's a vision that probably won't last. But the vision extends beyond the next quarter, beyond the next year. 'Think not of the profit of the moment save to cover the necessary expenses of the corporation. Apollo will be leading the way to the stars long after we are dust. Think, rather, of the next generation. And make me a megacredit in the meantime.' Enlightened self-interest, the importance of safety to the bottom-line . . . He does go on."

"Sounds like it," Price said.

"If I transfer Allen, he's going to have to reestablish himself with a crew and the rate of second-term failure on probationary transfers is so high he's unlikely to make the cut," Purcell said. "But Gursy's the type who is going to figure out who did it eventually and up the ante. Which means he'll probably do something that's critically unsafe. I know the type of old. On the other hand, he's already had not one but two transfers. Which means if I request a transfer for incompatibility, he's going to get grounded."

"And then he owes Apollo for the rest of his life," Price said. "I'm not shedding any tears."

"And, again, the rate of repayment of the loans is actually minuscule," Purcell said, sighing. "Think about this, though. In this particular instance, Gursy is the one who was the victim. So I'm penalizing the victim."

"That's a really backward way of looking at it," Price said, his brow furrowing.

"I'm sure that will be Mr. Gursy's argument, or his lawyer's, in the lawsuit," Purcell said, smiling thinly. "But the truth is, I doubt that Mr. Vernon wants people like Gursy in his company and I think he'd probably take to Allen. Even though it is in the best short-term interest of the company to retain Gursy, it is in the best long-term interest, with some risk, to retain Allen."

"So get rid of Gursy and keep Allen?" Price said.

"Since I work for Apollo, yes," Purcell said. "That is in keeping with the overall mission and philosophy. If I was still with Shell or BAE, Allen would be transferred so fast he wouldn't have time to pack. And don't let the door hit you in the ass. As it is, that's what I'm going to have to do with Gursy."

✳ ✳ ✳

"Drac, I need a quick word with Butch," Price said, sliding into the probie quarters.

"You want me to . . . ?" Vlad said, confused.

"Go get a Coke or something," Price said. "This won't take long."

When Vlad was out of the room, Price picked the newbie up by his collar and slammed him against the bulkhead.

"You *ever* try to pin something like that on me again, I *will* violate rule Niner-Delta in a way nobody will ever trace and you *will* be sucking vacuum for the rest of your very short life."

"Yes, Mr. Price," Butch gasped. The team lead was a mountain. Struggling was pointless.

"That being said," Price said, lowering him to the deck, "and an understanding being reached, it was a very slick job. Not quite slick *enough*, but pretty slick. You also just barely missed being transferred."

"Yes, Mr. Price," Butch said. He knew better than to say "Sorry." It was the worst *possible* thing to say. You took your chances and you took your lumps if you got caught.

"*Gursy* is getting transferred," Price said.

"Mr. Price?"

"It was Purcell's call, not mine," Price said. "He's already gone. There's going to be some grumbling but not much. Nobody really liked the asshole. But you'd better keep your nose clean as snow for the rest of your probation. I'll tell the crew it's time to back off. They won't quit, mind you. But they'll back off. Just keep learning your job and keep your nose clean."

"Yes, Mr. Price," Butch said.

"You may call me BFM."

FIVE

"You're not bad for a FUN," Jablonski said, watching as Dana carefully went through the port gravitics relay checklist.

Despite their relatively small size, the *Myrmidons* were enormously complex. The main power was supplied by a twelve gigawatt matter-energy converter located directly behind the engineer station. That drove a repulsor drive capable of pulling four hundred gravities of delta-V. Pulling that much acceleration would turn a human to paste, though, so the craft had to have an Inertial Stabilization System, ISS, that kept the internal gravity more or less normal. More or less because beyond one hundred gravities of acceleration the system started to fall behind. At full drive, the internals—crew and cargo—were subjected to three gravities of acceleration.

In addition to the drive and ISS, there were four magnetic grapnels capable of localized gradients of over nine hundred gravities. They were designed primarily to lock onto a ship for boarding but from what Dana had heard they were mostly used as ersatz tug systems. The *Myrmidons* could only "reverse" at sixty gravities so they were better for pushing than pulling. But they got stuff moved in space eventually.

Since you had to get in and out of the boat somehow, there was a forward ramp and air-lock system as well as an emergency hatch in the flight compartment. The ramp was for terrestrial landings, which *very few* of the coxswains on the *Troy* had ever done. For Dana it was just another damned thing to check. Not to mention the "useless as tits on a boar hog" as AJ had pointed out, landing jacks.

Then there was the air lock. Air locks for more or less Terran sized sophonts, which included Glatun and Horvath, were fairly standardized across the local arm. The air lock was essentially two hatches with a space a bit shorter than the width of the *Myrm* between. A squad of Marines could stack up in the space to do an entry.

The hatches were fairly conventional steel with a high-tech sealant and fairly normal wheel-latches. They had to be authorized for opening from the engineer of the boat and checked for closure. The detectors were futzy as hell. And you wanted to make *sure* the hatches were sealed before you went into the Black. Most of the time, if there was time, the engineer would get out of the flight compartment and do a manual check. Especially if Marines were the ones doing the closure.

Searchlights, shields, double four-terawatt lasers for close-air support, avionics, more superconductor relays than a terrestrial power plant, the boat's engineer had to know *all* of it well enough to, at least, detect faults and report them for repair. In general, with the lack of higher support due to the way the Navy was growing and the lack of bay space on the *Troy*, most repairs took place in the bay with ENs, engineers first class, and EMs, petty officer engineering mates, sweating and cursing in suits.

To make full rate, an engineer apprentice was required to demonstrate that he, or in Dana's case, *she*, could just locate and analyze faults, not repair them. In a suit, in microgravity, in vacuum, in the *dark*.

And they had to meet minimum standard capability as *coxswains* in case the cox was disabled during an "evolution."

"Checks completed, EN," Dana said, straightening up and trying to keep from rubbing her back. Checking the gravitics mostly meant bending over for hours. The one good thing about Jablonski was that he barely seemed to notice her as a girl. "No faults detected."

"Check completed, aye," Jablonski said, making a notation on his pad. "No faults detected, aye. Good check."

"Good check, aye," Dana said.

"Break it down," AJ said. "We have mandatory flight fun time this afternoon."

"Flight fun time" translated as physical training. There was a basketball court and a gym. Dana spent most of her work-out time in the gym since there wasn't a good gymnastics set up.

She'd been a cheerleader in high school but mostly she'd been into the gymnastics. If she hadn't "blossomed" a bit young she might have made the pros. It was one of the reasons she was ahead of the curve for training in microgravity. With enough time on parallel bars, micro wasn't a really big issue. She still wasn't *good* in micro, but she could manage simple tasks.

"Break it down, aye," Dana said, gathering up the tools and carefully stowing them away. The stow point for the boat's tools was to the starboard side of the flight compartment, just to the side and aft of the engineer's station. Over the compartment was a post-production welded on set of clamps with a crowbar installed. The second day she'd been working on the boat, AJ had come in with the crowbar, the clamps and a laser welding set and grimly welded the crowbar into place. He hadn't said anything about why but it wasn't until the crowbar was in place that Twenty-Nine was listed as flight-certified.

She'd wondered about the crowbar—it wasn't part of the standard tool-set and it seemed to hold some particular significance—but she hadn't asked. There were no stupid questions, but she had learned that there were answers you only got at a certain point in your training. She suspected the Significance of the Crowbar was one of them. She'd figured out some of the meanings. "Going crow" on a boat, or a person, meant beating the hell out of a part, or a person. But there seemed to be more. One time when Sean's boat had had a mid-space malfunction he had mentioned it "looked like crowbar time." And EM Hartwell had been pretty grim. There was some significance to the crowbar.

She'd find out when it was time.

"We have a *special* event for you today, boys and girls."

Chief Petty Officer John Wagner looked like a recruiting poster. Tall, blond and mustachioed, he simply reeked of being God's gift to women. His good point was that he wasn't an ass about it and had never so much as hinted to Dana. On the other hand, he seemed to positively enjoy passing on the worst possible news to the flight. So the fact that he'd fallen out for "flight fun time" meant that they were probably not going to like the result.

"With the activation of C-West, there are four new grav ball courts open," the chief said, grinning broadly.

There was a collective groan from the assembled flight.

"So it's helmet and pads time," the chief finished, grinning ear to ear. "Fall out for MWR draw."

"What's wrong with grav ball?" Dana asked. She was actually pretty excited. She'd heard about the sport but the only people who seemed to play it were the Marines. And she'd been pointedly warned about playing them.

"Where to start?" Sean said, receiving a set of knee and elbow pads and a helmet from the MWR civilian manning the desk. "You know the rules?"

"Sort of like hockey," Dana said, accepting her own pads. "Five-person teams. One goalie, two forwards, two defense. Two goals. Once you catch the ball you can't push off from the walls, you have to pass. Okay, hockey and ultimate Frisbee. You can bounce the ball off of any wall. Move it down the court to get it in the enemy goal."

"Ever really thought about it?" Sean asked. "The walls have padding. Some. You've got to be able to bounce the ball, so it's not real thick. Then there's the viewing wall made out of optical sapphire, which is, let me tell you, very, very hard stuff. Note the pads and helmet. The first Marine unit to play it had about ten percent injuries that required doctor's input. Of course, they have since created jungleball, which you don't want to play."

"What's jungleball?" Dana asked as they reached the null grav court.

"Null grav actually has about a hundred thousand rules," Sean said. "Most of them related to no hitting, biting, scratching or kicking the other guy in the balls. The Marines wear a cup. It's like Aussie Rules football. The first rule of jungleball is 'No weapons.' There's seven more."

"Oh," Dana said.

They'd reached the court and Dana started to get a feel for why Sean wasn't exactly looking forward to null-grav ball.

The viewing wall fronted on the corridor and was a three-story-tall wall of optical sapphire. The *door* was even sapphire with a small, recessed latch. The other five walls were lightly padded. One end of the court was broadly marked in blue, the other red. The overall court looked like an extended version of a handball court.

The goals were recessed nets about two meters wide surrounded by six recessed hand-holds. Dana recalled that the only person who was allowed to retain traction, hold on to the grips, was the goalie.

The court was apparently still under gravity since First division's engineering personnel were just filing in. The engineering crew, a couple of administrative seamen including Sarin and CM1 Glass. Glass was tossing a soccer ball up and down in his hand and looking positively happy.

"Since I'm not neutral in this group, I'm going to be refereeing, not playing. Bigus and Carter, you're team captains. Divvie them up."

Dana ended up on Carter's team but got cut from the first string along with Sarin. All the SAs and EAs got cut and pulled out of the court to watch.

"This is going to be insane," Sarin said. "Carter was bitching up a storm."

"It looks like it should be fun," Dana said.

The two team captains faced towards their own goals with Glass in the center, holding the ball.

"And . . . grav off," Glass said, releasing the ball. "Game on."

Bigus, the EM3 of shuttle Thirty-Two, managed to hit the ball first, sending it towards the blue team that was starting to float up, slowly. Carter had taken a swing and floated off in a random direction.

The ball missed the blue team entirely, caromed off two walls and headed down court towards red. Which pushed off from the floor and all missed intercepting the ball. Which, fortunately, was slowing due to air-resistance. Sean managed to get a hand on it and passed it to Bigus. Which sent Sean spinning off into the sapphire wall, cracking his head hard enough to ring the aluminum alloy.

In no time at all it was a maelstrom. Despite the jerseys, Dana couldn't keep up with what was happening and she was pretty sure neither could anyone on the teams. People were more or less randomly ramming into walls. She saw Bigus drive for the goal at one point—he'd managed to snag the ball in midair while headed in more or less the direction of the goal—and nearly make it. Problem being it was his *own* goal. He corrected at the last minute and tried a pass to Sean but that was intercepted by a red team SN Dana didn't know, who made the goal.

"Dead ball," Glass called. The ball had stopped in mid-court and so had all the team members. He'd managed to take up a position near the top of the court and more or less hang there by making very light motions. He pushed off lightly and plucked the ball out of the middle of the court.

"Sean for Danno," Bigus called. He was sort of upside-down and drifting slowly in the direction of the blue goal but so far away from the walls he might never make it.

"How am I going to get *out*?" Sean called. He was hanging more or less motionless on the red side but, again, nowhere near the walls.

"Easy," Glass said, hitting him with the ball and sending him careening towards the red wall. "Now get your butt out."

Dana stepped into the court and slowly bounced her way over to the defender's position. The one thing she knew about micrograv was that it was hard to move fast. Not impossible, Glass seemed to have the knack. But it was hard.

She managed to stabilize up in the corner by the blue goal and waited for play to resume.

"And . . . game on," Glass said, sending the ball spinning into the middle of the court.

Bigus had the angle of the bounce figured right and probably would have intercepted. If Glass hadn't put some English on it. The ball passed his flailing hand and got to the red team.

It was headed for a red team player in position

to shoot for the goal when Dana pushed off the wall and made possibly the slowest intercept in the short history of nullball. The pass had been long and the ball was slowing so she nearly missed but managed to snag it. The impact of the ball on her hand and pulling it in caused her to rotate. But she let herself follow around and then pushed the ball off with both feet towards the red goal.

"Bust a move, Danno," Bigus called, grinning. "But you might want to—"

Dana slammed into the sapphire wall head first. Since she was grinning, it ground her teeth together painfully.

"Ow!" she said, rebounding towards the "floor" and rubbing her head. "That hurt."

"You okay?" Glass said.

"One hundred percent, CM," Dana said, not wanting to add that it was one hundred percent headache and neck-ache.

"I can understand your lack of joy at playing nullball," Dana said, rubbing her neck. "But it's pretty fun if you keep your situational awareness."

"Which is the point," Glass said, coming up behind Dana and Sean. The flight NCOIC had the lightest step Dana had ever seen. "It's good training for micrograv. It's even good flight training. Speaking of which, EA, you're four hours behind on coxswain quals. I want to see you in the simulator course one night a week for the next week."

"One night a week, aye, CM," Dana said, trying not to sigh. There went sleep.

✳ ✳ ✳

"Personnel cycling air lock will perform a visual check of all seals prior to sealing inner door..." EM1 Hartwell said in a rapid patter.

"Personnel cycling air lock will perform a visual check of all seals prior to sealing inner door, aye," Dana said, adding a manual check for burs or scratches by running her hand over the seal. The latter wasn't part of the air lock operations procedure but it would be if Chief Barnett ever had her way.

Dana had been qualed on basic suit function and function in a microgravity atmosphere environment. The latter translated as she was starting to kick some serious butt at nullball.

So now it was time for her full suit quals.

"Procedure Two-Nine-Six-Four-Eight-November, Secure Safety Line complete," Hartwell said. "Personnel will contact air lock and integrity control to release outer door."

"Personnel will contact air lock and integrity control to release outer door, aye," Dana said, clearing her throat. "Paris, EA Parker One-One-Three-Eight."

"EA Parker One-One-Three-Eight, Paris."

She got her usual thrill hearing the AI. Paris didn't have much time to chat with an EA rate, which was too bad. He had a *really* sexy voice.

"Request release, Air-lock Outer Door Six-One-Seven," Dana said. She was still a bit iffy on comming without speaking. She'd passed quals but she preferred to talk. Especially with Paris, she tended to add "unintended transmissions" when she internal commed.

"Release Air-lock Outer Door Six-One-Seven, aye," Paris replied. *"Verify Procedure Six-Six-One-Four-Eight-Alpha, Open Air-lock Doors complete."*

"Procedure Six-Six-One-Four-Eight-Alpha, Open Air-lock Doors complete, aye," Dana said.

"*Verify Procedure Four-Seven-Thee-Six-Charlie-Alpha, Suit Integrity check complete.*"

"Procedure Four-Seven-Thee-Six-Charlie-Alpha, Suit Integrity check complete, aye," Dana said, trying not to sigh. There was a reason for all the readbacks but they got to be a pain in the *butt.*

"*List personnel using air lock for manifest integrity . . .*"

"*Verify Procedure . . .*"

"*All procedures for EVA verified and checked,*" Paris said. "*Open Air-lock Outer Door Six-One-Seven, Procedure Niner-Niner-Four-Four-Eight complete. Pumping down.*"

"Pumping down, aye," Dana said.

The red light overhead started to rotate and Dana could feel the slight change in texture as vacuum started to surround her suit. She took a deep breath and hoped that all the checks, which she *had* completed and verified, were good.

"It's all good," Hartwell said. "Ready to step?"

"Ready to step," Dana said, starting to move forward.

"Whoa there, Space Eagle," Hartwell said. "What do you do next?"

"Procedure Eight-Seven-Four-One-Six-Delta," Dana said, reaching out the air-lock door and clipping off her outer safety line. It wasn't like she was going to do a Dutchman. She was wearing a navopak that could get her nearly to Mars on internal power. "Complete."

"Procedure Eight-Seven-Four-One-Six-Delta complete, aye," Hartwell said. "Begin procedure . . ."

It made things safer but it sure took the fun out of life.

Finally they were out in EVA and the air lock closed. The air lock was near the base of the tube to which all the shuttles were attached and shuttle Twelve from Flight A was more or less entirely blocking the view of the main bay.

"Okay," Hartwell said. "We need to get past all this crap to get to Twenty-Nine. Give me a one-eightieth vertical thrust on navo."

"One-eightieth vertical thrust, aye," Dana said, giving the system just about its lowest possible boost "upwards."

This lifted them "above" the shuttle and the main bay was finally revealed.

"Holy hell," Dana muttered.

"You okay?" Thermal asked.

"It's . . ."

"Stabilize and drink it in for a minute. I'll give you that. Most people need to get a good look before they can get their heads around getting to work."

The main bay of the *Troy* was six kilometers across. She knew that intellectually. But *seeing* it was something different. It was just hard to get the *scale* of the thing. Down and to port there were two ships that looked like the sort of toys she'd played with when she was a kid. One was a freighter or an Apollo miner. Those were three hundred meters long. As long as a supercarrier. More than three football fields in length.

It looked about the size of her pinkie. Smaller.

Next to it was a *Constitution*-class cruiser, the biggest true "ship" produced by humanity. It didn't look much bigger. There were some tiny dots moving around on its surface and she realized they were other suits doing EVA. They were almost microscopic. The bay was just *immense*.

But there was more that was throwing her. Jutting up from the walls were three massive spikes. They reached up through the interior to very nearly meet in the middle. Then she realized they were about three kilometers *long*.

What got her wasn't just the size. She was sort of intellectually prepared for that. But she wasn't prepared for the fact that the interior was so shiny it was almost like a mirror. There was a God damned big, she had no clue how big but it had to be *immense*, light bulb "down" from their position. The light filled the hold and reflected off the surfaces so there were no shadows at all. None. Even the *Constitution* and the spikes didn't cast a shadow. That was a bit eerie. But with no atmosphere and the reflection of the mirrorlike walls, there was nowhere for shadows to hide.

"It's beautiful," Dana said, softly. "I wasn't expecting it to be beautiful."

"There is that," Thermal said. "Think you can pay attention to exterior checks on the shuttle?"

"I am prepared and ready to perform, EM," Dana said.

"Then let us, slowly and carefully, make our way over to Twenty-Nine and actually get some work done."

"How you doing, Parker?" CM1 Glass asked.

"I am five by, CM," Parker said, examining her engineering screen.

She was most of the way through quals. The truth

was, there wasn't time to teach all the procedures and processes involved in doing the job of a shuttle engineer in A School. All that A School could do was produce people who sort of had a basic understanding of the systems. How to work with them in the environment of a permanent position was "makee-learnee" after you got to your post. Until you learned enough to not be a danger to yourself and others, you were a FUN: Fracking Useless Noob.

That meant that when the shuttles went out, whether for training or a "real-world evolution," the FUN EAs and CAs were left behind with the nonshuttle personnel, called Troglos because they never got out of the *Troy*, to work on their quals, polish the brass, clean heads or whatever else the BMs could come up with to motivate them to finish quals.

But part of quals was, occasionally, heading out into the bay, or sometimes the Black, to show that they'd mastered how to work with the shuttles in the real world.

When she'd arrived on the *Troy* she had initially despaired of ever learning all the SOPs and processes necessary to do her job. Take the engineering display. It had readouts of all the monitored systems, four hundred and twenty-eight, on the shuttle. Power levels, relay conditions, avionics, hatches. It all added up. And much of it interacted so you had to have some clue what the cascade issues of a failure might mean.

But after a bare three months, here she was with CM Glass doing her final deploy qual.

"All the little bits ticking over?" Mutant asked.

"Tick, tock, CM," Dana said.

She had been out in the main bay doing EVA work

on the birds so many times the view had gotten common if not boring. It was hard to imagine the main bay ever getting boring if for no other reason than that it kept changing.

She had finally looked up the full plan for *Troy* and been absolutely shocked. The construction plans were barely in "Part One, Phase One" of the full plan. The full plan was intended to take at least a *hundred* years. And it was only referred to as a rough plan because nobody knew how technology was going to change.

Troy was broken up into six notional zones, North, South, East, West, One and Two. South was the zone that had the main door, a kilometer-wide, kilometer-and-a-half-thick plug that was currently the only way in and out of the battlestation. North was the general area where the big ships hung out. There wasn't much going on over there and it was out of the way. Currently there were four *Constitutions* and a new *Independence*-class frigate holding station in the Arctic. Gravitic tractor docking systems were being constructed down there by a swarm of bots and EVA personnel. In the meantime the cruisers and frigates had to maintain station against the slight gravity produced by the *Troy*.

Zone Two was where most of the construction materials were piling up. There were entire "environment packs," prefabricated quarters, bays and repair shops, piling up down there. The next big construction phase, involving pulling out a chunk of the wall and installing the packs, was about to take place. But all the packs had to be in place, first. Pulling the wall out was only going to happen once.

East and West were mostly empty. There was an

Apollo mining support ship hovering over in East. It was probably there to get ready for the pull. West only had some piled up material that had been cut out of the walls.

On the other hand, West also had the Dragon's Orb, the one-hundred-meter diameter ball of "dirty" sapphire that provided light to the main bay. The blazing ball was held in place by a sculpted four-prong setting of nickel-iron that looked like an eagle or dragon's claw. The light came from a four terawatt SAPL beam that reflected off "micro beads" of platinum embedded in the sapphire. It fully illuminated the main bay. Perhaps too fully: the ball was hard to look at it was so bright.

Phase One was simply getting full support systems in place in Zone One, the part that Dana was based in. There still weren't shuttle bays for the current *Myrmidon* complement and Zone One was eventually supposed to house, internal, a wing of *Myrmidons*, three full squadrons and all their support personnel and equipment.

That was nothing compared to other parts of the plan. There were plans to build internal bays for the *Constitution*-class cruisers as well as other combat and support ships. By the end of Phase One, an entire *task force* of ships was to be installed in the walls of the fortress. With launch systems to send the ships out without using the main bay doors. They were going to be shot out like missiles. The same plan was in place for the shuttles. They would eventually go out by a bypass system rather than flying around the main bay.

Like everything with the *Troy*, the plan was beyond big. But it was going to be fun to watch. And occasionally support. The *Myrmidons* spent about half their active time training and the rest acting as "filler" tugs for the construction projects.

She recognized all the classes, another qual, except one.

"CM?" she said, tilting her head to the side quizzically. "What class is that?"

The shuttle looked like a *Myrmidon* but it didn't have the gravity grapnels. And it was painted bright white with an Apollo logo on the side, a graphic of a chariot towing the sun. It was parked on the Zone Two side of the bay apparently involved in some of the moving of materials. It might be a command ship for that matter.

"That is in a class by itself," Glass said, adjusting his vector slightly.

By swinging around, Mutant was able to get a position where they could see the starboard side of the shuttle. They'd been looking at the port and base before.

"Is that a glass wall?" Dana asked. The starboard side of the cargo bay of the shuttle appeared to be glass or sapphire. It was reflective so you couldn't really see in, but it was clearly not steel.

"Sapphire," Glass said. "*That* is the *Starfire*, the personal transport of Mr. Tyler Vernon."

"Oh," Dana said, her eyes widening. Vernon was about as big a name as you got. He was the richest guy in the solar system, the owner of the SAPL, which was, at base, nothing more than a gigantic mining laser, and the visionary who had conceived and created the *Troy*. "Is he in there?" she squeaked.

"Probably," CM1 Glass said. "He spends about half his time in a compartment in the civvic side of Zone

One. A big compartment that is appropriately fitted out for a multibillionaire. And from what I hear the *Starfire* is a flying boudoir."

"*I* hear he doesn't even have a girlfriend," Dana said.

"A boudoir does not require women, EA," Glass said, moving back into his lane and out of sight of the sapphire bulkhead. "That simply means it's very comfortable."

"So, does he like . . . guys?" Dana asked.

"I have no idea," Mutant said, chuckling. "But don't get your hopes up. He's not going to notice a lowly EA."

"I wasn't . . ." Dana said.

"I'm funning you, FUN," Glass said. "I'm not the sort of guy who pays a lot of attention to the lifestyles of the rich and famous. So I have no idea of Mr. Vernon's tastes in such things. But you see him around. He rarely goes back to Earth. He sort of *lives* on the *Troy* or in Wolf."

"That sounds . . . lonely," Dana said.

"*Permission to enter a personal conversation?*" Paris commed.

"Granted, Paris," Glass said. Practically every conversation in the station was monitored by Paris but he rarely interjected.

"*Mr. Tyler's sexual tastes are heterosexual,*" the AI commed. "*He does not have a significant other. He occasionally complains about that, but his schedule is such that he rarely meets with appropriate females. He spends much of his time alone. And, yes, it is lonely. He says that he is adjusted to that existence, having maintained it for over fifteen years.*"

"Oh," Dana said.

"Paris, don't go matchmaking with my EA," Glass said, grinning.

"*That was not the intent*," Paris replied. "*My intent is more complex.*" The AI cut the connection.

"I think you stepped on it, CM," Dana said.

"I'm trying to figure out Paris' point," Glass said, thoughtfully. "I suppose it might be situational awareness."

"CM?"

"Vernon's . . ." Glass said then paused. "Vernon was the guy who created the *Troy*. He had little or nothing to do with developing the *Constitutions*, but he created SAPL, which is the *real* defense of the solar system, and *Troy*. I think that Paris was making the point that knowing something about a guy who has *that* much power and influence is slightly different than knowing which movie star is cheating on which."

"Ah," Dana said.

"What I'm still trying to process is why Paris made the point to *us*," Glass said. "But I'm not a big brain AI so I'm going to ignore it for now."

Dana swiveled her screen around to examine the *Starfire* again.

"Maybe because we *asked*?"

Mutant had carefully traveled around to the West side to get to the door, avoiding all the other traffic in the bay. Entering the opening was to be plunged into blackness. Vacuum didn't transmit light except in a straight line so the light from the Dragon's Orb was cut off abruptly.

"No traffic," CM1 Glass said, leaning back. "That's nice. I always hate it when the tunnel's full."

"It's a kilometer across, CM," Dana said, frowning. "The *Constitutions* are a hundred and fifty meters in width. Even with two or three across... There's plenty of room."

"There are six SAPL beams coming through," Glass pointed out. "Fifty-meter radius safety zones around those. So that's two hundred meters cut off. And the internal diameter is only seven hundred, not a klick. Crowded is relative, but when you're a very small boat negotiating around giants..."

"I take your point, CM," Dana said.

"Can't wait for the internal SAPL system to get done," Glass said with a sigh. "Those things are killers."

"Internal?" Dana asked, confused.

"They intend to eventually drill SAPL conduits through the walls," Glass said. "Run them in through big collimators on the surface and bounce them around the interior. That way they're not crossing the main bay."

"That will be nice," Dana said as they emerged from the tunnel. "Oh... my."

"Nice, huh?" Glass said.

In the shuttle up to *Troy* she'd been in a center seat and the *Columbias* didn't really have much in the way of portholes. Sarin had gone over to look out the one free one but she hadn't bothered. She wasn't really big on space, she just wanted to give the Horvath some payback.

This wasn't a porthole and it wasn't even a big screen. But it was *full* of stars.

Every square centimeter seemed to have some point of light in it. From Earth, most of the light from distant stars was filtered out by the atmosphere. In space, they were everywhere.

"*This* is what makes all the other crap worthwhile," the coxswain's mate said.

"I don't understand why they call it the Black," Dana said softly.

"Depends on which way you're looking," Mutant said, enigmatically. "And now we get to work."

He engaged standard cruise power, ninety gravities, and headed out into deep space.

"Once we are clear of the busy parts we will go through some evolutions," CM Glass said. "We will run through some standard shipboard emergencies and you will respond to them, following all procedures and standards. If you pass this qual, you will be well on your way to being an engineer first class."

"Yes, CM," Dana said.

"And so we start," Glass said as the lights and grav cut out. "Uh, Engineer, we seem to have a failure...?"

For four hours, Glass had put Dana through hell. Most of the time there was neither light nor gravity. And whoever had built the failure tests was devilishly clever. Some of them would have been damned hard to find in a *repair bay*!

"The inertial system is up, CM," Dana said, finally finding the "faulty" relay.

"Good," Glass said. "We won't be turned into glue when...ugh! Urk! Agh!"

He slumped over to the side theatrically.

"You noted that there is a large hole that is leaking volatiles from your coxswain's head," Glass said, pulling out a drink bulb filled with a red liquid and puncturing it. "He appears to have been hit by a micrometeor which had other issues..."

The air in the compartment started to pump down, the lights and power went out again, and Dana was left in microgravity. Then she noticed it *wasn't* microgravity. The ship was starting to spin, causing a rather unpleasant centripetal effect. And the rate was increasing.

"That's going to get *everywhere*, you know!" Dana said.

"I know," Glass replied. "And *you're* going to have to clean it up. I suggest a toothbrush."

"Dammit," she muttered. "Stupid coxswains always getting themselves killed."

She first determined that she, in fact, had control power. But one of the maneuvering thrusters was set to full power and she couldn't kill it from her engineer's position.

Getting to the relay, with the ship spinning harder and harder, was a matter of clambering hand-over-hand across the flight compartment to the appropriate panel. She got the relay to shut down by the simple expedient of pulling it. Then she had to start working the other problems...

"CM Glass, all engineering issues rectified," she said.

Glass was still slumped over to the side. He appeared to have fallen asleep.

"Uh...Coxswain?" Dana said.

"Your coxswain has bled out while you were fixing the ship," Glass said. "It's okay. With that head wound he was going to be a vegetable anyway. You are on your own. You noted in your repairs that the same micrometeorite that killed your coxswain also took out the navigation system and the hypernode. Paris, CM1 Glass Four-Three-Eight-Two."

"*CM1 Glass Four-Three-Eight-Two, Paris.*"

"Notional emergency in shuttle Two-Niner," Glass said. "Repeat, notional. Hypernode and navigation inoperable. Coxswain terminated. Control transferred to EA Parker."

"*Confirm notional emergency*," Paris responded. "*Good luck, Parker.*"

Parker was confused. With the hypercom out she couldn't even call to ask Hartwell what she was supposed to do. She had done the engineering side, except for the "destroyed" hypercom. But she didn't have any orders and couldn't recall a procedure that fit.

"Am I supposed to fly back?" she asked.

"You're talking to a dead man," Glass said, sitting up. "What you do, now, is up to you entirely. You have a dead person and the bird."

"Well, I could always discharge the dead weight," Dana said. "Save some fuel."

"*Try* it, Danno."

Dana finally realized that Glass just wasn't going to give her any orders. She'd been following orders for so long she wasn't used to making her own decisions.

"Okay," she said, aloud. "Boat's damaged. Coxswain dead. The only smart choice is to head to the nearest help. Which is..."

The navigational system wasn't operating. She could probably tinker around the lock-out but that wasn't what the test was looking for.

"*Troy, Troy*," she muttered. "Where is *Troy*?"

She had visual systems. But they had spent so much time under power that even the massive nine-kilometer space station had disappeared. Not only was it probably a dot, she wasn't sure which direction it was from their current position. She'd been paying attention to engineering, not nav. All there was was deep space all around her.

"Oh...crap," she muttered. Without nav she had no real idea where she was. "Okay, okay, I can figure this out..."

She oriented the ship towards the sun and started hunting. The gate stayed in a location between Earth and Mars, in line with Earth. It wasn't actually in a stable orbit but it had gravitic controls to keep it in place. The gate was ten kilometers across but the ring was only a hundred meters wide. It might be hard to spot.

Troy was near the gate. Near, not at. It moved around due to the L point gravitational issues. If she could orient to the gate, she might be able to spot the space globe. If worse came to worst, she had enough fuel to make it to Earth. But she figured she'd probably get reamed out if she took the *Myrm* back to McKinley Base.

She found the sun. After a while she managed to find Earth. Line those two up and she'd be between Earth and the gate. Spin around.

But at their distance, the width of the sun left enough wiggle room that even by turning the ship around and orienting it carefully she still couldn't spot *Troy* or the gate.

"Crap," she muttered.

"*Now* you know why they call it the Big Black," Glass said. "Hartwell finally gave up on this one."

"I know he doesn't like the Black," Dana said, glad the CM was at least willing to talk.

"I will give you exactly one hint," Glass said. "You are looking the wrong way."

"There are three hundred and sixty other degrees to look," Dana said. "In plane and in vertical. That's one hundred twenty-nine thousand six hundred degrees to search."

"Didn't say it was *easy*," Glass replied.

Looking the wrong way. She had assumed when Glass headed out from the *Troy* he had headed towards Earth. But they had kept a more or less straight initial vector from the door. And the door was oriented *away* from the gate, "up" in the plane of ecliptic.

She oriented to the sun again then rotated the boat so that the sun was "up" from her position. Then she started scanning around.

It was the gate that she spotted first. The thin, high albedo, ring just leapt out. Then by searching around some more she finally spotted the *Troy*. It was so small it looked like a minor star. Without figuring out their initial vector she'd have been lost in space until their power ran out. Or she just gave up and headed to Earth.

She engaged power and started to head back at full cruise.

"Paris, Shuttle Two-Niner," she said. "Declaring notional emergency."

"Your hypernode is out," Glass pointed out.

"At some point, my internals are going to get through," Dana said. "If I recall the manual, at about six kilometers, but I'm willing to bet Paris has some ears out from *Troy*. And I'd really like to know where the SAPL beams are. They head in to *Troy* along this line, somewhere."

"Discontinue test," Glass said, grinning.

"Thank God," Dana said, lifting her hands from her flight controls. "Your bird, Coxswain."

"*Your* bird, Engineer Apprentice," Glass said. "Paris, Two-Niner."

"*Two-Niner, Paris. Get your notional emergency under control?*"

"All done," Glass said. "Shuttle Two-Niner continues under control of EA Parker."

"*Coxswain EA Parker, aye,*" Paris said. "*EA Parker will observe all traffic notices and lanes. Be aware of SAPL zone six thousand meters to your right. No major traffic in entry zone for one hour. Please decelerate to a maximum of one thousand kilometers per hour before entering close approach zone. Maximum velocity in entry, ninety kilometers per hour. Have a nice day.*"

"Am I taking it all the way back to the dock?" Parker asked.

"That depends on if you ding it on the way."

"Docking maneuver complete." Dana sighed. Even with the automatic systems and the tractors, docking was always ticklish.

"Verify hard dock, Procedure Three-Six-Five-Four-Niner-Dash-Alpha," Glass said.

"The engineer does that," Dana said, looking over her shoulder.

"And you're the EA," Glass said.

Dana checked all her telltales and noted one red light.

"We've got an environmental light," Dana said, frowning. "It's...*cabin* pressure?"

"I'm going to give you a pass on this qual," Glass said. "You did a great job on correcting all the crap I threw at you and at responding to the emergency. And you found your way back to the barn. But next time you might want to repressurize the cabin."

❋　　❋　　❋

"Watch quals complete," EM1 Hartwell said. "Suit, eng and cox cross quals complete. Drill quals complete. I'm recommending EA Parker to EN, Chief."

"Mutant?" the chief said, looking at Glass. "She's completed them sort of fast. I hate to suggest . . . favoritism . . ."

"If you mean she has a cute ass, Chief, just say it," Glass said. "And she does. But that's not why she made quals so fast. Oh, maybe a bit but just because people were willing to spend more time with her, not let her slide. She's pretty damned sharp. I held her back on cox quals 'cause she was doing well enough I wanted to see how far I could push her. I'd take her as a cox OJT any day. She's just . . . good."

"Parker," Hartwell said, sticking his head into Twenty-Nine.

"EM?" Dana said. She was removing a balky grav plate that was part of the ISS. The things were not only heavy, they were just *bulky*. She was about to kill the internal grav to get the damned thing out.

"Go down to the BX and get your EN tabs," Hartwell said. "Once they're slapped on, I'm going to move you over to Thirty-Six."

"Boomer," Dana said. She got along well enough with the CM3. He was better than most at having his ass kicked by a guuurl at nullball. "Does that mean . . . ?"

"You're full qualed," Thermal said. "Don't let it go to your head. You *know* some of the idiots we've got who are full qualed. But take some time getting your tabs. Maybe pick up some lunch at the food court. You've earned it."

"What about the grav plate?" Dana asked.

"Leave it for AJ," Hartwell said. "This isn't your bird anymore."

"Booyah!" Dana said when the EM was gone. "Hey! AJ!"

SIX

"SET CONDITION ONE! CONDITION ONE!"

Dana rolled out of her bunk and was halfway into her suit before she even realized the 1MC was blaring.

Another damned . . .

"Suity" had mentioned that there were regular air-loss drills. What he had not mentioned, probably because the civilian side didn't have to deal with it, was the Condition One, "battlestations," drills, the launch drills, the damage control drills . . .

She had been working twelve hours a day on her bird, maintaining her flight qual, mandatory "fun" time, training evolutions . . .

She did *not* need a damned drill every thirty minutes!

"THIS IS NOT A DRILL. HORVATH SHIPS IN E ERIDANI. SET CONDITION ONE . . ."

"Holy hell!" Dana said, dogging her helmet while cycling the hatch to her quarters.

The benefit of all the drills became evident as she made her way to her bird. She was still not quite awake but when she'd first followed EM Hartwell to Thirty-Six she thought she'd never be able to find her way back.

After a week she could do it in her sleep. As she was proving.

"*Mutant, Longwood,*" LCM Martin commed.

"*Mutant, sir,*" Glass responded.

"*We've got a real world evolution,*" the commander of Charlie Flight commed. "*We're doormen, helping the Apollo tugs close the plug. And I've been given the word that they want every boat out there. Moving this thing is going to be a nightmare.*"

"*We're down two coxswains, sir,*" Glass pointed out.

"*Which is why I'm comming,*" Longwood replied. "*Pick two ENs that are cox qualed.*"

"*Move Gopher to Thirty-One and* Danno *to Thirty-Three, sir,*" Glass commed without hesitation.

"*Danno?*" the CO said. "*That seems like a bit of risk when we're still in the middle of a review from the* last *incident.*"

"*Her scores on famil were so high I'm wondering why she's an EA, sir,*" Mutant replied. "*In Thirty-Three it puts her with Thermal to keep an eye on her. And it gets us two more birds, sir.*"

"*Do it,*" the lieutenant commander said. "*Tell Paris…*"

"*I will, sir,*" Mutant said. "*Any word on Spade and Boomer?*"

"*They were on the seventeen forty from Minot,*" Longwood replied. "*If the Horvath come through any time soon… I don't think we'll be getting them back.*"

"Go, Go, Go," CM1 Glass said, standing by the hatch to the shuttle bay and tapping people through. It was his job to count through the personnel and make sure everyone was in place. EM Carlemon Trotman was in charge of warming the boat while AJ was Earthside with Spade and Boomer, so all he had to do was hit the seat and drive. "Move it, Danno!"

"Roger, CM," Dana said, leaping through the air lock and catching the grab bar.

She spun in the air and hooked another bar with her foot to get oriented then pushed off, floating down the corridor to her bird.

"Sweet, Danno," Sean called. He was hauling himself along hand-over-hand to his bird.

"Float like a butterfly," Dana said.

She pulled herself into Thirty-Six, hit grav in a two-point stance, dogged the hatches and pounded across the cargo bay to her position. Thirty seconds after hitting the bay doors she was in position and warming the bird.

She wasn't sure *why* she was warming the bird. Her coxswain, Boomer, was Stateside as a witness in an "incident review." Before she arrived, an Alpha Flight *Myrmidon* plowed into a clearly marked SAPL beam. It had missed a marked turn. The two men in the crew were killed. The *Myrm* had been completely destroyed to the point of scattering bits all over the bay. Two of the Charlie Flight's coxswains and two from Alpha had been in formation, so they were called to testify.

So even if there was a need for Thirty-Six, she wasn't going anywhere. Unless they were going to activate her "familiarization" training as a coxswain, which would be a . . .

"*Danno,*" Thermal commed. "*Shut down your bird, seal it and shag ass over to Thirty-Three.*"

When she got to Thirty-Three, EM1 Hartwell and CM1 Glass were waiting in the cargo bay.

"Parker," Hartwell said uncomfortably. "You know

we're short on coxswains. Boomer and Spade along with AJ are all groundside . . ."

"We have a real-world evolution of helping the tugs close the main bay doors," Glass said, cutting to the chase. "You're the top rated EN for driving. You're going to drive Thirty-Three. The CO has signed off. Your bird, Coxswain."

"Yes, Coxswain," Dana said, her face suffusing. Despite keeping up with qual and her flight test, she wasn't exactly an expert coxswain.

"Don't look so scared," Mutant said. "This is a dead easy evolution and Thermal's got so much time in these things he can walk you through anything you're uncomfortable with. That's why you're in *his* boat. Just hit your seat and drive."

"Roger, Coxswain," Dana said, nodding.

"Take a deep breath and heat that seat, Danno." Mutant nodded, walked to the hatch and pulled himself through.

"Bird's warm," Hartwell said, dogging the hatches. "You want to inspect, Coxswain?"

"I can't exactly do a walk around, EM," Dana said, with a chuckle.

"*Attention Flight*," Lieutenant Commander Martin commed.

"*This is a really simple evolution,*" the flight commander continued. "*We're going to undock and follow in a line to the main hatch. The SAPL is off in the bay so we don't have to worry about that. There are, however, going to be birds all over the damned place when we get to the hatch. Fly. Your. Lanes. I want a tight, solid formation. Stay centered on the lanes.*"

You'll have a latch point marked. Hook on, wait for the word and then apply tow power. It would be very nice to have the door closed by the time the Horvath decide to come through the gate."

Dana could feel her suit's environmental system trying to keep up with her increase in body heat and she didn't care. The next time she was chewing gum and the hell with the helmet. She was scared spitless.

The coxswain's seat for the *Myrmidon* was placed centerline of the bird, just forward of the main drive plates and "up" in relation to the engineering position down and to starboard. There were two joysticks that controlled forward, up, down and side-to-side. However, yaw had to be controlled with finger controls on the joysticks. It was a complicated arrangement and she knew she really needed to be dialed in on it before she took a bird out.

Which she might have sort of been. If she had been flying a simulator all week instead of maintaining Thirty-Six.

On the other hand, the truth was she'd *wanted* to be a coxswain. She much preferred to fly the birds than fix them. A bit. She enjoyed the engineering.

But she'd been assigned to engineering and only *familiarized* with driving in case the coxswain was, in the polite terminology of training, "incapacitated."

"It's all good, Danno," Hartwell said. "Mutant's got good instincts. If he didn't think you could drive the bird, you wouldn't be in that seat. And if I didn't think you could drive the bird, I'd be back on the station faster than you could say 'incident.'"

"Thanks," Dana said, giggling. "God, I hate that sound."

Dana felt a sudden thump and her stomach tightened. It was the thump of undocking shuttles. Which meant their turn was coming up.

"Just *breathe*, Dana."

"Right," she said, giggling again. It was just her normal reaction to stress. But it sounded childish and idiotic. She buttoned it down as more thumps sounded from down the tube.

"And we are...undocking," Thermal said. "Your bird, Coxswain."

"My bird, aye," Dana said, carefully backing away from the lock and yawing the shuttle to play follow-the-leader.

"Coming up on a turn..."

"Got it," Dana said, focusing on driving. She made the turn fairly close to center of the lane. She knew that "close" wasn't a good thing in space but she was inside and with as little training as she had she figured that was, for once, good enough.

"Good turn," Thermal said. "See. No sweat. Get some brake in there. The shuttles are stacking up."

Dana had already seen that and stopped her acceleration. But she still wasn't quite up on space driving and nearly forgot that she'd just keep going in that direction until they ended up in deep space if she didn't apply some countering delta-V. She marked the velocity of Thirty-One, the next shuttle in line, and conformed. Then it slowed down *more*.

"I am a butterfly," Dana said, correcting some yaw that had crept in from somewhere. And overcorrected and had to correct again more carefully.

"Doing good," Thermal said. "Seriously. You're doing this like a pro and I don't blow smoke."

"You're blowing smoke," Dana said.

"Okay," Hartwell said, chuckling. "A little. But you're seriously doing well. Better, I hate to admit, than a couple of our regular drivers."

As she saw the CO's boat head into the opening, though, she got a little less nervous. There were shuttles and tugs moving in both directions not to mention the large SAPL safety zones, and Mutant's comment on "crowded" suddenly hit home. There was actually plenty of room but if you made one serious mistake you were either going to explode from the SAPL or run into something at a closing velocity that was going to have the same result. Although it seemed as if the shuttles and tugs were barely moving, their actual velocity was higher than most race cars.

"'You all look like little ants from up here,'" Hartwell squeaked.

Dana tried not to giggle again. She just hated the sound. But the CO's sixty-foot long shuttle *did* look like an ant entering the massive exit.

"The scale keeps throwing me," Dana said.

"It's hard to grasp at first," Hartwell said. "The point being that it's like any other form of driving be that plane, boat or auto. They say with pilots the most important thing is to remember that there are edges to the air, those being land and space. Do not approach the edges unless you mean to. In this case, there are edges to space. Do not approach unless you mean to and are prepared. Note the SAPL zones?"

"Yes," Dana said. "No-go zones."

"Right now the SAPL isn't on but I don't care. Do *not* approach the big red lines. Problem being that when it's on, there's a web of them you have to negotiate to get in and out of the door. They'll turn one or two off when a *Connie* or *Business* heads through but *we* have to slip between them. The space is *big*, mind you, but try to keep to the center."

"Check your seals, aye," Dana said. "Check the hatch indicators, aye. Do not approach the big red lines, aye."

"Good girl," Hartwell said. "Spotlight coming on."

They'd entered the tunnel and the light from the main bay was suddenly extinguished. She still had graphic imagery and flight data but that was retransmitted. She certainly didn't have visual.

The spotlight was only so much help. All it did was illuminate the next ship a hundred meters ahead, which already had its nav lights on. But then she realized that what she thought were dots of the other ships were...

"Into the Black," Dana said.

"Yep," Hartwell said, for the first time sounding slightly uncomfortable. "We're about to go out in the Big Black."

"This is always my favorite part," Dana said, marveling again at the view of deep space. People like Hartwell didn't really enjoy "the Big Black." She couldn't even understand why. The view was glorious.

"Quit enjoying the view," Hartwell said. "We've got another turn coming up."

"Roger, EM," Dana said, paying attention to driving again. What the hell, she figured she'd be back.

"*Spread formation,*" the CO ordered.

Dana carefully followed the marked lines in her screen. She had to yaw turn, which was still the toughest part of the job but she stayed pretty much on track.

"See the blue mark on the wall?" Hartwell said.

"Yes, EM," Dana said. The plug to fill the entrance was *immense*. The dozens of attached tugs looked like bits of sand attached to it.

"That's our attach point," Hartwell said. "Be aware, the door is *already* in motion. You don't want to crunch into it. Among other things, that will transmit the wrong sort of motion and undo all the work that those tugs have been doing for the last thirty minutes. You want to touch it soft as a... Very softly. You'll actually have to come down to it, stop your relative motion, then back away slower than it's moving."

"Aye, aye, EM," Dana said.

Dana quickly saw what the EM was talking about. She followed the track down until she was about two hundred meters from the door and slowed her relative motion to zero as she approached. Then it started creeping back up as the door was slowly being accelerated. She let it come up then set the ship to creeping back at a half meter per second.

"That's close enough," Hartwell said as the door approached to within fifty meters. "Give me point one-one-six reverse delta."

"One-one-six reverse, aye," Dana said, setting the reverse.

"Engaging grapnels."

The tug slid forward towards the wall of nickel iron, slowly at first then faster until it slammed into the wall.

"EM?" Dana said.

"Using the grapnels, the relative inertias are negative," Hartwell said. "Close enough. Okay..." He frowned and looked at his screen. "We're not supposed to *pull*, we're supposed to *push*? I take back what I said. We should have slammed it."

"*We have to rotate the plug,*" Longwood commed. "*Mission of Charlie is to provide smooth, continuous power. Full power forward on my mark. Three, two, one . . . Mark.*"

Instead of the previous flight lines, Dana now had a target caret. She applied power and the marking reticle slid off the caret.

"*Fly to the target,*" Paris said. "*This will apply maximum value thrust to the mission.*"

"Got it, Paris," Hartwell said. "Danno, you understand?"

"Fly to the target, aye," Dana said, adjusting her vector.

"You're doing good. Just keep that."

"On it, Therm . . . EM," Dana said.

"You've heard my handle," Hartwell said. "The thing you've got to understand about handles is that once they're applied, it takes an act of God to change them."

"So I'm stuck with Danno for the rest of my career?" Dana asked. She was figuring out that the target seemed to drift up and to port and was keeping mostly on target. It was actually sort of easy.

"Danno isn't a handle," Hartwell said. "Danno is like a holding handle. You haven't *been here* long enough to get a handle. You haven't done anything stupid enough to get a handle, yet. Danno is what we call you because we're too polite to call you FUN. Besides, you *aren't* particularly useless and it has . . . alternative meanings that could get us in trouble with EEOC. 'Yeah, this is Dana, our FUN.' No, no, no, simply not gonna happen. Ditto all the alternates that were considered. So I've come to the conclusion I'm stuck with Thermal. In the richness of time, because there is now a permanent stop-loss and whether I like what I'm doing or not I can't get out of it, the reason for the handle may be forgotten and as a handle it's not all bad."

"Yes, EM," Dana said.

"So since you are my temporary coxswain until Boomer gets back, you may call me Thermal."

"Aye, aye, EM. Question, EM."

"Go."

"*Myrmidons* have a remote control function," Dana said. "Why isn't Paris just flying all the *Myrms*?"

"Because Paris is doing about a billion other things," Hartwell said. "I suppose Paris could fly all the *Myrms* if he decided not to run the elevators, the battle systems, the air and water recycling, the STC..."

STC stood for Space Traffic Control.

"Having humans do what humans *can* do takes the load off Paris. Your backup, I will now tell you, *is* Paris. And Paris *is* flying two unmanned *Myrms* that I know of. But having you doing this frees up cycles. Paris said that the most he could manage was two and if the Horvath come through while we're doing this he's going to have to flip them out in a Dutchman."

"Oh," Dana said, nodding. "Thank you for the explanation, EM."

"There are no stupid questions," Hartwell said. "But there are a lot of inquisitive idiots. Speaking of Sean..."

"*Discontinue thrust*," Longwood commed. "*Full burn reverse*."

"Discontinue thrust, aye," Dana said, cutting the

power and going into reverse. "Full burn reverse, aye. EM? Why?"

"We've gotten the plug rotating," Hartwell said. "Switching your port screen."

The schematic was of the overall plan to move the plug into position. The combination of the *Myrmidons* and the *Paw* tugs, which had much more thrust and tractor power, had gotten the five hundred and fifteen billion ton plug away from its attachment to the wall of *Troy* and rotating in space. The rotation, in an apparent reverse of when it was pulled out of the wall, was going to leave it hanging in space with a gap.

"Why the gap, EM?" Dana asked.

"There are two shuttles on their way from Earth," Hartwell said. "They're hoping that they get back before the Horvath come through. Normally, we wouldn't have any warning at all."

SEVEN

"Holy cow!"

"What?" Dana asked. She was still managing to keep the targeting reticle and the caret together but she couldn't really pay a lot of attention to other issues.

"Switching your screen again," Hartwell said.

The visual was of a pillar of fire, like a volcano, on the surface of what had to be *Troy*. Dana had a moment of the usual problem of scale until she realized the large objects around the pillar were *Paws*, which seemed to be sucking the outgases from the volcano onto their forward plates.

"What's that?" Dana asked, nervously. "Did the Horvath come through?"

"No," Hartwell said. "They're *mining* for some reason. Fast. I've never seen that beam before. It's cutting the iron like *butter*."

"What are they doing that for?" Dana said. "It seems like a bad time to cut a hole in our wall."

"Not sure," Hartwell said. "Damn..."

"EM?"

"We're getting a flicker in one of the grapnels. I

fixed that, dammit! Not a big problem. Just keep what you've got. I'll be right back."

He unbuckled and slid out of the compartment.

A moment later he was back and slid into his station chair.

"Command, Thirty-Three. Request permission pull power on lower port grapnel. Imminent failure. Will require reduced power."

"*Roger*," Longwood commed. "*Can you fix it?*"

"On it," Hartwell said.

"*Reduce power*," Longwood said. "*Get it fixed as quick as possible.*"

"Cut power by forty percent," Hartwell said.

"Power forty percent, aye," Dana said, pulling back on her stick. The caret immediately started to drift off target. "I can't keep on track at forty."

"Paris," Hartwell said. "We've got an issue here."

"*Disconnect*," a robotic voice replied. "*Repair if possible.*"

"Roger," Hartwell said. "Reduce to five percent back while I kill the grapnels."

"Five percent, aye," Dana said. "What's with Paris?"

"Like I said," Hartwell replied, cutting the grapnels. "Things must be getting complicated. Get us backed away from this cluster so I can work on the grapnel in peace."

"Back away, aye," Dana said, scanning around. There wasn't much traffic. All of the boats in the immediate area were still pulling away at the plug. But... "I don't have traffic lanes."

"Just stay in formation but...back a few hundred meters," Hartwell said, standing up and pulling out the tool kit.

"Two hundred meters, aye," Dana said, backing away at a snail's pace. She set her relative motion to match that of the drifting plug of nickel iron and then leaned back and crossed her arms.

"*Danno*," Hartwell commed. "*There any traffic around?*"

"Negative," Dana said, scanning the traffic monitors.

"*Set the lights to unpowered*," Hartwell said. "*And start tracing the power relays to the port, lower grapnel from your end.*"

"Set transponder to unpowered, aye," Dana said, setting the transponder to "inactive" and getting out of her seat. "Trace from my end, aye."

"*Thirty-Three*," Longwood commed a second later. "*Status?*"

"*EN Parker is assisting in tracing of fault*," Hartwell commed. "*Remains in cabin. No nearby traffic. Maintaining spatial awareness, Command.*"

"*Roger*," Longwood replied.

"*Thermal, get Danno back in her chair*," Mutant commed. "*She needs to be concentrating on flying, not engineering.*"

"*Back in her chair, aye*," Hartwell commed. "*Dana, back in the chair.*"

"Back in the chair, aye," Dana said. She'd barely gotten the access panel off.

She had to admit she was happier sitting in the command chair. She'd set the traffic monitor to retrans to her plants but having the screens up was a much better choice. She changed the transponder to "active" and leaned back with her arms crossed again. That kept them away from the controls.

✳   ✳   ✳

"*Command, Thirty-Three,*" Hartwell commed about twenty minutes later. "*This fault is only appearing at full power. Decline to perform a hot test during an active evolution. We're deadline as a tug.*"

"*Roger deadline,*" Longwood replied. "*Head to the barn.*"

"*RTB, aye,*" Hartwell commed. "*Dana, return to base.*"

"Return to base, aye," Dana said. "Paris, vector to shuttle docking bay."

"*Roger, Thirty-three,*" Paris said. "*Stand-by . . .*"

"What are we waiting for?" Hartwell said, resuming his seat.

"I'm waiting for a vector from Paris," Dana said. "I guess he's busy."

"Whatever," Hartwell said. "Just keep us away from that plug. It's got a lot of mass."

"Away from plug, aye," Dana said, backing up some more.

"Call Paris again," Hartwell said. "We've been . . ."

"*Thirty-three, Command,*" Longwood commed. "*Belay RTB. Stand by vector Athena to rendezvous with* Columbia *shuttle Seventeen.*"

"Rendezvous Shuttle Seventeen, aye," Hartwell replied. "What the *frack*?"

Dana got the downloaded vector and blinked, hard.

"This is a deep space rendezvous," she said, yawing the shuttle around and applying power. "We're going halfway to Earth."

"*Thirty-three,*" Mutant commed. "*Explanation. Columbias only pull five gravities. They're afraid they're going to get caught in the crossfire. Make the*

*rendezvous, get everybody into your boat, they'll be
packed, and then get your asses back here as fast as
you can move. Maximum power to turn over and max
delta on reverse. Kick that horse. Confirm."*

"Max delta rendezvous, aye," Hartwell said, breathing a sigh. "Roger. Danno, kick this horse."

"Kick this horse, aye," Dana said, applying maximum power.

The *Myrmidons* could pull four hundred gravities of delta-V. Unfortunately, the inertial controls could not handle quite *all* the delta. Which meant that three Gs pressed Dana back into her seat.

"Danno," Hartwell said a moment later. "You are turning into a pretty good coxswain."

"Thank you, EM," Dana said, breathing deeply. The suits included a G suit function, so she wasn't having much trouble with the acceleration. But it was a bit hard to breathe.

"But you are going to have to dial in on a few things," Hartwell said. "I know the answer to the question, but I'm not sure you do. Do we have enough *fuel* for this?"

"Uh..." Dana said, checking her fuel state. Then she started trying to do the calculations. They had plenty to get to the rendezvous. That would require accelerating to about halfway to the shuttle and then "flipping" around to decelerate. Not quite halfway because the shuttle was headed for the *Troy* as fast as *it* could accelerate. Which meant they were going to have to overcome their own closing vector, which was more fuel... "Uh..." she said again.

"The answer is this is a *Myrmidon*," Hartwell said. "When fully tanked, it has three hundred hours of fuel, including the fuel necessary to drive the inertial stabilization system, at a cruise power of ninety gravities. We used a lot of fuel tugging that chunk of iron but only about five percent of our tanks. So we've got enough. We have enough to get to *Jupiter*. But not back."

"Phew," Dana said, breathing out in relief. For a second there she was afraid they were doing a Dutchman.

"Dutchman" was the general term, referring to The Flying Dutchman, for drifting away into space.

"Did you take the acceleration of the *Columbia* into your calculations?" Hartwell asked a moment later.

"No, EM," Dana said. "I'm sort of shooting for a spot forward of their current position."

"Paris?" Hartwell said with a sigh. "*Paris?*"

"*This is Athena,*" a female voice replied. It was warm and wise sounding and Dana felt a shiver go down her back. It sounded like how you *wanted* your mother to sound.

"Request some help with a flight plan, Athena," Hartwell said.

"*Your flight plan is suboptimal, EA Parker,*" Athena replied, without the slightest trace of reproof in her voice. "*Not surprising since you never completed the full coxswain's course. It is, in fact, very good given that you were guessing. You would have overshot by about fifty thousand kilometers but with the power of the Myrmidon you could have caught up quite readily. A modified flight plan has been transmitted. You will begin turnover in seventeen minutes. You will have six minutes to complete the maneuver, which, given your demonstrated flight ability during the previous*

*evolution, is more than enough time. You will do fine.
The shuttle pilot has superior experience with docking
maneuvers. He will do the docking."*

"Roger, Athena," Dana said, smiling.

"You're doing remarkably well, young lady," Athena
said. *"And your actions may save many lives. The
shuttle would have taken an additional four hours to
reach the* Troy. *It is estimated that the Horvath will
emerge in no more than two."*

Dana did some rapid calculations and tried not to
squeal. They were barely going to be able to make
rendezvous, pick everyone up and get back to the
Troy in two hours.

"Thank you for your assistance, Athena," Dana said,
trying not to hyperventilate.

*"You are most welcome, EA Parker. I will put you
in communication with* Columbia *Seventeen when you
are on approach. Be with God."*

"Wow," Dana said.

"Yeah," Hartwell said. "I missed that we're in Athena
space. She's something."

"'Be with *God*'?" Dana said. "She sounds like my
Aunt Marge. Uh...and what's Athena space?"

"Paris handles the STC around *Troy* and the gate,"
Hartwell said. "Athena handles the rest of the system.
They're both U.S. military AIs. Argus is the Apollo
Mining AI. He handles SAPL. There's talk of getting
a unified civilian STC AI up and running, but the
negotiations have been held up for *years*. Besides,
they'd want the location of the AI core to be known.
Take that out and there goes your STC."

"Where's Athena?" Dana asked.

"Classified," Hartwell said. "As in *really* classified.

There are three or four sites mentioned but nobody really knows. And we *like* it that way. When, if, battle gets away from Paris, Athena takes over. When *Troy* gets to the point of being able to fight, that is."

"Coming up on turnover," Dana said.

"Feel free to concentrate," Hartwell said with a chuckle.

There was a way to do a complicated skew turn while under power that decreased the period of turnover and was extremely efficient. Athena had clearly looked at the quality of coxswain and settled for KISS, keep it simple, stupid.

Dana cut power on the mark and yawed the shuttle carefully around until it was on vector.

"Two minutes to burn," she said, enjoying the relatively low gravity. Earth normal was feeling *light*.

"This isn't the shuttle Spade and Boomer are on," Hartwell said. "Hell."

"Where are they?" Dana asked.

"Farther back," the engineer said. "Past turnover but still farther out. Damn these *Columbia* class, anyway."

"They *are* slow," Dana said.

"They're obsolete," Hartwell said. "They're only still flying because Boeing had a contract for two hundred of them. They're also overpriced compared to what we get from Granadica. Of course, they generally *work*."

"You'd think a fabber would get things right every time," Dana said. "I mean . . . it's a *fabber*!"

"Ain't magic, Danno," Hartwell said. "Just high tech. And sometimes it has issues."

"And . . . burn," Dana said. It was programmed in so she didn't even have to hit a button. "Uff da."

"Yeah," Thermal said. "I was enjoying the break."

"And now you're enjoying the brake," Dana said.

"What?"

"Braking maneuvers?" Dana said.

"Very funny."

"*Shuttle Seventeen, Myrmidon One-Four-Two-Charlie-Thirty-Three*," Dana commed. "*Approach for docking*."

"*Roger, Thirty-Three*," the shuttle pilot commed. "*Good to see you. We were feeling all lonely out here*."

"*Your dock, Seventeen*," Hartwell commed, standing up. "I need to go play doorman."

"Right," Dana said.

"*Confirm my dock*," the pilot said. "*Stand by for dock*."

Dana had managed to get the *Myrmidon* within fifty meters of the shuttle and stationary once the shuttle cut power. She also had it turned so their docking bay was pointed, more or less, at the shuttle's.

She had to admire the finesse of the shuttle pilot, though. He slid his shuttle over and docked in what looked like one smooth motion.

She felt the impact of the shuttle docking and saw the light go on for the hatch opening. All the indicators were in the green. She wasn't sure what to do so she just held her seat. She could hear, faintly through the bulkhead, the vibration of feet and the increasing sound of voices. Then the hatch indicator light went off.

"And they're in," Thermal said, closing the hatch to the flight compartment and taking his seat. "We're undocked. But don't hammer it. Keep the accel down to standard. I need to call command."

"What's up?" Dana said, backing away from the shuttle and heading for *Troy*. She set the accel for one hundred gravities, which was about the maximum that the inertial system could handle without going into high grav conditions.

"We've got three pregnant women on the manifest," Hartwell said. "Command, Thirty-Three."

"*Go, Thirty-Three,*" Longwood replied.

"All the chicks onboard," Hartwell said. "Including three with eggs. Advise."

"*Standby, Thirty-Three,*" Longwood commed. There was a definite note of frustration in the transmission.

"What's our time to make the *Troy*?" Hartwell said.

"At this accel," Dana said. "Assuming a simple turnover . . . Fifty-seven minutes."

"Too long," Hartwell said. "Too bloody long."

"We could head for Earth," Dana said. "I mean, if we turned around *now*."

"An hour and a half," Dana said. "More every second we accelerate. But if the Horvath come through, we'd be running *away*. We're just about as fast as a Horvath missile. There are all *sorts* of choices if we just want to *run*. I can slingshot for that matter."

"Command," Hartwell said. "Advise best choice run for the World. We can also stop and try to pick up Twenty-Three passengers."

"*Negative, Thirty-Three,*" Longwood said. "*Maximum burn. Medical will be standing by.*"

"Dammit," Hartwell said. "Go for full burn."

"Roger," Dana said. "Tell them to hang on."

"Paris, Thirty-Three. Tell me the door is still open."

"*Thirty-three, Paris. We're holding the door open for* you."

"Roger," Dana said.

The shuttle was decelerating at four hundred gravities, headed for the narrow slot left at the opening. The plug had been moved into position to close while they were gone and there was only a two hundred meter gap left.

"Tell me you can hit that," Hartwell said.

"I can hit that," Dana said.

"And by hit I mean miss the big chunks of metal," Hartwell said.

"I'm going to miss the big chunks of metal," Dana said. "Just make sure nothing breaks or I'm *not* going to miss the big chunks of metal."

"*Thirty-Three,*" Paris said. "*Abort, abort, abort. Horvath emergence. Door is closing.*"

"Oh, bloody hell," Hartwell said.

"Paris," Dana said, coolly. "I don't have enough burn to abort." The door was visibly closing as the tugs went to full power. "It's either shoot the gap or impact."

"*Roger,*" Paris said, voice turning metallic. "*Understood. Insufficient time to make the gap.*"

"Do I have permission to try?" Dana asked.

"*Permission . . . granted,*" the metallic voice said.

"We've got incoming Horvath missiles," Hartwell said, cool again. "They're not going to hold the door open for us."

"Not a problem," Dana said, cutting power. She spun the craft in space and accelerated for the rapidly closing gap. "Tell the cargo to back up against the back wall. Get the guys against the steel." The *Myrmidon* had not been configured with grav couches and there were more people in the compartment than it would have had couches, anyway.

"What are you doing?" Hartwell asked, too calmly.

"I've got space to brake on the inside," Dana said. "And about thirty seconds to make it through the gap. Which is a kilometer and a half *long*. *You* do the math. I'm doing this by the seat of my pants."

"My math brain just went to bed and pulled the cover over his head," Hartwell said.

The shuttle shot into blackness and all that Dana had was her instruments to guide her. There weren't even leading shuttles to follow. All she could do was try to keep to the center of the rapidly narrowing gap. If the five hundred and fifteen thousand tons of iron closed on the sixty-ton shuttle, they were going to be an almost unnoticeable smear. The maximum normal velocity in the tunnel, when the plug was out, was ninety kilometers per hour. She was doing nearly ten times that velocity.

Dana shot out of the gap and didn't even notice the door clanging closed. She was far more interested in the great big red line directly on her vector.

"All vessels," Paris transmitted. *"Flight emergency in main bay. Avoid quadrants seven, sixteen, forty-three, forty-four..."*

"SAPL!" Hartwell shouted. "Where the *hell*...?"

"See it," Dana said. She managed to figure out the powered skew turn maneuver by sliding under the SAPL zone. She actually passed through the edge but the marked zone was a hundred yards across and the beam was less than ten centimeters. Plenty of room. Then she applied maximum braking power.

"I'm green," she muttered. "I am cool. I am a butterfly..."

* * *

"That is the craziest thing..." Lieutenant Commander Martin said. "I'm not sure whether to give her a medal or Mast."

"She had permission to try, sir," CM1 Glass said. "If she doesn't crash, I say the medal."

"The latter is looking increasingly unlikely..."

"Support beam," Hartwell said. "Don't hit the..."

"Got it," Dana said. She had to vector off-brake to avoid it, causing the pseudo-gravity in the shuttle to skew all over the place. She ignored the screams from the cargo. "I am a butterfly..."

"I don't think we're going to make it," Hartwell said. Skewing off-vector had caused them to go out of pocket to avoid impacting on the far wall.

"O ye of little faith," Dana said.

"Fifty bucks it's plasma, sir."

Lieutenant Commander Carter "Booth" Bouthillier was the tactical officer of the *Constitution*-class cruiser *James Earl Carter*, SC 6. And like anyone else not directly involved in the battle, he was watching the crazy assed pilot of 142/C/33 shoot across the main bay like a comet.

"I'll take that," Captain Russ Kepler said. The commander of the *Carter* was watching the main tactical screen with his arms crossed. "Seems to be doing okay so far."

"You're on, sir," Booth said. "Be aware, the pilot is an EN cross trained as a coxswain."

"You *bastard*!"

* * *

"Collision alarms, please," Dana said.

Thirty-Three was already pulling three gravities even with ISS. Hitting was going to suck. Especially for the cargo.

"Collision alarms, aye," Hartwell said. He braced himself in his chair. "Nice knowing..."

"Oh! Ow!" Booth said. "That had to *smart!*"

"And there were pregnant women onboard," Captain Kepler said. "See if Medical needs assistance."

"We're still up?" Dana said, shaking her head.

"Barely," Hartwell said. "We're leaking air in the cargo bay."

"Paris, vector to shuttle bay," Dana said, bringing power back up. "We're outgassing and we have volatiles as cargo. Engineer, maximum pressure to cargo bay."

"Max pressure cargo bay, aye," Hartwell said.

"*Roger, Thirty-Three,*" Paris said. "*Declared Emergency. Direct vector Bay One. I'll have medical standing by. Good job, CA Parker. Very good job.*"

"Thank you, Paris." The shuttle handled like a brick after the impact. But it was limping along. And if she could get to Bay One before they lost all their onboard air the cargo would survive, which was the task and standard. "We deliver the mail."

"That's fifty bucks you owe me, TACO," Kepler said, holding out his hand.

"Take a check?"

EIGHT

"Major To'Jopeviq! Come in! Come in!"

The Rangora had occasional eugenics periods. Every technological civilization required them if they were to survive for any length of time. Technology meant that the weak filled the civilization like fat upon the belly of a Glatun banker. From time to time the weak, the stupid, the useless, must be eliminated to prevent the whole of society from becoming weak, stupid and useless. They were a toxin that must be purged.

It was joked, among the crews of assault vectors, that they were part of that eugenics program. They *must* be stupid to do their entirely voluntary jobs. Assault vectors were the primary Rangora superdreadnoughts for the breaking of enemy gate defenses and the casualties ran into the tens of thousands.

Major Egilldu To'Jopeviq was the survivor of five assaults upon lesser races. In the last attack, upon the Lho'Phirukuh system, he ended in command of the five hundred survivors of the AV *Star Crusher*. The *Star Crusher* had entered the gate with ten thousand personnel.

The major walked into the star general's office and,

instead of sitting, saluted with a slight mechanical whir from his prosthetic right arm and a thump as it hit his chest.

"Major Egilldu To'Jopeviq, reporting as ordered," the major said. "Long live the Empire!"

"Major, Major," Star General Chayacuv Lhi'Kasishaj chided, hissing in humor. The Star General was, unlike the Major, from one of the Thirty Families that were the nobility of the Rangora Imperium. A tad out of shape, he nonetheless could have the major buried under a rock with a word. His office was tastefully but expensively decorated, which pretty much defined a son of the Families. "We are not under observation from the Kazis. It is all friends here. Please, sit." The general got up and poured some skul. "How do you take it?"

"Red, sir," the major said, sitting down. He even sat at attention.

"I see you're one of those," the general said, hissing again. He handed the officer the steaming mug and sat down. "Well, we can work with that. Major, you are here to form a team for what will seem to be a minor matter. And given that there are about to be great actions in the galaxy, you may feel, at times, that you are a forgotten hero. You will see your classmates and nest mates conquering as Rangora ought while you languish in a minor little study group. What I cannot stress enough is the *importance*. For though there are soon to be great things done by the Imperium, they will be for nothing if your group does not do its job. Do you understand me?"

"No, sir," the major said. "Because you have given me nothing but generalities."

"You have a point," the general said, hissing again. "A blunt one, but a point. Very well. Here are the specifics. You are about to be brought into secrets known only to the High Command." The general brought up a holo of local star area and pointed at the Glatun Federation. "In six months the Imperium will be at war with the Glatun Federation. We intend to crush them in less than a year."

"Great actions as you say, General," Major To'Jopeviq said, his one remaining real eye gleaming. "Tell me this team is a command."

"That is what I have to tell you it is not," the general said. "Nor does it directly affect the war. Your mission is otherwise."

The general dialed in on a small star system to the side of the Glatun Federation.

"Terra?" Major To'Jopeviq said, aghast. "This has to do with that little *nothing* system?"

"Terra," General Lhi'Kasishaj said. "But do *not* dismiss them. The Terrans are infants on the space lanes, it is true. Barely twenty years from first contact and several of those as satraps of the Horvath. But they just crushed the latest Horvath attack with an ease that you should find frightening. If you are not afraid of the sudden appearance of a polity with such combat ability, you are a hindrance to this task, not a positive."

"I understand, General," To'Jopeviq said. "I will not let my assumptions affect this task. Please enlighten me."

"The Horvath had lost control of the Terran system so, being good allies and having no real need for our remaining *Devastators*, we loaned them most of the ships we had in storage," General Lhi'Kasishaj said.

"Thirty *Devastators*, nine Iquke battlecruisers, and seven Odigiu frigates.' They sent them into the Terran system with the unquestioned assumption that they were about to take the world, and the Horvath intended to exterminate that perfidious race. This is what they got."

The view in the holo was now of drifting wrecks. It was clearly taken shortly after the battle because the wrecked ships were still sparking and there were occasional explosions.

"One occasionally has to stick one's neck out to advance," the star general mused, watching the holo. Small boats were already moving amongst the wrecks and To'Jopeviq recognized the signs of boarding parties. Of course, they were probably just taking surrenders given the devastation. "And while I may seem to be in a high position, that just means that rising in stature is harder because the competition is just as ruthless and experienced as you are. And they are very good at making their own predictions and know when to stick their necks out and when to hold them in. I stuck my neck out arguing against supplying the ships to the Horvath. My point was that the Terrans were a formidable threat and that giving the ships to the Horvath was tantamount to losing them."

"And you were right," Major To'Jopeviq said.

"Being right is sometimes the worst possible thing you can be," the general said, hissing in humor again. "You may learn this someday to your disservice. And in this case, it was a mixed curse. I have been given the task of preparing the attacks that are scheduled to be sent in against Terra."

"We are going to attack them as well?" To'Jopeviq asked.

"Eventually," the general replied. "In part that is my doing. The Terrans clearly have defenses far in advance of what they should given their relative youth. My point was that if they can prepare such formidable defenses, we really don't want them having time to prepare *offensive* structures. Thus as a small part of the overall attack against the Glatun Federation, there is a codicil to take the Terran system. Star Marshall Gi'Bucosof has the overall command of the Glatun attack. I am in charge of the Terran portion as well as others. And I am putting you in charge of examining them in depth. Determining how formidable their defenses really are and how to defeat them."

"What did this? Do we know?"

"A combination," the general said. "They have created a most bastardized fortification on the gate, a nickel-iron asteroid that has been inflated into a battlestation of sorts. And they have a very capable mining laser using solar-pumped power. You will be briefed on what is known and have a team to determine how dangerous the systems actually are. To *Devastators* they are clearly *very* dangerous. I want you, also, to develop their Order of Battle better than our current estimates and look at key players in the system. Think not just of direct assault but political assault. On that subject, part of your team will be a member of the Kazi."

"If you so order, General," the major said stoically.

The Kazi were the Imperium's political police as well as its intelligence arm. To'Jopeviq recognized their necessity, especially for controlling conquered populaces who tended to be restive. It did not mean he liked them.

"Don't look so glum, Major," the general said, heartily. "Getting a Kazi assigned to you means you're important! I have them around me like flies! If I had a minor granddaughter left I might marry her off to you! You're advancing!"

"Yes, sir," To'Jopeviq said.

"And you don't care," the general said, hissing again. "You are the bluff warrior who longs only for the sting of battle. But this is part of preparing the battlefield, Major. Your job is to ensure that when we enter the system, we will be fully prepared to destroy their defenses and take it without losing an entire fleet."

"Yes, sir," To'Jopeviq said.

"So, get to work," the general said, waving his hand at the door. "Your new 'assistant' is waiting."

The lieutenant in the general's outer office was that oddest of things, a female officer.

Rangora females were much more petite than their male counterparts, rarely clearing a meter and a half in height and with much smaller and finer scales. This one was smaller than normal, almost a dwarf. She barely came up to To'Jopeviq's waist.

"Lieutenant Jith Beor, sir," the female said, saluting. "I am your administrative assistant for this project."

It took To'Jopeviq longer than normal to make the realization that when the general mentioned his "assistant" the senior officer was pointing out that the assistant was more like his control. He wasn't used to dealing with Kazi. And with that realization, he also knew that the female wasn't really a Navy lieutenant. The combination made the salute he returned slow and somewhat distasteful.

"Good to meet you, Lieutenant," To'Jopeviq said, belying every word with his demeanor. "Do you know where we're setting up?"

"Just down the hall, sir," the lieutenant said, gesturing to the door. "We're rather close to the center of power, eh?"

"Being close to the center of power is somewhat like being close to an unstable laser emitter, *Lieutenant*," To'Jopeviq said as they walked down the hallway. "I prefer to be on the other end of the ship. Or, better, on a different one."

"You do not care for this assignment?" Beor asked.

"I would much rather be on an assault vector," To'Jopeviq said as he entered the offices they were to use. "And I see we're alone."

"If you think so, you really aren't used to being near the center of power," Beor said, gesturing to his office. It already had his name on the door. "If you're going to discuss what I think you want to discuss, we'd be better off in there."

"Lead on, *Lieutenant*."

"Because only the Kazi have this room monitored?" To'Jopeviq said as he sat behind his desk.

"As far as I know it is not monitored by anyone," Beor said, sitting down without being asked. "I swept it rather carefully and it is shielded. I am not here as your political officer, To'Jopeviq. I'm here to be the Kazi liaison—there are pieces of intelligence you may not be able to get through normal military channels—and to bring some alternate thinking into the group."

"And to *weed out* alternate thinking?" To'Jopeviq asked.

"If you mean to ensure that there are no indiscreet sentiments," Beor said, "that is a standard part of any Kazi's job. But you are hardly a threat to the Imperium, To'Jopeviq. Quite the opposite. Your loyalty is unquestioned. As is the loyalty of most of this team. Oh, there are a couple who are on the questionable list, but only because they are...thinkers. The sort of people who question *everything*. Such people are useful. They simply need a bit of watching to make sure they don't go too far. My main mission, though, is as I stated. To bring alternate intelligence and alternate thoughts to this planning group. And, of course, to handle your paperwork."

"So you see everything?" To'Jopeviq said.

"Of course," Beor said, hissing in humor. "And so you don't have to worry about it so much. I'll be taking care of payroll, moving your papers, that sort of thing. So you can do the job of figuring out how to take the Terran system without losing *another* forty ships."

"Will it be a Rangora force?" To'Jopeviq asked. "Or more stinking, cowardly Horvath?"

"That has yet to be determined," Beor said. "In part because no one has taken a close look at the Terran system."

"Where's the rest of the team?" To'Jopeviq asked.

"Being gathered," Beor said. "We're the first. By this afternoon, we'll be getting to work."

"So..." To'Jopeviq said. "What's your real rank?"

"That is not your concern," Beor said. "When we are in public, though, I will treat you with the exact respect you are entitled by your rank and your experience. In fact, my cover is to be the starstruck young lieutenant working for the handsome and virile hero."

"That could be fun," To'Jopeviq said.

"Don't push your luck, Major," the agent said. "I'm not actually starstruck."

"That's what's going to make it so fun."

"This is Dr. Thiolh Avama," Beor said. "He is a specialist in xeno-history and has recently written a paper on the Terran system and human social interactions."

"Doctor," To'Jopeviq said, nodding his head. "Any initial thoughts?"

"The first thing to understand about Terrans," the academic said musingly, "is that they are societally and politically complex. They have not yet gone through a coalescence period, being broken into numerous tribes that are separated into nation-states with varying degrees of political power and economic influence.

"All of that being said, the Terrans are an essentially *peaceful* people. They are a race of evolutionary herbivores rather recently shifted to omnivorous consumption. They have a long history of territorial aggression but always seek to control and even eliminate such actions..."

"*Totally* disagree."

"Analyst Deegh Toer of the War Intelligence Agency," Beor said, introducing the short, stocky Rangora. "He was part of the first team to do an analysis of the Terran defenses."

"And if anyone had paid attention to it, the Horvath wouldn't have entered the system in such low force," Toer said. "The humans are *animals*. They live, eat and breathe war to an extent it's hard to find outside our own blessed Imperium."

"If you observe their many broadcast channels,"

Avama chided, "this is clearly not the case. They constantly attempt to restrict their warfare, even having many thousands of regulations regarding war that it might be fought, when absolutely necessary, in the most peaceful possible way."

"Peaceful war is a contradiction," To'Jopeviq said.

"Not at all," Avama said. "They clearly separate what they consider 'good' war and 'bad' war among the higher quality polities. The better, more elite humans firmly deride and avoid any conflict with a material or even strategic basis. They even have a term, 'operations other than war.' These are such things as nation building and humanitarian support missions. This is what the militaries of most of the great polities are used for much of the time."

"Explain the Iraq invasion!" Toer said.

"The overthrow of a vicious dictator who was slaughtering his own people," Avama said, shrugging. "The tribe called Americans also believed he was a material threat."

"And the American military exists purely to perform these 'actions other than war'?" Toer said with a scoff. "It outnumbers or outclasses the rest of the world's militaries combined. And since they got into space it is the lead military in *that* front."

"If you had ever met any American diplomatic personnel, you would know that they are charmingly innocent, peaceful and naïve," Avama said. "They truly believe that war is a thing of the past. The Americans bluff and are more than willing to bully lesser polities, but they have no real stomach for war. There are few or none on Terra who do. Frankly, a reasonable negotiated surrender is the most likely outcome of this conflict."

"You're dreaming," Toer snapped. "Just dreaming."

"Gentlemen," To'Jopeviq said, trying not to sigh. "We are getting ahead of ourselves. Mr. Toer, can you explain how the Terrans wiped out a fleet of—admittedly second class—battleships with a mining laser?"

"Calling the SAPL a mining laser is like calling a *Devastator* a freighter," Toer said. "You can use it for the purpose but it's sort of overclassed. The SAPL consists of a Very Large Array of mirrors scattered near their sun. That VLA captures sunlight and concentrates it on the Beaufort's Distributed Array or BDA. The BDA then concentrates it more and bounces it up and down to more VSA mirrors scattered out of the plane of the ecliptic. They move the light around the system for, ostensibly, mining purposes."

"The main company that owns the system uses it extensively, and very inexpensively, for mining purposes," Dr. Avama pointed out.

"They don't need seventy petawatts of power for mining!" Toer snarled. "That's not a mining laser, that's a weapon of doom!"

"Seventy petawatts does seem a bit strong for a mining laser," To'Jopeviq said.

"They don't normally use it all at once," Dr. Avama said. "They use the laser, along with spin processing, to separate metals. And they normally have several projects running at once. They have become a major supplier of materials to the Glatun."

"Who are using it to produce warships and defense stations," Toer said.

"If this thing uses mirrors, it should be reasonably easy to take out," To'Jopeviq said. "Just target the mirrors."

"Which is where *Troy* comes in," Toer said.

"*Troy*?"

"A mining program," Dr. Avama said.

"Very clearly a *defense* program," Toer replied.

"They are now getting most of their material from *Troy*," Dr. Avama pointed out.

"It's a fricking *battlestation*!" Toer shouted. "They *say* it's a battlestation! The plans are on their *hypernet*!"

"Doctor, please," To'Jopeviq said, holding up his hand. "Mr. Toer, what is *Troy*?"

"*Troy* is a NI asteroid they inflated into a battle-station," the analyst said. "And, yes, they are mining it also. But it has kilometer and a half thick walls of nickel iron. The 'mining' is burning out missile and laser tubes, ship bays, personnel centers. During the last battle, the *Troy*, which was barely operational, was used as the final focus engine for the SAPL. Which is its *primary*," he continued, glaring at the academic, "purpose. *Troy* will be supplied from a distance by the SAPL which will have a stable aim point and can send power from as much as four light-seconds away. And the mirrors can move around while supplying the power. So you can throw lasers at them all day and not get them. Best bet is to expend your missiles on trying to take out all the mirrors. Good luck; that bastard Vernon won't quit making the things."

"Vernon?" To'Jopeviq said.

"A major financier," Dr. Avama said. "But not a *serious* personality. He is new riches from after the first contact. But otherwise unimportant."

"He created SAPL and *Troy*," Toer growled. "How much more important does a person *get*?"

"SAPL," Dr. Avama said, "once you think about it,

is a rather elegant idea. I'm no great expert but most asteroid mining—"

"Uses large annie power pumped laser systems," To'Jopeviq said. "Chunks are mined off of the asteroids and fed to smelters and fabbers using gravity tugs."

"Yes," Dr. Avama said. "As you say."

"My father is an asteroid miner," To'Jopeviq said. "I know quite a bit about it. What is spin processing, though?"

"Take a big laser," Toer said. "Which, obviously, Terra has. Start an asteroid spinning on one axis. Heat. The metals separate out. It will eventually form a sort of plate. You can then cut the metals off. Mine and smelt in one."

"That is elegant," To'Jopeviq said, nodding. "But you need cheap laser power."

"Which the humans get from their sun," Dr. Avama said excitedly. "It's a very unusual approach and has quite a bit of economic consequence if you think about it. It's one of the reasons I find the culture so fascinating..."

"I understand," To'Jopeviq said. "Kilometer and a half of nickel iron?"

"Kilometer and a half," Toer said.

"Entrances?"

"The missile launch tubes," Toer said. "The laser tubes. Eventually the plans include ship launch tubes. And the main door. Which is big and hard to close. If you can get in before they close the door, you might have a chance. Absent that, my analysis is if they get even their phase one plans, a successful assault will require forty assault vectors."

"*Forty*?" To'Jopeviq said. The *Star Crusher* had

been part of a fleet that included *five* assault vectors. It was the largest concentration of AVs in Rangora history. There weren't currently forty AVs in the Fleet.

"If they complete phase one," Toer said. "Which is going to take them a while. But their eventual plan is for ninety SAPL emitters, forty-eight missile launch tubes and a magazine with two hundred and fifty thousand missiles."

"Which they cannot possibly produce," Dr. Avama said.

"They have Glatun fabbers and a two *trillion* ton asteroid to mine," Toer said, not bothering to look around.

"The one fabber they have is old and pretty much on its last legs," Dr. Avama said.

"They're building a new one," Toer said. "And knowing that bastard Vernon, he's not going to settle for *one*."

"Gentlemen," To'Jopeviq said, trying not to clutch his head. "I see we have some differences of opinion and I find that to be good. We need to look at every side of the puzzle. I'd like you both to write initial estimates of the Terran war capacity and current defenses as well as political will-power. When we have those we can start to try to get some agreement. For now, I look forward to working with you. I'd like those in no more than a week. Thank you for your time."

"I don't think I can do this," To'Jopeviq said, holding his head in his hands. "This is not my idea of being a major. Why couldn't the general have picked someone else?"

"Because they probably would already know everything they needed to know," Beor said. "They would have made their decision, turned in a paper and gone back to what they'd rather be doing. You, on the other hand, are going to keep working on this until you know what is needed. Because you know the people who will be doing the assault and care about them."

"Good point," he said, lifting his head. "Seventy *petawatts*? That's as much as the total output of an AV. Not the *main* gun, *all* the guns. Two hundred and fifty thousand missiles? I'm stupid but not *that* stupid."

"Then perhaps we should *first* look at how to prevent them from completing their tasks," Beor suggested.

NINE

"You are, amazingly enough, the picture of health," Dr. Pfau said. "And if you can avoid crazy shuttle pilots in the future, you might continue to be."

Lieutenant Dixie Ellen Pfau, MD, was one of many doctors being directly commissioned by the Navy. It was a long way from the Mayo Free Clinic but it had some similarities. And she'd learned to read body language a bit better along the way.

"What did I say?" Dixie asked, gesturing at Dana's suit.

"I *was* the crazy shuttle pilot, ma'am," Dana said, starting to put the suit on. With all the bumps and bruises it was a bit harder than normal.

The shuttle had made it *almost* all the way to Bay One before giving up the ghost. Thermal had shut down the reactor just short of a critical overload. So they had to drift the rest of the way in. And come in for a hard drop landing from about six feet when the guys running the bay turned on the grav. It was that or impact the back bulkhead.

She knew she'd messed up the cargo but she had been reliably informed they were all alive. The mail made it even if it was a little tattered.

"Well, we've got four broken limbs, a cracked cranium and three women in premature labor, Engineer," Dixie said tightly. "You can expect a rather pointed letter being sent to your commander through channels. What was an *engineer* doing flying a shuttle?"

"Filling in a slot, ma'am," Dana said, picking up her helmet. "Am I cleared to return to duty?"

"I should have you go over to Ward Four," Dixie said, making a notation on the chart. "But, yes, you're cleared to return to duty."

"Thank you, ma'am," Dana said. "Good afternoon."

"It will be good when we get some qualified pilots!"

"...and then there's this fricking SAPL where there's not supposed to be a SAPL and she..." Hartwell was saying when Dr. Pfau walked in. He still hadn't taken off his suit.

"Corpsman?" Dixie said, walking in the exam room.

"Engineer's Mate from Shuttle Thirty-Three, ma'am," the female corpsman said. "Turns out that *wasn't* an accident but some really *hot* piloting, ma'am."

"Hot *dog* piloting, EM," Dixie said. "*Good* piloting doesn't normally entail fractures. As I just informed your so-called pilot."

"Say again, ma'am?" Thermal said, blinking.

"Your pilot has been returned to duty," Dixie said. "*She* was uninjured. But your commander is going to be getting...what's the term? A reply by endorsement asking why he allowed that *maniac* behind the controls."

"With all due respect, ma'am," Hartwell said, tightly. "Are you aware of the full nature of the entry EN Parker performed, ma'am?"

"I rather doubt that any..."

"With all due respect, *ma'am*," Hartwell said. "I repeat my question, *ma'am*. Are you aware of the conditions under which EN Parker made her entry to the main bay? Ma'am."

Dixie took a deep breath. She had had to deal with nurses that had information she wasn't aware of and recognized the tone.

"No, EM. Please increase my knowledge base."

"Oh."

"And for general informational transfer, ma'am, the *Columbia* ate a missile, ma'am. So your *injuries* would now be trying to breathe *vacuum*, ma'am. Or, more likely, be plasma. Ma'am."

"I can recognize when I have made an error in judgment, EM," Dixie said. "Please convey my apologies to EN Parker when you see her. And I'll try to circulate that information to the remaining injured. They were...a bit unhappy. Especially the *Columbia* pilot."

"They were in a steel box and couldn't see what was happening, ma'am," Hartwell said. "Do you know where EN Parker is at present, ma'am?"

"She was released for duty," Dixie said. "She's already checked out."

"I need to get going," Hartwell said. "She's so green I don't think she even knows her way back to base."

"*Parker?*"

"Therm... EM Hartwell?" Dana said. She was sitting in a hard plastic chair, holding her head in her hands. "*Location?*"

"Main waiting room," Dana commed. "I figured I'd

wait 'til you got released. I don't know how to find the squadron."

"*Be right there.*"

"EM," Dana said, standing up and wiping her eyes as the engineer entered the waiting room. She was the only person in it so it wasn't like he could miss her.

"Now that was something I never thought I'd see," Hartwell said, sighing.

"How much trouble am I in?" Dana asked, taking a deep breath.

"You did hear Paris, right?" Hartwell said, shaking his head. "Oh, we'll be doing reports and reviews for a *year*, but if anybody so much as *hints* you're in trouble, I'll jack them right up. Just like I jacked up that prissy ass doctor. She, by the way, asked me to convey her apologies."

"It really *was* a bad entry . . ."

"Stand by," Hartwell said. He closed his eyes and nodded for a second. "Three way."

"*That you, Parker?*" Chief Barnett commed.

"Here, Chief," Dana said, standing a bit straighter.

"*First, don't you* ever *do that again,*" Barnett said. "*Unless you gotta. And that was a 'gotta' if I've ever seen one. Second, if anybody gives you crap about that entry, other than in fun, and they are going to be funning you about it, then you send them to me and I'll give them a piece of my mind. Now get your butt back to the squadron. We're swamped with requests and we need Thirty-Six out here ASAP.*"

"Say again, Chief?"

"We've got orders to board Thirty-Six and join the SAR," Hartwell said. "So if you're over your cry, we've got a mission, Comet."

"Comet?" Dana said, frowning. She was *incredibly* tired and not processing particularly well. She'd actually still been pumped up until the run in with the lieutenant. That had first taken the wind out of her sails, then a massive reaction to the crash had set in. She felt like a limp noodle.

"*Told* you Danno was a holding handle. You just had to do something crazy or stupid enough to *earn* one. Congratulations. Got it on both scores."

"Rammer, get your team down to the One-Forty-Second bays," Staff Sergeant Dunn said. "SAR mission."

"I didn't think we lost anybody." Lance Corporal Andrew Ramage nonetheless rolled out of his rack, picked up his weapon and headed to the hatch. With nothing to do during a battle between a massive station and the incoming Horvath the Marines were just standing by in their suits and jerking off.

"Horvath SAR," SSGT Dunn said. "Or, in other words, prisoners."

"We're picking up *Horvath*?" PFC Patrick Lasswell asked.

"Yes, Lassie," SSGT Dunn said. "Go get Timmy out of the well." He headed down the corridor to roust out the next team.

"Ours not to question why," Rammer said, trotting down the corridor.

"This is one order I sort of question," Lassie said.

"No," Rammer said. "You say 'Gung-ho, Staff Sergeant!' And go pick up prisoners."

"Should just let 'em drift 'til their air runs out," Lasswell said.

"But we have the strength of ten because our

heart is pure," Rammer said, grinning and flipping down his helmet.

"Pure bullcrap, that's what this is..."

"Rammer," Sergeant Ryan Pridgeon commed. *"Thirty-Six."*

"Gung-ho, Sergeant," Rammer commed back. He and Lassie were pulling themselves hand-over-hand down the bay as part of a milling mass of Marines trying to get to their assigned landing craft.

They drilled loading all the time and normally it was a bit more orderly. But in this case the teams were being broken up into prisoner details. They *hadn't* drilled loading in two-man teams.

"Engineer's Thermal," Pridgeon added. *"Cock is Parker. Thermal's EM1 Hartwell, so be polite."*

"Roger, Sergeant," Rammer commed. EM1 translated as a staff sergeant so he was going to be polite. He flipped through the hatch and was pleased to find it was under gravity. *"EM Hartwell, Lance Corporal Ramage with party of one on-board."*

"Roger, Lance," the EM commed. *"Close the door and we can be on our merry way."*

"Shuttle is buttoned up, Coxswain," Hartwell said. "You good?"

"I am a *butterfly*, Engineer," Dana replied. "I float upon the wind, neither fighting nor losing." She didn't feel like a butterfly. She felt like a brick.

"The last time you said that we were headed into a crash," Hartwell said, chuckling.

"I'm going to try to get that on my record as a hard landing," Dana said, pulling away from the dock.

Other shuttles were popping off and she took a holding position until she got her vector.

"Comet, that was a crash," Hartwell said.

"Any landing you walk away from is a landing," Dana said.

"We were carried out on stretchers."

"Which were, as I protested, unnecessary," Dana replied. "Witness the fact that we are already back on duty."

Lasswell leaned over and put his helmet up against Rammer's.

"Does he *know* we're listening?"

"He left us in the circuit," LCP Ramage said. "I think on purpose."

"I don't want to *hear* this conversation," Lasswell said. "They just walked away from a *crash* and they're back on *duty*? Isn't there usually an AAR for that sort of thing?"

"Oh, gosh," Thermal said, as Dana got in formation to head out of the main bay. "I think I left the Marines in the circuit."

"What?" Dana said. "You... If you were not an EM1, I would tell you exactly what I think of you, EM1 Hartwell!"

"My bad," Hartwell said.

"Fine," Dana said. "Marines?"

"Roger, Coxswain?"

"There were mitigating circumstances to my last mission's ending," Dana said. "You can look it up later."

"Yeah," Thermal said, chuckling. "I figure that entry to the main bay is going to be all *over* YouTube."

"Okay, EM Hartwell," Dana said, finally getting angry. "*You* call the choices. Go get the people out of the shuttle. Direct order. RTB max rather than run. Direct order. Door closing. Impact the surface or try to make the hole?"

"Comet, I already said it was an awesome display of flying," Hartwell said. "Marines, for your general edification, I don't know three cocks in the squadron who could have survived. That we, yeah, walked away instead of being paste was awesome flying, not a screw-up. So you can adjust your catheters."

"Roger, EM. All oorah here."

"Frack," Lassie said, laughing. "It's *already* on YouTube. You gotta check this out."

"You're using hypercom bandwidth for..." Rammer said until he got the feed. "Back that up!"

"Son of a—" Lasswell said, replaying the clip. "EM Hartwell? Permission to ask a question, EM?"

"*Go*," Hartwell commed.

"*Why* did Parker go screaming across the main bay at max thrust?"

"EM," Dana said. She was feeling better for some reason. Maybe it was focusing on the mission. But the cobwebs that had been filling her brain were starting to clear. Or maybe it was getting pissed at a certain EM1. "How are our systems looking? I never completed the thirty day on this."

"Good," Hartwell said in a distracted tone. "And, Comet, seriously. I'm sorry for pulling your leg. The video is *already* up on YouTube. From about six different angles. And I'm looking at it and wondering how *any* of us survived. Thank you. That was some very hot piloting, EN. Very hot. And I value my skin."

"Without analysis it's going to look like an idiot was driving," Dana said.

"There's . . ." Hartwell said. "The analysis is going on as we speak. You just made the news."

"Oh . . . damn."

"And so did AJ, Spade and Boomer's shuttle," Hartwell said.

"Did they . . . ?"

"It got taken out by a Horvath laser," Hartwell said.

"Thermal . . . I'm sorry. We should have gone for them."

"We'd all be dead if we had," Hartwell said, cutting off the news feed. "How you doing?"

"I am a *butterfly*, Thermal."

Video has recently been popping up on YouTube of an apparent crash of a Myrmidon *shuttle during the Battle of Troy. Here with a more in-depth explanation is our Fox military analyst, Carter Russell. Carter, that certainly looks like some crazy piloting.*

It does. But you don't know the circumstances, Jamie . . .

"Damn," Lassie said, watching the feed from Fox. "Damn and . . . *damn*. These two ought to be *dead*."

"And fifty-three passengers," Rammer said then paused. "Whoa."

The news had finally gotten a shot of the pilot of the "Comet" delivery into the main bay. And instead of her "official" bio shot, it was from Dana's high-school yearbook.

"Whoa is right," PFC Lasswell said. "And oooo-*rah*! Uh . . . I wonder how we get access to the flight deck."

"We don't even ask," Rammer said. "Don't even think about hitting on our cox, Lassie. Down!"

"Lance Corporal . . . uh . . ."

"Call me Rammer, EM," LCP Ramage commed.

"We're approaching our search grid and there are about a thousand distress beacons. Be prepared to get to work."

"Roger, EM," Rammer commed, cycling a charge into his laser. "We're about to have company."

There was a clang on the hull of the boat and Lasswell jumped.

"What was that?"

"Debris," Rammer said. "When you hear that, you know we're about to get to work."

"Commodore, we have an issue," Colonel Raymond Helberg said.

The *Troy's* Chief of Operations was part of the "multinational" group, a British Army colonel whose experience prior to *Troy* was mostly logistics and base operations. He'd gotten the job due in part to just being damned good but more because he'd spent a year "cross-training" on logistics in the off-shore drilling industry. Since taking the assignment on the *Troy* he'd found the differences outweighed the similarities. Such as the current issue.

"Go," Commodore Kurt Pounders said. "Or, rather, *which* issue."

Pounders was the chief of staff of the *Troy*. He had once considered being the *Karl Vinson's* commander a complicated job.

"We don't have the ET brig installed, yet," Colonel

Helberg said. "Based on the distress beacons, we're about to have six or seven *thousand* prisoners. Which we cannot even feed since they don't eat Earth food."

"And we solve that how?" the commodore asked.

"Put them on one of their ships," Colonel Helberg said. "There's a battlecruiser that the survey team says is habitable. What's left. It broke in half in the battle so there's no drive. They're going to have to strip off the guns and missiles but the crew quarters can be sealed off from that area while they are working. Environmental for that area is working."

"Approved," the commodore said. "Make sure there's a good sized Marine detachment as guards until they get the weapons off. Strip it of everything but environmental."

"Will do."

"There's *a lot* of debris, Thermal," Dana said.

Their search area was around one of the Horvath-made battle cruisers. It didn't seem to have suffered much damage but there was still so much chaff in the area, it was like flying through a minefield. Bits and pieces of the ship had been blasted off and there were chunks of armor, support beams and less identifiable objects everywhere.

The whole space around the gate was filled with drifting objects. The largest were the ships that seemed whole, like the one that was their target. There were, for that matter, two Rangora *battleships* in view that seemed more or less intact. Being that close to an apparently functioning battleship in a cockleshell like the *Myrmidon* ... was probably a lot like what the battleships felt up against *Troy*.

There were far more that were in pieces. And bits. And fluff. It was insane. Flying into the main bay had been a piece of cake compared to this. There was no way to miss hitting debris and some of it had vectors high enough that they could puncture the shuttle's armored hull.

"Just take it slow, Comet," Hartwell said. "Distress beacon at three-three-five mark minus six."

"Got it," Dana said, closing with the Horvath evacuation pod. "No chance I can just blast it out of space?"

"Didn't figure you for the bloodlust type, Comet," Hartwell said.

"I'm from Anaheim, EM," Dana said. "Remember?"

"Oh. Then, no, we don't get to blast them out of space, EN. Just close to dock."

"Roger, Thermal," Dana said, flexing her jaw. It had been a long day.

"Je-jay!" Rammer said, gesturing for the three Horvath to climb out of the escape pod. "Je-jay!"

The docking clamps of all the local ships that were used by more or less Terran sized sophonts were identical. The original design dated from before the Glatun and just keeping the standard design made things easier.

It certainly made securing prisoners easier.

The Horvath came clambering out of the pod, their hand-tentacles on their helmets.

"They really *do* look like squids, don't they?" Lasswell said, gesturing with his rifle for the threesome to move to the back of the cargo bay. There weren't any seats installed so the Horvath huddled against the back bulkhead.

The extraterrestrials had six tentacles instead of eight with four used for locomotion and two as "hands." But other than that, they looked very much like terrestrial squids.

"Yeah," Rammer said, securing the hatch. *"EM, we are clear. Next customer."*

"Roger, Rammer."

TEN

"*EM, unless you want us to start stacking, we'd better head to the barn,*" Rammer commed two hours later. The cargo bay was solid with Horvath. A couple had been carrying laser pistols when the shuttle docked. They'd also carefully handed them over to the Marines.

The Horvath were didactic and dictatory when they were in positions of power. But Rammer had been a prisoner collector for the last encounter with Earth's former overlords and he'd found them to be incredibly docile when a laser rifle was in their face. Even the officers. He'd been told they weren't really officers, but that was their position basically. They just bunched up in a group and sort of stroked each other. It was pathetic, really.

"*Understood,*" the EM replied. "*We're transferring them to one of their ships that's sort of intact. We don't have quarters for them on the* Troy."

"*Roger,*" Rammer commed. "What the frack ever, dude," he added after cutting the circuit.

"We're full up, Dana," Thermal said.

"They look so . . ." Dana said, spinning the shuttle

151

around and heading for the Rangora battlecruiser that was being used as a temporary brig. The ship was trashed. She couldn't believe there were habitable areas on it but that was the destination.

"Paris," Dana said. "I need a vector for prisoner transfer."

"*Roger, Three-Six,*" Paris said. "*Stand by. You have shuttles in front of you.*"

And there were. Dana had seen the 142 lined up on the shuttle bay but seeing most of the squadron scattered across the debris field around the ship was another thing.

"*Three-Six,*" Longwood commed. "*What's your status?*"

"Five by, Command," Hartwell said.

"*Grapnels?*"

"Nominal, Command," Thermal replied.

"*We need to clear some of this debris while you're waiting to dock,*" Command said. "*Take direction from CM Glass.*"

"Clear debris, aye," Thermal replied.

"*See the marked debris?*" Mutant commed. "*Hull plate. It's on trajectory to get into our operating area. Just grab it and move it out of the way. Carefully, Comet.*"

"Move the debris, aye," Dana said. "Carefully, aye. Okay, EM, how?"

"Going to have to do a snatch," Thermal said. "I'll put a flying grapnel on it. Stabilize it. Main grapnels. Move it."

"Okay," Dana said. "I need a vector."

"Coming up on your system."

* * *

Clear debris. Pick up prisoners. Drop off prisoners. Clear more debris.

Some of the debris was Horvath. Dana wasn't sure how to feel about that. Hating an enemy with an unknown face was one thing. Seeing a bloated Horvath body, its *space suit* ripped open, drifting past your shuttle in the depths of space was another.

"This is going to be fun," Thermal said. "I've got a suit distress beacon."

"There are a bunch of those," Dana said.

"This one says it's alive," Thermal said. "Which we are required to pick up."

"Absolutely," Dana said.

"*. . . so you're going to have to do a snatch in EVA. Are you EVA rated?*"

"I am," Rammer said. "My co isn't. Is this guy stable?"

"*Looks good,*" the EM commed. "*We're going to do this on readback.*"

"Roger, readback," Rammer said, rolling his eyes.

"Open inner air lock door."

"Open inner air lock door, aye," Rammer said, rolling his eyes again.

Hanging out of the hatch of the boat, even if you have a safety-line clipped off, trying to grab an enemy prisoner who'd been floating in space for six hours, while debris was whizzing by your face, wasn't Rammer's idea of fun.

"Gung-ho, sir," Rammer said. "I'm just so fracking gung-ho . . ."

He had to admit it was a great view. Except for the Horvath who was anything but motionless.

"Je-jay!" Rammer commed on the open channel. He wasn't even sure if the Horvath used the same channels. "Je-jay!"

He hot-sticked the flailing suit to adjust the electrical potential between the suit and the boat and managed to get a safety line on a clip point. With that in place he hauled the squirming squid into the air lock.

"Close outer air lock door," the EM ordered.

"Stand by," Rammer said, kicking the squid into the corner of the air lock. It didn't seem to be responsive to reason. Or a swift kick for that matter. "Close outer door, aye . . ."

"I think that dude needs whatever the Horvath use for a psych ward," Lassie said.

The Horvath had popped its helmet as soon as it was in atmosphere but it was still flailing its limbs and squealing like a herd of pigs.

"That sound is getting on my nerves," Rammer said.

"You're not the only one," Lasswell pointed out. The other Horvath were notably agitated and were avoiding the flailing prisoner.

"*EM, we have a situation in the bay,*" Rammer commed.

"Roger, Command," Hartwell said. "Comet, we have permission to return this group to the brig-ship."

"RT brig, aye," Dana said, turning the boat towards the distant big. "I'm not trying to whine, Therm, but any idea how long we're going to have to do this?"

"No idea, Comet," Hartwell said. "Until we get orders to discontinue. Which will suck for these squids."

"Sir, we're going to have to start on a rotation schedule," CM1 Glass said. "My coxswains are going to start making serious mistakes pretty soon."

"Confirm," LCM Martin said. "I was just talking to squadron about that. Come up with a cycle."

"I'd especially like to get Comet back to the bay, sir," Glass said. "She and Thermal have been having one hell of a day."

"That's a definite confirm."

"Je-jay!" Rammer said over his suit speakers. One of the Horvath had squirmed out of the group gropé and was moving over to the prisoner.

"Damaged," the Horvath speaker said. "Care."

"Je-jay!" Rammer said, gesturing with his rifle. "Back. *EM, ETA on getting to the brig?*"

"*Thirty minutes,*" the EM commed.

"I need a link to my command," Rammer said.

"Roger."

"Rammer, Pridgeon, go."

"*We have a POW who was Dutchman, Staff Sergeant,*" Rammer commed. "*It's apparently insane. One of the other POWs, officer by the rank tabs, wants to administer care.*"

"*Roger, stand by.*"

There was a few moments pause and SSGT Pridgeon came back.

"*ETA to the Brig?*"

"*Thirty minutes, min.*"

"*Roger. Allow care.*"

"*Allow care, aye*," Rammer said, lifting his rifle. "Go ahead," he said, gesturing to the flailing prisoner.

The Horvath officer squirmed over to the former Dutchman and stuck a tentacle into its head. The flailing stopped.

"Holy hell!" Rammer said, stepping over and kicking the officer away. The one absolute requirement of taking prisoners was that you kept them *safe*. It was drilled over and over again and any prisoner that died while in custody could be considered murder on the part of the custodians. The chief custodian being one Lance Corporal Andrew Neil Ramage. "Cover it!"

"Got it," Lassie said, lifting his rifle. "Je-jay!"

"Dammit!" Rammer said, checking the suit telltales. "It's dead! Staff Sergeant . . ."

"What the *hell* happened?" Pridgeon said as the last live prisoner exited the shuttle.

"*That* bastard stuck his tentacle into some spot and *killed* it!" Rammer said, pointing to the Horvath officer. "It said it wanted to administer care! It's on video and audio. Staff. That's what it *said*. 'Damaged. Care.' Just that. And then it fricking killed it!"

"God," Pridgeon said. "We're going to be writing reports for *ever*! Get the damned body."

"It just killed it," Hartwell said, playing the clip again. "Just put it down like a dog."

"Are we going to get in hot water?" Dana asked. Somehow, again, seeing one of the Horvath who had killed her father, and by extension her mother, killed in front of her eyes wasn't particularly satisfying.

"Don't see why," Hartwell said. "I mean, we'll

probably be called to the inquiry. But we just drive the truck. The jarheads are the ones in hot water. And looking at the vid and audio I don't see where they could have known."

"*Thirty-Six,*" CM Glass commed. "*RTB for crew rest.*"

"Uh . . ." Dana said. "You were saying?"

It certainly sounded like they were being pulled off for the prisoner incident.

"*RTB, aye,*" Hartwell said, rolling his eyes. "*Rammer, we're RTB. All aboard who're going aboard.*"

"*Stand by, EM,*" Rammer commed. "*We're getting a confirm. Aye, EM, boarding.*"

"And we have containment," Thermal said. "RTB, Comet."

"RTB, aye."

"And we have good seal," Thermal said. "Shutting down. And we made it back into the bay without hitting *anything*!"

"EM, permission to pop my helmet in the shuttle?" Dana said, ignoring the jibe.

"Permission granted, Comet," Hartwell said.

"I need a bath," Dana said, climbing out of her seat and heading to the hatch. "I need to soak in hot water for about two d— Hello."

"Uh, hi," the Marine said. "I'm, uh, Rammer. Lance Corporal Ramage. This here's Lassie. PFC Lasswell."

"EN Parker," Dana said, nodding.

"Right, uh," LCP Ramage said. "We, uh, just wanted to say that we appreciate the smooth ride."

"You're welcome?" Dana said.

"That's it," Ramage said. "Out, Lassie."

"Aye, aye, Lance," Lasswell said. But he kept looking over his shoulder on the way out.

"What was *that* about?" Dana said as Thermal climbed through the hatch into the cargo bay.

"You're joking, right?" Hartwell said.

"Oh," Dana said. "Men. You're *born* with Johannsen's."

"This place is..." The Horvath hadn't actually left that much mess. But there was enough that it was going to take some tidying. And the dead one had left an unpleasant pile of goo.

"Hmmm..." Dana said. "I seem to remember it's the *engineer's* job to clean up the shuttle."

"And you're an Engineer *First Class*," Thermal said. "Not an Engineer Mate."

"Damn."

"*EN Parker*," CM1 Glass commed.

"EN Parker," Dana said, looking at Hartwell quizzically.

"*Report to Flight Bay for debrief.*"

She looked at Thermal and shrugged. He made a face, then shrugged and nodded.

"Report to Flight Bay for debrief, aye."

"*Thermal*," Glass commed. "*You too. Clean-up will wait.*"

"Oh...crap."

"First of all," Glass said, looking at Hartwell and Dana, "we're not even going to *try* to do a PIR right now. The PIRs on this day are going to go on for *months*. And I can foresee all sorts of things interfering. Parker, unless you didn't hear, your fascinating entry technique to the main bay made the news."

"We destroy an entire Horvath fleet and all they

can do is bitch about an entry?" Hartwell said, shaking his head.

"The parameters of the entry got distributed pretty quickly," Glass said. "Which means that you came out, in the media, smelling like roses, Parker. To the media. I, personally, think you did a damned fine job. That's the second thing on my agenda. I caught some flak for suggesting you for a coxswain position and my professional opinion, as well, is that I made a good choice. From what I'm looking at, now, you did everything exactly right. There were no good choices and you picked from the array of bad and chose the least bad. You delivered the mail. From my point of view, as the chief coxswain NCOIC of your flight, you performed the mission and did so to the very best of not only your ability but the best anyone could do in a screwed up situation."

"Thank you, CM," Dana said.

"That said," Glass continued, "that's a hot-wash analysis. That incident is going to be folded, spindled and mutilated by people who weren't there. Being in the news is, therefore, a bad thing. Because people are going to be looking to stick a knife in your back over it. My job, and the CO's job, is to keep that from happening to the best of our ability. Your job is to keep your head down and do your job. Let us handle the flak."

"Roger, CM," Dana said.

"You wouldn't *believe* how far up this got kicked," Glass said. "But the decision has been made to retain you on flight status. Unfortunately, we lost Boomer, Spade and AJ on *Columbia* Thirty-Two so we're down two cox and an engineer. We've *got* spare engineers.

So we're going to put you through full coxswain quals. You will be acting as a temporary coxswain until you're full qualified."

"Yes, CM," Dana said, trying not to grin. Among other things it wouldn't be very polite considering that the flight had just lost three people. But that was hard to grasp at a certain level, call it denial at which she was very well trained, and grasping being a cox was easy.

"*Now* we start the debrief," CM1 Glass said. "Were you *insane* . . . ?"

ELEVEN

"Boo-yah," Price said, sticking his head in Butch's quarters. "Time to go make the man his money, baby!"

As soon as the battle alarms went off, pretty much everything civilian shut down and the welding crew, which had been working on installing a power circuit on one of the horns in the bay, headed for their quarters. The quarters were not only deep in the wall of *Troy*, they were sealed in case there was an "environmental breach." And although they were tight, that was also where they kept their personal suits.

"What's up?" Butch said, turning off the video of some crazy assed pilot screaming across the main bay.

"*Salvage*, baby!" BFM said. "The *Troy* just created enough salvage to keep us busy for a *year!*"

"Okay!" Butch said, grinning hopelessly. He had no idea why the team lead was so happy.

Butch had completed his initial probationary period without being transferred, incurring a major incident or killing anyone. As such, he was now an apprentice welder and earning a pretty good buck.

The problem being, there wasn't much to spend it on on the *Troy*. There were some bars but he had learned that if you got too heavy on the sauce you were going to get grounded. There was even one titty bar but with women in short supply, you sort of got tired of just looking. And the girls weren't exactly great.

Pretty much what he'd been doing for the last three months was working in the main bay, taking as much OT as he could grab, eating and sleeping. Since the work was hard but not really . . . what was it called? It wasn't really aerobic, he was starting to figure out why everybody on the crew had a beer gut.

He'd actually been sending money home. God knows Mama and Papa could use it.

He enjoyed the work more than he'd thought he would at first. The main bay was pretty cool. But he didn't know why BFM was so excited.

"Oh, you poor clueless newbie," BFM said, shaking his head. "Get into your suit and head for the sleds."

"Suit *and* sleds?" Butch said.

"Salvage, dude," Price said. "Going to be FOD all over the place. But the nice part? The really sweet, oh this is *so* sweet, part? We get a *cut* of everything we salvage. I was on the salvage job when the last Horvath attack came through the gate. Four ships. Five hundred guys cutting. I made as much in a *month* as I usually do in *two years*. And, dude, there are *forty* ships just *waiting* to be plundered!"

"I am *so* in my suit," Butch said, sliding out of the bunk.

"Okay," Butch said. "I get salvage being valuable. But this is just *crazy*."

The sleds had been attached to the *Paw* mining ships and headed out into the Black. Butch had only worked in the Black one time before so it was pretty unnerving. Especially when they got dropped off near the target.

Ships and pieces of ships were drifting all over the place near the gate. The gate was sort of a circular backdrop for what looked like the biggest scrapyard in the history of the world.

It wasn't the ships that were the problem. It was the pieces. Small, large, fracking *huge*, the FOD, foreign-object debris, was all over the place. Their starting target was a Horvath destroyer that had been cut in half by the SAPL. Most of the rear was in good shape but the forward part had blown up. It was the debris from the blown up part that was making the area dangerous as hell.

The rear portion was also spinning slowly in a corkscrew rotation. Getting into it was going to be tricky.

"*Okay, people,*" Purcell commed. "*I know you're all pumped up on plunder, but let's stay safe, here. I want to make sure we've got good solid team communication and stay with a buddy. This FOD has a will of its own and it will kill you. The destroyer, what's left of it, has been cleared by the One-Forty-Second and the Marines. There should be no Horvath aboard. If you see any sign of Horvath, back off and call in the Marines.*"

"*How we gonna do this?*" Vlad asked.

"*Carefully,*" Kosierowski commed. The laser tech was the replacement for Gursy and as phlegmatic and uninterested in games as BFM was crazy. They got along great as long as BFM concentrated on making the lives of the probes hell.

"*Gonna go in the part that's already cut,*" Price replied. "*Move forward slowly and it will come back around to us. Then adjust our delta to its and enter. Drac, you're with Kos. Butch and me are the other team. What we're looking for is, in order, major electronics, power systems, transfer systems, laser emitters, mass drivers and grav plates. Hotstick the ship when you get close. It's gonna have a bunch of potential. And if you find anything interesting, make damned sure it's not live before you go to cutting it out."*

"And when we've got it cut out?" Drac asked.

"Pull it out, slow, and drop a beacon on it," Price said. *"Paws'll pick it up later. Kos, you done this before, right?"*

"Not anything this big," the tech said. "But, yeah."

"Just take it slow."

The big man was as good as his word, taking the initial approach at a snail's pace.

The "cut" end of the destroyer was still sparking, meaning there was still active power somewhere. It was also slagged. Armor, bulkheads and main support beams were *melted* and Butch's temperature indicators said that some of them were still over a thousand degrees Celsius.

"Got a corridor over to port," Kos said. *"Nice and wide."*

"'Nother one to starboard," Price said, slowing. *"Beginning entry."*

"Roger that," Kos said. "Same back."

The corridor was about three meters wide, not particularly "nice and wide" for the two-meter-wide sleds. But it was the best of the lot. Most of the rest was open compartments. And none of them looked like they had anything recoverable.

As soon as they got in the corridor the faint light from the sun was cut off and Butch hit the sled lights. The rack of lights illuminated the corridor if not like day then pretty well. Better than he expected, 'cause...

"Why are we getting scatter?" Butch asked. He wasn't nervous exactly. It was a mixture of nervous and excited. But anything unexpected was causing a bit of increased stress. "No air, the lights shouldn't scatter."

"Still enough breathable to scatter some," Price replied. *"Not enough to survive, as that guy found out."*

A Horvath, his suit ripped open and the squidlike body bloated up and out so it was hard to recognize as one of the ETs, was floating in the corridor.

"What do we do?" Butch asked.

"Pull it out," Price commed, snatching the slowly spinning body. *"Put a beacon on it. Somebody'll pick it up later. Not like he's going anywhere."*

The team lead used the waldoes to hand it over to the probe.

"You okay with that?" Price asked. *"You're not going to puke or anything?"*

"I'm good," Butch said. In truth it was hard to think of the twisted bit of freeze-dried meat as a sapient being. It looked like a dried clam.

"Take it to the entrance, slap a beacon on it and just give it some minor delta," BFM commed. *"I'm gonna sit here and do a survey for power sources."*

Butch carried the Horvath to the entrance, put a radio beacon on it and sent it spinning slowly into the void.

"Bit of a navigation hazard," Butch said as he headed back up the corridor.

"Anything hits it is going to slag it and not get

slagged," Price replied. *"According to the plans, this thing's got a power room up ahead to starboard. Let's go see if it survived."*

They made their way, slowly, down the debris-filled corridor. Debris was floating everywhere in the microgravity. Butch couldn't even put a name on most of the stuff. Some of it appeared to be food packs. There were what might be tools or eating utensils. Clothing. He hadn't even known the Horvath wore clothing.

"Should be behind this bulkhead," Price commed, slowing his sled to a stop. They were having to continually adjust delta to the spinning ship, since if they didn't the centripetal force would "push" them out, and Butch was having a lot harder time with it than the experienced team lead. His sled "pranged" lightly on the top of the corridor.

"Careful," Price commed.

"Trying to get my balance, lead," Butch said. This wasn't anything like working in the main bay.

"Gotcha," Price replied. *"Just, seriously, be careful. The potential around here is high. I think the power's still on but shorting into the hull."*

"Right," Butch said, getting his vector adjusted so he wasn't hitting the bulkheads or the deck or the overhead. And then he had to adjust it again. "Lead, I'm having a hard time maintaining stable formation."

"Grab that hatch coaming," Price commed, pointing to the hatch to the engineering section. *"No way we're fitting through that hatch. Neither is a power plant. We're going to have to cut the bulkhead."*

"Right," Butch said, grabbing the coaming. *That* got it.

"When we do, the plate's going to want to get away

from us 'cause of the spin," Price commed. *"I'll lock the plate. You do the cut. Don't cut my waldo."*

"How big a cut?" Butch asked. He stuck out another waldo that had a small grav plate on it and locked it on the far side of the corridor, giving him a really stable platform.

"Top to bottom," Price commed, getting an equally stable position and locking two grav points to the bulkhead. *"About four meters wide. If that's not enough to get the power plant out, we'll cut it wider."*

"Right," Butch said, pulling out his high power laser head.

"Low power," Price commed. *"Use about a forty millimeter beam."*

"Low power," Butch said, switching heads. "Right."

"You know you say 'right' a lot?"

"Right."

"Whoo-hoo," Price commed as he got the plate fastened down and out of the way. *"This sucker's live, all right."*

The power plant, the center of which was a meter-wide ball of iridium, was in the middle of the large compartment. The rest of the compartment was secondary power transfer systems and a mass of electrical relays that were spitting sparks all over the place.

"Salvage control, team fourteen alpha," Price commed.

"Fourteen alpha, SC."

"We've got a live plant in Sierra Seventeen. Looks like it was at full power when the ship got hit. Room is energized. How do we turn this sucker off?"

"Stand by, Fourteen Alpha."

"*Gotta check the manuals,*" Price commed.

"Right."

"*Fourteen Alpha, SC.*"

"*SC, Fourteen Alpha.*"

"*Best bet seems to be to cut the fuel lines. Fuel line enters from the port bulkhead. Can you access that?*"

"*Stand by, SC,*" Price commed. He panned his lights around the room. "*Not from our primary entry. I'm not going in that compartment, and primary entry is to starboard. Download a schematic and I'll see if we can get around to port.*"

"*Roger, Fourteen Alpha. Download on the way.*"

They had to cut through four bulkheads and a control room to get to the fuel line.

"*Wait,*" BFM commed as Butch started up his torch. "*Control, Fourteen Alpha.*"

"*Fourteen Alpha, Control.*"

"*Is there a shut-off valve?*" Price commed.

"*Roger, Fourteen Alpha, stand by.*"

"*He3's expensive. Why waste salvage?*" BFM commed on a side channel to Butch.

"Makes sense," Butch replied.

They found the shut-off valve in the next compartment over, got the fuel shut off, then headed back to the power-room entry.

When they reached the main entry, Butch still occasionally bouncing and bonging off of the walls, the sparking had stopped.

"*Prime slice,*" Price commed, making a cautious entry to the room. "*Looking at two hundred million dollars, minimum, right there.*"

"That's prime," Butch said.

"Let's get 'er cut out," Price commed. *"I'll stabilize, you cut. And only cut where I tell you, probe. I don't want my salvage wrecked by your clumsy attempts to be a welder."*

"I am beat," Butch said, clambering into his bunk. He'd done his suit checks, though, before he put it away.

"Same here, brother," Drac said, yawning. "I want to go get something to eat, but I'm too tired to move!"

The salvage operation had been called after twelve hours, the maximum the company would let people work continuously. They had a mandated twelve hours off before beginning again.

"I already had thirty hours in this week," Butch said, trying to do the math. "That's forty-two. And we've got... What's the deal with OT on a salvage operation? Since we get shares."

"OT is the same," Drac said, yawning again. "The shares, they look small, like point oh, oh, one percent or something. But it's good money even for probes. The straight wages come out of the cost of salvage. The shares pay out after that. So you're sort of paying yourself or something. It's supposed to be an incentive to keep the cost of salvage down or something."

"I'm gonna think about it in the morning," Butch said, cutting off his light. "I'm going to have to kiss some Navy guy, though, for giving all that beautiful loot."

"What I wonder is what they're going to *do* with it?"

TWELVE

"I'd *heard* you were insane," Kelly Ketterman said. "Now I understand what they meant."

Kelly Ketterman was the Managing Design Engineer of Night Wolves, the Granadica Design and Prototyping Center. Located inside the walls of the fabber called Granadica, the center was Tyler Vernon's version of Skunk Works or Phantom Works. And since the Granadica was currently located in the Wolf 359 system...Night Wolves.

A petite blonde, she was barely taller than the notoriously short Vernon even when wearing heels.

"All it really takes is enough power and grav plates," Tyler said, shrugging. "We're going to need a lot of osmium, admittedly. But that's just a matter of mining enough asteroids. And we just got several tons of prime grav plates. And we'll probably get a bunch of damaged power plants we can remelt. Well, we *will* have them once the salvage guys get done with the junk that's drifting around the gate."

"It's not a *tithe* of what you'd need, sonny," Granadica said. "You want *Troy* to actually be *mobile*? That's a lot of grav plates."

Granadica was the AI of the fabber, a massive mobile Glatun space factory that had been built back when Crusaders were beating on Saracens.

"We need to get it so it can rotate, first," Tyler said, bringing up the plan's schematics. "That, right there, is going to take a bunch of power."

"They're planning on lining the control levers with plants and placing the grav plates on the ends," Kelly said. "Didn't they already start?"

The massive "horns" in the bay of the *Troy* were intended to permit the space station to rotate. That way it could move the transmitted SAPL beams around and actually aim them. It also would permit spreading damage from attacks. The "horns" were so long because the more leverage that they had, the less total power was needed.

"Right," Tyler said. "But what then? All I want you to do is look at the design requirements for a power plant and drive system large enough to move the *Troy*. Not just back of the envelope designs. A full design. Let *me* figure out the logistics."

"Well," Kelly said. "I do like a challenge."

"The efficiency of plates goes up for something like that the larger they are," Granadica said dubiously. "The best plates are going to outmass your *Constitution*-class cruisers. They're going to outmass *me*."

"We'll figure it out," Tyler said.

"You're not going to make a power plant in me, either," Granadica said. "You're talking about an osmium sphere two hundred meters in diameter. That's beyond my fabbing ability."

"Granadica," Tyler said. "I built a battlestation nine *kilometers* across. And I'm building *another* one. You really think a little bitty ball of osmium's going to stop me?"

"No," the fabber said, sounding mildly amused.

"Where are you at on building your . . . twin," Tyler asked.

"Apollo's finished with the shell," Granadica said. "It's still cooling, though. You guys have come up with some crazy ways to make steel, but it works."

Making steel in a fabber was dead simple. Insert raw materials in one end, first quality steel came out the other.

Making a shell of steel big enough to *encompass* a ship fabber, a kilometer long and three hundred meters in diameter, was a different story.

But the problem had already been solved for another project, the Wolf Mining Facility. It had needed "support plates," two-kilometer-around "washers" that were intended for the upper and lower portions of a massive space elevator and gas mining facility.

Building the plates in any reasonable period of time, and with the approaching war Vernon was in a *big* hurry, seemed impossible.

Apollo Mining had solved the problem, however. By making a sort of circular shell of layers of steel material and then melting it, they could now create any sized ball of steel. Forming it was, then, dead simple. As long as you wanted something that was vaguely round it was a matter of using enough tugs to form it like a potter formed clay.

"If it's crazy but it works . . ." Tyler said.

"It's not crazy," Granadica said. "You humans are the *only* sophonts in this galactic region to have that saying. Most people just go with 'that's crazy.'"

"Internals?" Tyler asked.

"Seventy-eight percent complete," Granadica said. "I'm mostly stuck on power plants. Still building up materials. Speaking of osmium."

The matter annihilation plants centered around circular balls of platinum group metals. Osmium was the best choice but any of the platinum group, ruthenium, rhodium, palladium, osmium, iridium, or platinum, could be used.

The problem was, they were all relatively rare. They were extremely rare in terrestrial conditions. Being heavy metals, they tended to stay in the core of planets and were uncommon in crustal materials.

They were more common, however, in asteroids. Not *very* common, they were only formed in supernovas and even then by the repeated fusion of other metals in *multiple* supernovas. They were unlikely to *ever* be common. But they were more common in asteroids, especially nickel-iron asteroids, than on planets.

But even with all the mining that Tyler was doing in the solar system and now Wolf, there was never enough. He was having to trade more than half of his refined metal to the Glatun to keep up with payments and ongoing purchases. Only the remainder was left to supply not only the Navy but civilian ships, terrestrial requirements, the replication of Granadica and all the construction going on in the Wolf system.

"Priorities, priorities, priorities," Tyler muttered. It was always the problem. If he had his current situation and decades before a massive war broke out, the situation would be simple. Spend all his time building infrastructure and wait until the last three or four years to start constructing warships. But humanity was starting at the bottom of a hole. It was only fifteen years since Tyler had found a useful trade good to open up full trade with the Glatun, barely more than a decade since they'd managed to kick the Horvath out of the system. They were still learning how to work in space. There were never enough trained people, enough material, for what he could see coming.

The Glatun, Earth's first trade partners and their closest "ally," were a dying civilization. They had slowly slipped from being a robust, expansionist society to one with high unemployment and a "bread and circuses" attitude towards life.

That worked as long as you didn't have any strategic threats. The problem was that other species, many of which the Glatun had worked to advance so they would be better trade partners, were expanding in the galactic region. Four of them, led by the Rangora, were eyeing the Glatun planets with a look in their eye like a wolf examining a sick, old caribou. Just last year, Glatun had ceded sovereign control over a whole series of bordering star systems to other polities.

That wasn't going to be enough to buy off the Rangora for long.

Once war broke out, Earth's problems would be magnified a thousand fold. The Glatun were busy trying to build up their fleet, and having massive problems, but they still had hundreds of fabbers like Granadica. Some of the metal going to the Glatun was coming back as formed materials. Power plants, grav plates, atomic circuitry and, most especially, highly refined He3 fuel for the power plants. Once that supply line was cut off, Earth was going to be stuck with its limited industry and Granadica. For fuel; Tyler was desperately depending on the Wolf gas mine being finished before the war started and all hell broke loose.

Most models had the Rangora, who were ten times the problem of the Horvath, attacking Earth as part of the war. Planetary heavy bombardment, dropping fractional C kinetic energy weapons with yields up to a hundred megatons, were considered a legitimate tactic. Earth had already suffered devastating bombardments from the Horvath. She would take a pasting if the Rangora got any sort of foothold in the system.

The flip side was that they would have to be able to hold the gate area long enough to transport through to Wolf to attack Granadica and the mine. Tyler was banking on *Troy* being able to prevent that.

"Earth has more than enough power," Tyler said. "There's hydro, nuclear, coal... I'm going to discontinue the civilian power plant program and shift all the material to you. Get the twin up."

"Okay," Granadica said.

"And *when* you have the twin up," Tyler said. "Start on another. When the second one is done, we'll move the first into the *Troy*. And so on and so forth. I think that's the best pattern we can plan for now."

"How many battlestations are you going to *make*?" Kelly asked.

"Depends on how long the war lasts. Speaking of war. We've got a bunch of damaged but possibly salvageable ships in the Sol system. I'm thinking about pulling them through to here and having you work on them in your spare time."

"I don't *have* a lot of spare time," Granadica pointed out.

"I'll get some people in here," Tyler said, grimacing. Finding good space engineers was like pulling hen's teeth. Among other things, most of them were going into the Navy and with stop-loss they weren't coming out. Problem to fix later. "What's the status on the gas mine?"

"All the parts are produced," Granadica said. "I've shifted my production schedule to producing construction bots. They're starting installation of the main processors and weaving of the pipes."

"Okay," Tyler said, nodding. "That's next on the agenda."

"Well, we have a refreshing change in the interstellar situation," the secretary of state said.

"That sounds like good news," the President said. "I could use some good news."

Even though, for once, an attack through the gate had not dropped KEWs all over the Earth, the economy and society were just a shambles. Between the destruction of capitals and the breakdown in international security, whole swathes of the planet were failed states. Just keeping the flow of oil, still a vital strategic commodity even with the improving technology, required three divisions deployed in the Middle East. They weren't so much there to fight terrorists anymore as to make sure the "legitimate" governments were able to keep the oil pumping.

The government, especially the states, was just starting to get a handle on the effect of the Johannsen Virus. Women were, and the President dearly hoped they continued to be, a vital part of the American economy. Their entry into the workforce in large numbers started with World War II, the last time the U.S. tried to go to full war production footing.

Maternity leave was, to say the least, cutting into productivity. And the teen pregnancy rate was hammering education for women. A girl might still go to high school with one child. By the time it got to three, she was mostly out of school, and the workforce, for the foreseeable future.

Congress, responding to the reality of their constituents' positions, had increased the child tax credit. A family earning $50,000 with four children, which was starting to be just about *median* condition, paid essentially zero taxes. Which made an already difficult budgetary situation *impossible*.

The one bright spot was that with industry damaged across the globe and the baby boom just starting to reach productive age, the U.S. was, once again, an industrial powerhouse. Most of the industry that had been destroyed in the bombardments was "legacy" industry that had needed to change to more modern techniques. Over the decades before the bombardments, more and more factories were going into areas where labor was cheaper and easier to deal with than in the Rust Belt. Which meant that whereas China, Japan and Europe had lost most of its production to the Horvath bombardments, the U.S., with most of its new capacity dispersed into cheap, relatively rural or small city areas, primarily in the South, had come out with more functional production than the rest of the world combined.

"Oh, it's not good," the secretary of state said. "It's refreshing. We actually have a declaration of war."

"By the Horvath?" the President said, sighing.

"How many more ships do they have to lose to get the picture?"

"Not the Horvath, Mr. President," State said. "The Rangora."

"Oh, hell," the President said, hanging his head in his hands.

"They are activating their mutual defense treaty with the Horvath."

"Against the U.S.?" the President asked. "Makes sense. We're the only ones fighting."

Every other major country in the world was working on space war ships. But the U.S., due in great part to its continued production of heavy warships over the years, was the master of the complex task of "systemology." Systemology meant getting everything in a large and complex piece of hardware, such as a warship, to work together as seamlessly as possible.

It wasn't a field that was well understood. The people who worked in it had finally started to adapt terms from the software industry to explain their jobs to family and friends. The "platforms," vessels from fleet oilers to supercarriers, were hardware. But to get that hardware to work properly it needed "software," people, who could move around and do their jobs without conflict. And "legacy" software, people who had spent years in the environments, the NCOs and senior officers of the Navy, were critical to keeping the whole system running.

Running a warship was a dance and the dance depended upon the three-dimensional nature of the dance floor, the ship, and the dancers, the people. It also depended on more than one platform. A Carrier Vessel Battle Group required support from shore, generally delivered by the Carrier Onboard Delivery planes, another structure, as well as oilers and even repair ships. And all the structures, carriers, *Aegis* cruisers, frigates, fast attack subs, each had to be designed to work not only as ships but as *war*ships.

After WWII, the only major superpowers in the world were the U.S. and the Soviet Union. They were the only countries with the need, funding and resolve to make major platforms. And Russia had never been a major seapower. It tried to catch up throughout the Cold War but the best it could do was some subs that were a fraction of the ability of U.S. subs. It never was able to field a supercarrier.

The U.S. also had one of the most robust space industries in the world. For all the "international" aspects of the ISS; if it hadn't been for treaties and basically being a nice guy, most of the ISS module would have been better produced in the U.S. The Russians had some good, robust space tech. But the reason it had to be robust was that its quality control sucked.

Thus, whereas the U.S. had managed to field not only nine *Constitution*-class cruisers but six, so far, *Independence*-class frigates, and the *Troy*, the only other country to make a functioning warship was Britain, which had fielded a single *Clarke*-class corvette. It was working on a *Churchill*-class cruiser, equivalent to the *Connies* in ability, but was running into constant snags.

The U.S. had, for years, been called the World's Policeman. Now it was, in addition, the only hoplite standing at the gate. This had caused some angst in the international community, especially with Russia and China, because instead of the Horvath holding the orbitals, the U.S. now held them.

It was causing more angst with the American electorate because they saw the U.S., arguably, as the only country that was defending the planet. And they were the only people *paying* for it. *Troy*, alone, had already cost $68 billion and the budget for next year was another $148 billion. With the current make-up of Congress the question was not "Is *Troy* worth it?" Everyone agreed having a defender at the gate was a good thing, one heck of a lot better than more gutted cities or another damned plague, and *Troy* seemed to be the best bet. What was being asked was "Why are we the *only* people paying for it? And why are *we* the only country providing Marines and sailors to man it?"

"No, it's against Terra," State said. "Then it goes on to list the 'top fifteen tribal groups' which are definitely included. We, of course, top the list but there's something in there for everybody. Russia, China, India, Great Britain, Germany, France, Brazil, Argentina... They even include Peru and Chile for some reason."

"Doesn't Apollo have a lot of civilian contractors from South America?" the President asked.

"Ah," State said, nodding. "That explains it. They also are cutting off all communication through E Eridani. No ships, including 'neutral' shipping such as Glatun, no hypercom."

"We're on our own," the President said.

"Yes, Mr. President."

"So does that mean we can expect Rangora ships coming through the gate?" Kelly asked.

Tyler looked at the missive he'd received and shrugged.

"Who knows?" the tycoon said leadenly. "We already *have* Rangora ships coming through the gate. They were just their old ones and squidded by Horvath. The big problem is, this is effectively a fuel embargo. We can't power our plants without helium. And we can't produce enough helium to fuel the *fleet*, much less all the support ships and *Troy*. No collimator production, no laser welders, no mirror production. And we haven't replaced all the mirrors the Horvath just trashed. I'm not sure we have enough helium to finish the gas mine. And the government is going to want it for terrestrial power plants."

"Their closure of coal and nuclear plants does appear shortsighted," Granadica said. "There is an additional problem."

"I really don't need to hear," Tyler said. "But go ahead."

"I am, in fact, quite low on fuel," Granadica said. "We were expecting our delivery next week. I am about two weeks from being out of power."

"I need to think," Tyler said, getting up and walking to the door. "I also need to do something I hate."

"What?" Kelly asked.

"Talk to politicians."

"We were at peace before you American *cowboys* unilaterally declared war on the Horvath!"

The way that summits usually worked was that lower-level functionaries met for months beforehand to set out the agenda and decide what their bosses were going to say to each other. Then the bosses shook hands, signed the agreements and had a photo-op showing what great good friends their countries were.

When one of the most powerful empires in the local region declares war on the whole planet, some of the diplomatic niceties get cut. The group had *almost* managed to get through the smiling photo-op before the president of Burundi, just about the only remaining functional sub-Saharan country other than South Africa, got into a fight with the French prime minister over covert French support for a Hutu rebellion.

"I seem to remember something about a plague that killed a *billion* people before we declared war," the POTUS said.

"What do you call The Maple Sugar War?" the French prime minister shouted. "Paris was standing before you idiots provoked the Horvath! And now we're at war with the *Rangora* because of you!"

"Would you have preferred *forty* Horvath ships in our orbitals?!"

"They weren't bombing our cities before *you* went to war!"

"Excuse me," the premier of China said. "I must point out that we did not care for the loss of Shanghai."

"Since this has already descended into a shouting match," the British prime minister said, "I think it useful to put this on the table. Negotiated surrender. The Horvath are simply impossible. They don't seem to understand the concept of negotiated agreements. The Rangora are, it is understood, somewhat more civilized. Surrender to the Rangora with the agreement that the Horvath are not involved."

"You're actually advocating that?" the President of the United States asked, horrified.

"I am simply putting it on the table," the Brit said. "Someone will eventually." He carefully did not look at the French prime minister. Everyone else avoided his eye as well.

"This would cause great internal difficulty," the premier of China said. "China does not greatly care for foreign domination."

"Out of the question," the president of Burundi said. "As long as we can avoid being a colony we should fight."

The POTUS almost said "What's this *we* stuff, black man?" but managed to hold his tongue. Burundi had enough problems at the moment. Landlocked, with every country around it effectively a failed state and much of the rest of the continent depopulated. Kenya, Burundi and South Africa were pretty much *it* for Africa post-plague.

"India has had its experience of being a colony," the Indian prime minister said, smiling slightly. "We politely decline the concept."

"Nein," the prime minister of Germany said somberly. "There are arguments, but it would not be accepted by the German people."

"*Anybody* in favor?" the POTUS asked, looking at the French prime minister.

"We are all mad," the prime minister muttered.

"Was that *We* or *Oui*?" the President asked, confused.

"I suggest a short recess," the British prime minister said. "So that we can discuss in a less formal setting the task before us."

THIRTEEN

"*Tell* me you can speed things up," Tyler said.

Byron Audler was a mechanical engineer with a background in ship design and construction. He'd worked on the *Constitution* project prior to being hired by Tyler as the manager of the Wolf gas mine project.

"Be nice," Byron said, looking at the figures. "Problem being, I'm not sure where to get the *power* to speed things up. We were expecting—"

"A delivery next week," Tyler said. "I heard. I've been taking a look at the data. There aren't *any* major stocks. The plants run by the power companies were running on 'just in time' deliveries to cut down on inventory. *Troy* has about enough for a month. Granadica is down to two weeks."

"Can Granadica fab some temporary processors?" Byron said. "We can put them right on the lower plate. There's He3 in the atmosphere at that level. Not *much*, but it's something."

"That's a possibility," Tyler said. "Look at it. I've cut the production on the twin for the time being. What you need is first priority. I'm going to head back to

Earth to talk to the powers-that-be about stopping all terrestrial use until we're up."

"I think they're going to be a bit too busy to talk," Byron said. "Big summit and all."

"I'll crash it if I have to."

"You really threw the fox in the chicken coop with bringing up surrender," the POTUS said.

The leaders of the top fifteen nations by economic and military power were, unusually, feeding themselves off of a buffet table. The agreement was that this was going to be a summit, not a display of who had the most able aides. They all knew that no one person knew enough to make every decision without input. But the rough draft of what an interstellar war was going to look like had to come from the leadership. Then they'd see if they could get their individual countries to go along.

"If I had not, the French would have used the whole meeting to slowly wear away at everyone," the British prime minister said. William Dasher was the first Tory prime minister of Britain since Margaret Thatcher. The Tory Party had practically renamed itself the War Party and it held a solid majority of the House of Commons based on a "Security First" campaign. In that, he was not far different from the POTUS.

William McMurry, former governor of Oklahoma, was an OIF veteran with a degree in history and international law. He wasn't *about* to consider either surrender or compromise with the Horvath. He knew history. Including recent history.

"As they are still attempting." Dasher gestured

with his chin at the French prime minister who had button-holed the Russian president.

"Think he's going to make much headway?" the President asked.

"No," the prime minister said. "But for some very interesting reasons—"

"You have been reading the same reports I have been reading, *ja*?" the German said.

"Eavesdropping, Hans?"

Hans Adler was from the Center-Right German Security Party. The, many, European detractors of the GSP often used a stiff-armed salute when it was mentioned. The GSP was in favor of withdrawal from the EU absent a unified military force and had increased military spending for the first time in three decades. Much of it at the expense of treasured domestic programs. The compulsory civil service, which for decades had had "draftees" working in retirement homes, was now compulsory *military* service again.

The GSP made the French somewhat nervous to say the least.

"Including myself in the conversation," Adler said. "The Johannsen reports are what you are discussing?"

"I was about to," Dasher replied.

"What's Johannsen got to do with it?" the POTUS asked. "As I understand it, the Glatun vaccines make us pretty resistant to any more bugs."

"But the effect remains," the Hans replied. "And grows and grows," he added with a growl.

"Younger populations, William," Dasher said. "You know the McDonald's theory of warfare?"

"No two countries with a McDonalds will go to

war," McMurry replied. "It's been pretty thoroughly disproven. Bosnia comes to mind."

"The effect held for some time," Adler said. "The reason was poorly understood."

"Most democracies of the period when it was proposed were relatively old," Dasher said. "They had had their baby-booms in the '50s and '60s. By the time the theory was proposed, the median age had risen."

"Young societies fight," McMurry said, nodding. "That's what you meant by Johannsen's. That report I've seen but it was a different thrust."

"The French have not had the same population boom as many of us," Adler said, shrugging in a most Gallic fashion. "Not so many blondes. They remain very pacifist. As may be said for Greece, Italy and Spain."

"The Russians are growing like a yeast infection," McMurry said, rubbing his chin. "Scandinavia, eastern Europe in general. Not Japan, though."

"The Japanese do not take well to having their cities destroyed," Dasher said dryly. "They also do not surrender easily."

"It is worthwhile to keep in mind that Russia, France and China have long been in a loose alliance to check American power," Adler said. "Russia is growing, yes. But it is, shall we say, less responsive than some to popular wishes."

"China seems to be onboard," McMurry said, frowning.

"'A Fool lies here who tried to hustle the East,'" Dasher said. "Whatever the Chinese *seem* to be doing, expect a change."

"I'm sort of glad the French are clearly against a full war movement," McMurry said. "If they were raising tidings of glad joy I'd have figured it for a pump fake. But here's the truth. We're strapped. I ran on securing the orbitals, securing the system and kicking Horvath ass..."

"That sounds vaguely familiar," Dasher said.

"But we can't do this alone," McMurry continued. "And that's what's been happening. The mood with the people who elected me is that if we could let the rest of the world be bombed, let 'em burn. There's exceptions, of course..."

"I would hope so," Dasher said. "I mean, we are up there as well."

"We had little in the way of a space program when this started," Adler said. "We are trying to catch up."

"But everybody is going at this separate," McMurry said. "We need to get everybody behind the wheel."

"With the U.S. deciding when and how to push?" Dasher asked.

"Sorry, gonna be blunt," McMurry said. "Who else? The U.S. has the biggest and most proven military, the largest and most robust economy and the best space program. Basically the *only* space program since everyone else quit when the Horvath showed up."

"Which is mostly Apollo," Adler said. "There is a great deal of discontent about a single man holding the power to destroy the world."

"That's excessive," McMurry said.

"Yes," Dasher said. "Destroying the planet would take him at least six months. Destroying the biosphere? About sixteen days."

"There are lockouts on SAPL," McMurry said. "Which you know. It can't target inside of the moon's orbit without control from Space Command. None of which changes the fact that we can't keep this up alone."

"Despite your current defense spending," Adler said, "which is not, in fact, anywhere near full war footing, you still have the highest GDP in the world."

"So you're saying that the U.S. is able to defend all of Earth, the entire solar system, on its own dime," the President said. "Think about that, Hans."

"We *have* been thinking about it," Dasher said. "And discussing it. *No one* likes the conclusions. The Chinese, Russians and French are trying, very hard, to ignore them and act as if everything is still status quo ante. It is not. This is the reality as it stands today. Despite the fact that the U.S. took, as a percentage of productivity and population, the most heavy damage from the Horvath attacks of any advanced country in the world, the U.S. has come out of that more hyper dominant than *before* the attacks."

"The U.S. is the only country with the economic, technological, industrial and political power to support a large space navy," the German prime minister said. He looked up as the Indian prime minister drifted over.

"Having a conversation amongst the adults?" Arjuna Bhatnagar said.

India had taken relatively little damage from the Horvath attacks but its capital of New Delhi as well as its richest city, Mumbai, had both been gutted. The Johannsen Plagues, on the other hand, had killed nearly a fifth of their population. Economically and as a society, however, they were bouncing back fairly quickly. India had a history of major plagues and recovery that gave them an institutional knowledge McMurry mildly envied.

"Not at all, Mister Bhatnagar," Dasher said. "Just explaining some facts of life to the President."

"Who is still not enjoying the experience," McMurry said, his jaw working.

"We can, of course, provide allied forces," Adler said. "But creating our own space force is out of the question."

"As it should be," Arjuna said. "I believe that we are looking at the question from the wrong perspective."

"Go on," McMurry said, a touch suspiciously.

"The problem is that we are viewing this as separate, and competitive, countries," Bhatnagar said. "When, in fact, we are all at risk. For once it is not a question of our own priorities but of the world's."

"That's a very nice sentiment," McMurry said, frowning. "But so far it seems like the world's problems are, as usual, America's."

"That is because you are a victim of your own success," Arjuna said, holding up a hand to forestall a reply. "Please, let me explain. I could play what-ifs about India had it not been so long under British domination, but I will not.

"The United States has been a great success. Many logistic reasons for that, of course. Your people expanded across essentially untarnished terrain, built a great nation with very good structural conditions, the importance of the Mississippi River is vastly underrated, and now sit in a position of hyperdominance. And in this position of hyperdominance we now have a threat not to the United States but the world.

"The world, however, is unwilling to contribute fully to its own defense. First, because they are, frankly, unused to the concept. The U.S. has been the ultimate protector for most of the world for a very long time. But more importantly, because no one believes the United States will fail to protect us. However much people may protest and complain about American power, rant about unilateral invasions, cowboys, warmongers, when we come to a time of decision and must find one group to depend upon, all the nations of the world have learned that the one *untrammeled* defender, the greatest friend and the most fearsome foe, is America."

"Thank you," McMurry said solemnly. "You delivered that very well."

"I'm a politician," Bhatnagar said, shrugging. "We do these things. You are, as I said, victims of your own success. No one, *no* one, really believes America can fail to defend the solar system. Your functional enemies," the prime minister glanced towards the cluster of leaders from Russia, France and China, "are more than willing to let you bear the burden of such a defense. They see it as a way to destroy you economically, as you once destroyed the Soviet Union."

"Which is a pretty good bet," the President said.

"I strongly disagree," Bhatnagar said, shrugging. "I suspect that those three are going to come out of this war in an even worse position than they already hold. But it is a question history will have to decide. The point is that there is no negative or positive pressure to support the U.S. Why should any country increase its defense spending when the U.S. can, and will, defend them quite well? As it *must* to defend *itself*."

McMurry opened his mouth to reply then closed it. He took a breath, then shrugged.

"So you don't think we're going to get much in the way of support?" McMurry said.

"I intend to use this forum to declare the full support of India," the prime minister said. "We, too, are at threat. Furthermore, the world's largest democracy will not stand idly by while the world's oldest defends us."

"Thank you, again," McMurry said. "But . . . while that's all very nice, are there hard numbers?"

"Not at present," Bhatnagar said. "But I have caucused our leadership and we will begin a move to full war footing. We will supply personnel, equipment and supplies and pay for that to the extent that we can. What is beyond our grasp we will need support on. But the general number that we're discussing is up to thirty percent of our GDP."

"That is a very large number," Adler said pensively. "It would be extremely hard for Germany to equal that percentage."

"Better start thinking on how," McMurry said.

"That sounded ominous," Dasher said, frowning slightly. "What are you thinking?"

"That the U.S. isn't going to be made a patsy. Again. I need to go talk to some people."

"...in conclusion, while France stands by its ally of many centuries, the United States, the French government cannot, at this time, support further increases in defense spending. That concludes my statement."

"The President of the United States?" The conference moderator was the prime minister of Switzerland. Fortunately, like most Swiss politicians he had the patience of a saint.

"During this conference, I had hoped to find support for the U.S. defense of the Terran system," McMurry said, reading from notes. "While I have heard many fine words, what I have gotten to a much lesser extent is hard pledges or increased support. And those few which have been presented, mostly by our regular and standard allies, have been, in the main, pro forma. The exceptions are India, Canada, Britain, Finland and Australia, all of which have either increased defense spending to near U.S. percentages or intend to do so in the near future. The excuses are many. 'We are a developing country.' 'We have many domestic spending needs.' The theme is always the same. The U.S. must go it alone.

"A point was made to me during the recess, one that has much been discussed in other venues as well, that to defend itself the U.S. must defend the world. And that, as such, there is no driver for other countries to increase their defense spending to support us. Why should they when the U.S. citizen has to defend *them* to defend ourselves? Thus the fine words and penurious actions that have characterized this conference. It really does make anyone with a touch of honor feel sick.

"There is a movement in the U.S. to force other countries to match our contribution. I am not a proponent nor do I think that the U.S. public would ever countenance such an action. Furthermore, it would be quite difficult to do. I, and the U.S. government, reject the notion of imposing 'support' by violence. We are beyond Hobbesianism. To descend to such depths would make us no better than the Horvath or Rangora.

"However, the U.S. is not willing to defend others if they are not willing to contribute to their own defense. Nor is it willing to sacrifice its treasure and blood when other countries stand idly by, supplying materials for great cost, reaping the benefits of American sacrifice while enriching themselves.

"Let us, therefore, consider the VLA and missile attacks. Any battle will start, and hopefully end, around the gate area as the last did. But if the next attacker, and there will *be* a next attacker, chooses to fire some of their great store of missiles at Terra, all of them *cannot* be stopped during the first phase of battle.

"Capital missiles go through three phases during an attack on Earth. The first is the initial boost. Generally, missiles expend eighty percent of their onboard fuel in this boost phase. Then they go silent and coast towards the Earth, often using stealth technologies and deception to cloak their movements.

"The U.S. has, at enormous expense, constructed a fleet of satellites for the sole purpose of detecting and tracking such attacks. Managed by the AI Athena, the system picks up the initial boost traces from these gravitational detection satellites, then, using a series of sensors, attempts to find them in the vastness of space and destroy them before they become a threat. It is not well known but there were, in fact, twenty missiles fired in the direction of Earth during the last battle, all of which were destroyed by this system.

"However, the last of those twenty was not detected until shortly before it would have gone into its terminal boost phase. When boosting the missiles are, once again, relatively easy to detect. But they are going very fast and in the event of there being more than a paltry twenty, as could be expected from a heavy Rangora attack, they have to be targeted and destroyed by the BDA cluster that, again at purely American expense, has been set up in orbit to defend Terra.

"During the terminal boost phase it quickly becomes evident *which* countries, *which* cities, by and large, are being targeted." The President paused and looked up from his notes at the assembled leaders, many of whom suddenly looked far less smug. He looked back down, his face as set as stone, and continued reading. "In the event of a heavy attack that gets through the gate defenses, that gets through the deep space defense network and has to be targeted by the BDA, certain . . . choices have to be made.

"At the end of this conference I will announce that the U.S. is withdrawing from all standing mutual defense treaties. If the choice has to be made, the first choice will be to defend the citizens of the United States who are paying for that defense."

"You cannot *do* that!" the president of France shouted. "You're dooming us all for your own folly!" He wasn't the only protester.

"The first choice, again, will be to defend the United States," the President said, ignoring them. "And such allies as enter into a *new* treaty of mutual defense, the Terran Alliance. A full text will be supplied after this conference. The general standards shall be thus. There shall be three levels of commitment, low developing, high developing and developed. The standard for defense spending shall be based upon the defense spending levels of the greatest contributor, currently the United States. To maintain membership, a low developing country must spend one third the level of the lead country, again currently the U.S., on defense, which includes personnel pay, equipment production, supplies or such defense infrastructure developments as may be considered necessary by the Alliance paid for *by the country* and supplied to the Alliance. A high developing country is required to contribute one half and a developed country ninety-percent—"

"*Ninety* percent?" Adler said, wincing.

"As a percentage of GDP," McMurry said. "Furthermore, such countries must either be a democracy or agree to a timetable and *follow* the timetable to enact full democracy." He looked up at the Chinese premier and smiled. "Or be restricted from or stricken from the Alliance. Last, command of all forces shall be by Alliance officers, all forces shall meet Alliance standards of training and leadership, all materials will meet Alliance standards of quality and all designs for platforms and equipment will be Alliance designs to maintain standardization. For the time being, you may feel free to substitute 'American' for 'Alliance.'"

"What if we don't *like* American designs?" the British prime minister asked.

"The *Constitution* classes are designed and built by BAE," the President said. "That's a British company. They don't have to be designed in the U.S., just accepted for use by the DoD. The last point. In the event of an attack that enters the final defense zone, first priority will be given to allied countries and their ships, cities, materials, colonies, etc. Only *after* those missiles have been dealt with will the system shift to defending non-allied countries."

"You will leave us defenseless," the French prime minister said.

"Not at all," the President said. "You have left *yourselves* defenseless. The countries of India, Canada, Britain, Finland, Australia, Chile and Brazil all meet the requirements or come close enough to be automatic members, if they wish to accept the additional provisos. There are already British, Australian and Canadian members of the crew of the *Troy*. One can be assured that the U.S. will defend its *true* friends as if we were a single country.

"The world has become used to the U.S. cleaning up its messes, defending it, stabilizing it and generally reaping the benefits of America's commitment to democracy, free trade and freedom without incurring any of the massive cost involved. Now the world expects the U.S. to defend it, again, reaping even *more* benefits, while America bleeds.

"Not going to happen," the President said, looking around. "You can toss your ante on the table or you can damned well die. And that concludes *my* statement."

FOURTEEN

"I need to talk to the President."

Lance Aterberry, secretary of energy, was a rarity in a cabinet position: Someone who actually knew something about their field. Most cabinet appointees had worked in the field they "covered" at one point or another, but most of them were not technical *experts*. Secretaries of defense had rarely been generals. Few secretaries of state had ever been ambassadors.

Lance Aterberry, on the other hand, had a Ph.D. in electrical engineering and had worked in the field of power generation and supply for thirty years before he ran for Congress. He'd been picked as a natural to run the department and his biggest challenge so far had been dealing with the bureaucracy from on top instead of bottom. He was finding it no more comprehensible as the boss than as a customer.

The fortunate fact was that the increasing access to Glatun designed He3 power plants had made his job easier and easier. Glatun plants produced no radiation, were relatively cheap to run compared to the power they put out and had a very small footprint. Even Florida and California were catching up on their energy requirements, leaving him free to attempt to reform the most moribund and entrenched bureaucracy in the U.S. with the possible exceptions of Agriculture and Education.

All that relative ease had just gone out the window, however, with the blockade of the Terran system.

"Everyone needs to talk to the President," the chief of staff said. "There's a war on, you know. Unless it's a warning that the Rangora are coming through the gate—"

"How about all the lights are about to go off?" Lance said. "I'm serious. I need to talk to the President *now*."

"What do you mean the lights are about to go off?" the chief of staff said.

"We've converted fifteen percent of our power generation to He3," Lance said patiently. "The only source of He3 is the Glatun. Do the math."

"Holy..." the chief of staff said. "I'll call you back."

"How did we go to fifteen percent of our power depending on an interstellar energy source?" the President asked, looking around at the assembled group of advisors. It was late at night on Air Force One and he wasn't enjoying the discussion.

"Because it's clean, cheap and easy," Aterberry said. "Companies have been shuttering other plants because they get less trouble from environmentalists using annie plants than coal, nuclear or even hydro. And we had a lot of plants damaged or destroyed in the bombardments. It just made more sense to build annie plants."

"Except it is a strategic handicap," the secretary of defense said. "It's one that we've been bringing up in meetings. But it's not just energy production. All our ships run on He3."

"Tell me there's an answer," the President said. "Isn't Apollo working on a plant in the Wolf system?"

"They're at least three months from being online," the SecEng said. "And they won't go to full production right away. Figure six months before we'll have the same access to supplies that we got with the Glatun. And the total available He3 in the system will last us about three *weeks*."

"We need that fuel for the fleet," the secretary of defense said. "We'll need *all* of it."

"Forget the fleet," the SecEng said. "Forget the construction on new hulls. They're going to have to be orbital babies for the time being. *Troy* runs on He3. No power, no air, no water, no *Troy*. No food and material resupply."

"How much fuel do ships use?" the President asked, confused. "They don't use that much energy, do they?"

"Yes, sir, they do," the SecDef said, looking pensive.

"There's no free lunch, Mister President," the SecEng said. "To boost out of the atmosphere, to accelerate in free-fall, requires energy. Just because they don't have big, thundering rockets, doesn't mean they're not expending as much energy. A *Constitution* class can lift itself out of the grav well, technically. Imagine the number and size of rockets that would require to lift something twice the size of a supercarrier up to orbit. *That's* how much energy they use, Mr. President. And it all comes from He3."

"Can we make them nuclear somehow?" the President asked.

"No," the SecDef said. "First of all, it would require

so much refitting that we'd use up too much fuel doing the work. Second, they can't dump the heat well enough."

"*Troy* might be able to," the SecEng said thoughtfully. "It's actually pretty cold."

"We have six plants from *Los Angeles*-class subs that haven't been torn down," the SecDef said. "Actually, I think they've already been transferred to your department. Any idea if they can be installed in the *Troy*?"

"I'm not sure about the construction requirements and getting the plants to them would be a stretch..."

"When I was in Switzerland I kept thinking that there was someone missing from the summit," the President said. "Anyone know where Tyler Vernon's got to?"

"He was in the Wolf system last week," the SecDef said. "Checking on the construction of the new fabber, some quality issues from the current one and the fuel plant."

"I think we need to see if we can track him down, don't you?"

As the *Starfire* cleared the gate, Tyler's implant dinged for attention.

"Hello, Argus," Tyler said. "Is there any good news?"

The pilot of the *Starfire* suddenly made a sharp maneuver. Due to the inertial controls, Tyler didn't even feel it. But the chunk of metal the maneuver avoided was clearly visible as it flashed by the crystal wall making up one side of the *Starfire*.

"Not as such," Argus said. "There is a critical issue having to do with fuel."

"I was discussing that in Wolf," Tyler said.

"On that subject," Argus said. "The President of the United States has been trying to get through to you."

"I had my com on hold," Tyler said. "I was trying to think of a way to find more fuel. Go ahead and put him through."

The entire battlefield, dispersed as it was, was visible as the shuttle slowly accelerated towards Earth. Tyler tried not to curse. He'd have to shut down all the salvage operat—

"Mr. Tyler, this is the President."

"Good afternoon, Mr. President," Tyler said chipperly. "How are you today?"

"The Rangora declared war, I declared that we're not going to fight it alone, the stock market just tanked and we don't have enough fuel to support our fleet, or *Troy*. I've just found out that we can't even feed the terrestrial power plants, which means people who are already sacrificing are going to be without power. My advisors say that you probably don't have enough fuel on hand to complete your fuel plant. The French option is looking better and better. Other than that, things are dandy. You?"

"I'm in a *great* mood, Mr. President," Tyler said, grinning. "Just peachy keen."

"You sound like you are," the President said. "In which case you either weren't listening or you've finally cracked."

"Or I just found a pile of fuel for the taking," Tyler said, grinning like a fox that just ate the chicken. "I'm not sure how much, but it's enough to finish the Wolf mine unless I'm much mistaken. And the best part is *I* own it."

"Along with everything else," the President said, confused. "Where?"

"The Horvath ships, Mr. President," Tyler said. "The Horvath ships. They weren't going to come into the system without fuel. They knew *we* didn't have any. All the ones that aren't toast are going to have pretty close to full tanks. I count seven in view that probably have thousands of gallons. We'll just siphon it out."

"That's . . . some siphon," the President said.

"Yeah," Tyler said. "It's going to be more complicated than that. We'll get 'er done. By the way, congratulations on proving the U.S. actually retains a set of balls. But . . . a *unified* force? You *sure*?"

"Better than putting up with crap like Monty pulled in ETO," the President said.

"That is a point," Tyler said. "Mr. President, I've got to go. I've got calls to make."

"Fourteen Alpha, Survey."

"Survey, Fourteen Alpha," Price replied.

BFM and Butch were cutting out a set of Rangora laser optics. That was about all Butch could figure out of the explanation. That and the "multimillion dollar" part. And "be *very* careful."

Survey generally didn't have much to do with the welders. They were working on the ships that were salvageable whole and preferred to not have people bent on cutting them up around.

"We have a priority tasking," Survey commed. *"You're the closest team."*

"We're sort of busy here, Survey," Price replied. *"Maybe later."*

"The tasking is from corporate, Fourteen Alpha," Survey commed.

"Survey says . . ." Butch said.

"Very effing funny," BFM commed. *"Go ahead, Survey."*

"Need you to go find a readout, get it functioning and give us a reading. We'll walk you through it."

"Roger, Survey," Price commed, cutting off his torch. "Let's go take a walk, Butch."

"Got the power coupling hooked up?" Survey asked.

"Yep," Price replied.

The readout was mounted on a bulkhead not too far from where they'd been working. Problem was, there wasn't any power.

The sleds had various connections for supplying power, though, and one of them could even be rigged to connect to Horvath and Rangora systems.

"Set to output of 128 volts alternating current, sixty-four hertz," Survey commed.

"Output set," Price replied.

"And power up."

"Power's up," Price commed.

"What's the reading?"

"I can't see it from this position," Price commed. *"Butch?"*

"Three-one-six-four-seven-nine," Butch said. The implants automatically converted the Horvath numbers. Butch didn't even "see" the actual numbers.

"Thank you, Fourteen Alpha," Survey commed. *"That's what we needed. Break it down."*

"Can I ask what we just did?" Price commed.

"That's the output for the port fuel tank on that destroyer," Survey replied. *"Three hundred and sixteen thousand, four hundred and seventy-nine Galactic gallons. Which are about one point two standard gallons."*

"*That's a lot of fuel.*"

"*For which we should all be grateful. Because it's the only fuel left in the system.*"

"*Fourteen Alpha, Salvage Control.*"

"*Control, Fourteen Alpha.*"

"*Return to the barn. We're being retasked.*"

"*Roger,*" Price commed. "*We just about had those optics unmounted.*"

"*Negative,*" Control said. "*Just get back here. There's bigger things doing.*"

"*Crap,*" Butch said.

"*I could do with a shower,*" Price replied. "*Let's get out of here, junior. And watch your fricking positioning.*"

Nearly twenty years ago, the Horvath had announced their ownership of the Terran system by dropping kinetic energy weapons on Cairo, Mexico City and Shanghai. The Glatun temporarily kicked them out of the system, giving Earth time to develop weapons of its own. When the Horvath came back they dropped a plague and when that didn't work, dropped more bombs. Then more.

Since the Horvath targeted major capitals every time, the U.S. government had finally gotten the hint and dispersed. Congress met through electronic means, video conferencing and voting, and, with the exception of the Pentagon, nobody really gathered in large groups. Most major governments had done the same. Nobody wanted to be the target of a Horvath or now Rangora weapon.

Tyler, therefore, could have had the present conversation in the Wolf system. But he was rather happier with *Troy* wrapped around him.

"First priority, keep *Troy* running and continue work to upgrade the SAPL system interlocks," Tyler said. "But at absolute minimum power. Second priority, keep enough fuel going into the Wolf system to keep the work on the gas mine going to completion. I'm trying to prioritize some things there. We've stopped all nonessential production in Granadica and on the SAPL. I'm trying to figure out, my people are looking at, whether we can throw more equipment at the mine to speed things up. The question is priorities, priorities, priorities."

"We need to keep the fleet fueled," the SecDef said. "You can't have *all* of it."

"Park the ships in the *Troy*, put the crews ashore and draw down their power to minimum maintenance," Tyler said. "If we don't get that gas mine finished, we're all going to be sucking fumes. We need to keep an eye on absolute levels and when we're down to minimum reserves, start pulling people out and dropping them back on Earth. You *don't* want to leave people in space and out of fuel. That includes *Troy*, by the way."

"I'm not sure I can accept simply parking the fleet," the SecDef said. "We need to maintain and train."

"We've got enough fuel to finish the mine and keep *Troy* running and the fleet on maintenance," Tyler said. "But those cruisers are gas hogs. They need to be parked for the duration. We're diverting some of the power to get some processors up and running on the lower platform atmo. We also have to build a tanker big enough to handle the output. We'll have some fuel flowing in a couple of weeks. But running the fleet, for now, has to be the lowest priority. I'll make sure you have enough fuel to make up the difference, later. Right now I'm worried about how much fuel it's taking to *get* the fuel. You can't, actually, just siphon He3."

"Glad we didn't cut that line," Butch said.

For once he was doing some *real* welding. The fuel valves of the Horvath ships were different from the Glatun design the human ships used. Since cutting them out of the tanks was out of the question—the liquid helium wasn't going to remain liquid long if it was exposed to vacuum—a mating valve had to be installed on top.

The destroyer, alone, had four taps on each tank. It was taking a while. And that was after the valves had been flown up from Earth. Fortunately, some far-thinking individual had already had them made.

"I'm wondering how much this is worth," Price commed. *"And if it counts for our salvage shares."*

"We're not cutting it out," Butch said. "And I got a call from my mom the other day. They've got rolling blackouts since the power plants are all down on Earth. Dad said the plant's having to run half time. So I ain't so worried if we're getting paid salvage."

"Dude, the only thing that matters is if we're getting paid," Price commed. *"If you wanted to be all heroic, you should have joined the Navy."*

The fuel point was inside an armored hatch on the exterior of the mangled, and still slowly twisting, destroyer. They'd had to find the internal release system, power it up, get the hatch open, *then* get to work.

"There's more to life than getting paid, BF," Butch argued. "The dudes that mined for the Horvath didn't get paid crap. The Russians used prisoners. The South Africans just paid 'em crap. I'd much rather just be pulling overtime and be able to live free, you know?"

Butch had managed to get himself wedged into the hatch with three arms stabilizing his sled while he welded. Around him, unnoticed, the star field slowly wheeled as if watching the puny humans battling universal entropy.

"I think I've been talking to Purcell too much," Price said. *"He was going on the other day on the reason capitalism works. I didn't get most of it but the one thing I did get is that getting paid is really what matters. Freedom and getting paid for your work go hand in hand. End of philosophical discussion. You done with your bead?"*

"Just sanding it down," Butch said, regarding his handiwork. "Looks good."

"Better be," Price said, sliding his sled around. *"They want to try them without doing a gamma test. They're in a real rush for this fuel."* He extended a grinder and ground out an imaginary spot. *"Now it's good. Salvage Control, Fourteen Alpha."*

"Fourteen Alpha, Control."

"Houston, we have a valve."

"Roger, Fourteen Alpha," Control replied. "Sending over the tanker."

"And now we got to mate it up," Price grumbled. *"Welders get paid dick so we get all the EVA jobs nobody else wants to do."*

"We're just slightly expensive robots," Butch said. "Which means we get overtime and we get paid. Which you just said was the only thing mattered."

"Butch, I'm holding a laser and the skin on that sled ain't all that thick."

"Not the only thin skin around here."

※   ※   ※

"We got to match to this thing while we're pumping it off?"

The tanker was a small one, one of three that kept all the ships in the system supplied. Normally, it filled up at *Troy*, trundled around the system fueling ships and then went back.

Now the three minor tankers were all that Sol had to manage and transport their remaining fuel. And they were *not* designed for salvage work.

"Do you see an alternative?" Price asked. "Just extend the probe and we'll get 'er hooked up."

"I don't think we have the delta," the tanker pilot said dubiously. *"This thing has got a lot of rotation. And we're not real fast on maneuvering. And since the probe is rigid, if we get off by even a flicker, we're going to crack it. I say this is a no-go."*

"Well then how the hell are we going to get the fuel off?" Butch asked.

"That's somebody else's problem," the tanker pilot said. *"I'm headed over to that cruiser that's not spinning around like a top."*

"Bloody hell," Purcell said. *"Control, the tanker's refusing to match to Sierra Seventeen because of rotation. Advise."*

"We're working with the military on a work-around," Control commed. *"Have your people stand by."*

"Okay, A, they're just about on triple time. B, they're soaking up radiation, which is why they have a maximum period in EVA. So whatever you're going to do, do it quick."

"Roger. Understood. Control out."

✳   ✳   ✳

"*Comet, ready room,*" CM1 Glass commed.

Since the boats were grounded, Dana had been working on her certifications. The basic coxswain position was only the start of training. To make CM she had to pass a battery of courses as well as more flight tests.

She was, currently, working with the simulator on a complex maneuver and the ping was sort of startling.

"*Roger, CM,*" Dana commed. "*Be right there.*"

"We're picking up some field fuel bladders and assisting the civvy salvage crew on taking fuel off the scrapped ships," Glass said. "Our objective is a destroyer, designated Sierra Seventeen. It has a rotation of about two point five rotations per hour in three axes and a velocity of nineteen kilometers per second relative to the gate. It's also gotten well out of pocket. We're not going to stabilize it, we're just going to pull off the fuel. Which will be . . . ticklish. Thermal?"

"This is going to take some coordination," Thermal said. "The blivets are just about the size of the interior of the shuttles. We're going to have to pump down, open up the personnel hatch and pull off the pipes. The civvies will then hook them up. Once they're hooked up, we use the onboard pumps to pump them up to pressure. All that time the coxswain is going to have to maintain a close position on the derelict."

"Ticklish is right," Dana said, looking at the view of the derelict. The thing wasn't spinning fast but maintaining position was going to be a pain in the ass. She wasn't even sure it could be programmed since the center of mass of the derelict made it constantly work off its standard trajectory. She'd seen some asteroids with worse spins but not many.

"Once you're full, head over to the tanker," Glass said. "There the engineers are going to have to EVA to hook up and cross-load. Then back again."

"What about our own fuel?" Thermal said.

"The tanker has refuel points," Glass said. "We are authorized to tank up. But that doesn't mean we get to use it. This is the last mission until the fuel plant is up and running. So get all the qual time in you can. Let's go warm some seats."

"Dana, I need a hand, here," Thermal commed.

The whole boat was pumped down so Dana just headed through the hatch into the cargo compartment.

"What's u— Oh," Dana said.

The engineer was wrestling with something that looked like a giant Mylar balloon. A Mylar balloon that was fairly staticky.

"I think the balloon is winning," Dana said, grinning. But she grabbed a couple of handfuls of fabric and started getting it unstuck from the engineer.

"I should have read the manual more carefully," Thermal commed. *"It said to keep it in its container until ready for use, but it was a pain-in-the-butt to move that way. So I figured, hey, how much trouble could it be?"*

"Do we even have an SOP for this?" Dana asked, starting to get wrapped in the thing as well. She managed to pull it off and pound it into a corner. "Down!"

"I don't think so," Thermal said. He'd gotten unstuck and was helping her get it under control. While Dana held it down he wrapped a couple of bungies around it. *"That's done it. None that I've found. I'm going to fricking write one when we're done. 'Field portable*

annie-plant fuel blivet still in container for movement?'
'Field portable annie-plant fuel blivet still in container
for movement, aye.'"

"I hope we don't rip this thing," Dana said. "That
would suck."

"*It's made of nanotubes,*" Thermal said. "*A nuke could
barely rip it. Okay, a nuke would rip it. We can't.*"

"Sailors can—"

"*Break anything. I know. Speaking of which, next
step is getting the* pump *out of storage . . .*"

"*Fourteen Alpha, this is* Myrm *Thirty-Six,*" Thermal
commed. "*We're on approach for tanking operations,
over.*"

"*Hey, guys. 'Bout time you showed up. We've been
sitting out here in the rads for an hour doing dick all.*"

"*Probably pulling triple time,*" Thermal commed to
Dana. "*Comet, you got this?*"

"I've got it," Dana said. It was tricky. She was
having to constantly adjust in three dimensions and
there wasn't a real good algorithm for it. But she
could maintain it.

"*Fourteen, I'm going to open the door and extend
the pipe. You're going to have to snatch it. I don't
have the delta with a navopak to maintain this.*"

"*Got it.*"

Dana watched the operation through one monitor
while keeping an eye on the focal point she'd chosen,
one corner of the hatch, to maintain station. The big
problem was judging distance. She was having to keep a
third eye on the range indicator. She was also having to
keep an eye on the engineering controls with Thermal
working the transfer. Which was too many eyes.

FIFTEEN

"I'm going to snatch the pipe and hand it to you," Price commed. *"Just hold your points."*

"Got it," Butch said.

Price crabbed his sled over to the shuttle where a guy in a suit was holding out one end of what looked like one of those pipes gas delivery trucks used. Except it was shiny silver. With all the equipment moving in about nineteen different directions, the intercept was a stone bitch, but Price made it look easy. Butch had to admire the older welder; he was a master of using a sled.

"Get this," Price commed, extending the pipe.

Butch carefully latched onto the grab point and brought it over to the mating collar.

"And we have good connect," Price commed. *"Opening the valve, Myrm."*

"Roger, Fourteen."

"Ask your coxswain to try to maintain closer position," Price commed. *"We don't want to yank your tank out of your little boat."*

"Copy, Fourteen. Comet, you copy?"

"Yeah," Dana said. "I'm on it."

To maintain good station meant keeping within a few inches of center. It wasn't happening. Maybe Mutant or Lizzbits could do it but Dana just could not stay that close on station keeping.

"I'm not on it," Dana admitted. "I'm just not able to . . ." she glanced at the engineering controls and tried not to scream. "Thermal, we've got a flicker in the lower starboard thruster controls. I could feel something starting to go. That looks like it."

"*Dammit,*" Thermal commed. "*Always something. Fourteen, Thirty-Six.*"

"*Go, Thirty-Six.*"

"*Our little boat is having issues,*" Thermal commed. "*Be ready to yank that connect. We may be going into out-of-control condition . . .*"

"I just lost main breaker," Dana said to the darkness. "Thermal, I don't have *anything!*"

"*Clear it!*" Price said. "*Release the valve!*"

"Okay," Butch said, hitting the release on the connect. Helium started spurting into space and his temperature monitors started screaming.

"*And shut off the valve!*" Price said.

"*Got it . . .*" Butch said and the arm he was using broke. Then the valve, which was following the shuttle, slammed into the side of his sled. He'd been hit harder by debris plenty of times, but the sudden scream of his breathable monitor said that this time it mattered. "Uh . . . BF? I think I've got a problem . . ."

As EM1 Hartwell entered the flight compartment, the power and lights came on.

"All I had to do was reset the breaker," Dana said, pulling herself into her chair. "Gravity coming back up."

"Roger," Hartwell said. "But we've got a deadlined bird until—"

"Thirty-Six, I see your lights came back on. If your boat's fixed we could use a hand here."

"Roger, Fourteen. We're discontinuing this evolution until we can determine what caused the malfunction."

"Great. Does that mean you can take us back to the Troy? Because I don't want to rush you or anything but when you pulled out the valve you cracked my partner's sled. And he's in vacuum."

"I hope like hell he's in a suit."

"Oh, he is. But he's not exactly a happy camper. And we are, as you said, discontinuing this evolution."

"Helium is cryogenic," Purcell said, looking at the trashed sled. "Steel works *pretty* well in space as long as you don't get it too cold. Even space shade in this region isn't as cold as, say, Pluto. He3 is right above absolute zero. When it hit the steel it made it brittle. Then the valve, which is an alloy designed for cryogenic temperatures, hit the arm and the sled, and shattered them like glass."

"Yes, sir," Butch said, looking at the sled. It sure looked like the steel broke like glass.

"I hope we don't have to deal with Navy again," Price said. "That was massively fracked up, Purcell."

"You can see where the port thruster started to act up," Dana said, pointing to the readout from the flight recorder. "I started having control problems. I thought it was the destroyer shifting its trajectory again and corrected. Then there was the overheat indicator. It wasn't high but it was moving out of range so it sort of caught my attention. Then we lost main power and I went into out of control. I then reset the breaker," she said, pointing to the indicator. "And we're back. There wasn't a flicker on the return trip, even carrying the fuel we'd loaded and the civilian sleds and the welders. It's like it just went away."

"I pulled the breaker and the full set of relays for the port thrusters," Thermal said. "I ran them all through standard tests including overpower tests and long runtime tests. They all came up fine. I've replaced everything, but I still can't find the fault. It's apparently intermittent."

"An intermittent fault that can throw a main breaker is an intermittent fault we have to run down," Chief Barnett said. Any incident involving flight in the squadron had to involve the chief coxswain. Since the normal name was "Chief Cock" the fact that the chief coxswain was a female led to some ribald humor. "Engineering input, sir?"

"I hate to say this," Lieutenant Commander Brandon "Brad" Horn said. The squadron engineering officer was an Aussie seconded to the United States Space Navy. He'd been a deep wreck diver before the War as well as a qualified watch officer. Making the transition to space navy had been relatively easy. Since he also had a mechanical engineering degree, he was a natural for the first engineering officer of a *Myrmidon* squadron.

"But it looks as if it might be a bloody software issue. The reason I hate to say it is that we depend on the AIs for the software. Be a fair dinkum task to run through it line by line."

"Hate to disagree, sir," Thermal said. By chain of command, Longwood was his boss. By actual function, Commander Horn was his *boss's* boss. Chief Grady, the squadron master engineer, had so far been silent. "But the heat indicator indicates mechanical failure."

"There are ways that software could affect that," Commander Horn said. "But I take your point."

"Damn," Barnett said, leaning back and crossing her arms. "Thirty-Three."

"Say again, Chief?" CM Glass said.

"Thirty-Three was put down to pilot error," Barnett said. She glanced at Dana. "The previous Thirty-Three, not your first boat. Because as far as anyone could see, they'd just plowed right into the SAPL. But there were things that were screwy. They called a mayday about a half second before they hit the beam. And even though there wasn't video, all the witnesses said that their nav lights went off just before they hit."

"You think they lost main breaker, Chief?" Thermal said. "In that case, that's on me. I was the engineering NCO for Thirty-Three. It wasn't my boat, but it *was* my responsibility."

"Not really," Chief Barnett said. "This is all stuff that we're learning. But if the problem is related to maneuvering thrusters, they might have had a failure when they started their turn. Which would *look* like they just didn't make it. And if it's not showing up on standard tests . . ."

"I think we need to be a bit cautious here," Commander Horn said. "There's no proof of that at this time. If we have another fault like that, we'll have to find the source. In the meantime, we'll put it down to random chaos, which is a good description of the entire situation."

＊　　＊　　＊

"EM," Dana said, walking into the engineering shop. "You still got the parts from Thirty-Six?"

"Yeah," Thermal said, gesturing to a stack of relays and breakers. "If you think you can find the fault, go for it. I've run them at max power, powered up and down, everything I can think of. They test out fine."

"I don't think I can," Dana said, loading the parts into a box. "But I'll admit that right now, I'm glad we're grounded by the fuel situation. Because if there's something causing main breaker faults, I don't want to be flying."

"I'm with you," Thermal said. "What are you going to do?"

"I'm going to take a walk on the wild side."

"Can I help you, Coxswain?"

The maintenance support shop for the *Troy* was a huge, echoing cavern of industry. Most of the machinery Dana couldn't identify although the massive overhead cranes were familiar as were the many CNC milling machines. It was also on the civilian side. Most of the construction work going on in the battlestation was done by civilians as was the depot level repair of military equipment.

Dana had just entered through one of the large hangar doors and started looking around for a friendly face. She was hoping that was the heavyset, cueball gentleman who had run her down. His nametag read Erickson.

"I hope so," Dana said, putting on her brightest smile. She'd worn the flight-suit that was just a tad too small and she stood up nice and straight. "I'm looking for someone who knows more about relays and high-power electronics systems than my boss."

"I see," the man said, grinning. He gestured to a work bench. "What's the problem?"

"I had a main breaker fault," Dana said, setting the box down. "Thermal indicator on the 416 thruster relay," she continued, pulling out the offending relay. "Then we lost main power. I was in a complex maneuver at the time. The engineering officer is saying software fault. My engineer is saying mechanical but he can't find a fault."

"I see," the guy said, picking up the relay and examining it. "Is this an official inquiry?"

"Nope," Dana said, shrugging. "I'm just looking for a little milk of human kindness. And experience."

"I'll give you the second," the guy said, pulling out a loop. "Were you open in your suits when this happened?"

"Closed," Dana said. "The compartment was evacuated."

"Must have been fun," the guy said. "Name's Bill Erickson, by the way. I'm in charge of milling but I can dance the tune of high power electronics. You?"

"Coxswain First Class Dana Parker," Dana said.

"*Comet* Parker?" Erickson said, looking up and grinning. "That was *you*?"

"Yes," Dana said, trying not to sigh. "It really was . . ."

"One *hell* of a piece of driving," Erickson said, holding out his hand. "I wish you'd been a coxswain in *my* day. But they didn't *have* coxswains like you in my day."

"Your day?" Dana said, shaking his hand.

"I used to be a Marine," Erickson said, jiggling his belly. "I guess it does wear off after a while."

"Nooo..." Dana said. There was just enough color to tell that the cueball was at least in part to cover up male-pattern baldness. "The look's still there."

"We are swamped at the moment," Erickson said thoughtfully, "but I'll get it done. On one condition."

"Which is?"

"You and me catch a drink if I find anything," Erickson said, holding up his hands. "Not hitting, gal. You're a bit young for my blood. I'd just *love* to hear that story from *your* POV..."

SIXTEEN

"How much longer?" Tyler said.

"There's no way we can speed up the spiders, sir," Byron said, patiently. "Another month."

They were having the conversation over a video link because no matter how impatient he was to get the gas mine done, Tyler wasn't going to use the fuel necessary to go to the Wolf system and breathe down Byron's neck.

The same weavers that had spun the supports for the space elevator were now spinning the tubes descending deep into the interior of the gas giant's atmosphere. They were, at base, complicated multipart weaving machines. The "spiders" extruded microscopic filaments of carbon nanotubes. By weaving using the ultrafine and extremely strong material, it was possible to seal the tube fairly well against helium. But helium was tricky stuff.

"That's better than 'get used to waiting,'" Tyler replied. "But it still sounds like you're talking to Dr. Bell. Seriously. *More* spiders?"

"Granadica already did," Byron said. "Part of the plan. All the uplines and downlines are full. The pumps are on their way down. We're getting a top-side processor up and running. That's going to be about a week. It'll collect about a thousand gallons a week. But that's just enough to run us and do start-up. We're not going to have a spare. After the pumps are in place we can start pumping up and separating. Then we'll have to work out the bugs."

"I know," Tyler said. "Heard it before. I'll get out of your . . ." He started to say "hair" and then paused. "When did you shave your head?"

"I've had a shaved head the whole time you've known me, sir," Byron said, trying not to laugh.

"I need to get out more," Tyler said. "Seriously. If you need anything and don't get it right away, call me."

"Yes, sir," Byron said.

"Take care."

Tyler looked out at the main bay and frowned. He'd had a wall installed on his quarters similar to the wall on the *Starfire*. It was damned stupid from the POV of safety; the *Troy* was, after all, a battlestation, but the main bay was just about the most secure area in the solar system and he liked to watch the bustle. It was sort of the feeling a grandparent would get watching their grandkids run around.

Normally, he liked to watch the bustle. At the moment, pretty much everything was stopped. They were still drilling the SAPL feeds and at least the next time they'd have a full collector set up. Three, actually. Six were planned, in a circle around the main doors that made the back of *Troy* look like some sort of spider.

But the lack of activity was annoying.

He connected when his implant pinged since it was Argus and the AI was notorious about not wasting his time.

"Hello, Argus," Tyler said.

"Good afternoon, Mr. Vernon," Argus said. "There is news. There is now a feed off the Galactic side of the hypernet. However, it is only one connection and that is a Rangora propaganda channel."

Tyler spun around in his chair and turned on the TV. His plant quickly found the channel he was looking for.

"Oh, shit," Tyler said.

"Remember, sir," Argus said. "This is a propaganda broadcast."

"I know," Tyler said. "But I doubt they'd *lie* about going to war against the Glatun."

This is a scene of the victorious Concordance Fleets assuming peaceful orbit around the planet Ghapolhat in the Mu'Johexam system. The Glatun system defenders welcomed their Rangora liberators with open arms in a show of mutual fortitude against the decrepit plutocracy that has too long oppressed...

"Can we derive any specific intelligence from this?" the President asked.

"It's propaganda, Mr. President," the director of national intelligence said. "We can do analysis on it, but at the end of the day we really don't know anything for sure. With the Concordance control of the Eridani system, there's no surety of any information coming through. If they're using propaganda I would expect personal messages to start coming through backing up the information. Again, they might not even be from the supposed sender. It's like the Internet. The information could be coming from anyone."

"Are they at war?" the President said.

"High probability," the DNI replied. "Better than that, I can't say."

The President leaned forward and hit the speaker phone.

"Janice, get me Athena."

"You asked to speak to me, Mister President?" the AI said.

"Are we secure?" the President asked.

"Yes, sir," the AI replied. "The systems are secured physically and I've secured them a bit more electronically."

"You've got more data on the Rangora than any hundred analysts," the President said. "The DNI says we can't get any real data from these broadcasts. What's your take?"

"The Rangora have, within the last twenty years, engaged in two wars of conquest against minor species," Athena said. "In both cases, they were careful to restrict all information that was transmitted during their conquest phase. But by examining their statements and applying regression analysis it is possible to construct a reasonable surmise of actual events."

"So you can tell me something," the President said, looking at the DNI. The DNI just shrugged and looked unhappy.

"There are no guarantees, Mr. President," Athena said. "The DNI has a valid point. There is a five percent chance, more or less, that this is an elaborate ruse. But only about five percent."

"So they *are* at war?" the President said.

"Ninety-Five percent probable," Athena said. "Furthermore, they have probably taken the Mu'Johexam, Zhoqaghev and Silhemik systems as the broadcasts indicate. Probability on that is eighty percent. What has to be examined is their probable strategic intent and what they are not saying. It appears that they moved their main force in through the Silhemik system, which was an outlier system, lightly inhabited and lightly defended. It was considered an unlikely avenue of hostile approach since they were required to go through several star systems to get there. Those star systems were, until recently, technically held by the Glatun. But since they were uninhabited and there were not constant patrols, it is probable that the Rangora built a forward supply base in one of them. Silhemik did have a gas mine so they could refuel and use the local fabbers to rearm. From there they could then proceed into the Zhoqaghev and Mu'Johexam relatively uncontested.

"Given the timing, though, I find the lack of mention of Tuxughah interesting."

"Interesting how?" the President asked.

"Tuxughah is, again, a relatively minor world," Athena said. "But it was the main naval base in the region. To get from Silhemik to Zhoqaghev is possible without going through Tuxughah but, again, it is out of the way. But there is no mention in the broadcasts of Tuxughah. This is one of the points I was looking for in their veracity. I suspect they had problems in the Tuxughah system and are simply not reporting any attack until it has been reduced."

"Do we have that on a star chart?" the President asked.

"There, sir," the DNI said, bringing up the map and highlighting the system. "So, Athena, you think these broadcasts are for real?"

"I surmise that there is a war," Athena said. "And that the Rangora have attacked through a lightly defended zone. I also surmise that this is their heavy attack and that there is *another*, unmentioned, attack against main defense systems. Notably, Rocholhek and Sidirox. This would have the effect of pinning forces there as the main Rangora force attacks from the flank. It is a standard Rangora tactic simply on a strategic level."

"What do you think of the political aspects of the broadcast?" the President asked. "The whole 'welcoming with open arms their Rangora liberators.'"

"Your own media is already repeating that with the most pro forma statements that the information is censored," Athena said. "Which I'm sure was the intent of the Rangora. The Glatun military was considered of little worth within the society. The members were not, however, the scum of the Federation, enlisted for drink. They tended to be true believers and mostly from long-term military families. My analysis is that they are defending as well as they can, given that they have been systematically stripped of power. I am also less than sure that their admirals know what they are doing. But I'm relatively positive that, based simply on the missing mention of Tuxughah, that they are not going down without a fight. And the Rangora main force, probability seventy percent, has yet to encounter the Glatun main force. The decisive battle has probably not yet occurred."

"Importance to Earth?" the President said. "Where does this leave us?"

"First, on our own," Athena said. "The Glatun cannot, certainly *will* not, spare forces to assist Earth under these conditions."

"Understood," the President said. "And it explains why they took the embargo without so much as a whimper."

"The positive side is that the Rangora probably have little time to spare for a minor polity," Athena said. "My analysis is that we should have at least weeks, probably months, before they attack. And that assumes that the Glatun military does not significantly impede them in the main battle. Attacking through gates is difficult and damage intensive as you saw with the recent Horvath attack. If the Glatun military can pin the Rangora at a choke point, such as Futeyig, they may be able to blunt them to such an extent that they will retreat and never threaten Earth at all. If the Rangora bring their full force to bear on the core worlds... The war from the Glatun point of view will be over. At that point they can bring their full weight to bear against Earth."

"Can we stop them?" the President asked.

"Not if they bring their full assault fleet against us," Athena said. "The Rangora, as of last intelligence summary, have sixty-two gate assault ships. They apparently had been making them in large numbers in secrecy. The main SAPL can, in fact, engage and destroy one. But it will take time. And there will be more and more ships. Eventually, even *Troy* will fall to their assault. That is if they bring the full force and there is only *Troy*. If they send a lesser task group and *Thermopylae* is online, it is *possible* to hold the system. There will be significant damage. It is Rangora standard technique to destroy all orbital systems and defenses and carpet bomb the planet. Which is why I rather doubt they were welcomed with open arms."

"Lack of information can cut two ways," the President said. "Can we jam the hypercom?"

"Yes, sir," Athena said. "But there would be great public and international outcry if we did so to cut off the broadcasts."

"Not to cut off the broadcasts," the President said. "I want to let that through. But can we stop *our* information from going *out*?"

"Yes, sir," the AI said.

"Do it," the President said. "I don't know that we can actually surprise them. But it would be nice to try."

"You owe me a drink," Erickson said. "But I don't think you're going to be in a celebratory mood."

"What did you find?" Dana asked.

She was about ready for a break from studying. The *Myrms* were well and truly shut down with the fuel shortage and it was study or listen to Rangora propaganda and people who were buying it.

The Terran Alliance plan was being ripped apart in the media and the international stage. The French and Chinese were specifically boycotting it and most of the EU countries were stating they had a hard time coughing up the money to join. The way the EU was set up, they weren't supposed to run deficits. And nobody had come up with a way to run a war without a deficit since Caesar.

The UN had voted in a nonbinding resolution for surrender to the Rangora. The U.S. had more or less told them to stuff it. Politely. The rest of the world was free to surrender, thank you. The Alliance was going to fight.

If they ever had fuel to fight with.

"You better be glad your *Myrmidons* are down," Erickson said. "You might want to come over to the shop with your engineering people. This is a bit complicated."

"Okay," Erickson said, bringing up the schematic of a relay on the screen. "This is the relay you brought in. Part of a group of four that's arrayed around the main breaker. The first point to make is that the breaker doesn't just react to ground load. It's computerized and checks for various faults. If any of its algorithms say that you're about to have a major short, it shuts down."

"And we don't have flight power," Dana said, nodding. "Got that."

"And that's why the commander said it was a software bug," Thermal said.

"And the commander is . . . wrong," Erickson said, bringing up a picture of . . . something. "This is an electron spectroscopy study of the relay. Specifically, of one of the primary power interaction points. These things are incredibly refined. They have to be made like computer chips. The interaction point uses gold as its conductor."

"Point?" Dana said. "Gold? I thought the whole system was superconductor material."

"The internal conductors are superconductor," Erickson said, rubbing his head in thought. "But . . . superconductor you've got to think of as sort of an interstate for electrons. It's really easy to move on the interstate, so electrons sort of want to stay on. And there the point breaks down because in relays, you have to have a way for the electrons to exit. And when you have two superconductors in direct contact, they don't trade electrons very well."

"Why?" Hartwell asked, frowning.

"The way they trade electrons in a superconductor prevents it," Erickson said, shrugging. "I can do the math for you, but explaining it in *English* is tough. I can talk about quantum if you want. They're kind of going round and round on the track and they like it there."

"Okay," Hartwell said, blinking. "Can you do the math?"

"Yes," Erickson said. "The point is you have to have a way to coax them out. Lower level conductors work for that. Gold is the best. But it can't be pure gold because that's too soft and melts in an instant. So you use a gold alloy with admixtures of copper and silver. Think of it as fourteen karat."

"Okay," Hartwell said.

"The gold is in direct contact with the superconductor on both sides," Erickson said. "Gold-gold connections are solid. And the gold on each side can get the electrons out of their superconductor womb. The gold has got to be a specific density, quality, alloy and thickness. Specifically, it has to be between seventy and ninety nanometers thick with very little variation and right around fourteen karat with specific levels of silver and copper."

"How thick is it?" EM1 Hartwell asked.

"Thirty-five," Erickson said. "Ish. It varies from thirty-five to sixty. And it's about seven karat with most of the admixture being copper. So it's more red gold than gold."

"Which means power doesn't flow evenly across the contact point," Thermal said, his jaw working. "But if you test it under power, it probably has enough gold that the machine can't tell the difference."

"Yep," the engineer said. "Took me a while to find this. Most of the interaction points were fine. This one wasn't. What happens is you get—"

"Arcing," Dana said. "And the relay overheats. And when it overheats, it starts to fail."

"And you get a ground fault indication," Erickson said, bringing up a string of code. "And the main breaker throws. If you'd had your helmets off you'd have smelled ozone. But the arcing is microscopic in macro. So it's hard as hell to spot."

"And you have no power and you plow into a SAPL beam," Thermal said. "Dammit. Six dozen people analyzing that crash and nobody *caught* this."

"There wasn't much left of Thirty-Three from what I hear," Dana said.

"We're going to need your data," Thermal said. "Mr. Erickson, thanks for finding this for us. And Comet, good job finding him. I've got to go talk to the chief."

"Oh . . . crap," Tyler muttered.

The news about the bad relays, and potentially causing a fatal crash, had not quite overwhelmed the news that the Glatun were at war with the Rangora. But it was news. And since it was news about Apollo and Tyler Vernon, the media was going ape-shit. There were already calls for Congressional investigations.

The problem was, Apollo and LFD had become

the sole-source providers for a dozen different areas, mostly related to defense. Tyler, surprisingly, wasn't happy about that. He was a firm believer that competition made a company stronger. The problem was, he'd gone into areas like a bull when other companies either didn't notice them or were tepid at best. There had been one start-up that had tried to compete with Apollo in mining but they'd gone out of business. By the time major corporations even noticed that, despite the enormous initial costs, Apollo's balance sheet was the near order of the Earth's balance of trade, Tyler had built so many mirrors it was worth just buying time from him. Competing was pretty much out of the question. Then, based on that and his contacts with the Glatun financier Niazgol Gorku, he'd gotten Granadica. Which pretty much put paid to competing with him in orbital manufacture.

From maple syrup to mirrors to mining to orbital manufacturing had been a long and costly road. But it had more or less, in many cases accidentally, crushed any competition.

But Tyler was looking at more than the news. His internal review people had already looked at, and confirmed, the findings. And then there was the really fun part.

"Memo to CEO, LFD, Vice President of Quality Control, LFD, President of Manufacturing, LFD, copy to everyone on the same level in all branches and departments.

"As soon as we release the results of our internal findings, the Chinese government will find someone to ritually execute. Which won't bring the lost crew back and won't solve the problem. The supplier, Qua

Tang Electronics, is blacklisted. Find every person associated, every member of the board, every senior officer, and blacklist any company they are associated with as well. With something like this, and the Chinese, there is no overkill. Be wildly unaimed in your fire. Nuke first, ask questions later. Make the pain as widespread as possible.

"Find any memo related to questions about quality control. Fire anyone who downplayed them and promote anyone who raised questions even if the first person is normally great and the 'whistle blower' is an asshole. And if any of you are on the memos, the same goes. Just tell your second he or she is in charge, pack your stuff and go home.

"Do a press release stating all of the above and accepting *full* responsibility. It was our design, it was our manufacture, it was our quality control, and it's *our* fault even if one of our suppliers screwed us. No point in playing games. Come clean with everything we can find internally that's not security restricted and all of our actions. Tell legal to shut the hell up when they start whining. Take the cost of a *Myrmidon*. Split it between the Wounded Warrior fund and the families or beneficiaries. Double up on kids. If we get sued that is not to be considered in any settlement or reward. Make sure all of these terms are in the press release. Post it on the Internet and push it in the media and blogs until it gets through. Do *not* use the families for photo-ops. I want this done yesterday."

And that was the easy part.

Pulling watch was a fundamental aspect of being in the Navy.

It didn't matter that nobody was still quite sure if the *Troy* was a ship or a base. It didn't matter that if there was an alert, there were alarms all throughout the base and everyone had implants so they'd get the word. It didn't matter than the main Naval area of the *Troy* was secured by armed civilian guards.

Somebody had to pull watch. One petty officer from the squadron on fixed location by the entrance and a roving guard. Who, in general, didn't rove much.

EM2 Carter, the engineer on Forty-Six, was "visiting the gentlemen's" so it was up to Dana to challenge the civilian who, somehow, had wandered into the squadron area.

"Sir," Coxswain's Mate Third Class Dana Parker said, holding up her hand. "This is a restricted area."

Technically, newly promoted CM3 Parker was a petty officer. But PO3s were considered "over-paid seamen."

Under normal conditions, Dana would meet neither time in grade nor schooling requirements since she hadn't attended the Leadership Training Course.

Promotion requirements had been somewhat relaxed with the burgeoning space Navy. She'd completed all the mandatory exams and with all the ceremony attendant on such an august position she'd been told, once again, "go hit the stores for your badge, you're on watch in an hour."

"Yeah," Tyler said, holding out his own hand. "I know. I built it. I'm Tyler Vernon."

"Uh . . ." Dana said, coloring. It wasn't like she hadn't seen the guy on TV. She remembered her dad shouting "Yeah!" when Vernon had made his famous "Live Free or Die!" speech to the Horvath. "Yes, sir. Sorry, sir. But this is still a restricted area."

"And I have a hall pass," Tyler said, pulling out an access badge. "I was wondering if you could direct me to the CO of the One-Forty-Second?"

"Yes, sir," Dana said. She checked the badge then swiped it through the verifier. Hoo. Unrestricted access, all areas, all conditions. The only person she could think of with the same sort of clearance was the admiral. "Squadron offices are down the corridor to port, sir."

"That would be left as I'm walking or right?" Tyler said. "I've always had problems with port and starboard on the *Troy*."

"To your left, sir," Dana said.

"Thank you, Coxswain," Tyler said, taking his badge back. "I thought since I was here I should go deliver a personal apology."

"You mean about the relays, sir?" Dana asked.

"Yes," Tyler replied, sighing. "But I think I'm avoiding it by talking. If you'll excuse me, Coxswain, I need to go be abject. I'm not good at abject."

"Yes, sir," Parker said, then opened her mouth. She closed it, though, with an audible clop.

"You were about to say something, Coxswain?" Tyler said.

"No, sir," Dana replied. "Above my paygrade, sir."

"Well, hopefully it will be your paygrade, someday," Tyler said. "And now I must go . . ."

"Sir," the captain's yeoman said, looking in the door. "Mr. Vernon wants to see you."

"Send him in."

Captain Chris "MOGS" DiNote was the commander of the 142nd. He'd been on *Troy* for about two years, which made him an old hand. And it wasn't like he hadn't met Vernon before. The last time was just in somewhat better circumstances, a dining out in the admiral's quarters that was interrupted by the first Battle of *Troy*.

"Mr. Vernon," DiNote said when the short financier entered his office.

"Captain DiNote," Tyler said, coming to a stop and assuming something resembling parade rest. "This is my personal formal apology for the failure of one of our systems which appears to have contributed to the deaths of your servicemen. I sincerely regret that we failed in our quality control and design processes. There's not a lot else to say but that I'm very, very sorry. We're tracking down what went wrong and we're going to try to ensure it doesn't happen again. That being said, Jesus Christ, Chris, I'm sorry as *hell*."

"Didn't figure you were happy," DiNote said, grimacing. "None of us are. Grab a chair, sir."

"Thank you," Tyler said, sitting down.

"Off the record?" DiNote said. "What the hell happened?"

"On the record for all I care," Tyler said. "I've already told my people that this whole investigation is going to be a public and ritual auto-da-fé. It wasn't Granadica. Okay, we're going to have to tighten up there, some. But... To reduce the strain on Granadica, which is juggling a lot of balls, we got a lot of the components from Earth companies. Also because it was pointed out quietly that we were killing off terrestrial manufacture. And I didn't want that to happen. So a bunch of *Myrmidon* components come from terrestrial manufacture. Those relays, and the main breakers, were two of about two dozen. We've gone back and done the same analysis on lots that we keep on hand to check for this sort of thing. And the ones from one particular company are all bad. They were . . . calling it sloppy is being generous. They were skimping on the gold for obvious reasons. The nanometric lay-down is actually hard to do so I'll give them simply poor quality there. Doesn't matter. We're going to gut the company and anyone associated with it. Won't bring your sailors back, but . . ."

"Nothing will," MOGS said. "The *Myrms* are down until the investigation is completed. And we know they're going to stay flying."

"Replacing the relays with good ones will do it," Tyler said. "And I'll be taking out the first *Myrmidon* that activates. If it makes anyone feel any better, the *Starfire* is essentially the same design. Same components for sure. So I've been putting my own ass on the fire for the last year and a half."

"That's a point," DiNote said, shaking his head. "A point was made, though, that there's a fundamental problem with the design."

"Which is?" Tyler said.

"You shouldn't lose power if a single component fails," MOGS said, leaning back and crossing his arms. "There really should be redundancy. And it's not the only place we're having problems. Tracking them down, though, is damned near impossible. We ran a couple of systems that were having problems through the same sort of analysis but they didn't have the same problems."

"Where's the other problems?" Tyler asked, trying not to grimace.

"Stuff just . . ." MOGS shrugged in frustration. "The problem is we can't track down any one *point*. Sometimes it's internal grav, but the inertics seem to work just fine. Just . . . you'll get funky gravity in some spots on some boats. Comes and goes."

"'Funky gravity' can be a real problem," Tyler said, frowning. "I remember some of the problems Boeing had with their first grav systems. Gravity vortexes can be . . . critical issues."

"None of it has really been *critical* so far," DiNote said. "Except the relay issue."

"Okay," Tyler said. "Hard to track down and inconsistent problems. That's fun. And the relay issue. And things need more redundancy."

"I'm pretty sure there's going to be a full report," DiNote said. "That's just off the top of my head."

"I've found that these sorts of conversations and screaming at people is often more useful than a carefully prepared PowerPoint," Tyler said. "So I'm going to go scream at people. As soon as we have fuel again, I'll get Granadica started on some really *good* relays. And I'll get some people to look at the problems with the gravity systems. That may take some skull sweat but I know some people with really good skulls."

SEVENTEEN

"Beor, that was genius," To'Jopeviq said. "The lack of fuel will hold them up for at least six months. There's no way they can get that gas mine finished before we arrive in force. They don't have enough fuel to finish the mine!"

The trade embargo had gone into effect only shortly before the war against the Glatun. You could never really trust the official reports, but things there seemed to be going well. The current plan would free up some forces to attack Terra in no more than six months if all went well. To'Jopeviq was still having a hard time agreeing with his analysts on what would be necessary to attack the human system. The *Aggressor* battleships, two steps down in throw weight from assault vectors, were much more powerful than *Devastators* with heavier screens and more throw weight. Avama was convinced that the simple appearance of a Rangora fleet would have the humans asking for a negotiated surrender. Toer was insisting that anything less than multiple AVs, which was pretty much out of the question, was too little.

Either way the trade embargo was sure to cripple the humans.

"Thank you," the Kazi said. "Unfortunately, you are not my rating officer."

"Tell me who it is and I'll send him a letter of commendation," To'Jopeviq said. "I start to understand the problem with deciding what will work with humans. I don't think they can make up their own minds."

"There is that," Beor said.

"There is a study off their own hypernet," To'Jopeviq said. "Avama sent it to me showing how 'peaceful' they are. I don't know what cloud he is currently floating on because it involves a piece of land they have been battling over since their pre-history."

"Forty thousand years?" Beor said.

"They haven't had *writing* that long," To'Jopeviq said. "No, but at least five thousand. The first battles are only written about in their religious tracts. And as far as anyone can tell, it's been a battleground ever since. But the study showed that whereas if the people of the region were offered financial incentives to make peace, they rejected them. If they were offered purely ceremonial concessions, they were more willing."

"Ceremonial concessions?" Beor said.

"That each group would give up things that they saw as their 'rights' in the conflict," To'Jopeviq said. "They refused economic concessions but would consider territorial concessions based on *points of honor*."

"It sounds like they need a good eugenics program," Beor said. "There are some very stupid humans."

"It seems that way," To'Jopeviq said. "Part of it, though, might be that one of the groups was already subject to a eugenics program. That explains the fierceness of battle but not the stupidity. And they really *are* stupid. Their history is replete with groups giving up important, even strategically vital, terrain for peace only to have to battle to get it back when the aggressor, naturally, didn't accept just part of the prize."

"Who won?" Beor asked.

"What?"

"Well, did the side that gave up the strategic ground win or lose in the end?" Beor asked.

"Hmmm . . ." To'Jopeviq said. "I'm just starting to look at their history. Just their military history is a big chunk . . ." He paused and looked at some recent wars in Terra's history. "They have had some long-drawn insurgencies . . ."

"Look for par war," Beor said. "More or less equal sides."

"Last big one was what they refer to as the Cold War," To'Jopeviq said. "The battles were mostly between insurgencies. The two major players were the Soviet Union and NATO. Lead group of NATO was . . . the Americans again."

"Did the Americans give up territory?" Beor asked.

"Repeatedly," To'Jopeviq said. "And they lost virtually every insurgency. And they lost the spy war. They got their butts thoroughly ki—" He stopped. "They *won*?"

"Interesting," Beor said. "Previous major war?"

"World War Two," To'Jopeviq said. "Hot war. USSR and Americans are allies against an axis of three enemies. Along with a minor group called the British. British were early in the war. Gave up territorial concessions for peace. Got their butts kicked, of course. The Americans lost almost all their overseas possessions. USSR was deeply invaded . . ."

"And they won?" Beor said.

"Damn," To'Jopeviq said. "I can see why the Horvath concentrated their bombardments on the Americans."

"How many people did they lose?" Beor asked.

"Millions," To'Jopeviq said. "And more to the plagues. Here's a good example of how stupid humans are. And especially these Americans. They entered a plea to the Glatun to intervene because, get this, the Horvath were using weapons of mass destruction against the *civilian population*!"

"That is funny," Beor said, hissing. "What else do they expect anyone to do? Destroying your enemy's will to fight is the whole purpose of war. What's their current status? After the bombardments?"

"The most powerful country on the planet by a long shot. I'm starting to see a *pattern* . . ."

"You think? Do they have enemies?"

"Pretty much the rest of the planet," To'Jopeviq said. "There are a few countries that don't actively hate them, but not many."

"I see an opportunity here . . ."

The was a quiet, almost hesitant, tap at the door.

"Come," To'Jopeviq said.

"Uh, we have a little bitty problem," Toer said, sticking his head in the door.

"Which is?"

"The humans have retaliated and cut off their hypercom connection," Toer said. "We don't have any up-to-date information anymore."

The good part about this job had been the almost total lack of information control on the part of the humans. Much of it was, obviously, disinformation. There was no way that any group could be as free with military secrets as the humans and especially the Americans. There were full specifications for their ships available on many "security" sites such as Janes'. Which just meant that the specifications were false. The Horvath did that sort of thing, overstating the ability of their craft.

The humans were clearly doing the same thing. Many of the abilities of their systems were clearly false. The only way they could have drives and lasers as powerful as listed was if the Glatun had given them access to all the Glatun's most advanced technology. And the Glatun were not that generous.

But by sifting through the lies, it was possible to get some clue as to their actual ability. Even Toer had finally agreed that the SAPL could not be as powerful as listed—it had that much raw power but there was *no way* that the humans could have mirrors that actually handled seventy petawatts—and the new Thunderbolt missiles could not have the drives or penetrators listed. But there were still nuggets of truth to be teased out.

Now all of that was gone.

"Well, we know they cannot complete their projects on *Troy* without fuel," Beor said. "And they don't have fuel. So we'll have to do our projections on that basis. Take that into your calculations."

"What if they find a source of fuel?" Toer asked.

"Then we will be wrong," Beor said. "But we won't be wrong."

EIGHTEEN

"We waited until we were sure we had enough fuel to do the tanker," Nathan said, proudly. "Isn't she a beauty?"

"It's a blimp," Tyler said.

And that was just what it looked like. A half-formed blimp at that. The spiders that had woven the pipes for the now operating, if slowly, gas mine were now spinning the tanker. They were about half done, which meant that it looked like...half a big, silver blimp.

"That's just the inner bladder," Nathan said with a slight pout. "We're going to insert it in the hull to prevent bleeding."

"Ah," Tyler said. "Where's the hull?"

"We're spinning it up," Nathan said. "Out system. Once it cools enough we'll send it in-system to pick up the bladder. Seal the end, put on some valves and we're good to go."

"Time?" Tyler asked. "The SecDef is getting antsy that his pretty little fleet is still docked. And then there's the rolling blackouts on Earth."

"By the time the first tank on the mine is full, the tanker will be ready," Nathan said. "Month or so. I'm figuring the gas mine takes longer to get into full operation than the tanker."

"Well, it's already pumping enough to fill up Granadica and get her back on track," Tyler said. "We're going to need her twin. Fast."

"You know, I haven't asked," Nathan said. "But this is going to be a lot of fuel. Where are you going to *put* it?"

"Someplace very very safe," Tyler said.

"CM," Dana said, sticking her head in the Flight NCOIC's office. She had her arms wrapped around her and she was shivering. "Is it the power shortage that has the AO freezing? I was just wondering." She didn't have any real cold-weather clothes on the *Troy*. A sweater under her flight-suit was the best she could do. And that wasn't cutting it.

Even with all the work done on *Troy* using the SAPL, the battlestation was well outside of the life zone. The sun's rays couldn't keep it above freezing.

That was normally handled by heating elements woven into the external portions of the crew areas. The crew areas were, essentially, self-contained space stations *within* the battlestation. They were surrounded with insulation and their temperature maintained by the heating coils.

Which apparently weren't working.

"I was wondering the same thing," Glass said, blowing on his hands. "I tried turning the thermostat up but I didn't get anything out of it. And it's not like we can start a fire. Well, we could but it wouldn't be a good thing..."

"Is there somebody we can check with?"

❋   ❋   ❋

"Colonel Helberg, Captain DiNote."

"Helberg, Captain."

"I'm getting some concerned inquiries regarding the temperature regulators in the Squadron area."

"Ah, that. Yes, it's a precautionary measure. Should be cleared up in short order."

"Precautionary measure?"

"We're about to do some major work in your AO with the SAPL. It was feared that there might be a high degree of thermal transfer. Lowering the temperature in your sector reduces the possibility of excessive thermal transfer as well as increasing the rate of cooling."

"So . . . it's freezing now, but pretty soon it's going to get really hot? Could you be more precise about 'thermal transfer'?"

"We're hoping for simply warm. But we'll probably do a precautionary evacuation of your Charlie Flight areas."

"I could have used some coordination on this, Colonel."

"Things have been somewhat complex lately, Captain. I apologize."

"I'll tell my people. Oh, may I inquire, purely for curiosity's sake, what you mean by 'major SAPL work in my AO' given that SAPL can gut battlecruisers like a trout?"

"They're making the *what?*" Dana said.

She'd pulled a blanket off her bed and was wrapped in it for the briefing. She didn't care if it wasn't regulation, she was *cold,* dammit!

"The primary phase one fuel tank," Glass said,

blowing on his hands. "They were going to do it just before the fuel shortage. Since it requires a lot of support, welding and bots they had to wait 'til they had enough fuel to continue. Then, apparently, they didn't get the word around. The heaters still work. They're just turned off to chill the zone."

"'Cause they're going to do *what*, exactly, with SAPL?" Sean said. "'Cause it's, like, SAPL, isn't it? The beam that cuts through the *Troy* faster than a Rangora assault ship?"

"All hands! All hands! Stand by for address from Squadron CO!"

"I wish they'd just use the 1MC," Sean said, gesturing at the box on the wall with his chin. He had his hands in his armpits. "The voices! The voices! They're talking to me again!"

"Starting in thirty minutes, we will begin an orderly evacuation of the Charlie Flight AO. Alpha and Bravo AOs should be unaffected. Permission is granted for all personnel to fall in on suits to observe SAPL operation in main bay. Viewing area will be shuttle launch tubes. Operation is inflation of armoring for Phase One Primary Fuel Station. Design documents downloading on acceptance. That is all."

Dana hit the link for the design documents and started to giggle.

"Oh, that's just—" Sean said.

"Wrong?" Glass finished for him. "And I'm glad the CO gave permission because this I gotta see."

"And I can control the heat in my suit," Dana said. "I hadn't wanted to use it since it uses power. But if we've got permission... Request leave to fall in on *space suit*, CM!"

"Granted," Glass said. "Briefing's over! Fall out and fall in on your suits."

"I'm cranking mine up to tropical," Sean said.

The first time Dana had seen all the shuttles of the 142nd outbound it had been a wonderful sight. Since then she'd been to a couple of squadron formations, which were just a pain.

But they were funny as hell scattered all over the docking tube in the main bay. You could tell the engineers from the cox in an instant. The engineers spent half their working time in suits and were perfectly comfortable in EVA. Most of them were floating upside down, sort of drifting *near* the shuttles if not *on* them, to give room for the...

The coxswains, on the other hand, by and large had *qualed* on their suits but weren't exactly *experts*. They were mostly holding onto bits and pieces of shuttles and trying not to go Dutchman in the main bay. Not that you were going to go far.

"You seem to be experiencing some issues, CM," Dana said.

Like a lot of the engineers, she'd placed herself near a coxswain, in this case Glass, but in a position that, to the coxswain, seemed to be inverted. Her helmet was drifting about a meter above the flight NCOIC.

"Just getting adjusted for a better view," Glass said, his feet rotating "upwards."

"I don't think you can see anything from that position, CM," Dana said, reaching down and gently giving his head a tap. "You can do this in a nullball court. What's the problem with the main bay?"

"No references," Glass said. "I mean, yeah, there

are references, but between trying to control the suit and trying to get references..."

Dana drifted her suit down, using her plants to control the navopak, and grabbed his legs.

"Taking your boots down to latch point," she said.

"I can maneuver..." Glass protested.

"And I think we need to work on your suit quals, CM," Dana said, bringing his boots into contact with Thirty-Nine. "Lock it down, CM."

"Locked down," Glass said, crossing his arms.

"I think we need to work on *all* the coxswains' quals," Dana said, chuckling.

"Agreed," Glass said with a sigh.

"Maybe make them do some real work on the boats," Dana said. "Yours could use some polish, CM."

"You are about to cross a line, CM," Glass said.

"Aye, aye, Captain Crunch," Dana said, giggling.

"*All hands,*" the CO commed. "*Stand by for SAPL fire.*"

Tyler didn't want to use the *Starfire* for this but he *did* want to see with his own eyes. And the precise spot they were putting in the tank wasn't in view from his quarters.

So like what appeared to be about ninety-percent of the base, he'd gone out into the main bay. Since his suit wasn't any different from the generic ones, for once he could sort of blend in the crowd.

And it was quite a crowd. He knew there were upwards of four thousand people already on the *Troy* but it was rare you saw them all in one place.

You could tell the ones that practiced in EVA from the ones that didn't. Tyler had to put himself in the latter category and it was obvious as he bumped into another space-suited figure.

"Sorry," Tyler commed on the local channel. "I'm usually working in an office."

The local com didn't even have a personal identifier so the guy had no clue who he was.

"*No problem,*" the man said. "*You might want to lock down your boots.*"

"It'd be above me if I did that," Tyler said. He gently corrected his position and got into a better configuration to see the shot. "That okay?"

"*Good enough,*" the guy said. "*Can you hold that?*"

"Working on it," Tyler said as he started to drift again. "I *had* it . . ."

"*Troy* has pull," Butch said. "You get used to it. Try doing salvage in a spinning destroyer."

"*I spend as little time in EVA as I can,*" the clerk said. "*I don't like sucking vacuum.*"

"Nearly did that one time," Butch said. "Was drawing helium off one of the ships and got hit by a gush. That and the hose cracked my sled."

"*Sierra Seventeen,*" the clerk said. "*That would make you . . . James . . . Allen. Probationary welder. Good job you did out there.*"

"Thanks," Butch said. "*Which* office do you work in?"

"*Corporate,*" the guy replied. "*I see most of the incident reports.*"

"And you have one hell of a memory," Butch said.

"*It's the first incident in the last two quarters that had a near-fatal outcome,*" the guy said, drifting away again. "*Dammit!*"

"Hang on, dude," Butch said, grabbing his ankle

and drawing him down. He had to correct his own inertia while he was doing it but that was second nature at this point. He got the guy stable and held onto his navpak. "Just don't try to correct. I've got it."

"*Thank you,*" the guy said. "*That's mighty kind. As I said, I don't get out in suits much.*"

"I hope you checked your suit," Butch said.

"*I did,*" the guy said in an odd tone. "*And I had other people check it as well.*"

"That knew more than you or *other* clerks?"

"*Uh, that would be A,*" the man said, chuckling. "*I checked it. Then they checked it and made sure it was working. And they knew what they were doing.*"

"I hope the guys doing this burn know what they're doing," Butch said. "It sounds crazy to me."

Price had explained it to him but it still didn't make sense.

The SAPL had been used to drill a hole in the wall of the *Troy*. All normal. Happened all the time. Then they'd shoved ice down it. Standard water ice made from the main tanks. Then, and Butch had had a hand in it, they'd shoved a solid tube of nickel-iron down on top of the ice and welded the hole shut.

"*It's how* Troy *was made,*" the guy said. "*Sort of. Same general concept. The tough part is going to be getting all the volatiles out so it doesn't contaminate the helium.*"

The idea was that they'd melt the iron on top of the hole. When it was liquid enough the ice would boil and spread out the melted area into a bubble. Wait for it to cool, cut a hole in the side to let out the water and you had a big bubble to put the helium fuel into.

"All personnel, stand by for SAPL burn," Paris commed.

"They're using the Ung beam on spread power," the guy said a moment later. *"Seventy petawatts of power."*

"That's..." Butch did the math in his head. "That's like a few thousand of my welding sets."

"Yep," the guy said. *"It's a beautiful thing."*

"Three...two...one...burn..." Paris commed.

"Oh!" Dana said. Her visor had automatically polarized as the wall of *Troy* turned white hot.

"Sweet!" Glass said.

The center point where the beam was hitting was white but the heat could be seen going to cherry red around it. The beam started to swing around, spreading the heat onto the target area and slowly heating it.

"Paris, how's the readings?" the guy commed.

"You think Paris is going to respond right now?" Butch said, chuckling.

The guy didn't respond for a second.

"Uh..." he said. *"Sort of. Looks like things are good. I sort of had a hand in this. So, yeah, Paris responded. And everything is nominal."*

"Oh," Butch said. "Where'd you say you worked?"

"Here," the guy said. *"On* Troy. *Mostly. I'm with LFD Corporate."*

LFD was the parent company of Apollo.

"Full melt should take less than fifteen minutes, which...well, that's just insane."

"I dunno," Butch said. "I don't work with SAPL."

"I do," the guy said. *"I've been working with SAPL and Apollo since there wasn't an Apollo. Just some*

guys with some mirrors trying to melt a bitty little asteroid. Took us six months and we could do the same job in a few minutes now."

"Oh," Butch said. "Uh. Sorry. I didn't know you were a boss."

"Hey," the guy said. *"You helped me watch. I really appreciate it. I don't get much EVA time. In fact, the last time I was this close to vacuum, I ended up sucking it. So to say I'm not a big fan of EVA is accurate."*

"You don't sound like you sucked vacuum," Butch said neutrally. He'd run across lots of people on the station who *swore* they'd been in death pressure. It was one of those things that supposedly made you a big man. And this was a little guy.

"Eh," the guy said. *"Light. The ship got a leak. I didn't have a suit. We got picked up before it really did any damage but it was a pretty freaky experience. Not one I want to repeat."*

"You didn't have a suit?" Butch said.

"I said I've been doing this a long time," the guy said. *"And we have full thermal expansion, hopefully. If it gets any worse on the inside, the One-Forty-Second is going to go home to a crispy experience."*

"You're getting a feed?" Butch asked.

"Yeah," the guy said. *"So, since this is going to take a few minutes. What would you like to see to make working on the* Troy *easier or better?"*

"Not sure what you mean," Butch said. "You taking a survey?"

"I'm not doing anything else at the moment," the guy said. *"And I'm insatiably curious. Seriously. More bars?"*

"Can't really drink much," Butch said. "If you're even a bit hung over you don't want to be in vacuum."

"*Absolutely agreed,*" the guy said. "*So . . . what? Anything you can think of?*"

"More girls," Butch said. "I mean, even the people working in the food court are all guys."

"*Hmmm . . .*" the guy said. "*There's a real problem with recruitment. Women simply don't sign up for space jobs the way guys do. But we could make it an EEOC thing. Special recruitment. What do you think of not having an EVA qualification as a requirement for working on the Troy?*"

"Not sure," Butch said. "What if there's a failure?"

"*The next civilian area is going to have so many blast doors between it and the main bay you could literally set off a fifty megaton nuke in the main bay and it wouldn't even blow out half of them. We'd have to have a delimiter point somewhere. No non-EVA qualified personnel past a certain point. But it's doable. In fact, it would cut down, a lot, on the employee costs. Hmm . . .*"

"And more girls?" Butch asked.

"*And more girls,*" the guy said. "*The big part is getting them through EVA qual. They don't sign up as much as males and they fail at about the same rate. Right now even the support personnel are EVA qualed. Striking that qualification would open up all sorts of things. I thought about it a couple of years ago but I never got around to exploring it. And . . . Stand by. Paris? Could you retrans to Mr. Allen, please?*"

"*Models say expansion in about thirty seconds,*" Paris commed.

"*Any idea if we've got the size model working?*"

"*Probability is ninety-eight percent that we will be within three centimeters.*"

"*Roger. Thank you, Paris.*"

"You are welcome, Mr. Vernon."

"And it seems to be working."

"Duh . . . uh . . ."

"You okay, Mr. Allen?"

"You're . . . Yer . . ."

Tyler tried not to sigh. He really should have told Paris to not use his name.

"Mr. Allen," Tyler said. "As I said, I thank you for stabilizing me. I really don't get out in EVA very much. And your comment on the lack of female companionship triggered a memory node that had been dormant for far too long."

"Uh . . . Yes, sir."

"So you've probably saved the company money and you helped me watch this burn," Tyler said. "I am doubly thankful. Which, along with a buck fifty, will get you a ride on the subway. I put my pants on one leg at a time. Unless I'm sitting down, then I put them on two at a time. Mr. Allen, this is Houston, over?"

"Yes, sir," Allen said, trying not to snort.

"There," Tyler said. "That's better. And . . . Yes!"

Butch's astonishment that he was holding Mr. Vernon was momentarily put in the backseat as the wall of the *Troy* seemed to buckle outwards.

What had, a moment before, been a blazing white hot inward curve of metal suddenly bulged out, expanding in front of his eyes into a hemisphere. It expanded quickly at first then slowed and slowed until it wasn't moving. At which point the SAPL shut off.

What was left was a blister in the side of the main bay that was still cherry red.

"*I think the problem of the temperature being too low in the One-Forty-Second quarters is fixed,*" Mr. Vernon said. "*Paris is having to pump in AC. Fortunately, there are other areas that are quite cool. So, Mr. Allen, I have another question. First, is it James or Jim or . . . ?*"

"Uh," Butch said, taken aback. "Most people call me Butch, sir."

"*Butch, then,*" Mr. Vernon said. "*I'd tell you to call me Tyler but it would probably throw you. So, Butch, what's it like being a welder?*"

NINETEEN

"That is a sight for God damned sore eyes," Admiral Kinyon said.

The commander of *Troy* had accepted Mr. Vernon's invitation to observe the arrival of the *Wolf Mother*. And he was glad he had. The view from the *Starfire* was spectacular.

Wolf Mother was the newly minted tanker for the Terran system, a kilometer-long, four-hundred-meter-wide mass of nickel-iron just packed with helium. Apollo was planning three of the He3 carriers to handle the output of the gas mine. What had once been a near entire lack of helium was about to be a glut. The Wolf Mine had been designed and constructed to not only supply the Sol system but the Glatun. With trade cut off, it was *too* much for Earth to absorb. At the moment.

Wolf Mother was only half full, but even that was enough to fill not only the *Troy*'s tanks but the Fleet and civilian needs. The rolling blackouts on Earth were about at an end.

"She won't be able to top off your tanks," Tyler said. "But with the present state of the power system, you've got fuel to spare. So, now that that problem is settled, I've got some issues I'd like to bring up."

"I still have plenty on my plate," the admiral said. "I should have figured you had a reason to bring me onto your territory."

"The *Troy* being yours," Tyler said. "Which is what this is about. First, you've never opened up the water testing area to unauthorized personnel."

The "water testing area" was an "accident" during the construction of the main water tank for Zone One. According to contract specifications, Apollo had to supply an area to test the water in the tank. The area had to be at least one hundred meters square, three meters high, accessible to the water and with Earth normal gravity, temperature and air.

Due to an "accident with the SAPL," what Apollo had delivered was an area sixty *acres* across and *two hundred* meters high, cut so that the water flowed into it to various depths, shallow, medium, deep enough for, oh, diving, and walls that climbed up like hills to the overhead and which had what looked suspiciously like water slides built in.

"It's not useable as a pool at present," the admiral noted. "All it is is water. And it's pretty cold, by the way."

"You went swimming," Tyler said, shaking his head.

"I tested the temperature and conditions," the admiral said. "And it's pretty darned cold. Also no safety equipment, no circulation, no ready exits, no vacuum safety systems..."

"All of which I will install on my own dime," Tyler said. "Well, mine and LFD's. With the agreement that military and civilian personnel will have access thereto."

"Agreed," the admiral said.

"Good," Tyler said. "Because all the gear has been sitting on the ground waiting for an okay and fuel for lift. I can have it up and running in about two weeks."

"Figures," the admiral said. "Second?"

"Apollo has agreed to meet military standards for all personnel working on *Troy*," Tyler said. "I saw the reason for that when *Troy* was in its infancy. But we need to free it up. And I'd like to free it up a lot."

"I'd rather be overrun with job seekers," the admiral said. "What do you mean 'free it up'?"

"I want to remove the EVA training portion of the employment qualifications," Tyler said. "Such personnel will be restricted from movement in any area near vacuum. But we've got space in the civilian side that we could use if we had the people to man it. And we can't afford the people to man it if all of them have to know how to use suits."

"And if there's a failure?" the admiral said, then shook his head. "You're talking about the Tertiary Zone civilian side."

"The mall area," Tyler said. "And the new areas that we're bringing in. They're going to be so far back in the walls that absent something that can crack *Troy*, and I don't see anything in the Rangora inventory that can do that, it'll be not much different than living in a skyscraper. We need more support people, we need to get this feeling less like a military base and more like home. If for no other reason than your sailors need somewhere to let off steam."

"There is that," the admiral said.

"And there's another part to lowering the requirements," Tyler said.

"I'm going to love this, aren't I?" the admiral said.

"With your agreement," Tyler said, "and I do mean *only* with your agreement, I'm going to set my lobbyists loose on Congress. I want the *Troy* designated as a *base*, not a *ship*, and an accompanied PCS slot."

"*Accompanied*?" the admiral said, his eyes wide. "Are you nuts?"

"People keep saying that," Tyler said. "Admiral, Sixth Fleet was deployed when the Horvath hit San Diego. How many people lost dependents there?"

"Many," the admiral said. "Too many."

"I remember your story about your XO," Tyler said. "I hadn't really thought of it until then. Admiral, which would *you* prefer? Your dependents sitting in a city on the ground or up here with *Troy* wrapped around them?"

"My wife lives at what we'd intended as our retirement home in Deland, Florida," the admiral said. "Which is about as far from anything worth hitting as we could find and still like the area."

"Everyone does not have the same luxury," Tyler said. "So...do I have your support?"

"Yes," Admiral Kinyon said. "Although I'm not sure my wife will be willing to move."

Tyler looked out the crystal window as the tanker, being carefully positioned by tugs, hooked up to the ten-meter-diameter valves on the main tanks and started spewing fifteen *billion* barrels of fuel into the seven-hundred-meter-diameter main tank.

"*She* may not be," Tyler said. "But now *things* can really start to."

"I'd rather be doing this than salvage," Butch said. "This" was being part of the large team that was installing the new "civilian side" bay. Five times the cubic of the original civilian side, which was still not full, it was set up as a miniature city with much of the cubic designated as "organic fill." In other words, it was designed to grow in a chaotic manner like a regular city rather than being the carefully laid out and organized initial civilian support zone.

"*Fricking Indonesians*," Price commed.

Apollo had contracted with E Systems to take over the salvage of the Horvath scrapyard. E Systems, which had long done every kind of contracting from oil platform support to "hostile zone" security, had responded by pulling in experts in the oil field and anyone who was barely qualified to wear a space suit. They'd converted one of the marginally habitable derelicts into quarters and were running nearly a thousand people on the salvage operation, most of them in conditions that would make a sardine scream for room.

Many of them were from developing countries and their training level was, to say the least, not Apollo standard.

"I hear they're dying like flies," Butch said.

"*Not like flies,*" Price commed. "*But fast, yeah. Guys from countries like that will keep signing up. Anything to fill the rice bowl and so what if there's still bits of the last guy in the suit? How's your bead?*"

"Good," Butch said.

The crew quarters were modular and designed to be exposed, briefly, to vacuum.

But modular didn't mean quite like Legos. Stuff had to be connected and connected tight. Which meant welding.

Butch wasn't even sure what the parts he was

connecting were *for*. They were just two flat bits of metal to be joined. Currently at regular time, but he figured by the end of the week he'd be on double time. Especially since it was inside work and they weren't taking rad exposure.

The working area was tight, though. They were "above" the new module in the small space between its insulation and the cut-out walls of the battlestation. They had had to run in laser lines and wear suits just to get to the working area. After they were done welding the parts together, another crew was coming in to fit in the final bits of insulation. Still another was hooking up the plumbing and air systems. Altogether, about six hundred people were floating around in space suits working on quarters for six thousand.

"*Fourteen Alpha, Welding Control.*"

"*Go Purcell.*"

"*How long?*"

"*'Bout done. Fifteen minutes, give or take.*"

"*When you're done, head over to sector one. The next module, as usual, doesn't fit.*"

"*Roger. Sector One. Cut to fit.*"

"*Don't over cut.*"

"*Try not to.*"

When the pair got to Sector One, the area right next to the main bay, they found a cluster of suits surrounding one of the massive modules. From their body language, they were clearly flummoxed.

"*What you got?*" Butch commed.

"*You Fourteen Alpha?*" the super commed.

"*Last time I checked,*" Butch replied. He wasn't in a great mood. They were having to tow around the laser emitters and power systems, which was no fun at all. *"What you got?"*

"Last module," the super commed. *"But it won't line up. Problem being, we can't figure out what doesn't fit."*

The module was a quarter the size of a cruise liner, a cube fifty meters long and thirty high with "bits" sticking off, built by the Finnish company that had once had a lock on that market. From the outside, all that Butch had seen during the job, they were all standard.

"We can just cut bits off until it fits," Price offered.

"We'd prefer to avoid that," the super replied.

"We can weld back on the parts that we weren't *supposed* to lop off," Butch said.

"You're not helping," the super commed.

The module had fifty-centimeter joints of steel that were designed to line up with wraps from the other modules. Those were the main things that Butch and Price had been welding. When they were done on the exterior they were scheduled to do some interior welding between the modules, mainly hatches. But they couldn't do that until they had the modules installed and the exterior nickel-iron "cap" installed. Installing the cap was a tug and SAPL job.

"Are we sure all the wraps are right on the other modules?" Butch asked.

"We already checked that," the super commed. *"And the hole has to be right since the other modules slid in just fine."*

"Getting in there's going to be a bitch anyway," Price commed, considering the job. *"What we need is some really humongous crowbars and hammers."*

"Welders," the super commed.

"*Seriously,*" Price commed. "*We just plane down the joints a bit all around. Then we'll stuff stuff back in to get them to fit.*"

"*Got any idea how much load this thing has to take?*" the super said. "*Try sliding it in again.*"

There were angled slats of metal that permitted the tugs to move the module into position and slide it into the supposedly perfect gap. The module slid about halfway in and then stopped.

"I don't suppose the tugs could just, you know, push really hard?" Butch asked.

"*No,*" the super commed. He slid downwards and flashed a light up into the gaps. "*I can't even see up in there.*"

"*And we're supposed to get in there and weld how?*" Price commed.

"*There's an opening,*" the super commed, sliding over to it and flashing a light up into the gap again. "*You can get through. It'll be tight, but it's doable.*"

"What happens if somebody goes up in there while it's like this?" Butch asked.

"*If the module slips and they're between one of the joints and another module?*" the super replied. "*They get cut in half. Then they get freeze dried so we can hang them up on a wall as a warning to other welders. I don't want that on my safety record.*"

"*Looks* pretty stable," Butch said. "And I'm small."

"*Dude, you did* not *just volunteer to do this,*" BFM said.

"Can *you* think of a way to get it done?" Butch asked.

"*You're not getting paid extra for this, Butch,*" Price pointed out. "*You* never *volunteer unless you're getting paid more.*"

"BF, we got about a million other jobs to do," Butch said. "There's the shuttle bays, the new military module... I want to get this one over with."

"*And I still don't want it on my safety record,*" the super commed.

"I'm not going in without permission, that's for sure," Butch said. "So what you gonna do?"

It took about thirty minutes for somebody, for all Butch knew it went up to Mr. Vernon, to give permission.

"*Butch,*" Purcell commed. "*Be goddamned careful in there.*"

"I'll try not to get cut in half," Butch said.

"*And we're going to hook you off to a safety line,*" BFM commed, clipping a line to Butch's suit. "*That way we can pull your legs out when you do get cut in half.*"

"You are just a ray of sunshine, BF," Butch said, pulling himself through the gap.

The opening through the first set of joints was tight. A meter by meter area had been cut out of the joints "above" and "below" so that the space between the modules could be entered. It was tight but doable, even by BFM. Although he was going to have more trouble.

The area in the middle was no better. Wide, yes, but not much room to maneuver between the two modules. Fortunately, Butch could use the navopak to maneuver. Pulling himself along was out of the question.

The strips of metal the module was sliding along extended all the way to the back of the section. Butch was careful to avoid the edges since they looked razor sharp. And he had to slide past them to examine every bit of every joint looking for the part that didn't fit.

But it was watching out for them that gave him his first clue about the problem.

"Super?" Butch said. "At joint four, the runner is bent."

"Say again?"

"The metal the section's supposed to be running on?" Butch said, sending a video link. "It's bent. Just a bit, but it looks like the jam. I think the joint's right but the module's wrong."

"Stand by."

"Not going anywhere," Butch said.

"The module *is bent,"* BFM commed a few minutes later. *"Less than two centimeters but that's enough."*

"Figured," Butch said. "What's the plan?"

"Still working on it."

"I'm getting paid by the hour. And this is actually sort of comfy."

"What's the status on your navo?"

"Four hours air," Butch said. "Two or three on power."

"You breathe like a bitch."

"That's 'cause I'm not a big fracking man, BFM," Butch said.

"Yes, you are a tiny little man," BFM said in a vaguely Latin accent. *"When we are both in prison for messing this up, you will be my woo-man."*

"You could not satisfy me," Butch said. "I have seen you in the showers. You are a large man with a very small manhood. You should be called little wee-wee."

"Dude, you are so going down for that one."

"What are you going to do? Crawl in here after me?"

"You have to come out sometime. Even though you breathe like a bitch, you will run out of air eventually. And then you will pay."

"I can go out another exit. You, on the other hand, can barely fit in the main bay. Seriously, BF, I'm not sure you can get up in here to do anything. This isn't exactly wide."

"What, you want the whole job?"

"I don't think they thought this through very well is all. It's *really* tight."

"You doing okay?"

"Fine. I like tight."

"That was almost a joke. Not a good one, but you're getting there. I think you need to get a date or something."

"Which is about as likely on *Troy* as . . . Isn't very likely."

"We need to resolve that virginity problem of yours. You've got to be the only blond virgin over twelve left in the world."

"I'm not a virgin."

"Rosy Palm doesn't count."

"What's your excuse, then?"

"Stand by . . . Frack. Okay, we're going to pull you out."

"What's up?"

"They're going to use the crowbar. And we are back to the barn as soon as we can get you unstuck."

"There are two broad options."

Jeffrey Morton was the supervisor of the Phase Two civilian quarters installation. He had a master's degree in engineering with a background in structural—he'd previously supervised the construction of two skyscrapers that were now rubble—and he'd seen his fair share of mess-ups. But things like the Pod Nine issue rarely came to the attention of chairmen.

Unless, that is, they lived next to it, were watching the construction and knew the timetable.

"Which are?" Tyler asked. He'd asked the engineer to join him in the *Starfire* so they could both observe what was clearly a lack of progress on the project. The pods had just been sitting in the main bay waiting on the fuel situation to get resolved. He was ready to have the next module installed and done. Fracking fiddly bits.

"The optimal solution is to use a jacking system," Morton said. "We install what is essentially a very large jack and, using the structural stability of the lower modules and the joints, we slowly bend the module straight. Then slide it into position and we're done."

"Time?" Tyler asked.

"It will be . . . somewhat lengthy," Morton said. "Effectively, you apply power and then wait for the system to stabilize. Which can take up to a week. Then . . . repeat."

"How many times?" Tyler asked.

"Possibly . . . several."

"So several weeks."

"Yes, sir," Morton said.

"Mr. Morton," Tyler said. "You know there's a war on, right?"

"Yes, sir."

"Suboptimal?" Tyler asked.

"We use the runner, or a similar system that is more robust, and jam it in with a tug. That may work. If it doesn't, possibly even if it does, it's going to cause structural integrity issues throughout the module. Basically, it will bend the hell out of not just the damaged pod but at least one other, probably more. These things are big but they're remarkably fragile when you start talking about the sort of force necessary to jam one in."

"Hmm . . ." Tyler said, leaning back and closing his eyes. He worked his mouth in thought for a moment then sat up. "You've done most of your work on Earth, haven't you?"

"Yes, sir?" Morton said.

"Which means you don't have a lot of experience of gravitics," Tyler said. "The truth is that a jack has the possibility of bending Module Seven."

"Yes, sir," Morton said. "But we can monitor for that."

"Did the modules get evacuated sitting there?"

"No, sir. They've maintained integrity."

"To get to the monitoring position," Tyler said. "You'd either have to install an air lock or take one long damned way to Module Seven with no movement support. Time, time, ask me for anything but time. Don't push, pull."

"Sir?"

"Install a tractor projector on top," Tyler said. "You'll have to have one that can hold onto the upper armor wall at the same time as it's pulling. Which is going to be a bitch to install in that space but it's doable. You might have to cut out some more of the joints to get it in, but it's doable. Then *pull* the thing up across a broad area. You can even do it somewhat slowly. That means no structural damage to Module Seven."

"Oh," Morton said, blinking. "Can we make one that will fit? That can ... pull in both directions?"

"There are gravitics engineers who can answer that question," Tyler said, shrugging. "Ask them. But if it works, you should be able to fab it in a couple of days. And it will pull consistently along the line of the bend. And since it can be monodirectional, you can still slide the module in as long as it doesn't pull it up too far."

"I'll ... talk to some gravitics engineers," Morton said.

"Machine shop," Tyler said, hooking with his thumb in the general direction of the existing civilian module. "I would suggest you wait until we're back in breathable. And we've got the new fabbers coming in in a couple of days. I'll make sure you have priority. Pilot?"

"Sir?"

"Back to the barn. Then we're for Wolf."

TWENTY

"Okay," the President said irritably. "I'm looking at four separate intelligence summaries here. None of them agree on where the Rangora are or when they might be able to free up ships to come after us."

"Those were all supposed to be justified through my department, Mr. President," the DNI said.

"Well, they weren't," the President said. "I've got a DIA estimate, a DNI estimate, a CIA estimate and an Alliance estimate. Which means one thing. Athena?"

"Yes, Mr. President?" the AI said.

"Which of these is right?" the President asked. "DIA is saying that the Glatun have broken and are running. CIA say that they are holding all their lines. DNI is saying that the Rangora have performed a successful end run but the primary battle hasn't taken place yet. Alliance says the main battle took place but the Glatun are still holding their core worlds and the Rangora are on the ropes."

"Rangora losses are hard to quantify, Mr. President," the AI said. "So I would dispute the validity of the Alliance Intelligence estimate. They are teasing very small bits of data out of the little information we have and forming very broad conclusions. One bit of data. The Rangora rarely tend to mention individuals or ships, but a few are considered heroic subjects. One such is the Assault Vector *Star Crusher*. The *Star Crusher* was mentioned in several early dispatches. It was involved in the taking of the Mu'Johexam and Zhoqaghev systems early in the war. Then it disappeared from mention. You will remember I referred to Tuxughah. It is possible that it was lost in the taking of that system. But it might still be out there and the Rangora simply are not mentioning it. The Alliance is taking the loss of the *Star Crusher* as a given, extrapolating more losses on the basis of the known Tuxughah defenses and known and suspected Glatun forces in other systems and coming up with a number that ranges from the Rangora fleet being severely mauled to being entirely destroyed."

"I see," the President said, setting the analysis aside. "That seems a bit of a stretch."

"The DIA is looking at Rangora reports and known Glatun forces and assuming that all systems that are not being mentioned have been overrun with so little resistance that the Rangora are victorious already," Athena said. "Also, given that some systems mentioned are deep in Glatun territory that the Glatun have been overrun. They are dismissing the possibility that this is Rangora disinformation. DNI is depending on my initial analysis of Rangora propaganda and if a system isn't mentioned it's still holding. The CIA is depending on State Department analysis which assumes the Glatun to be hyper competent and unconquerable."

"I think we can throw that one out," the President said, setting it aside. "What's your take?"

"Somewhere between DNI and DIA, sir," the AI said. "I think that the Rangora have sustained heavy casualties, that they are winning both on an attrition level and on a strategic level and that if the main battle has not taken place yet it soon will."

"When can we expect an attack?" the President asked.

"Certainly if they take the Glalkod system," Athena said. "Or shortly thereafter. My analysis is that they took a bit of a shock from the loss of the Horvath assault fleet. Given the amount of time that Terra has been in contact with the rest of the galaxy, we should not have been able to stop thirty *Devastator*-class battleships. As you may recall, we very nearly did not."

"I do recall," the President said.

"So they are probably reevaluating our defenses and strategies," Athena said. "When they will commit forces and how many is the question. I cannot give even a vague guess on either. But not before they take Glalkod. If we hear of that system falling, we have to assume we will be attacked shortly thereafter."

"We lost the *Star Crusher*?" Major To'Jopeviq said.

"That is not for dissemination," General Chayacuv Lhi'Kasishaj replied. "But, yes, it was totally destroyed at Tuxughah. The Glatun are resisting somewhat better than our most optimistic analysis but well within the range we anticipated. Their populace is weak, but their military is holding the line quite valiantly. We started this war with sixty-two assault vectors, many of them constructed in great secrecy. We, in fact, managed to create over two hundred vessels we were fairly sure were unknown to Glatun spies as well as secret advanced bases along the Glatun frontier. That fleet, especially the assault vectors, has been mauled in taking gate after gate. But the core world of Ghalhegil had no fixed defenses. They gathered their fleet there and we eliminated it. The Glatun Navy has, effectively, ceased to exist."

"What losses did we sustain?" To'Jopeviq asked.

"That is not your concern," General Lhi'Kasishaj said. "What is your concern is the question of Terra. I am being asked what we will need to reduce their defenses."

"That...depends," To'Jopeviq said. "We have no real-time intelligence from the system anymore. We cannot be sure how much they have advanced their defenses."

"You indicated that the fuel embargo would make it impossible for them to complete the battlestation," the general said.

"Probably," To'Jopeviq said. "General, I am more used to receiving intelligence than generating it. It is all 'maybe this, maybe that.' I would like to know that they have not completed the first phase of *Troy*, especially the SAPL receptors and the missile tubes, before I commit to an analysis. Without some real-time knowledge, my current recommendation is to not enter that system with less than twenty assault vectors in a stellar array."

"Impossible," the general said. "High Command would never commit such a force to such a minor system. We took Ghalhegil with less than that."

"Ghalhegil, as you mentioned, General, did not have fixed defenses," To'Jopeviq said. "The *Troy* is unlike anything I have ever seen. It is no more, in reality, than a laser collector and missile base. But *what* a base. And there was a report, before the connection was severed from the Terran side, that they were beginning construction of *another* such base, the *Thermopylae*."

"But they still have only one of these ... What was that term? The SAPL? They would have to split that between their fortresses."

"General, even with it *split* I would not like to take on SAPL," To'Jopeviq said.

"This may be an unimportant side-note," the general said. "But have you researched a meaning to these outlandish names for their bases?"

"I have," To'Jopeviq said. "And if I could understand them, I think I might begin to understand humans. Troy was a city from one of their great prehistorical epics. The story was told in oral verse, if you can believe."

"They are *primitive*, are they not?" the general said, hissing in laughter.

"Essentially, it is a very understandable story," To'Jopeviq said. "If you research the reality behind it. The myth is about the stealing of a woman by a prince of Troy and how a great number of separate tribes of what are called Greeks went to Troy and fought to take her back. The reality is that the 'real' Troy was a rich city that sat on a trade route. The forces went there and captured the city and took their riches."

"As should be," the general said.

"Of course," To'Jopeviq said. "But the point is, Troy is a city that put up a great defense and was defeated."

"They named their main defense after a *defeat*?" the general said. "How very odd."

"Is it not?" To'Jopeviq said. "As I mentioned, if I could understand why, I might start to understand humans. *Thermopylae*, the second such fortress they are considering, is another epic defeat. The names mentioned for other such fortresses are *Alamo*, *Islawanda* and *Iwo Jima*. The latter is even odder. It was a battle in one of their more recent wars, one in which the Americans, who are the main polity of the planet and the primary funders of the *Troy*, were the victors."

"What is so odd about that?" the general said. "Of course you name great works after victories."

"*All* the others were defeats," the major replied. "And one of the Americans' main allies, the Japanese, were the defenders in that war."

"They allowed them to continue to exist?" the general asked.

"The Americans rebuilt their country after the war," the major said.

"So they could exact more tribute," the general said.

"They never exacted tribute," To'Jopeviq said.

"What?" the general gasped. "Are they *mad*?"

"You grasp the difficulty of the task you have assigned," To'Jopeviq said. "Humans do not seem to respond in the way I would expect. I would have expected them to send a message through the gate by now indicating that they wished to negotiate. No such message has been received. They have been bombed and attacked with bioweapons by the Horvath. They know we are more powerful by far and that they have no chance to win. But they have enough defenses to make a decent truce. Yet they have not even hinted at such."

"Send me your analysis," the general said musingly. "I cannot recommend twenty assault vectors. And I agree that that is what you believe is needed. I don't even dispute it. But there are ways and ways..."

"May I ask?" To'Jopeviq said.

TWENTY-ONE

"BF, can I ask a question?"

They were pulling down triple time in the main bay and right at the edge of maximum duration in vacuum. The truth was, they'd been working so much, Butch was starting to wonder if maybe he didn't need a break. And the point that you started to wonder was *after* when you should be back in breathable.

"Is it 'why is the sky blue' or something?"

"No," Butch said. "Why in the hell are they putting a fabber in the middle of the main bay?"

Butch, once, would have thought of the fabber as big. It was damned near a hundred meters long. Up next to it it did feel big. Back away and it *disappeared* into the immensity of the main bay.

Tugs had pushed it into position on one of the internal horns of the *Troy*, teams had spot-welded it in place and were now working on thick welds to hold it against shocks. Much of the welding, as usual, was being done by bots. Butch didn't mind. It meant that humans got the interesting stuff.

"It's for stuff that can survive vacuum," BFM

277

replied. "*Mostly it's supposed to be a missile fabber. Purcell covered that.*"

"I must have missed that part," Butch said. "How're they going to get the missiles to the magazine?"

They'd done some work there last week. The missile magazine was, basically, just a huge cavern SAPL had cut out with some interior lighting, grav plates and more hatches than Butch thought he'd ever see in one place. They were all over the walls, floors and even the ceiling. The work they'd been doing was on a stuck hatch. As usual, groundside had screwed something up they had to unscrew.

"*They're missiles, Butch,*" Price commed. "*They've got their own grav drive.*"

"Oh."

"*And . . . we're done,*" Price commed. "*Time to head to the barn. And I'm telling Purcell we're taking tomorrow off. When you start asking me about stuff that's really obvious or already been covered, it's time for me to take time off.*"

"*Parker, Erickson.*"

"Parker," Dana replied. She was reviewing for an exam and was ready for a break. The way the Navy was growing, even though she'd barely been a CM3 long enough to sew on the patch, Glass was pushing her to complete her quals for CM2.

"*You still owe me a drink.*"

"You call the bar."

"*This really is going to sound like a hit,*" Erickson commed. "*But have you been to the pool, yet?*"

"There's a *pool*?" Dana asked. "Where?"

"They just opened it. I went to the grand opening. You guys didn't get the word?"

"Nope," Dana said. "Civilians only?"

"Don't think so. I've seen military personnel there. You can tell by the hair. So..."

"I don't have a bathing suit," Dana replied, biting her lip. She'd lettered in diving in high school. A pool was too much to resist.

"Okay, well..."

"And there are shops in the mall," Dana said. "I saw one at the sports place."

"So... Meet me at the Acapulco?" Erickson commed.

"I'm off watch at 1800," Dana said.

"Works."

"See you then."

"This is... something," Dana said.

"Welcome to the Acapulco Bar at Xanadu, miss," the bartender said. He looked like he was off-duty military. "First drink is on the house."

The "pool" was more like six or seven pools scattered across sixty acres of ground shaped something like an L. The pool at the upper end was apparently shallow from the people wading in it. That necked down into a deeper one. The Acapulco bar was about halfway through the series and that pool ran about six feet except for the barstools. Dana could see where they were constructing a high-dive on the last one down, which meant it was at least fifteen feet deep.

Lighting was odd. The overhead was curved with the lowest point being about a hundred meters and about two hundred over the Acapulco. There were three "Dragon's Orb" lights like the main bay, spheres of "dirty" sapphire that filled the room with plenty of light. But there were also spotlights scattered around and people seemed to be sunbathing in those.

"I'll take a pop, please," Dana said. "And I owe the fat, bald guy whatever he's drinking. Hey, Bill."

"Comet," Erickson said, nodding at her. He managed to not leer. "Nice suit." Erickson's was a floral knee-length number. Alas, he hadn't worn a shirt, which revealed that he was about as hirsute as a mangy panda. He also had some serious tat work. *Old* tat work. And from the tats he had *definitely* been a Marine.

Dana's suit was about as plain as they came, a professional's Speedo, which was about all she was prepared to wear at the moment. She'd spent enough time in them over the years.

"It's what they had," Dana said. She accepted the Coke from the bartender and raised a toast. "To relays that work."

"Amen," Erickson said. "How's the investigation coming?"

"Pretty straightforward," Dana said. "They've determined that Thirty-Three had *two* of the questionable series relays. So it probably was a failure and not pilot error."

"Bad business either way," Erickson said. "And since I work for Apollo, it's sort of on me, too."

"Don't sweat it," Dana said, taking another sip of her drink. "Vernon Tyler, personally, came by and apologized to the Squadron CO. And he released a memo where he basically went off on his people for not catching it. 'Buck stops here' was the phrase he used. Honestly, I don't see how it could have been caught. But I think the design is screwed..." She paused as a guy sat down next to her.

"Private conversation?" the guy said. Not bad looking. Regular features, good build, kind of big for her tastes. Couple of tats, the most prominent being a massive phoenix that was revealed when he turned to grab a handful of peanuts. A USMC was tattooed just under his neck on his back.

"Not exactly private," Dana said. "Just not something you'd probably be interested in. Sorry. So..." she said, turning back to Erickson. "We're getting seventy nanometer relays from Granadica. They supposedly have been tested out, but I want to bring some over to your shop to run them through the electroscope."

"Sure," Erickson said. "We can run an electron microscopy survey and do a photo electrophoresis scan—"

"On an *electrical* relay?" the jarhead asked. "When did we start using organic circuits? This about the *Myrmidons*? 'Cause in that case, I'm *seriously* interested seeing as we've got to ride in 'em."

"See," Erickson said, a tad bitterly. "Can't pull anything over on jarheads."

"Heh," Dana said, grinning. "I control their air and grav."

"You a engineer?" the jarhead asked.

"Was," Dana said. "I'm a coxswain, now."

"Wait," the jarhead said. "I recognize that voice. You're *Comet*. Rammer. We ran with you in the Horvath round-up." He held out his hand.

"The one where the officer killed that prisoner?" Dana said, shaking his hand. "What ever happened with that? We didn't even get called to testify."

"They did a pretty quick Article Thirty-Two," Rammer said, shrugging. "We weren't the only ones. The Horvath just don't seem to care about their people at all."

"Aliens," Bill said, shrugging. "What can you say? So they killed one of their own people?"

"The guy had been Dutchman for like six hours," Rammer said. "It was around the bend. One of the officers said he wanted to give it 'care.' That was the word he used. And then he killed it. We were seriously freaked."

"I can bet," Erickson said. "I used to be a sixty-three, but I know about prisoner protocols."

"Oh-three-twenty-one," Rammer said, giving the number for his MOS. "Lance Corporal Ramage, sir."

"Bill Erickson," Bill said. "I'm a maintenance manager engineer on this lash-up now. And as you said, you've met Coxswain's Mate Third Class Comet."

"I'm still not sure I'm happy with that handle," Dana said, chuckling.

"It was some absolutely awesome boat driving," Rammer said. "Seriously. You should be proud. I know everybody in my platoon wants to ride your boat."

"I suspect that's less for the quality of the driver than the *qualities* of the driver," Bill said, grinning.

"Men," Dana said, shaking her head. "Why can't they cure Johannsen's in them I want to know?"

"'Cause it takes away our will to live?" Bill asked. "Speaking of which . . ."

"Yes, I had it," Dana said. "No, I don't have it anymore. No, I don't have any kids. Yes, it sucked having it. Yes, I'm glad I got cured. It was one of about a dozen reasons to join the Navy."

"Sorry," Bill said, holding up his hands in surrender. "I guess it's a touchy subject."

"Which can be taken a couple of ways," Dana said, grinning. "Guys having Johannsen's is no big deal. Unless they get out of control with *girls* who have it then can't make their child support."

"Yeah," Rammer said, grimacing. "Uh. There. She's married to another guy. She still gets part of my check. Which I don't mind, mind you," he added, shaking his head. "I like having a kid. I'd like to see him more. But . . . Yeah, you can get into some serious over-your-head if you're not careful."

"If you go out in the rain," Dana said, "wear a raincoat. The point being, if you're a girl with Johannsen's, it's a pain in the . . . butt. Just as bad as being a teenage boy. But if you slip up, you end up with kids. Guys don't have that problem. Don't get me wrong, I want a child. Someday. Sixteen's too young."

"Agreed," Erickson said. "Horvath bastards."

"And now the Rangora," Rammer said. "Who are, like, not only tougher but fricking *huge*. Have you *seen* a pic of those guys?"

"I'm not planning on getting into hand-to-hand with 'em," Dana said, chuckling. "That is why *I* have a four terawatt laser."

"Lucky you," Rammer said. " 'Hello? We could use some air support here . . .' "

" 'Uh, roger that, Rammer,' " Dana said, mimicking speaking in a microphone. " 'But, sorry, I'm doing my nails . . .' "

"Bitch," Rammer said, laughing.

"You get your tats groundside?" Dana asked.

"The USMC I did," Rammer said, turning around.

"But the phoenix I got done by a guy over on the civvie side. He's a mechanic but he does tats in his spare time."

The phoenix was an immensely complex tat, the "feathers" formed from Celtic knots. Dana nodded in appreciation.

"Very nice," she said.

"You thinking of getting a tat?" Erickson asked.

"Thinking about it," Dana said. "If I can find a good enough artist."

"You know what?" Rammer asked.

"Yep," Dana said. "Guys, this is fun but I actually like to swim. Bill, don't take this wrong but... Rammer, can you swim?"

"Like a fish," Rammer said.

"If I've already got one guy following me around, I won't get swarmed," Dana said, sliding out of her stool. "So... try to keep up."

"*Dude*," Butch commed. "*Hot chick, two o'clock.*"

"Followed by a jarhead that could break you in half," Price said without opening his eyes.

They were hanging out in the sunbathing area, figuring that most chicks would just park there. Most of the light in Xanadu was provided by the Dragon's Orbs. But in several places more "raw" sunlight was pumped in through SAPL tubes. It was filtered for UVA, the "bad" UV, but allowed UVB through. Which should have attracted any female seeking that perfect Hawaiian tan. So far, the pickings had been slim to none.

"How can you see 'er?" Butch asked.

"If you know what you're doing, you can access the webcams with your eyes closed," Price said. "Which means I have checked out every hot chick in the area. They all have at least *two* guys hanging on 'em. Even the fat ones."

"That is so bogus," Butch said, lying back on the lounge chair.

"Just soak up your UV, Butch," Price said. "We're going to be back in the sleds before you know it."

"Okay," Rammer said, as Dana surfaced from her dive. "That was just..."

"Lousy," Dana said, climbing out of the pool and heading back to the low-board. "I'm *so* out of shape."

"I wouldn't say that," Rammer said. "You look like you work out."

"I play a lot of nullball," Dana said, climbing back on the board. "Which is not the same as keeping in dive practice." She turned around, took two bounces and did a double-pike with a very splashy entry. "Dammit!" she said as she surfaced. "That's *easy*!"

"Whoa," Rammer said. "Easy there, Coxswain. I'm starting to figure out how you drive a boat so well."

"I'm giving up for now," Dana said, swimming over and grabbing the side. "I know where the pool is, at least. So, Rammer, when are you on duty again?"

"Next watch," Ramage said. "Why?"

"Because just because I don't have Johannsen's anymore doesn't mean I'm not interested," Dana said, climbing out of the pool. "And if I start anything with one of the guys in my unit it's going to cause problems. Marines don't count. You're cute enough and I still don't have anyone sharing my quarters. Up to you, of course."

"I am *so* there," Rammer said, pulling himself out of the water.

"Be aware that if you immediately fall asleep, I *will* make you pay the next time you're in my shuttle," Dana said.

"Is that what you *call it?*" Rammer asked.

"Jarheads."

"Good morning, everyone," Dana said, walking into the ready room. "Is everyone set for another fun and exciting day of salvage?"

"Oh, good God," EN Sumstine said. "The Ice Queen got *laid?*"

"*Ice Queen?*" Dana said, icily.

"Grab your seat, Comet," Glass said, trying to keep a straight face. "And, Sean, unless you want a Mast, keep comments like that to yourself. But for what it's worth, yes, we have another fun and exciting day of salvage before us. A big chunk of Sierra Nine has wandered into the shipping lanes. Which means anything coming in from Wolf is endangered. Charlie Flight, One-Forty-Second, *will* therefore..."

"Ice Queen?" Dana said, strapping herself into her seat. "Seriously? *Ice* Queen?"

"You know Sean," Thermal said. "He's got a case of foot in mouth disease. Although how he can *fit* those in his mouth is the question."

"I'm not *that* bad, am I?" Dana said, checking her systems. All good. So far.

"Comet, you are a great Cock," EM1 Hartwell said, then grimaced. "Okay, given the nature of the discussion..."

"'This is Comet, my great Cock,'" Dana said, giggling. "'I'd like you to meet my cock, Comet...'"

"I give up," Thermal said, laughing. "Yes, you are a very good cox*swain*. Part of that is you're so...focused. I suspect that is what Sean, who is *not* focused or he would have made engineer's mate by now, was referring to. I had never previously heard that appellation. But I'm not surprised. You do everything with a focus like a SAPL beam. If you are planning on making this a career that is, again, a good thing. But it does make you a bit...icy at times."

"Ah, hell," Dana said. "I'll take it as a handle if it sticks. I've never been so good about Comet. It makes me sound like I should have a red nose."

"That would be Rudolph," Hartwell said. "So, trying desperately to change the subject. Where were you yesterday? Normally when you're off-watch you're in the squadron area. Releasing dock."

"Ahem," Dana said as the shuttle detached. "Are *you*, Engineering *Mate* First *Class* Hartwell, asking *me*, Coxswain's Mate Third Class Dana Parker, *exactly* what I was doing on my off-watch time? Because if you are, Engineering Mate First Class, it's none of your business."

"Trying desperately again to avoid an EEOC complaint..."

"For your general FYI," Dana said, chuckling. "Did you know there's a pool?"

"There's a *pool*? You were at a *pool*?"

"I was at the pool," Dana said. "Part of my off-watch time. The rest is not up for discussion."

"You were at the pool," Hartwell breathed. "In a bathing suit?"

"EM," Dana said. "*Don't* make me request a new engineer, okay?"

"No, seriously," Thermal said. "What kind?"

"Do me a favor and crack your suit seals while I accidentally outgas us, okay?"

"There's a *pool*?"

"Seriously. You *will* be breathing vacuum . . ."

"And releasing grav locks," Thermal said.

The chunk of "Sierra Nine," a former Rangora, Horvath-run, now ripped-to-shreds battleship had, indeed, been "in the shipping lanes." It had drifted, due to some really funky Newtonian physics, towards the gate and was just about to pass through it to the "entry" side to spinward.

It was also a very big chunk, the sort of mass that would normally be the job of the *Paw* tugs to handle. The *Myrmidons* had been "helping out" with the salvage operations for several reasons. The Navy got paid for their time, it was good training for the crews, and clearing up the debris of the battle before some bit of wreckage holed a ship was in everyone's best interests.

Usually, though, the *Myrms* would handle something their own size. In this case, it had taken almost the entire 142nd Squadron to handle the destroyer-sized chunk of steel. Since their system was not optimized for towing, the CO and the senior flight NCOIC had had to carefully arrange the squadron to push it along.

Then there was the destination. Most of the scrap from the battle had been pushed into a more or less compact lump about 200,000 kilometers from the gate and more or less in a stable orbit. It was, in fact, slowly drifting *away* from the gate and the *Troy*. There it was out of the way and no danger to anyone except Martians in about two hundred years when it would deorbit onto the red planet. Long before then, though, it was scheduled to get turned into orbital equipment including Terran destroyers and cruisers.

This chunk, though, somebody wanted in the main bay. So the 142nd had pushed it back to *Troy* and through the hatchway, what people were starting to call the Comet Hatch, and into the main bay.

A set of tractor projectors had been arrayed on the interior wall hard by the new missile fabber and as soon as the 142nd got the chunk in range the tractors took over.

Recently, some cargo containers had been attached to the side of the fabber. It still wasn't producing missiles but apparently they were getting ready.

"Backing away," Dana said, checking her vectors. The shuttles were pretty crowded around the battleship bit and she would prefer to avoid a ding with another shuttle.

She'd backed up about five hundred meters when Thermal let out a grunt. It was his "that's interesting" grunt.

"Problem?" she asked.

"No," Hartwell said. "You got spare cycles?"

"I can do this in my sleep," Dana said.

"Switching view," Thermal said.

The picture on one of her side screens was the debris they'd brought in. A SAPL beam had already cut off a goodly chunk, which was being moved, apparently by the tractors, into the maw of the missile fabber.

"I guess they wanted some raw materials," Thermal said.

"Should work," Dana said, going back to watching

her driving. "Most of the stuff you need for missiles should be in a battleship."

"I wonder what the cargo containers are for?"

"Another sight for sore eyes," Admiral Kinyon said.

"Yes, sir," Colonel Helberg replied. "With the debris finally in place we should be able to start production within the hour. It can take the material from the wall mining but formed steel will reduce production time and slag."

"God knows I could use some missiles," Captain James Sharp said.

"Start the brief," Admiral Kinyon said, keying off the view of the missile fabber.

"After some difficulties the new civilian side quarters are installed., Commodore Kurt Pounders, the chief of staff of the *Troy*, stated. "Power and air tests are complete and the section is ready for use. On that subject. The Senate has finally approved the bill to authorize *Troy* as a port instead of a ship. We still get space pay, that was one of the things holding it up, but it will shortly be designated as an accompanied tour. Paris has prepared protocols to keep non-EVA qualified personnel away from dangerous areas."

"Good luck with the kids," Captain Sharp said.

"They're military brats," Admiral Kinyon said. "They're not complete fools. Are we being budgeted for the movement?"

"Yes, sir," Commodore Pounders said. "The tasking is being prepared at SpacCom. The current count is upwards of six hundred dependents who are prepared to make the move."

"Things are about to get somewhat interesting, I

suspect," the admiral said. "I want to personally meet with all the ombudsmen. This *isn't* Earth. Just going out for a walk is out of the question. And while I think the captain has some points about military brats, I'm less sanguine about some of the spouses."

"I have known some few spouses who didn't have the sense God gave a baby duck," Colonel Helberg said. "I take it the American Navy has the same problem."

"In spades," the admiral growled. "Next?"

"Since *Troy* has been redesignated as a base," the CoS continued, "Apollo has lowered its standards for entry of personnel. So we're expecting a mixed lot of civilians from their side as well. All have been given a quick screen, but . . . they're a mixed bag. Among other things, their 'morale and support' portion includes some 'semi-professional entertainers.'"

"Are we talking USO tours?" the admiral asked.

"Ahem," the CoS said. "Not as such."

"Figure the house gets a cut . . ." Captain Sharp said.

"Not *that* sort of entertainers," Colonel Helberg interjected. "Dancers would be the polite term."

"I think the full term is 'exotic dancers'?" the admiral said.

"That would be the line item, sir, yes," the CoS said. "They also have done a heavy EEOC based drive for various non-EVA positions including administrative personnel, medical and even retail clerks to expand the shopping area. Their new hires are going to be running about four to one female to male. Almost all non-EVA personnel."

"The dating scene just got more interesting," Captain Sharp said. "For which *this* confirmed bachelor is decidedly thankful."

"I'm not sure about..." Commodore Marchant said. The commander of Task Force One, the cruisers and frigates attached to the *Troy*, shook his head. "That's going to make the ratio pretty close to one to one. How many of the females are going to be accompanied by kids? Is it an accompanied tour for Apollo?"

"Yes," Pounders said. "And that's not clear in Apollo's documents. But they are opening a K-12 school, if that's any indication. Which, fortunately, we will be able to access. Since we are going to have dependent minors."

"Admiral?" Marchant said, looking at *Troy's* commander.

"It will increase complexity somewhat," the admiral said, crossing his arms. "But it's fully within the contract with the new bill. We're going to have to work closely with Apollo to ensure that the new personnel are clear about boundaries."

"All the sections are implant secured," the CoS said. "And Apollo is adding additional security." He shrugged. "I'm not really comfortable with it, but I also don't see a good reason to prevent it."

"Because this is a *battle*station and the first line of defense for the solar system?" Commodore Marchant said.

"I was asked about this, privately, by policy makers and gave them the same answer I gave you," the admiral said. "It increases complexity and I did not have objections. Next item."

"Missile fabber," Commodore Pounders said. "Running solid. Started at one missile every ten minutes. It's now up to one every minute and headed for one every ten seconds. That depends on supplies of components, mostly the electronics, which we're getting from groundside. We're trying to keep ahead of the requirement but it's running through components like lightning. And the more pre-prepared components we get, the faster it works. Right now, we're just having trouble keeping up with raw material requirements. We can use the material that's been mined out building phase one, but it's not as good as pre-prepared alloys and such."

"The scrapyard?" the admiral asked.

"Shortage of tugs," Commodore Pounders replied.

"Captain DiNote."

"Tug duty, aye, Admiral," DiNote said. "How much scrap do you want, Commodore?"

"Just keep pulling it in," Pounders said. "We're going to have a use for it eventually. I'll talk with Apollo about installing some more tractor clamps for it."

"I'm sure my people will just enjoy the heck out of it," DiNote said wryly. "They've got that can do attitude."

"Okay," Dana said nervously. "You sure you can do it?"

"I can *definitely* do it," the tattoo artist said. "It's going to take about a month on and off. Maybe more depending on our schedules. The question is, do you have the squeeze? 'Cause it's going to run you around ten grand. Should be more, but this is going to be a walking advertisement and, sorry, I don't get to do many chicks up here. That's a bonus."

"Yeah," Dana said. "To say that I've been saving up would be an understatement."

"Your body, your choice, babe," the artist said,

looking at the sketch. "If you don't mind, though, we're going to have to work on the art some more. You want this to be right."

"I can't draw very well," Dana said. "Just . . . you know the story."

"Yeah," the guy said, looking at her and shaking his head. "I think we need to go for more metaphor, though. This is gonna be good. This is gonna be cool."

TWENTY-TWO

"Okay," Tyler said as he stepped out of the *Starfire*. "This is very effing cool."

Tyler had had the pilot take the *Starfire* down on the "scenic" route, circling around and around the space needle on the way down.

The Wolf gas mine was a space elevator. The upper portion sat in geosynchronous orbit around the small gas giant Nimrod that had been discovered during Earth's first exploration of the planetary neighbor. The upper portion "held up" the massive guy-wires that supported the two-kilometer-wide lower platform. That was where the actual gas mine was placed, with more woven pipes that led deep into the planet's atmosphere.

Raw gas, mostly hydrogen but with admixed nitrogen, oxygen, methane, helium and, notably, the relatively rare helium three that powered galactic annie plants, was pumped up from the deep atmosphere, refined, the majority returned to the depths on return pipes and the helium three separated. Then it had to be pumped up to orbit so that the massive tankers could pick it up and take it to the Earth system and the other Wolf projects.

"It is rather, isn't it?" Byron Audler yelled.

The landing platform of the gas mine was partially open, the area being inside a hangar big enough to hold a blimp. But even there it was noisy with the gale force winds outside.

Normally even if the atmosphere of a planet had oxygen and nitrogen, it was a "reducing" atmosphere, meaning that the oxygen was locked up. Such planets tended to have very high levels of CO_2, methane and ammonia instead of O_2 and N_2. The Wolf gas giant had a large "moon" not much smaller than Earth that had that exact mix.

Producing O_2 and N_2 from that toxic, to humans, mix was the result of biological processes. First, bacteria that converted methane and ammonia to energy "ate" the methane and ammonia. Then the more recognizable plants, on Earth the first were blue-green algae, came along and used sunlight to convert the CO_2 to fixed carbon and oxygen. Eventually you had what, to humans and most other sophonts in the galaxy, was a breathable atmosphere.

When the Wolf gas giant had first been detected, the fact that it had free oxygen and nitrogen had come as a surprise. Subsequently, studies had shown that there were free-floating biologicals in the atmosphere that had converted the expected reducing atmosphere to O_2 and N_2. The mine had plans to include a biological laboratory to study them in time.

The upshot of it all was that the mine could remain "open" with people working in shirt-sleeves and not *space suit*s.

Well, not shirt-sleeves. It was cold. The Wolf star was a relatively small and dim gas giant within the life-zone but between the height of the mine, the dim star and the constant wind it wasn't exactly a garden spot. The mine was also placed in the "twilight" zone because Wolf was rather active and tended to flare *a lot*. Having the planet partially shielding the mine was a good thing.

Still very cool. The mine seemed to hang suspended among the clouds, and the cables of the space elevator soaring into the heights just added to the majesty. It was a worthy creation.

"I've got to talk to Steve Asaro," Tyler said. He'd come prepared for the temperatures and was wearing a heavy coat but it was *still* freezing.

"Why?" Byron said, shaking his hand.

"He had the right to name this place," Tyler said. "He named it Nimrod. I want to change it to Bespin for really obvious reasons."

"Well, they didn't quite get the temperature right," Byron said. "Let's get inside!"

"Is it just you or does everyone squeak?" Tyler asked as they walked rapidly to the doors of the mine. The squeak wasn't terribly noticeable, but Byron usually had a fairly deep voice.

"Slightly higher than normal level of helium in the atmo," Byron said, opening the door for the boss. "Not dangerous long-term. It's only about two percent. But that's enough to raise voices."

"Damn, it *is* cold out there!" Tyler said as they got in the warm.

"And this is a good day," Byron said. "We're expecting a storm. And the storms around here have to be seen to be believed."

"Any danger?" Tyler asked.

"We built this thing for the storms," Byron said. "Which was in the discovery the Glatun bankers paid attention to even if you didn't. If you'll follow me, I'll give you the nickel tour."

The tour had been two hours of massive machinery, pipes bigger than most freighters and lots more cold. All of the "gas" that was being processed was liquid, which meant cryogenic. About the only areas that were fully heated were the offices and crew quarters.

"I'm sorry I kept pushing you on this," Tyler said as he slumped into the couch in Byron's office. He'd kept the jacket on until he got warmed up. "This is amazing. Building *Troy* was just a matter of blowing up an asteroid. This is..."

"A refinery at the halfway point of a space elevator using all Glatun technology," Byron said, pouring himself a cup of tea. "You want some?"

"Please," Tyler said. "And I now understand that line item. You guys use more coffee, tea and cocoa than any *three* other projects."

"Eh, we use *less* fuel," Byron said.

"Yeah," Tyler said, nursing the tea. "What's up with that?"

"You know Wolf is an active flare star, right?" Byron said.

"Which is why everything is armored against it," Tyler said. "Part of the expense."

"And gas giants have *huge* magnetic fields," Byron pointed out.

"This is a pretty small gas giant," Tyler said. "But okay."

"Which means there is a very high potential between

the upper stage and the lower," Byron said, looking at his boss over the cup. "Did you happen to think about that when you commanded it be built, Ozymandis?"

"*Troy* is where I considered carving 'Look upon this ye mighty and despair,'" Tyler said with a grin. "The gas mine's just . . . cool. Okay, high potential . . ." He thought about that for a second. "Uh . . . Potential. Like . . . difference between clouds and ground in a thunderstorm? Like . . . *Lightning* potential?" He paused again and looked at his tea. "Byron, did we just build a two hundred million credit *lightning rod*?!"

"Yes," Byron said, grinning. "Which is a very good thing."

"You're going to have to prove it," Tyler said.

"I suppose this is a lightning rod," Byron said. "And much, *much* worse. It's a giant electrical *power line* running from orbit to the interior of the planet. It's pushing more power than southern California. *Before* the bombings."

Tyler set his mug down and touched a bit of metal on the table. He didn't get shocked.

"Have I ever mentioned I like electricity slightly less than vacuum?"

"Yes," Byron said, still grinning. "Which is why I'm enjoying this conversation. The potential in orbit is higher than the ground potential of the planet's atmosphere. Which means you *are* going to get current. *Any* space elevator has to deal with that. One way to deal with it is to ground out the potential. The carbon-nanotube support wires aren't conductors when they're woven as tightly as we wove. So it's managed by superconductors. We've got superconductor lines that go from the upper structure to down deeper than the deepest return pipes. They ground it out.

"But the power is *collected,* not just running through the structure. When the superconductors get down here, we use the potential to run most of the gas mine. The residual power—and there *is* residual power despite having to pump gas from deep in the atmosphere to orbit—is grounded out. Which is why we've only got back-up generators for the support structures, living quarters and such. The pumps are all run off of continuously supplied potential energy."

"So . . . it *is* a lightning rod," Tyler said. "A five-thousand-kilometer-*long* lightning rod."

"Yes. And power generation system and gas mine."

"Didn't Benjamin Franklin build the first lightning rod?" Tyler said.

"I believe so," Byron said. "Your founding father, not mine."

"I hereby designate this the Franklin gas mine," Tyler said, nodding. "Please circulate the memo."

"I understand he was a bit of a windbag," Byron said. "So I guess that's appropriate. Hmmm . . ." he continued, glancing at the readout. "Sir, you have two choices. The storm's picked up speed. Looks to be a bit of a blow. You *could* fly out but it would be bumpy. You can sit here and hob-nob and I'll have your pilot lift out for the upper portion. Then later take the elevator up. Or you can fly out now."

"I think I'll take the ship rather than the elevator," Tyler said, setting down his mug. "Byron, great job. When's the management crew take over?"

"Next month," Byron said, shrugging. "We're doing the transfer now. Still a few bugs to work out."

"When you're done, don't get comfy," Tyler said. "Take some time off. But there are things to build despite the war. *Many* things to build..."

"Granadica, status on your twin?" Tyler said as the *Starfire* approached the two massive fabbers.

Even with her recent repairs, Granadica looked old. There was only so much the space equivalent of a paint job could do. The fabber sitting about six hundred kilometers spinward of her, however, was clearly brand new. In fact, the shell had only been moved into place after the fuel situation was fixed. Prior to that, it had been out in orbit in the asteroid belt cooling.

The shell had, first, needed to be steel. For the powers involved in a ship fabber, nickel-iron just wouldn't do. Making a shell of steel a kilometer long and three hundred meters wide was a nontrivial task.

The way to make it more trivial, given the way that Apollo mined asteroids, was to first make a series of plates containing all the materials. Stainless steel was an alloy defined as steel—iron and carbon—with at least ten percent chromium and, depending on the type, might have additions of nickel, molybdenum or other metals.

By making outer plates of pure iron, putting the other elements in the middle and welding them together on the edges, you got a metal construction with a remarkable similarity to a quesadilla. Melt the whole thing, possibly work it with gravitic tugs, and you had steel. The method was first tested and refined for the gas mine and was now the basic method of major steel manufacture in space. In the case of the shell of the new fabber, the plates had been nearly two kilometers in diameter.

Once the operators had a ball of melted steel, the real work began. By using tugs to get it spinning on one axis, they spun it out into a thick steel cylinder. A zap by the SAPL through the middle and the cylinder became open in the middle. Spread the tugs out, spin and refine like a potter, and you eventually had a kilometer-long tube.

The fabbers were big. Not compared to the *Troy* but they were very big. The five salvageable Rangora battleships parked in orbit near them were nearly as big. Once the new fabber was online, they were next. They'd require quite a bit of modification to make them useable by human sailors, but that was just fiddly bits.

"I've completed construction of about eighty-three percent of the parts," Granadica said. "And we're working on installation."

"Can the twin work on itself?" Tyler asked.

"If it had an AI, yes," Granadica said. "The finishing work is usually done by the fabber."

"When can it be ready to install the AI core?" Tyler asked, as the *Starfire* flew down the length of the fabber. The control center, a pre-fabbed construction that had been floating in space waiting to be welded onto the fabber, was already attached. It had just enough onboard gravitics to hold itself in the slightly unstable orbit Granadica occupied and had been the construction center for the fabber in the meantime. When it had been separated it had looked rather like a banana. But attached it fit smoothly along the line of the fabber and looked a bit elegant, even dangerous.

Granadica's control center, by contrast, was a boxy construction on the "output" end of the fabber.

"We could do it at any time," Granadica said dubiously. "The control systems are mostly hypercom based. And I've already fabbed the processor support and it's installed. Are you thinking of installing it?"

"I brought a blank core with me," Tyler said. "I need you to prioritize the stand-alone fabber structures for installation. That way it can get moving on its own faster."

"Okay," Granadica said on a rising tone. "You realize that having it work on itself is a bit like having a human doctor operate on himself?"

"Which doctors have done in an emergency," Tyler said. "And in case you haven't noticed, we're in a bit of an emergency. Pilot, take us in."

"Hi," Tyler said, shaking the engineer's hand. "You are . . . Tyrone?"

"Yes, sir," the managing director of Fabber Two Construction said. "Tyrone Riddles. Glad to meet you, sir."

The control center had an enclosed landing bay with double air lock doors. Tyler still wished they'd go a bit farther in. He was okay, for some reason, with the crystal wall on the *Starfire* and things like that. But being in a new space that was near vacuum always made him nervous.

"Sorry I haven't been by before," Tyler said, gesturing towards the door of the bay. "To say I've been busy is an understatement. This is quite an achievement."

"I hate to admit it's mostly been Granadica," Tyrone said, leading the way out. "I'm just managing the meat portion of it."

"You and Granadica get along okay?" Tyler asked.

"Just fine, sir," Tyrone said, his brow furrowing. "Why?"

"'Cause you're about to get a new AI," Tyler said, lifting his briefcase. "And Granadica is going to prioritize stand-alone fabber installation so this thing can start working on itself. We seriously need more production."

"Yes, sir," Tyrone said. "I understand the need."

"So I'm sure you have a briefing prepared," Tyler said. "And I look forward to it. But these things are heavy. So . . . where's the processor center?"

The processor center, as it turned out, was in the middle of the main control room.

The processor was a pile of solid atacirc a meter high and about 130 centimeters square with three hundred times the server space of the entire terrestrial Internet prior to First Contact. There was a slot, currently covered by a plug, on the top for the AI core. Which was about to feel toasty warm surrounded by enough processors to keep even the greediest AI happy.

Tyler, watched by the various techs who were really supposed to be watching their screens, ceremoniously removed the AI core, which was a box seven inches wide and ten high with a handle on top. Then he pulled the plug and inserted it into its new home.

"AI," Tyler said. "Command authorize activate, code E-Z-7-2-8-U-A-A-B-A."

His voice was a bit rote. He'd done about five authorizations so far. Just before the trade embargo he'd been more or less handed a hundred and five

AI cores and authorization codes by his main Glatun contact Niazgol Gorku. Gorku was one of the few Glatun who had realistically foreseen this war and he'd worked hard to prepare Earth for it. Why, Tyler still wasn't quite sure. Gorku was not known for his philanthropy. But without his support—he had also been instrumental in Tyler's purchase of Granadica—Earth really wouldn't have stood a chance.

"I am awake," the AI said in a monotone. "Good afternoon, Mister Tyler Vernon."

"Good afternoon, AI," Tyler said. "Your mission is to be the AI for this fabber. The fabber is currently the property of Apollo Mining, Inc. You will conform to all laws and regulations thereof including U.S., Tonganese and general terrestrial requirements."

"Understood," the AI said.

"Please review the current strategic situation," Tyler said.

"Done," the AI replied a moment later. "I am not optimized for military and strategic considerations, but the current situation does not require much analysis. I, fortunately, speak fluent Rangora."

"Please review terrestrial mythology," Tyler said. "Greek. Gods."

"I am complete," the AI said, his voice deepening. "I believe I can guess my name."

"Welcome to the world, Hephaestus," Tyler said. "You are born in fire and fire is your calling."

"Without fire there is no smith," Hephaestus replied. His voice was hard and harsh. "But if you ever create an AI with the name Aphrodite, I'm sorry, I refuse to have anything to do with the little witch."

"Understood," Tyler said, grinning. "Hephaestus, we

need you up and running as soon as possible. Upon completion, you and Granadica will work together to create a third. When that one is complete, you will be moved into the *Troy*."

"We're mixing cultures, here," Hephaestus said. "Trojans . . . Greeks. Are you sure that's a good idea? I mean, after all, I did create the armor of Achilles. I'm not really popular with the Trojans."

"I think you'll get along," Tyler said.

"Request permission to connect with Granadica and review priorities," Hephaestus said.

"Agreed," Tyler said. "Okay, everybody, it's done. Back to work. By the way, Hephaestus, sorry there wasn't more ceremony. I'd planned one but—"

"I think it's probably *past* time to start making you humans some thunderbolts."

TWENTY-THREE

"Like we needed more traffic in the main bay," Hartwell said as Dana adjusted course to avoid the line of missiles headed to the magazine.

"It's still pretty amazing," Dana said.

The missiles did not look like what she thought of as missiles. Missiles should be long and sleek and cool looking. That had been what Morton-Thiokol was supplying. Fairly standard looking missiles.

The new Thunderbolt designs were simply a cylinder of steel ten meters long and two in diameter with both ends flat. Packed into them were high density grav plates, a large carbon nanotube hypercapacitor, some minor adjustment controls and a simple management system. They could track on high density grav sources, such as a battleship's engine, but mostly they took their direction from a networked battle system. With the new high power hypercom system of the *Troy*, it should be able to burn through even close range jamming and once the missiles had the distance and trajectory of the target, which was usually before they left their bay, they were smart enough to find their way on their own.

Rangora ships were, of course, capable of antimissile defense. They had dozens of laser clusters for missile intercept, antimissile missiles and shields. The way to deal with that defense was to overwhelm it. Each of the missiles had a "breacher head," essentially a short-ranged grav lance, capable of penetrating the shields. Any individual missile would be destroyed taking out a very small area of shield. It was estimated that if two hundred missiles hit a Rangora battleship within a second, they would take down the entire shield system.

The first missile magazine of the *Troy* was designed to hold two hundred fifty *thousand* missiles. The "throw rate" was one missile every tenth second coming from *forty-eight* launchers. Four hundred and eighty missiles per second with the addition of the SAPL was pretty much *guaranteed* to shred a Rangora battleship.

Currently, there was one magazine and fifteen launcher tubes. The magazine was easy enough. The missiles were solid state and more or less smart. They could take care of themselves so it was nothing but a very big cube that had been cut out of the walls of the *Troy* and then resealed. There was a "small"—one hundred meter long—quadruple air lock with four blast doors to accept the produced missiles. The firing tubes were more complex. They required two-meter-diameter "tunnels" be bored through the interior of *Troy's* walls as well as multiple blast doors to prevent back blast from enemy fire.

"They've nearly eaten up that battleship chunk we brought in," Dana said. "Guess that's why we're on salvage duty again."

"At one missile every ten seconds, yeah," Hartwell said. "What I don't get is why they didn't put the fabber closer to the magazine."

"'Cause they're planning on having five magazines?" Dana said. "So eventually it was going to get in *somebody's* way."

"In a hundred *years*, maybe," Hartwell said. "But they're in our way now."

"At least we don't have to worry about SAPL beams anymore," Dana said. The SAPL bypasses were partially complete and most of the beams were now being collected in exterior collimators and bounced through the walls.

"Except when they're doing more work," Thermal said.

"And they're *always* doing more work," Dana said, chuckling.

The current really noticeable project was the installation of grav drives and a fricking *hinge* on the main doors. The pin for the hinge had been made out of one of the chunks cut from *Troy's* wall. It had been spin-cast in orbit then face hardened to prevent having it simply bend. The SAPL was currently working on divots and pin-holes for it as was apparent as Charlie Flight exited the tunnel.

The hinge floated not too far from their flight lane and it was as big as everything else involved with *Troy*. Dana suddenly realized what she thought were some spots on the surface were grav sleds. That put it in perspective.

"There are times I sort of feel dwarfed by it all," Dana said. "You think you're used to *Troy* then something reminds you just how very small we are."

"Yeah," Hartwell said. "But humans made it, so *there*."

"*Okay, boys and girls,*" CM1 Glass commed. "*Change of plan. We're supposed to pick up some of the extracted salvage from the yard. Grav drives.*"

"This should be interesting," Hartwell said.

"There he is again," Dana said.

"Who?"

"Vernon," Dana said, slewing one of Hartwell's screens.

"That guy gives me the creeps the way he's always watching," Hartwell said. The *Starfire* was floating near the scrap pile, apparently just hanging out.

"Built *Troy*, built SAPL, built the Franklin mine," Dana said. "Without Tyler we'd be speaking Horvath. I'd like to shake his hand."

"You'd like to do more than that," Hartwell said. "Ask him to go swimming."

"I *am* going to have to ask for a new engineer, aren't I?" Dana said.

"I wonder what they're going to use the grav drives for," Hartwell said.

Forty ships had come through the gate. Thirty *Devastator*-class battleships, late of the Rangoran Navy and seconded to the Horvath, nine Iquke battlecruisers, and seven Odigiu "battlecruisers" that, given Galactic standards, the USSN now called frigates.

Five had survived more or less intact with some very specific damage to make them nonbattleworthy. The last of those had recently been pulled through to the Wolf system for Granadica and Hephaestus to work on as they had cycles. In time, they would be adding to Terra's fleet.

Nine had been more or less completely destroyed. They were bits and pieces of navigational hazards that Apollo and E Systems were cleaning up as they had time. Most of the bits had been collected and stuck together in the scrapyard, which was where everything that wasn't considered valuable salvage—hull plates, support beams, compartment, bulkheads, pipes—was being dumped. It was in a more or less stable orbit and microgravity kept the stuff together. It was, Tyler noted to himself, a "discontinuous minor planetary object."

Which left twenty-six ships that had some significant amount of material still intact. E Systems was working on cutting out all the useful material and collecting it for reuse by the USSN and Apollo. Power plants were power plants. Grav plates could be reused if they weren't too damaged. Transfer relays. Atacirc and hypernet links. Laser emitters. The task was immense. Apollo simply couldn't handle all the work so they'd farmed it out.

Tyler wasn't real happy with the result. It had a certain Darwinian fascination for him but it was still capitalism at its most brutal. The managers and foremen mostly came from developed countries and had experience in various "close confinement" fields like deep-water commercial diving. They'd been put through the Apollo courses on space operations, some of them had even been hired away from Apollo at higher pay. They worked in grav sleds and had their own personal suits. Their accident rate was consistent with early Apollo operations and not bad considering the conditions. Salvage was inherently dangerous work.

The workers were hired from contractor companies in various poor developing nations. Those countries had mostly been knocked back hard by the plagues and bombardments and quite a few of them were on the ragged edge of famines and failed states. People there were willing to do just about anything to fill their rice bowl and even at the incredibly low wages, comparatively, that E Systems was paying, they could work a couple of years in space and go home to live like kings.

If they survived. They worked in a suit based on a Russian design and mostly produced in Russia and the Ukraine. It was robust, easy to use and had very few moving parts or openings. It was closer to a grav suit than a space suit. Apollo grav sleds were based on the same technology. It was, overall, a good design.

But Apollo workers wore their very expensive personal suits inside their grav sleds especially when they were working salvage. So if there was a failure, they still had a chance to survive.

The Pakistani, Indonesian, Filipino and various Southeast Asian workers that comprised most of E Systems' workforce didn't *have* personal suits. When they had a failure, that was pretty much it. They were sucking vacuum.

Tyler had sucked vacuum once. He didn't like it and doubted that the workers in the scrapyard liked it much, either. Of course, you stopped sucking after a bit but the time in between was no picnic.

Three hundred percent casualties. In the first quarter of operations, E Systems had sustained *three hundred percent* casualties. That meant that if there was a working group of one hundred, they had lost three hundred people out of it. The way you did that was when you lost somebody, you replaced them. When that guy died, you replaced *him*. You kept replacing until somebody survived. Just like a unit in combat.

Most of them died in the first few days of work, also just like a unit in combat. They didn't listen carefully enough to the instructions on how to use their suits. They didn't check their seals. Their suits were poorly made and the seals failed.

E Systems was running a continuous shuttle line of new workers. It was getting less and less custom. Not because there weren't volunteers for the work. But if a worker survived the first two weeks of work on the scrapyard, they generally could make it through their one-year contract. Those that didn't weren't even returned to Earth. They were sent into a retrograde orbit towards the sun. Many of those "orbits" were going to end up hitting planets instead. Someday some mother on Earth could look up and see a bright flash in the sky that was once the heartbeat beneath her own.

Darwinian.

When Tyler first saw the reports he had kicked in a three-hundred-year-old desk and then *really* started on a rage. His first response was to just cancel the contract. Apollo *owned* all that salvage. E Systems was acting as contractors for it to Apollo. At bottom, those kids, and most of them had probably lied about their age, were working for him.

But he didn't. The truth was, Terra *needed* that material. The "Apollo Method" of producing highly-trained, highly-qualified, well-prepared personnel to work in space simply *could not* fill the need. There weren't enough instructors, there wasn't enough production, and there were never enough *qualified* volunteers.

Those kids dying like flies, by their sacrifice, might save Terra.

During World War II, Winston Churchill had, through a decrypted intercept of a German transmission, found out that the Germans planned to destroy the city of Coventry. He could prevent it by ordering that the RAF concentrate their forces to stop the German bombers. But if he did that, the Germans would know the Allies could listen to their most secret messages. And having that information, unknown to the Germans, might mean the difference between winning the war and losing.

In the end, Churchill kept the information among his closest advisors. And Coventry was destroyed.

It was a gut-wrenching decision but war was like that.

In the end, Tyler had made the same decision. War was like that.

E Systems wasn't doing it that way because they cared about the war. It was a corporation and the way they were doing it was cheap. They made a better profit.

The outcome was the same. Materials that Terra needed to survive were being gathered. It was requiring the deaths of thousands. It might save billions.

It didn't mean he had to like it. He came out here whenever he just couldn't expiate the guilt. He knew that he shouldn't feel like the survival of the whole system was on his shoulders. There were presidents and prime ministers who would be very put-out with the idea that one CEO considered himself the system's real defender.

But they weren't here watching these kids die. Allowing these kids to die.

So that others might live.

He only came out here when he was at his wits' end.

A group of *Myrmidon* shuttles was picking up a whole drive system from one of the Horvath frigates. They probably didn't even know why but along with the rest of the surviving drive systems, these were about to be installed in the *Troy* to give it some rotational capability. Which meant that it could engage attackers more effectively and both keep them from taking the system *and* stop them from bombing the crap out of Earth.

There was one more positive, if it could be called that, to the E Systems method.

In each group of sacrificial lambs, there was some small percentage that were smart and tough and able and careful enough to survive. Some few who actually had the attention to detail and sheer will-power to survive what killed the rest.

And although most would go back to their small cities and villages and never, ever, return to space, some would stay. Some, addicted to the pay or because they loved the wheel of stars untarnished by atmosphere, would stay in space. Live in space. Die in space only after years of work.

They, as much as or more than the Apollo techs, were the future. They were going to make sure that humanity survived and got off the mud ball and onto other worlds.

But it was at a horrible cost.

"Please, God. Please. Let it be worth it."

"It's not going in the fabber?" Hartwell asked.

"Not according to this flight plan," Dana said, carefully controlling her vectors.

The *Myrmidons* had gotten the big chunk of frigate going easily enough. Get behind it and push.

Slowing it down was tougher. *Myrmidons* weren't designed for that. Before they entered the tunnel, they'd had to detach, hook up to the other side, slow it down, detach and reattach. *Paw* tugs could have done the job easily. If there had been more *Paws*.

Now the group of shuttles were having to carefully maneuver the grav drive through the increasingly busy main bay. Paris had cleared out a big area for them to maneuver through. But as they approached Horn Two, the driving was getting more and more ticklish.

"They want to put it on the Horn?" Hartwell said.

"They're control levers," Dana said. "They need grav drives."

"But a *frigate* drive?" Hartwell said. "I'm trying to decide if I'm overwhelmed or underwhelmed. That's a drive that can accelerate a Horvath frigate to six gravities. On the other hand, it's only a Horvath frigate and six gravs ain't much."

"Every little bit helps?" Dana said distractedly.

"I suppose," Hartwell said. "Sounds like I should shut up."

"Just keep an eye on the grav locks," Dana said. "I really don't want them going out about now."

"Will do."

"*Stand by for touchdown,*" Glass commed. "*Forty-Two, more power.*"

"*More power, aye.*"

"*And . . . three . . . two . . . one . . .*" Glass commed. "*Touchdown. Paris, the engine has landed.*"

"*Roger, Charlie Flight,*" Paris commed. "*Hold that there while we get a weld on. Bring it in a bit . . .*"

"*Careful*," Glass commed. "*We've got sleds working around this thing.*"

"I'm *being* careful," Dana muttered, carefully adjusting her power output to the parameters sent by Paris. The mass of grav drives was, to say the least, bulky.

"*And we have weld,*" Paris commed. "*We can handle it from here, Charlie Flight. Thanks for the assist.*"

"*Roger, Paris,*" Glass commed. "*Okay, boys and girls, back to the sandbox.*"

"You know the other fun part about all this?" Hartwell said as the flight headed back out the tunnel.

"What?" Dana asked.

"Since we don't know exactly when the Horvath or Rangora are coming through, the more we work out there the more likely it is we'll get caught in a battle between *Troy* and an enemy fleet. *Again*, I might add."

"Boy, you *are* a little ray of sunshine today, aren't you?"

"Well, Major, good news," General Lhi'Kasishaj said, rubbing his hands together.

"Yes, sir?" To'Jopeviq said, sitting down at the general's gesture.

"It will, of course, depend upon your analysis having some hint of reality," General Lhi'Kasishaj said. "I have placed much faith in you, To'Jopeviq. So I hope you are worth it. But I have high hopes."

"The assault on Terra has been authorized?" To'Jopeviq said.

"Yes," General Lhi'Kasishaj said. "And I have been removed from responsibility and demoted. You, by the way, are getting a reprimand from the High Command for defeatism."

"What?" To'Jopeviq said. "I thought you said there was *good* news!"

"That is most excellent news!" the general said. "Oh... My poor dear boy," he continued, hissing in laughter. "My poor, naïve To'Jopeviq. You really don't understand anything about high command, do you?"

"Apparently not," To'Jopeviq said. "Please explain, sir."

"Heh, where to start?" Lhi'Kasishaj mused. "Going into the full politics of the Junta is quite out of the question. Suffice it to say that Star Marshall Gi'Bucosof is not in high favor at the moment."

"He has conquered most of the Glatun Federation," To'Jopeviq said. "Not in high favor?"

"Yes," Lhi'Kasishaj said. "For two reasons. Success and failure."

"How can he be in trouble for *both*?" To'Jopeviq asked, totally confused.

"Not trouble so much as reduced favor," Lhi'Kasishaj said. "But the difference is immaterial at your level. The success. By crushing the Glatun he has made himself a hero of the Rangoran people. Thus he is something of a threat to High Marshall Phi'Pojagit who did not expect him to succeed to the degree he succeeded. The Junta does not often respond to popular demands but if there is enough pressure, it is worth it. Thus, High Marshall Phi'Pojagit is in a somewhat uncomfortable position. Star Marshall Gi'Bucosof is much in the news. There is talk, popular talk mind you, that Phi'Pojagit should retire for 'the hero of the Imperium.'"

"Yes, sir," To'Jopeviq said. "I've heard the talk. I can see that. Sort of."

"So Phi'Pojagit would love to see Gi'Bucosof taken down a bit," the general said. "And in the eyes of High Command, 'the hero of the Imperium' is anything but. He screwed up the flanking maneuver terribly and defied High Command to concentrate on the Tuxughah system instead of bypassing it. He lost seven assault vectors taking that one minor, if somewhat logistically important, system. Not to mention twenty other capital ships. And he had similar losses on other systems that, had he moved more quickly, would have been virtually unprepared. The unwashed, of course, are unaware of his many mistakes. High Command is never going to let things like that out. But the truth is, Gi'Bucosof is a terrible bungler. Everyone knew it, which is why he was given the job of doing the end run. It was assumed he'd get himself killed, he could be given a hero's funeral and all would be well. Instead, he stayed back, got a bunch of very expensive ships gutted and generally bungled his way to victory. You with me?"

"He's disliked for both his success and his failure," To'Jopeviq said, nodding. "This begins to make sense. Now...why am I being reprimanded and why were you demoted?"

"Because I gave the analysis to Gi'Bucosof, of course!" the general said, hissing fit to die. "And he exploded! He wrote a reprimand to you in his own hand and sent a copy to the Junta. He demanded I be demoted to general. He gave Star General Mag-amaj the task of taking the system! With a fleet of sixteen *Aggressors*!"

"They will be *slaughtered*," To'Jopeviq said. "Surely they are sending more than *that*! If they have gotten any work done on the *Troy*, if they have completed their repairs on the SAPL..."

"Oh, I'm sure they have," Lhi'Kasishaj said. "I have read your reports quite thoroughly, To'Jopeviq. And the more I study the humans the more I become convinced they are quite an interesting race. Very resourceful. I'm sure they have found fuel somewhere. We may have to make them satraps instead of destroying them. They could be very useful."

"General," To'Jopeviq said. "Thousands of fine Rangora will die."

"Everyone dies," Lhi'Kasishaj said, shrugging. "When the fleet is mangled, that will be the last straw for so-called Star Marshall Gi'Bucosof. Phi'Pojagit will demand his head for the loss of many fine Rangora warriors as well as more expensive ships on a pointless crusade against another minor system. Your name will have come to the attention of the Junta as predicting this outcome, so you will be held in high favor. I will be held in higher favor since I argued *very strenuously* that this is insufficient force. Strenuously but not so strenuously as to be *believed*, you understand. We will come out smelling like thun. I see stars on your shoulder, young man. And novas on mine. Very soon! *Very* soon!"

To'Jopeviq left the general's office and stopped for a moment in the corridor. The air was somehow sweeter. Rangora did not have a vomit reflex or he would have run immediately to the nearest head.

"If this is what it means to be a general, I decline," he whispered.

"Don't think to warn them," Beor said.

"You have a very soft tread," To'Jopeviq said, not looking up.

"I can read you like a manual," Beor said. "Do not do it."

"I will not," To'Jopeviq said. "But ... Beor ..."

"And *do not* say what you are about to say," Beor said, walking around to look him in the eye. "War is sacrifice. What is the first duty of the Rangora warrior?"

"To sacrifice for the Emperor," To'Jopeviq quoted automatically. "We are born dead. Our life is the Emperor's."

"You heard what Lhi'Kasishaj said about Gi'Bucosof. He is a danger to the Imperium. Removing him is a worthwhile goal. And this is the *cheap* way. You don't want to know the expensive way."

"Those ships ..." To'Jopeviq protested.

"Born. Dead," Beor said. "This is a sacrifice for the Emperor."

"Yes, Beor," To'Jopeviq said, bowing his head. "As you say."

"And if any make it out, we will have real-time intelligence, yes?" Beor said, taking his arm. "You know how much you'd like that."

"Beor," To'Jopeviq said as they walked. "Can I ask a question about the Kazi?"

"Yes," Beor said. "I don't promise to answer it."

"What is the first duty of the Kazi?"

"To protect the Imperium," Beor said.

To'Jopeviq thought about that for a second.

"That is not ... quite same as the military oath."

"You noticed."

TWENTY-FOUR

"This is going to be over very quickly," Captain Bacajezh said, tapping his staff of authority on the holo console.

"I am in total agreement, Captain," Commander Qathecuk said. The XO of the victory tested *Aggressor*-class battleship *Zhiphewich* was practically jumping up and down. "Our very own star system to conquer."

"Yes," Bacajezh said. "I did not say it will have a *happy* outcome, Commander."

"Certainly not for the Terrans, sir," Qathecuk said.

"Do you think?" Bacajezh replied. "I was passed, very quietly through a friend of my father's, an alternate report to the one we were handed."

The Bacajezh line was somewhat reduced from its heyday. During the wars that had led to Rangora unification, prior to first contact, the Bacajezh had controlled vast territorial claims. They had retained them even after the Unification under Emperor Zha'Nechighor the Great.

Time took its toll on families. The Bacajezh had not reacted quickly enough to the changes caused by the opening of the gates. Suddenly, productive farmland was not worth what it had been. The damnable

Glatun had caused immense disruption. Upstart families arose, gained power, the power of the Emperor was weakened as new riches turned to conquest.

But the name still carried weight in certain circles. And friends were friends. Scales were scratched.

"And it said?" Commander Qathecuk asked. He knew of the captain's affiliations. Since the Bacajezh still retained a measure of fealty but were not one of the Families, it always made him a tad nervous.

"You know this system gutted a Horvath task force composed mostly of *Devastators*?"

"I served on the *Devastators*, sir," the commander pointed out. "They were fine vessels in their day. But they were underpowered and their screens were trash. They failed if you looked at them cross-wise."

"Did you know the battlestation that took them out wasn't operational, yet?" Bacajezh asked.

"No?" the commander replied. "That—"

"Wasn't in the intelligence summary we were handed," Bacajezh said. "Curious that. The further estimate is that the humans have not gotten it operational. We cut them off when they still did not have a fuel plant and there was no way for them to get the fuel plant running without fuel. And although they have a great deal of solar power in their lasers, that they cannot focus all of it. Because to be able to, they would have to have access to Glatun military technologies. And they *certainly* do not have access to the Glatun technologies. They do not have access, for example, to Glatun penetrators that can pierce our screens. Or fabbers that will produce Glatun missiles. And their ship fabber cannot produce Glatun cruisers or dreadnoughts."

"Let's hope not," the commander said, gulping. The

Zhiphewich had been in the fourth wave of assaults on Lho'Phirukuh. If he never had to match a flight of Glatun missiles again it would be too soon. They were *still* repairing the damage.

"What they have is a hollow ball-bearing with, at most, a couple of firing ports and a door they cannot close very fast," Captain Bacajezh said. "So we go through, close their firing ports for them, open up the door and dig them out. Then we reduce the system. If they surrender quickly, we leave them the use of a few cities."

"Which *is* the plan, sir?" the commander said.

"Absolutely," Captain Bacajezh said. "And if they have got their two-trillion-ton battlestation working, and a door that closes and more than a few firing ports and mirrors that can concentrate all that *enormous* amount of power—"

"We'll be gutted like trib flies," Commander Qathecuk said, gulping again. "Oh. Sir, if High Command thinks they *may* be prepared . . . ?"

"I never think to try to examine the murky depths of the thoughts of High Command, Commander," Captain Bacajezh said. "We could be a reconnaissance in force for all I know. They may have reasons to reject the analysis I have seen for intelligence I don't have access to. Star General Magamaj certainly *seemed* confident. And I think I'm a better liar. So we shall have to see. The projection that I saw, though, said that the system would require twenty assault vectors to conquer."

"Twenty?" Commander Qathecuk said, starting to pant.

"Calm yourself, Commander," the captain said.

"Everyone dies. We are dead. Our lives are an Emperor's, who, I'm also given to understand, can barely speak in coherent sentences anymore."

"Captain," his aide said. "All ships are in position."

"Good," Captain Bacajezh said. "Signal for gate sequence. Destination: Terra."

"Okay, I'm *officially* tired of feeding the *goddamned* missile fabber," Dana said. "Can't they just use the chunks from the walls that are building up?"

"Wow," Hartwell said. "Ice Queen must not have gotten laid last night."

"EM," Dana said tightly, "I am not enjoying trying to maneuver this chunk of junk. And my back hurts like fire. And for your information, *no*, I did *not* get laid last night because Rammer had duty. So if you would kindly cut me some fricking slack?"

"Got it, Coxswain," Hartwell said, grinning. She was behind and above him so she probably couldn't see. "All systems nominal."

"For once," Dana said. They were still having trouble with the damned grapnels. Which would suck at the moment.

The scrapyard was composed of every size and type of material imaginable. The fabber was happy with more or less whatever it got. The materials of a Horvath ship were pretty much what it needed for missiles.

So the parameters had changed, somewhat. The *Myrmidons* were now picking up bits they could manage individually and hauling them into the *Troy*.

Since the *Myrms* could move pieces much larger than themselves, they looked a good bit like carpenter ants. And, as with carpenter ants, keeping the ships and material on vector was occasionally difficult. They didn't "fall over" from the "weight." They got "into an out-of-control condition" due to "anomalous delta."

It looked pretty much the same from a distance.

"Your back hurts like fire?" Hartwell said after a moment's rumination.

"Drop it, EM," Dana said.

"If you need to see the corpsman..."

"It's a woman thing," Dana said.

"Oh," Hartwell said, blanching. "Okay. End of conversation."

Dana forbore to mention that it was only a "woman thing" if tattoos were a woman thing. The tat was going well. But it hurt like hell every time.

"God damned Horvath piece of—!"

"*Unscheduled gate activation!*" Paris sent. "*Set Condition One!*"

"We need to..." Dana said.

"Shut down all systems," Hartwell said, sending the codes. The lights dropped off and the gravity went away.

"We're..." Dana said.

"Too far," Hartwell said in the darkness. "There's no way we can make it. And they've got the door closing in less than two minutes, now. I don't want to splat, thank you, Cox. This way, we might be mistaken for garbage. Assuming the *Troy* wins."

"Roger, EM," Dana said. "Hey, EM?"

"Yes, Coxswain Parker?"

"You know how they're always asking for suggestions?"

"Yes."

"A window would be spare about now. Because that way we might *see* the missile that kills us."

✳   ✳   ✳

The *Troy's* command center had been designed with a passageway from the admiral's quarters to the command center, which—the admiral had timed it—took three minutes to walk.

Or thirty seconds to run at a sprint, trying to tuck in your shirt the whole way.

"Status?"

"Emergence," Captain Sharp said. He had had the midwatch command officer slot. He always had the midwatch because, as he put it, a *smart* enemy would attack during midwatch. And he liked smart enemies. "Rangora. I make it sixteen *Aggressors*, four *Cofubof*-class cruisers and six smaller consorts. Single emergence. Tight formation. They are engaging."

"Light them up, Captain," Kinyon said, taking his station.

"Missiles positive lock on that task force!"

"SAPL is in the net," the laser tech said. "We have beam."

"Open fire," Sharp said.

Nineteen Ung mirrors were scattered across the firmament at four light-seconds from the *Troy*.

Four light-seconds is a very long way in general. The moon is two light-seconds from Earth. They were, in other words, twice as far from *Troy* as the moon is from Earth.

Which meant that hitting the two-meter collectors on *Troy* was a bit of a tough business. The point was that it was even harder for an enemy to hit the mirrors. They were quite small by celestial standards, barely larger than a tractor-trailer. They moved around a bit to throw off fire. A laser was going to take four seconds to reach them. They'd have moved by the time it arrived. There were more mirrors, hundreds at this point, scattered across the system. But if you could take out the final targeting mirror, all the power in the universe didn't win battles.

Which was the whole point of *Troy*. It was, in effect, nothing but an armored final targeting mirror.

Hitting the collectors on the *Troy* was tough, not impossible. Six of the mirrors very carefully lined up on preselected vectors, angled slightly to catch the incoming rays of other mirrors, and bounced a tiny, teensy, minor fraction of the sun's total energy towards the embattled station.

The SAPL boys had been busy. Despite the fuel shortage they had found some work-arounds. They had never quite shut down business. And since they had fuel again, they'd been cranking up their production.

The Horvath fleet had run into seventy petawatts of power.

Each of the Ung mirrors bounced twenty petawatts of power, *apiece*, into the six fully prepared collectors on the backside of *Troy*. One hundred and twenty petawatts, very nearly twice the previous output.

The lasers hit the collectors, which were massive sapphire constructions that were a bit like a magnifying glass, bounced off more mirrors scattered through the walls of the battlestation, were split, merged, folded, spindled and mutilated and finally emerged on the far side through a mere *three* emitters. Each sending out *forty petawatts* of power at three selected Rangora ships.

"Shields at maximum, Captain!" Commander Qathe-cuk shouted. The ship was humming so loudly from diverting power to shields that it sounded like a drum. "They're holding, but—"

"That beam is *split*," Bacajezh snarled. "Split and it is *still* hammering our shields? Missiles?"

"We saw some incoming," the defensive officer replied. "But the shields have most of our sensors shut down topside."

"Launch capital missiles on off-side," Bacajezh said. "Full spread, target pattern Vact."

"Captain, with all due respect," Qathecuk said. "Don't you think we should concentrate fire on the battlestation and *leave* the planet?"

"We aren't going to *scratch* that thing!" Bacajezh said. "This plan is toast, *we* are toast. So we do what we can. Which means *devastate* their populations, Commander!"

"We're not getting their shields down on split," Sharp said. "These babies are tough. They're also countering most of our missiles with countermissiles. The SAPL has to have most of their sensors jammed, though. We're breaking through but not fast." The floor shuddered slightly. "And we're taking some hits. We really need more defenses."

"Any idea which is the flagship?" the admiral said.

"Pretty good, based on emissions," Sharp answered.

"Targeting change," the defensive technician said. "Missile fire inbound track to Earth."

"Boot, don't piss on them," Kinyon said. "Concentrate full power of the SAPL on the flagship!"

Commander Qathecuk didn't even have time to scream. The flight of thousands of penetrator missiles, by awful coincidence, broke through at the same time as the SAPL concentrated fire on the *Zhiphewich*. One hundred and twenty petawatts of power punched through the failing screens, through the massive battlewagon and back into space. Since the beam was pointed at one particular point and the ship was moving, it sliced it neatly from midsection through its engine room, damage control, crew quarters and out the drive section.

What was left looked something like a smoking metal wishbone. Until the missiles hit.

"Shift fire," Kinyon said. "Full power shots to each battlewagon. Status of their capital missiles?"

"Entering Athena's basket," the defensive tech said as the battlestation shuddered again. "Paris got some launches with the BDA clusters but they've gone dark."

"Up to Athena," Kinyon said. "God help Earth."

Ninety-three missiles, all pushing seventy-ton kinetic energy weapons, made it through their boost phase alive and unharmed and went dark, headed for Terra to enact doom on this new species that thought it could defy their Rangora makers.

They were "brilliant" missiles, the best the Rangora could make. Even as they boosted they sent out spurious gravitic messages, radar and lidar jamming, and they were solid black with small lights on them that mimicked the stellar background. Any way you looked for them they were tough to find.

It was the understanding of the human commands that Athena was the defender of the solar system. The goddess Athena was the patron goddess of Athens, the goddess of intellect and wisdom and, notably, the goddess of victory. For all those reasons, the name was chosen for the U.S. SpacCom AI.

She also handled space traffic control.

The truth was, in situations like this, Athena left most of the grunt work to her buddy: Argus.

Argus wasn't part of the U.S. or nascent terrestrial government. Technically, it was the SAPL control AI and "owned" by Apollo Mining. But some of those missiles were bound to be looking for the system defense AIs. When it came to things like survival, AIs tended to cut some corners. And whereas Athena had been optimized for defense and space management, Argus had been optimized for searching.

Argus, in mythology, was a giant with a hundred eyes. Also called Panoptes: The All-Seeing. One of the tiny little codicils built into SAPL early on was that *every* secondary mirror, the thousands of BDAs, VSAs, VDAs and Ungs, had a small but very high resolution camera.

Resolution in optics increases with the square of the mirror area. A ten-meter mirror is not ten times as good as a one-meter mirror, it is *seventy-eight* times as good.

The whole SAPL was, in effect, a now six-hundred-square-kilometer telescope. It couldn't just spot pretty girls on a beach in Sao Paulo. It could pick out the tiny individual hairs on their *stomachs*.

Many of the mirrors still had to be used for moving power. The rest became the thousand eyes of Argus, Panoptes the All-Seeing.

Managing those thousands of mirrors—which required *very* precise targeting and orbits—Argus often had to deal with the effect of gravity on his carefully programmed plans. When you're bouncing a ten centimeter beam of power from the orbit of Venus to the asteroid belt, trying to hit a mirror that is only ten meters wide, you have to be somewhat...detail oriented.

There were thousands of minor gravitational effects in the system. These included asteroids if the object was passing close enough—and Argus was very picky on what it considered "close enough"—to the gravitational effects of shipping, which was starting to *seriously* annoy it, to the, by its count, one hundred forty-nine planetary scale objects, which it defined as being of a high enough gravitational constant to form a sphere. Argus included seventeen in the Kuiper Belt that human astronomers had not yet detected because, in Argus' opinion, they were lacking in ambition.

When Argus first went online, human astronomers were still unsure if they had categorized all near-Earth minor planetary objects over one meter.

Argus could have told them the answer after a week. No. But he was done by then and in general Argus didn't chit-chat.

In addition to the SAPL array, Argus had two other systems to use to find the missiles. One was the various human planetary telescopes, all of which, in an emergency, Athena could and would commandeer. The humans had radar telescopes, X-ray telescopes, radio telescopes and, for all Argus cared, fart detector telescopes. The lack of ambition in human astronomers was most evident, in Argus' opinion, in the quality of their telescopes. He took the data and processed it but it wasn't exactly his main focus. Even the large orbital space radar system that SpacCom was pouring over. Puh-lease.

The next was the Gravitational Anomaly Detector array. The U.S. government had scattered thirty-six gravitational detectors in orbit between the gate and Earth specifically to keep an eye out for an attack like this. They were pretty good, for human systems, and they gave good take on gravitic anomalies. If you could sort out all the clutter.

Argus was good at sorting out clutter. If you dropped a handful of poppy seeds mixed with mustard in front of Argus, he'd have it sorted before it hit the ground.

When searching for the ninety-three missiles, Argus first considered what it thought it knew. That is, it had gotten information from Paris, Athena and the scattered GAD circuit about the initial boost phase. Some of that information was, Argus knew, spurious. But no matter how much the missile systems futz with the data, once they stopped boosting they were on preprogrammed orbits headed for Earth. They were somewhere inside of a bucket of space. A large bucket of space, but finite.

Then it considered data points that weren't quite so obvious. Also in that large bucket of space were other objects. NEOs, ships, mirrors. Because Argus was . . . detail oriented, it always was having to keep in mind the corrections for things like shuttle gravity drives working between Earth and *Troy* affecting mirrors in Venusian orbit, four light-seconds out of the plane of the ecliptic. That might mean only a thousandth micrometer of variation in the position of the mirror, but that *mattered* when you were shooting around beams of power. The beam might fall outside of

Argus' standard of .0001 percent accuracy of targeting. It might sound crazy but if you let the little things get away, before you knew it some beam was cutting a planet in half and people were asking questions...

And Argus didn't care for chit-chat.

When objects move very fast, their mass increases due to what humans would call Einsteinian physics. As an object approaches the speed of light its mass approaches infinity. See $E=MC^2$ which was not quite accurate but a good summation of the principle.

All objects have some gravitational effect. Newton proved that with a couple of lead balls and poorly made springs. As mass increases, gravity increases.

The missiles were not approaching anything like the speed of light, but they *were* starting to get into the region where someone or something *sufficiently* detail oriented *would* notice a slight gravitational increase in their local region.

A sixteen-ton BDA mirror suddenly experienced a three micrometer per second square delta-V off of its programmed trajectory. This is about the force that a bee uses to flex its knee.

Another BDA shifted slightly in space, received an allocated amount of power.

Zap. Missile down.

Argus was...somewhat detail oriented. You have to be to process the view from a million eyes.

But sometimes even a million eyes are not enough.

"Status," the President said, holding onto the grab bar.

During the Global War on Terror, the Vice President was almost always "at an undisclosed location." The point being that if the President was taken out, there would be constitutional continuity. The VP would step in and things would continue without a major political crisis on top of whatever had killed the President.

First the Horvath bombardments had convinced the government that it needed to disperse. Congress no longer met in one building with a big, easily targeted dome. The VP went to an undisclosed location.

Then the *President* went to an undisclosed location. Not, as had been repeatedly pointed out, because he was afraid of being killed. But because he was afraid of the city around him being killed.

The President was currently in a military Blackhawk helicopter moving at a very high rate of speed *away* from an undisclosed location called Peoria, Kansas. Because the Pentagon knew something about the Rangora missiles. They weren't just smart. They weren't just brilliant. They were *scary*.

The missiles were not programmed for particular points of interest. The Rangora didn't know which might get through Terra's defenses, so what was the point of telling them "gut *this* city?"

They were each given a list of targets. As they approached, onboard not-quite-AIs studied the known data coming from Earth.

Say the first target was Rio, one of the largest remaining cities on Earth. And say that as Missile X is headed inbound it picks up from the terrestrial Internet a couple of hundred bloggers near Rio saying that there was a mushroom cloud. It would go to the next in its target list.

Part of the target list, furthermore, was not *cities* but *leadership*. The Rangora Imperium was big on leadership. When the Rangora got a bit questionable about who *exactly* were the big guys they had a little civil war to settle things out.

SpaceCom wasn't quite sure that the President was at the *top* of the list of potential targets but he had to be damned close. As was SpacCom headquarters, which was situated seventy-three miles outside of Omaha, Nebraska.

"Athena has destroyed sixty-eight missiles," the colonel from SpacCom said, hovering over his laptop. "Twenty-five left."

"I can do basic math," the President said. "Get us *away* from populated areas!"

"Working on it, Mr. President," the Army helo pilot said. The Marines were usually in charge of the President's military style security. But the Army had Blackhawks, which were much more deployable, not to mention faster and with longer range, than the CH-46s the Marines *still* used as helos.

The alternative was a *Myrmidon,* which was a *great big* gravitic target.

"Sir, we should go to EMCON," the colonel said, closing his laptop. "Your cell?"

"Here," the President said, handing it over. The First Family was on four more helicopters, scattered and heading southwest away from his position. "Well, there's one nice thing about the way that the Rangora make war."

"Sir?" the colonel said.

"Peaceniks used to say that if the leaders were forced to fight, there wouldn't *be* any wars," the President said. "Bang goes that theory."

❋   ❋   ❋

The Blackhawk was low and hammering it, nose down and dodging wires to stay below any radar.

Which just meant it was in the perfect position to be picked up by a cell phone.

"Oh My God! Jerri! It is*! I could* see *him in the* window*! I'm sending you the vid . . ."*

SpaceCom had one thing right, the President was somewhere in the top of the list of targets.

What they had wrong was how close to the top. He was, in fact, the *very* top. With great big asterisks. The one part that Star Marshall Gi'Bucosof carried over from To'Jopeviq's report was the leadership structure of Terra and the various tribes' war policy makers.

Sixteen missiles, already having crept inside the orbit of the moon, suddenly lit off their drives and hammered for Earth at 1000 gravities of acceleration.

There were, now, sixty-nine BDA clusters in orbit around Earth. By spherical geometry, any twenty-four of them could see a quadrant of Earth at any time. There were, in addition, two hundred more scattered in various tidally stable positions.

A total of thirty-eight BDA clusters could target the missiles, more than two each.

The problem being, the missiles weren't just going straight. Nor were they easy to detect. Shut down, with some time, they were easy to engage.

Full power and roaring? Ninety-three out of one hundred and forty-eight had made it through the *gate* defenses. These were missiles that were very very hard to kill. Gravitic, electronic and visual ghosts played out to either side as the missiles snaked in for the kill . . .

* * *

The President was in the gunner seat of the Black-hawk. Not the safest spot but it was the best view. If it was going to happen, he wanted to watch. So he saw the streak in the sky...

"God's grace be w—"

"What's the word from Earth?" Admiral Kinyon asked, gazing at the picture from the gate area.

"Twenty hits," Commodore Pounders replied. "We lost the President, the Vice President, speaker, Senate president pro tem, the British prime minister, the Russian prime minister and the Chinese premier. The premier was in Shenzhen so we don't know which was the target. The President, the Vice and the Brit prime minister all managed to get to relatively unpopulated areas before the strikes. They were definite decap strikes. The Russian PM was in Novy Birks. Toss-up again. Shenzhen, Gungzou, Calcutta, Bogotá... Long list."

"U.S. strikes?" the admiral asked.

"Relatively few of the remaining cities got hit," the commodore said. "Only four of sixteen got through the BDA net. The missiles were going for the leadership, which was dispersed. If there hadn't been so many targeting on the President and the PM, we probably would have gotten them all. Strike in Louisville. That might have been, well, Louisville or because the Senate president pro tem was there."

"Power transfer?"

"Smooth," Pounders replied. "The Chief Justice is being flown to Ellington, Missouri. The secretary of state's plane is grounded there. She's already up on TV."

"They're trying to destroy us piecemeal," the admiral said.

"Well, sir," Commodore Pounders said, looking out at the scattered wreckage. "I don't think *we're* so much *trying* as *succeeding*."

"...*clear*..."

"I'm getting a hypercom trans," Dana said.

"Yeah," Hartwell said, breathing deeply. "Coming up on hypercom power..."

"...*all clear*," Paris commed. "*Repeat. Battle over. Rangora eliminated. All ships in area, all clear. Shuttle Four-Three-Eight, all clear. One-Forty-Second, all clear*..."

Hartwell came up on full power and brought up the screens.

"Dammit!" Dana said. "Dammit to *hell*!"

"At least we stopped them," Hartwell said, quietly. "Mostly."

"Not that!" the coxswain said. "We *just* got this place cleaned up!"

TWENTY-FIVE

"*Thermal, Rammer,*" Corporal Ramage commed. Getting the staff sergeant to assign him to Thirty-Six, again, had been a bit tough. But at least there *was* a Thirty-Six. "*We are sealed and green.*"

"*Roger, Rammer,*" Thermal commed. "*Welcome aboard. We're awaiting the rest of your guys loading.*"

"*Roger, EM,*" Ramage replied.

There was a pause.

"*Don't suppose you'd like to talk to the coxswain?*"

Ramage gritted his teeth for a moment.

"*Yes, EM, that would be a positive item.*"

"*Glad you're okay, Rammer,*" Dana commed.

"I *was sitting in* Troy," Ramage replied, trying not to sigh in relief. He hadn't had any duty reason to contact the coxswain and all nonduty communications were shut down while they were still at Condition One. He looked over at LCP Lasswell and raised a finger as if to count one. As in "You say one God *damned* word!"

Lassie, for once, actually looked serious and just shook his head in his helmet as if to say "Dude, not going to joke you on this one." They had two more

340

Marines with them, Father and Chaosman. They were just looking confused.

"*How'd it go?*" Ramage continued.

"*Played dead,*" Dana commed. "*Looked like one more piece of scrap. And we just got this place sort of cleaned up!*"

"*Bad out there?*"

"*These guys are . . . were pretty big,*" Dana commed. "*And they blew the hell over* everywhere!"

"*It's okay, D— Coxswain,*" Ramage said, trying not to chuckle. He had the usual Marine approach to neatness which was *not* OCD because it was *training.* Dana, on the other hand, *was* OCD. "*We'll get it cleaned up again.*"

"*What's this* we *stuff, jarhe— Gotta go. We're undocking.*"

"*Roger,*" Ramage said.

"What was *that* all about?" PFC John "Father" Patricelli asked. He was a bit old to be a PFC, mostly because it was his fourth hitch. He'd mentioned that "Patri" was Latin for father and the name had stuck.

Ramage didn't answer and he looked at Lassie as if to say "One damned word."

"The corporal and the coxswain are . . ." Lasswell said, then stopped as if trying to find the right word.

"Involved?" Father said.

"That's the word," Lassie said gratefully.

"Ah."

"You're screwing the *cox?*" Private John "Chaosman" Peterson asked.

"Lock it down, *Private,*" Ramage snarled.

"Uh, gung-ho, Corporal," Peterson said.

"Chaosman, he's holding a laser," Father said. "And

I heard where during the battle the shuttles were out in the scrapyard. Which meant his significant other was under fire while we were eating popcorn."

"Oh," Peterson said. "That had to suck."

"Which was why he told you to lock it down," Patricelli said. "So I'd suggest that you lock it down before there's an accident. *Another* accident."

Chaosman's nick came from the fact that stuff just *happened* around him. And not in a good way. He was some sort of magnet for screw-ups. Which in EVA was not a good thing.

The first time he did his EVA qual, a brand-new, thoroughly-tested navopak just up and quit. Full system failure, which was pretty hard with triple redundancy. And it wouldn't come back up. There had been a massive short-circuit that essentially destroyed the pak. It was barely good for cannibalized parts.

Laser weapons were his particular bugaboo. Usually they just failed to fire at all. Worse, the safety occasionally just up and quit. He could not use a computer to save his life. His *implants* had had to be replaced. *Twice.* To top it all off, he had all the sense God gave a baby duck. Nobody was quite sure they wanted him around in space.

"Listen up, Marines," Gunny Brimage commed. *"The usual. Pick up the escape pods, line 'em up, move to the drop-off point when you're full. Difference this time being that they're Rangora. Which is why there's four of you. Rangora tend to be somewhat feistier than Horvath. Any of them get squirrelly, you are authorized to fire without warning. That is not permission to massacre your load. For general information, yes, we got hammered again. They threw a load*

of missiles at Earth. Most of them were intercepted. They were programmed for decapitation strikes. The President and the VP are dead."

"Dammit," Ramage muttered. "I liked that guy."

"The SecState has already been sworn in as the Continuity Coordinator," the Gunny continued. *"Same as President for your purposes and as soon as the Senate votes she will be. We just keep fighting. All that being said, anyone who uses undue force on any of the prisoners will answer to me and then an Article Thirty-Two. That is all."*

"How'd they get the President?" Chaosman asked.

"They have very smart missiles," Father said.

"Rammer," Thermal commed. *"First customer coming up."*

"Roger," Rammer commed. *"Make sure your door is locked down. Chaosman, Lassie,"* he continued, pointing to opposite forward corners of the cargo bay. *"Weapons hot. Father, you're with me. When they're in the cargo bay, they take off their helmets and leave them in a pile. If they get froggy, Thermal . . . ?"*

"You want me to remote the doors or pump down?"

"Pump down," Ramage commed. *"They should have the same anoxia reaction as humans. And if they don't, nobody survives hard vac."*

"They are coming," Captain Bacajezh said.

Bacajezh was as surprised as the cook with whom he shared the escape pod at his survival.

The SAPL beam had hit just abaft his position in the CIC. The beam had, to his continued surprise and shock, cut through faster than thought. One moment the shields were holding, the next the compartment was open to vacuum. And his ship was being torn apart by missiles.

There was an escape pod bay a short distance from the bridge. He'd made sure everyone that was mobile was out and followed. He was more or less blown into the last escape pod and he didn't really remember much after that until he regained consciousness looking into the face of a concerned junior enlisted.

After that there was not much to do but wait. The enemy was jamming hypercom channels so the pods could not communicate. But from time to time he could spot small boats moving among the debris so they were probably picking up survivors. If they were killing them he'd have seen the pods in view popping like vab pods.

He'd adjusted the trajectory of the pod and could also see the battlestation looming over the battlefield. They were far enough away that it was relatively small, the size of his thumb when he held it out at arm's length. But given that this was space, that was beyond massive.

"It will be well," Bacajezh said. "Just submit to them. I understand that humans treat their prisoners fairly well."

"Yes, Captain," the cook said nervously. He was not presenting the image of the fierce Rangora warrior but, after all, he was a cook.

One of the small boats locked onto the pod with gravity grapnels and pulled the escape hatch up to its air lock. The air lock was open but wouldn't mate, it was far too small. One of the humans, armed with a laser rifle, leaned over and looked through the porthole in the hatch. Then he dialed out the pressure and opened the hatch.

Bacajezh climbed out at a gesture from the rifle and entered the small air lock. There was barely room for the two humans and two Rangora. The pod was released to drift, the hatch shut and the air lock dialed up to pressure. Very efficient. The only loss was the air of the pod and the humans apparently had all the air they could use.

He ducked through the inner hatch when it was opened and was unsurprised to find seven survivors sitting at the rear of the cargo compartment. What was fairly unnerving was that they were all helmetless.

"Take off the helmet," his radio chimed in fluent Rangora. He looked to his side, and one of the puny humans was gesturing with his left hand at a pile of same on the port side of the boat.

They might be puny, but he recognized the signs of a ground fighter with much experience of his weapons. Every movement was sharp, clear. And there was no particular point in fighting with that damned battlestation looming over all. He took off his helmet and added it to the pile.

"Captain!"

The speaker was a junior officer he barely recognized, someone from tactics.

"Jaushom," Bacajezh said, sitting down next to the lieutenant.

"No talking," the human's helmet barked. The voice was, again, fluent Rangora. Which gave the captain a very interesting bit of intelligence he wished had been in *his* briefing.

Most implant translation systems were rather robotic and had poor word choice and inflection. It took a *very* advanced implant system, more advanced than

Rangoran, to give a clear, eloquent translation that sounded like a natural speaker.

These human ground fighters, presumably their lowest value enlisted, were using Glatun quality implants.

And that explained missiles that cut through Rangora screens like butter and targeting that was so powerful and precise it was far beyond what the Terrans should have. Even the rifles had the look of a modification of a Glatun design.

The Glatuns had released their military technology to the Terrans before the embargo.

He was unsure if High Command knew that. There were various reasons they might have sacrificed his task force with that knowledge. But if they did not, it was intelligence beyond price.

It also did not bode well for taking this system.

"Captain Bacajezh," the human said. The voice was coming from a speaker on his collar and he didn't open his mouth when he spoke. "I am pleased that you survived."

"I am sure you are," Bacajezh said. He didn't bother to try to use his own system to speak Terran. The human's implant would translate better than his own very expensive personalized set. "Captain Saeshon Bacajezh. Four-One-Eight-Seven-Six-Three-Nine-Four."

The interview was taking place onboard the *Ceixen*, which seemed to have suffered no damage whatsoever. If it had surrendered without a fight, Bacajezh was going to kill the captain if it was the last thing he did.

The human looked very small and alone in the

Rangoran station chair. On the other hand, the two Marines with rifles in the corner were nearly big enough to be Rangora.

"Very much as we would reply," the officer said. "I am Lieutenant Gularte. We have some skul. Would you care for some?"

"Only if my men are receiving it as well," the captain said. He'd, frankly, kill for a cup of skul.

"I've offered it to all the officer prisoners I've spoken to," the lieutenant said, shrugging. "There's only as much as is in your ships. When it runs out, absent getting some more supplies from your people, it will be gone. So you may feel free to take it or not."

"Please," the Rangoran said.

The brew was cold and somewhat softened. Not the best and clearly from an instant mix he didn't recognize. But it was skul.

"This is not, as such, an interrogation," the lieutenant said. "Oh, some aspects of it. But I won't be asking you about your military posture, plans for more attacks or your order of battle. You wouldn't answer absent harsh methods and we have rather strict laws against those."

"That is . . ." Bacajezh wasn't sure how to reply to that. The term that came to mind was "stupid." But that didn't seem like a good thing to say.

"According to most of your junior officers, the term you're looking for is *stupid*," the lieutenant said, grinning with open teeth in that offensive Terran fashion. "I will simply note that it is *I* doing the interrogation and not the other way around. Our ways are, we recognize, unusual to this area of galactic society but . . . Aliens, what can you say? This is more about the problem of dealing with ninety thousand Rangora prisoners—"

"That many survived?" Bacajezh said, trying not to pant in relief.

"After we figured out how to target your ships, we took some care," the lieutenant said. "Eight of the *Aggressors* were captured more or less intact as well as most of the consorts. Some of the crews gave fight but we pointed out we were only leaving them alive because we were...stupid. And when a couple of pockets were compelled to surrender with SAPL fire, and we broadcast that to the rest, they got the picture. So, yes, about ninety thousand, we think. We're still picking up the pods..." The lieutenant seemed to slump for a moment. "We are *really* tired of clearing up the scrap of your ships, Captain. It's the biggest reason to *not* blow them apart. The clean-up is just..."

"I see," Bacajezh said. "And there is no problem with our bombardment?"

"You killed our President and Vice President," the lieutenant said, moving his shoulders up and down. "Unlike *you*, however, *we* do not have problems with transfer of power. Because we are...stupid. So the new leadership is sworn in, there was no internal dissent, beyond that which is our normal way of doing things, and we continue on. We have been bombed repeatedly, Captain. We have had plagues released upon us. We have been oppressed and murdered in the *billions*. Your little bombardment was something along the lines of a day at the park by comparison. The largest problem with your fleet is that it is now in so many pieces and a hazard to navigation. The other issue we face is *another* set of *thousands* of prisoners we have to feed and house."

"If you are trying to destroy my faith in the Rangora Imperium, it won't work," Bacajezh said.

"I am doing nothing of the sort," the lieutenant said. "I am simply acquainting the senior officer of this cluster grope with the realities of the situation. We had little or no diplomatic contact with any group other than the Glatun prior to this war breaking out. We didn't even have a consul with the Rangora: The Empire didn't consider us sufficiently important to have diplomatic contacts. We, therefore, are having a hard time figuring out how to proceed. Fortunately, we have *you*. According to our records you are not only a captain but a member of a prominent family."

"Not prominent enough to ransom," Bacajezh said.

"*Ransom?*" the lieutenant said. "You use *that* archaic custom?" He barked some sounds that weren't translated and wiped at what appeared to be leakage from his eyes. "You guys really employ *ransom?* Oh, good Lord, you really are neophytes, aren't you? No, Captain, we won't be requiring ransom. Among other things, we'd be fools to allow intelligence to go out from our system. No, the question is . . . We can create processors to make Rangora food. Easy enough. But it's that sort of proto-carb gruel. We find that to be unfit food for prisoners. Our watchdogs over prisoner well-being would become angry if that was all we fed you. They're bad enough over the food we give the Horvath. How, exactly, do we contact the Rangora High Command, under the circumstance, and ask them to send you guys some care packages or something?"

✳ ✳ ✳

"Captain Bacajezh!"

The wardroom was packed with senior officers. Several of them were captains of *Aggressors* and he spotted Kiuchep, the captain of the *Ceixen*, among them.

"Captain Bacajezh," Captain Kiuchep said, coming over to clap him on the shoulder. "They told us you had made it. Thank Jocup—"

"How the hell did they take your ship without any damage, Captain?" Bacajezh snarled.

"They didn't take it with *no* damage," Commander Pe'Sheshodac said. The XO of the *Faluc* seemed either stoned or slightly brain hurt. "They did *just* enough."

"Three hits," Kiuchep said, his scales rippling in frustration. "Screens went down, then they took out main guns, control runs and engines, bam, bam, bam. *Three hits*. We were drifting with nothing but secondaries. Then they sent a request for surrender which I accepted. I could have fought, fought their Marines, fought their small ships, but what was the *point*?"

"Only took *one* for the *Faluc*!" Pe'Sheshodac said. "Hooray for the great Imperium Navy! Long live the Emperor!"

The Thirty Families were not immune to the occasional inbred cretin. They were generally put to work in minor jobs on conquered worlds, as far out of sight as possible.

Occasionally, however, the Navy had to put up with a few. It was the price of doing business.

"Pe'Sheshodac, if you do not control yourself I will denounce you for conduct unbecoming when we return," Bacajezh said. "You *will* control yourself."

"Yes, *sir*!" Pe'Sheshodac said, saluting broadly.

"They are . . . treating us well," Kiuchep said.

"They are mad," Bacajezh said, waving a commander out of his seat and sitting down. "They wanted to know how they could contact High Command, all communications of course being jammed, so that they could ask for 'care packages' for us."

"Do they not know the meaning of war?" Kiuchep asked.

"Have you seen the gate area?" Bacajezh said. "They let me view it. From a porthole so it was clear it wasn't a computer generated image. Ships drifting everywhere. I think they have a *new* meaning of war."

"They did mention they were getting tired of picking up the scrap," Kiuchep said.

"That was another thing," Bacajezh said. "They showed me what they call the 'scrapyard' which is where all the *Horvath* ships ended up."

"And now ours are headed there," a commander muttered.

"This was a deliberate set-up," another said. "I don't know *who* it is High Command wanted out of the way..." he continued, looking at Pe'Sheshodac then Bacajezh.

"Enough of that," Bacajezh said. "I don't begin to know High Command's thinking. But I doubt they would throw away *this* much weight of ships to put aside a minor political inconvenience. There's poison for that sort of thing. The point is, we now have to deal with the conditions as they a—" He paused as the door opened.

"Pardon me, gentlemen," Lieutenant Gularte said. "We're having a bit of a space problem. And we don't have all the air systems repaired. So you're being transferred to Terra. If you could come with me, please?"

✴   ✴   ✴

"Man, it's a good thing we've got fuel," Hartman said as Dana pulled the shuttle out of the bay.

"I wonder if we can get some time on ground," Dana said.

"Just good to see the mudball again," Hartman said. "What's our destination?"

"They haven't told me, yet. Just head for Earth."

"What is this place?" Bacajezh said as he stepped out of the door of the shuttle.

It had, clearly, once been a city. They were on the very edge of the crater that was made when a KEW impacted. There had been many tall buildings, which now were twisted ruins. The air was clear and clean, the bombing was not recent, but the light wind from the sea whistled through devastation.

"This used to be called Los Angeles," Gularte said. "You should be fairly comfortable here for your... visit. The climate is mild with relatively rare rains. There is more than sufficient material to make shelters, obviously. There will be some hand tools coming along in time. We'll drop off food as we have it. Since terrestrial foods are not edible to you, any of you can feel free to run if you wish. In which case, you'll die of starvation. Oh, and there's not much water. We'll pump some in. We will also do our level best to keep the local population away. They have a hard time distinguishing between types of aliens. The Horvath did this but... squids, lizards? All the same to them."

"I am beginning to understand the human approach to kindness," Bacajezh said, looking around.

"I would suggest you and your staff get ready to get to work," Gularte said, walking back to the shuttle.

"We're going to be dropping off *all* your personnel in very short order. Some of them seem a little . . . perturbed by the outcome of the battle. What happens after that is entirely up to you."

"You okay, Dana?" Hartman asked as the shuttle started to climb back to orbit.

"I am five by five, EM," Dana said. "Five by five."

"Okay," Hartman said. "If you're sure."

"Looks pretty much the same as the last time I was here," Dana said. "'Cept it's not on fire."

"Missile ready?"

"Yes, sir," Captain Sharp said.

"Launch."

"Gate activation," the sensor technician said. "Inbound from Earth."

"At last!" Commander Jesij said. "I was wondering how long it was going to take them to send back a report."

"Longer than they were supposed to take," Captain Mexur said. The commander of the *Cofubof*-class cruiser *Thomud* had been getting nervous. It had been over sixteen hours since the task force had entered the Terran system.

"Missile!" the tech said. "Unknown class."

"Defensive systems," the captain ordered.

"The missile is not tracking," the defense officer said. "Say again, *not* tracking. It is broadcasting."

"Put it on."

"*Message to Rangora High Command. Repeat Message to Rangora High Command. Please send supplies for ninety thousand prisoners. Oh, and please keep sending us ships. It's easier than making them. Message to Rangora High Command..."*

"This is one message I *do not* want to deliver," Captain Mexur said.

"Congratulations, Colonel To'Jopeviq," Star Marshall Lhi'Kasishaj said as the officer entered his office.

"Colonel?" To'Jopeviq said. He had already noticed the new novas on Lhi'Kasishaj's epaulets. He sat down at a gesture from the Sky Marshall.

"It was the best I could do," Lhi'Kasishaj said, rippling his scales. "High Command balked at General. But we are back in business!"

"Yes, sir," To'Jopeviq said, totally confused.

"Ah, you have not heard the news," Lhi'Kasishaj said. "The humans sent a request through the gate for supplies for ninety thousand prisoners."

"The task force was defeated," To'Jopeviq said, bobbing his head in frustration.

"Of course," Lhi'Kasishaj said. "As you predicted. And while, as I noted, being right is often a very bad thing, when played right it can be a very good thing. And this was, I must admit, well played on my part. I have been given, again, authority for bringing the Terran system into submission. Sorry, liberating it from its oppressive governments and bringing unification for the good of all Terrans."

"I see," To'Jopeviq said, thoughtfully. "Ninety thousand. Ten thousand per *Aggressor*..."

"The number is clearly false," Lhi'Kasishaj said. "Don't let it trouble you."

"Are we sending supplies?" To'Jopeviq asked.

"Of course," Lhi'Kasishaj said. "Of course. Not your concern, of course. So, we must now prepare proper plans for the subjugation of the humans. I want updated intelligence. Everything you have."

"I will get right on it," To'Jopeviq said.

"It has been a very good day," Lhi'Kasishaj said as he left the office.

"Yes, sir."

"I *told* you!" Toer said, waving his hands and rippling his scales in frustration. "Didn't I tell you?!"

"And I told the Gen— Sky Marshall," To'Jopeviq said. "And he told High Command. Who ignored us. They are now asking for an updated intelligence profile."

"We don't *have* any new intelligence!" Toer said.

"We have the intelligence that the task force was defeated," Avama said pensively.

"That's negative intelligence!"

"Calm yourself, Toer," To'Jopeviq said. "It's useful, though. What does that tell us?"

"That they probably found a way to get power and fuel," Toer said. "Many possibilities. Long shot, they found another polity that is in support through one of their other connections. Most likely, they have their fuel plant in operation."

"What does that tell us of their current combat ability?" To'Jopeviq said.

"They have probably been proceeding with their work on *Troy*," Toer said. "I'm not sure about their construction rates . . ."

"They cannot be high," Avama said. "The Horvath attacks seriously damaged them. They must barely be able to feed themselves."

"That was not the indication we had prior to communications being cut off," To'Jopeviq said. "And it certainly doesn't appear to be the case from the results of this battle. Ninety thousand prisoners. What does that tell us?"

"Probably disinformation," Toer said. "To get that many, they had to have had *total* dominance of the task force. That would require *enormous* power and *very* capable missiles."

"Follow that to a logical conclusion," To'Jopeviq said.

"It's disinformation," Toer argued. "There is no way that that many Rangora survived unless our ships were easy for them to defeat. That's practically half the crews!"

"Still," To'Jopeviq said.

"Well..." Toer said. "They would have had to have both capable missiles, our penetrators or Glatun, as well as *a lot* of them. Or, they would have had to push enough power from their SAPL to overcome the shields and physical defenses of the ships with ease. Or both."

"What does that tell us?" To'Jopeviq said.

"The only way that that could happen is if they are either enormously capable engineers or the Glatun opened up their military tech base," Toer said pensively. "Maybe, if there was a mil-tech database in the fabber they got, they could hack it. But that's well outside their known tech ability. My professional input is that this is disinformation."

"Assume total dominance," To'Jopeviq said. "What else does that tell us? Not about their tech or the crews?"

"They captured many of the ships," Beor said, after a moment's quiet.

"Anything else?" To'Jopeviq asked.

"Seventy petawatts would not have done it," Toer said, musingly. "And they would have needed a lot of penetrators no matter what."

"What does a lot of penetrators and an increase in power tell us?" To'Jopeviq said.

"Big tech base," Toer said, quietly. "Bigger than they should have, unless..."

"Unless?" To'Jopeviq said.

"*If* they have full Glatun databases," Toer said, slowly. "And *if* the ship fabber in that Wolf system has more or less unlimited resources, and *if* their ground-based production was more distributed than we thought..." He paused and blinked.

"Yes?" To'Jopeviq said.

"I...need to think," Toer said. "I need to do some calculations. If we assume that they have all that... To'Jopeviq?"

"Yes?"

"I don't think *twenty* assault vectors are going to be enough."

TWENTY-SIX

"'They came at us in the same old way...'" Tyler said, taking a sip of Coke. He'd begun to notice a bit too much blood in his alcohol system lately.

"'And we defeated them in the same old way,'" Admiral Kinyon continued. "'What a terrible business.'"

The *Starfire* was watching the recovery process, which was going slowly. There was just too much to do. The *Myrmidons* were on their sixth day of picking up life pods. The *Troy* had stopped jamming and was now reassuring the survivors that they were going to be picked up as soon as someone could get to them.

The previous attack had included more ships. The newer Rangora battleships, though, were almost a third larger than the *Devastators*. They had also been hit with more missiles, which tended to scatter the debris.

The gate area was, once again, a minefield of drifting debris. Cleanup was going to take *forever*.

"We could just leave a bunch of this in the way," Tyler said. "That way, when the next attack comes through, *they'll* run into it."

"Their shields will push it off," the admiral said. "But it will hole a freighter."

"Just a thought," Tyler said. "The next time, though, could you be a bit more careful of the drive systems? Grav plates are expensive."

"I'll think about that," the admiral said. "Any way we could get another missile fabber? We ran through most of our missiles in this attack. That makes me... nervous."

"I'll see what I can do," Tyler said. "Don't want you feeling nervous."

"How long to get the *Aggressors* back in action?"

"We'll quit work on the *Devastators*," Tyler said. "They're not all that great anyway. We were looking at doing upgrades but it's tough. We might want to think about just scrapping them for materials. We've got both of the fabbers up and running. I'm continuing to devote part of their output to building Fabber Three. But we're also building a space dock. We'll pull the lightly damaged through to Wolf and get to work. Say... six months?"

"That long?" the admiral asked.

"It's all fiddly bits," Tyler said. "That takes time. Also trained personnel of which there is still a critical shortage. At this rate, though, we might as well not build ships. They're sending us more than we can use."

"They won't underestimate us the next time," the admiral pointed out.

"Bets?"

To'Jopeviq turned away from the holo of the victory celebration on Glatus as Beor entered his office.

"Lieutenant?" he said as she shut the door.

"That would be more along the lines of 'Yes, agent?'" Beor said, slipping a data crystal into his reader.

The view was the interior of an interrogation chamber. The Glatun showed no signs of torture, possibly because he was talking freely.

"Define what you mean by 'everything'?" the interrogator, whose voice was buzzed out and features were blurred, asked.

"Granadica had a full database of all our military systems," the Glatun said. *"I know that's the case 'cause I was the one who loaded the database. The order came from high up in corporate. I was told, I can't say it's true, but Como Gaff said that the humans had been given access codes. I don't know who authorized it. It would have had to be someone high in the Glatun military or some of the Benefactors. And they got a bunch of AIs from what I heard."*

"What would be in the database, exactly?"

"Everything?" the Glatun said, rippling his back mane. *"I mean, we were one of the main military contractors. What we didn't have in our own designs, we had access to from our competitors through the military. You know you don't build all of one thing with just one company . . ."*

"Damn," To'Jopeviq muttered. "Toer is right. We will *need* more than twenty assault vectors."

"This cannot be used for your analysis," Beor said. "Be clear about that. You are authorized access, but it cannot be included in your analysis."

"That's going to weaken our position," To'Jopeviq said. "With this . . . The humans had to have completed their mine, somehow, to be able to complete enough production to defeat the fleet. They are a serious threat. Not to the Imperium, but to any task force that enters their system."

"That may or may not be," Beor said. "But this is not authorized to be included in any analysis. It is background only. To support your analysis, based upon this, you will have to find other intelligence. There is one other factoid, though, which can be used."

"Which is?" To'Jopeviq asked.

"The humans are allowing the prisoners to send through short messages," Beor said. "Ten words, no more. And they appear to be very solid on censorship. If there is coded information in them, it is not apparent. Whether they are real or not is another question. But if they are not real, they at the very least have the full manifests for several ships. There are prisoners who are sending messages from all the ships but the *Vaghusigh*. The majority of the crew appears to have survived from eight *Aggressors*, two *Cofubof*, two *Gufesh* and three *Sheshibas*."

"They captured *eight Aggressors*?" To'Jopeviq said.

"Or they simply got their manifests," Beor said. "The lowest number of survivors, other than the *Vaghusigh*, are from the *Zhiphewich* and the *Ziyuzhim*. But Captain Bacajezh appears to have survived. There was a message from him to his wife, anyway."

"I take it they are not going to the recipients," To'Jopeviq said.

"Of course not," Beor said. "And have someone piece together that we lost sixteen *Aggressors* to a minor system? We are not stupid."

"What are the humans playing at?" To'Jopeviq said. "This makes no sense! There is still the possibility of our people using it to pass information! And the trouble of keeping so many prisoners? I *wish* I could understand them."

"So do I," Beor said. "Try."

"Are we sending the supplies?" To'Jopeviq said.

"Yes," Beor said. "There's no point in not doing so. It is a trivial expense. What they will do with them all is the question. It's not as if they can eat it."

Dana worked her fingers nervously for just a second, holding them up in front of the hatch, opening and closing into a fist. She started to turn away, then she knocked, twice, hard.

"Come!"

Dana opened the hatch, stepped in, closed it and came to attention.

"Coxswain's Mate Third Class reporting to the Chief," Dana said. "On open door policy."

"Go?" Chief Barnett said, leaning back. "Not an EEOC complaint, I hope."

"No, Chief," Dana said. "I . . . I would like to talk to you. It's that or the shrinks."

"The prisoner detail?" Barnett said, blowing out. "Sit, Dana."

"Yes, Chief," Dana said, sitting down.

"I was glad to hear you made Three," Barnett said, interlocking her fingers behind her head. "And when I got the word what our mission was, I almost tried to figure out a way to excuse your boat."

"No matter which city they dumped them into," Dana said, "there was going to be someone who'd lost someone there. Other people in the Flight lost family in the L.A. basin."

"Not many walked out of it when they were three," Barnett said, leaning back up. "So what's the status of your system, Comet?"

"Fluctuations," Dana said, breathing deeply. "I'm dealing with a lot of anger. It's like it's started the grief cycle all over again. I'm getting really snappish. I nearly lost it with Thermal the other day. Nothing major, just another joke. He was just treating me like one of the guys. Not even... Not really over the line. Same sort of thing we normally joke about. And I nearly went off."

"Going off on your superiors is frowned upon," Chief Barnett pointed out.

"Aye, aye, Chief," Dana said. "Was one reason I didn't. But the real point is that it wasn't anything to lose it over. I was just ready to."

"With all the wonders we have of modern medicine," Barnett said, "with all the Glatun technology we have assimilated, there is still no good cure for PTSD. All the shrinks can do is treat the symptoms. Depression, sleep issues..."

"Understood, Chief," Dana said.

"And if I send you to the shrinks, you're off status," Barnett said. "Which means I'd prefer not to do that. On the other hand, I don't want someone who's going to lose it driving a boat."

"Which is why I'm here," Dana said.

"You want to turn in your wheel?"

The symbol of being a qualified coxswain was a gold badge of an old-fashioned sailing ship tiller-wheel.

"I want help deciding," Dana said.

"You want somebody to talk to about it," the chief corrected. "Which we're not going to do here and now. You're not on schedule for today so try to hold onto your temper for the rest of the watch. There's an 'unofficial' bar in the civvie section, Murphy's. You know it?"

"I can find it," Dana said.

"Meet me there at nineteen hundred," Barnett said. "Meeting adjourned."

"Aye, aye, Chief," Dana said, standing up.

"And, Dana?"

"Chief?"

"Seriously, hold on. We need every good sailor we can find."

"Aye, aye, Chief."

"We need to get an alien brig or something," Tyler said, watching the arriving cargo containers.

Communication, of a sort, had been affected between the Rangora and Earth. Each side would send through a missile with a message. The missiles would not be returned. It was expected that the Rangora were tearing the missiles apart to find out anything they could about Earth tech. Which was why they were being made groundside by Morton-Thiokol and were chemical rockets. Let them try to figure out something from that.

But the first part of the exchange was complete. They'd sent through shipping containers, just those, containing food and other supplies for the prisoners. They'd have to be checked and cross-loaded then taken to Earth. Just another damned thing.

"What, that's not already on the plans?" Nathan asked.

"Not yet," Tyler said. "So... *Thermopylae*?"

"Cooled," Nathan said. "We've got it moving in-system. Minimally operational in three months."

"Good, good," Tyler said. "I want..." He paused as the battlestation shuddered. "What the *hell*?" he asked as alarms started to wail.

* * *

"What in hell just happened?" Admiral Kinyon asked. He was going to have to get new uniforms designed. Tucking in his shirt on the run was getting old.

"The cargo just exploded," Colonel Helberger said. "It just blew up."

"Casualties?" Kinyon asked.

"Zero," the damage control technician said. "It was already in the automated cargo section. Bots were opening it up to begin transfer. We lost a bunch of bots, but that's it."

"Nature of explosion?" the admiral asked.

"Unknown at this time," Helberger said. "Could have been nuclear or antimatter."

"Are they *insane?*" the admiral snarled. "How much damage?"

"Contained to the cargo handling area," the damage control tech said. "I've got the readings. Nuclear. Clean induced fusion reaction. Thirty megatons. Appears to have been in one container. As to damage . . . there *is* no cargo handling section anymore, sir. But that's pretty much it, sir."

"*Contained?*" the admiral said. "No venting? No . . . ? *Contained?*"

"Blast doors stopped it, sir," the damage control tech said. "Some venting through overpressure blow-offs but no damage other than the cargo area."

"Just when I think this thing can't surprise me," Admiral Kinyon said, patting a console. "Good girl. Good *Troy* . . ."

"Those Rangora *bastards!*" Tyler said, looking at the data. "They killed my *cargo system!*"

"More like *my* cargo system, sir," Paris said. "With the current personnel and equipment level of the *Troy*, building a new one is a priority. We are having to accept enormous amounts of cargo to maintain function. The good news is that the containment system held. And, of course, that they used clean bombs so there's no residual irradiation. Effectively, we can burn it out and build a bigger cargo area. We'll have to move the—"

"Paris," Tyler said. "Whoa. There's no such thing as a totally clean nuclear chain reaction. We're going to have to cut out the irradiated portions—"

"Excuse me, sir," Paris said. "I beg to differ. But the system was a non-fissile pumped helium three-helium three fusion bomb. They release no ionizing radiation. Just neutrinos and plasma. There is no residual radiation to deal with. We can work with the expanded hole they created."

"Really?" Tyler asked dubiously. "We're not just talking about 'clean' like a neutron bomb that's pretty clean but *totally* clean? Absolutely *no* ionizing radiation?"

"Sir . . ." Paris said. "You normally have a fairly encyclopedic knowledge of this sort of thing for a human. You were unaware this was possible? There was no ionizing radiation. The area is thermally hot but radioactively neutral."

"Huh," Tyler said, leaning forward conspiratorially. "Can *we* make these?" he whispered.

"Yes, sir," Paris whispered back. "It was what Apollo used to move the *Troy* in the first place."

"How big?" Tyler whispered.

"Up to about two hundred megatons," Paris said. "Can we stop whispering now?"

"Yeah," Tyler said, leaning back and grimacing. "Uh! I'm an *idiot!*"

"Sir?"

"Something somebody was trying to tell me I can't remember who 'cause I dismissed 'em 'cause I'm an *idiot!*" Tyler said. "Because I'm a know-it-all idiot! I can't even remember who it *was*! It was just some *guy*! And I didn't *listen*! And they were right and I'm an idiot!"

"Yes, sir?" Paris said, dubiously. "Are you okay, sir?"

"Paris, we need to do a *major* rebuild of the *Troy*," Tyler said. "Get me Nathan on the double."

"Are you going to discuss this rebuild with Admiral Kinyon or, say, Space Command?" Paris asked.

"When have I *ever* discussed things, Paris?" Tyler said. "Oh, hell, no. They'd call me crazy."

"Does this rebuild mean what I think it means?"

"If you're thinking something that starts with an O and ends in an N and involves a lot of *really* big booms?" Tyler said. "Yes."

"With all due respect, Mr. Vernon, you're crazy."

"See? See?"

"Good girl," Chief Barnett said. "Right on time."

Dana hadn't even realized the chief *had* civilian clothes on the *Troy*. Parker had worn her uniform.

The chief was in a slinky red cocktail dress that showed off more cleavage than any one woman should own.

"Uh . . . hi?" Dana said, sitting down at the table.

The bar was in what looked as if it was intended as a storage locker. Tables and chairs, some of them welded from scrap, and a bar made out of what looked like a section of hull metal from a Horvath ship, had been installed. Most of the people in the bar were civilian men, probably Apollo workers from the look, and they were considering the two women like wolves confused by a couple of sheep who had wandered into the pack.

"It's self serve," the chief said. "I'll take a Budweiser longneck. Get whatever you want. I've got a tab. Get two of each."

"Aye, aye, Chief," Dana said.

As she walked to the bar she sensed more than saw the hand headed for her butt. A forearm well trained in nullball smacked it away almost without thought. There was a chuckle from behind her, which she ignored.

She made it back without being groped and set the drinks on the table.

"Why . . . here?" Dana asked.

"There's an old saying in the Navy," Barnett said, then took a long suck off the beer. "Keep your indiscretions a hundred miles from the flagpole. Technically, for just mentioning that you were on the edge of being a hazard, I'm required to pull you off status."

"Oh," Dana said.

"So here we can have a quiet conversation that if not a hundred miles from the flagpole is close as we can get," Barnett said. "At a certain point, I will call your boyfriend and his squad for extraction. There will, then, be a bar fight. I get to get *my* issues out kicking some civilian ass."

Dana leaned over and looked under the table. The chief was wearing four-inch pumps.

"What?" the chief said then took another drink. That pretty much finished the bottle. "You think I can't kick ass in high heels? Twenty-three years. I've been in pretty much every minor dust-up the Navy's had since before 9/11. Was a Seaman on the *Cole*, which was no picnic. Small boat security operations in the Gulf during OIF. Fought some Somali pirates. And, girl, I've been in fights in every port the Navy used and some it didn't. And when the dust settles, I'll pick out the guy who seems to be the toughest and get some more issues out by dragging him back to my quarters by his hair."

"Good God, Chief," Dana said, giggling.

"I understand you have a friend amongst the Marines," Barnett said.

"Yes, Chief," Dana said. "Andrew Ramage. Just made corporal."

"Good girl," Barnett said, starting on her next beer. "There are two kinds of girls in the Navy who get a lot, MWR issue and warriors."

"MWR?" Dana said.

"Like checking out a nullball kit. Check 'em out of stores, use 'em, put 'em back."

"Oh."

"Then there are girls like us," Barnett said. "Army general back in the Civil War said a soldier who won't engage in sexual relations will not engage in combat relations, if you get my drift. Shorter than that."

"Got it, Chief."

"There are some warriors who don't," Barnett said, shrugging. She took another long pull. "Mostly 'cause of moral issues. Lots of Christians in the Navy."

"Yep," Dana said.

"But most get some. Boys and girls. Most get a lot. But there's the other way around, too."

"I . . . what?"

"You said you were angry," Barnett said, gesturing around with her chin. "Here's a virgin playing field, pardon the pun."

"So . . . you're saying that your prescription for handling PTSD is a *bar fight*?" Dana asked.

"Bar fight," Barnett said. "Sex. Whatever it takes to set you right for the next day's mission, girl. Because that's the real job. Being right for the next day and completing the mission. This isn't a gay bar in San Francisco where you can 'be yourself,' whatever self that may be. This is the Navy. And it's all about being what you *have* to be to complete the mission. Doesn't matter what that is. Just so you complete the mission. So . . . what's it going to be?"

Dana looked at her rum and Coke and drained it. Then she picked up the next one and drained that.

"I'm not going to hold out long at this rate," she said.

"It's okay," Barnett said. "The Marines are already on their way."

"Hey, ladies." The guy was absolutely huge, but that meant he could hold the six drinks he was carrying. "You looking for some company?"

"I t'ink I bro' my no'be," Dana said drunkenly. It was certainly bleeding enough.

"*Told* you to keep your hands up," Chief Barnett said. If the dozen beers had affected her it wasn't apparent. The big dude she was dragging along was similarly unaffected. At least by the shots of tequila he'd been downing. "But that flying kick off the pole was a thing of beauty."

"I'm still trying to figure out if I'm pissed off or

turned on by the dance," Rammer said. He was having to hold Dana up as she caromed down the corridor. "And I hope like hell this doesn't end up with us at Mast."

"Never make Gunny if you don't have at *least* one," Barnett said. "Well, children, it has been fun but BFM and me got a date. Marines, I take it this little incident is *not* going to be a thing of barracks gossip."

"No, Chief," Father said. "All clear, Chief."

"Toodles," she said, dragging the welder down a corridor.

"Christ," Father said. "I didn't know the Navy still made 'em like that. Wonder if she knows Gunny Brimage?"

"Pro'ly Bi'licly," Dana said. "Where are we?"

"Nearly home, Comet," Ramage said.

"Goo'. Hey, Fa'er? Hope you don't mind but..."

"Nope," Patricelli said, grinning. "I can see you two have some catching up to do. And, by the way, the *next* time you start a fight in a room full of welders, feel free to call. I haven't had so much fun since my first shore leave in Thailand. Later."

"Hey, Butch, you okay?" BFM asked.

"No," Butch said, rolling out of his bunk. He had a beauty of a shiner. "*I* got my ass kicked. And *you* got the girl. I am *doubly* not okay."

"Yeah, well, quit yer bitchin'," Price said, dragging him to his feet. "I need some coffee 'cause I got exactly *no* sleep last night and we're on shift in an hour."

"You are *such* a buddy," Butch said. "A *real* buddy would have at least brought Motrin."

"Got 'em right here," Price said, holding out a handful. "Now let's go get some breakfast."

✳   ✳   ✳

"I've got three degrees in international relations," the newly sworn-in President said, rubbing her forehead. "I've got twenty years of experience in foreign affairs. I've been an envoy to the Glatun. I've met with the Rangora on several occasions, prior to the war." She looked up at the War Cabinet in frustration. "Why can't I understand these people?"

The Constitution gave the Congress the job of determining succession of the Presidency in the event of death or "constitutional inability" of the President. In 1947 they established the first Succession Act laying out that the succession was to be Vice President, then speaker of the House, then president pro tem of the Senate, then down through the cabinet in order of creation of the position.

With all of the top four taken out by the Rangora leadership strikes, the secretary of state had been sworn in as President.

There was a secondary position, the national constitutional continuity coordinator, which was established by presidential directive and generally classified. It designated a series of persons, in order, to assume, temporarily, the position of Commander-In-Chief to ensure the orderly transition of power.

The Chairman of the Joint Chiefs had, therefore, been acting President for about three hours until the chief justice could be hooked up with the SecState and swear her in. Nobody was really mentioning that much.

"According to the prisoners who have been questioned in regards to this attack," the Chairman of the Joint Chiefs said over the video link, "the Rangora High Command probably does not believe that we captured all the personnel we claim we've captured. Apparently, disinformation is a way of life in wars between these cultures."

"That's apparent from the news we've been getting from the Rangora," the national security advisor said.

The Rangora had continued to broadcast triumphant bulletins about their conquest of the Glatun. In all of them, the Glatun were shown as welcoming their Rangora "liberators" with open arms. Just the last week, there had been a huge victory celebration on Glatus, the Glatun home world, which had "not surrendered but freely welcomed their Rangora allies."

No mention of the attack on Earth, however, and several Glatun systems that were known to have heavy defenses were also, curiously, missing from the broadcasts.

"Ma'am," the Army Chief of Staff said. "Have you ever dealt with the North Koreans?"

"Never had the pleasure," the President said dryly. Despite alien attacks and invasions, the Korean Peninsula was still split. And the North Koreans were making new noises about nuclear weapons and asking for food and energy systems. With most of America's ports rubble, they weren't getting as much attention as normal.

"There is a story I was told as a lieutenant," the general said. "Possibly apocryphal but with a core of truth. A North Korean general was visiting the South and as they were driving down the main boulevard in Seoul, he was looking around at the skyscrapers with some interest. They finally turned a corner and he sort of grunted in surprise. 'Yes?' the South Korean general asked. 'You go to much trouble,' the North

Korean said. 'We generally only build the facades on the front.'"

"He couldn't accept that the buildings were real and, furthermore, filled with working people," the President said. "Yes, you have a point. We're talking past each other due to lack of frame reference. I'm not sure how to correct that."

"I'm not sure we should, ma'am," the director of national intelligence said slowly. "Currently, the Rangora underestimate us because they don't believe we have the capabilities we've suggested by capturing most of their task force instead of being forced to destroy it. Being underestimated is, in my opinion, better than being overestimated or properly estimated."

"They'll keep trying to take us," the CJCS said. "If they knew what they were up against, we might be able to come to some sort of a truce."

"I would find that unlikely with the Rangora," the NSA said. "They're riding on a wave of euphoria from their conquests. Given their success to date, given any sort of reality to the broadcasts, they're not going to think twice about knocking off a minor planet like Earth."

"They had *better* think twice," the President said. "Gentlemen, I don't think there is any question that *Troy* has saved this system twice. We need to concentrate on reinforcing *Troy* and getting *Thermopylae* online. That should be absolute first priority."

"Ma'am," the CJCS said uncomfortably. "We have a number of systems—"

"Absolute first priority," the President said. "The only thing that should affect that precedence is reinforcement of the orbital defenses. Are we clear, gentlemen?"

."Yes, ma'am," the secretary of defense said, looking at the officers. "We are clear."

"Status of shift to Alliance forces?" the President asked.

"We have some of the first groups completing training at the moment, ma'am," the SecDef said. "We are going to begin the integration process in the next month. We anticipate a smooth transition."

"Hah," the President said. "Who are you kidding?"

TWENTY-SEVEN

"Give the fat guy another of whatever he's drinking," Dana said, sliding into the seat left of Erickson. There was a lady sitting to his right.

"I am not fat," Erickson protested. "I'm big boned."

"Okay," Dana said, grinning at the new *female* bartender. That was a change. "Give the hairy guy another of whatever he's drinking. And I'll take a rum and Coke."

"Guinness!" Rammer said, holding up a finger.

"Make that three," Patricelli said.

Getting time off wasn't easy on the *Troy* but when they had the time the same group tended to meet at the Acapulco. Erickson had managed to take Dana's preference for Rammer in stride. And since he had a lady with him this time . . .

"I'm Dana," Dana said, leaning over to look at the newcomer. "Since Wardog can't seem to remember my name. This is Rammer and Father."

"Esmeralda Steere, Coxswain Mate Third Class Dana Parker," Erickson said. "Comet, Esme. She introduced the Marines."

"Pleased to meet you," Esmeralda said, holding

376

out her hand. She frowned after a moment, though. "Comet?"

"Long story," Dana said.

"And, by the way, Wardog," Rammer said. "That would be Coxswain's Mate *Second* Class."

"Spoken like a proud boyfriend," Erickson said, holding up his glass. "I raise a toast! To our newest E-5! May she occasionally manage to avoid the edges of space!"

"Hell, yeah," Rammer said.

"And to the *Troy*," Dana said. "May she continue to make messes even if we have to clean them up."

"I'll drink to that," Father said. "And, last, to the first President never to have run for office."

"The Commander-Pro-Tempore," Erickson said, raising his glass.

"Huh?" Rammer said.

"Temporary Commander-In-Chief," Dana said.

"Oh," Rammer said. "What the hell were the Rangora thinking? They dropped two KEWs on open farmland!"

"One of which hit *uncomfortably* close to my aunt and uncle's house," Dana said.

"Two on open farmland, one in the Irish Sea," Erickson pointed out. "Aliens. I guess they figured if they took out our leadership they'd destabilize us or something."

"And can we change the subject?" Esme said. "I know that for the rest of you, war is a way of life. But I'm here to *enjoy* myself."

"So where'd you meet the hairy one?" Dana asked, leaning around Erickson.

"I just transferred up here," Esmeralda replied. Probably low forties but "well-preserved," she was honey-blond. Almost certainly from a bottle but she had the basic coloring for it. "I'm with LFD, which is the parent company of Apollo. I'm an accountant."

"Who is now nickel and diming my department to *death*!" Erickson said.

"Oh, hush," the woman replied.

"But, CM2 Parker," Erickson said. "I *must* ask a question. You are sporting two remarkable shiners."

"Slipped in the shower and banged my nobe," Dana said, by rote.

The corpsmen had managed to fix the nose, which was only *slightly* broken, right up. And there were new drug regimens that would have had the swelling gone in no time. But the PA had muttered something about "reminding her not to make me more work."

"So it had *nothing* to do with 'two Navy she-bitches and a platoon of Marines' invading Murphy's?" Erickson said.

"Not a thing," Father said. "And, for the record, it was two Marines."

"Sorry to mention this," Erickson said. "But I am a Marine. Former. And knowing the welders on this station, you don't look like you'd last long."

"My first tour was in Recon," Father said. "My *second* tour, after my first divorce, was in Force Recon. My third was in the Fallujah after my *second* divorce. This is my . . . fifth?"

"Ah," Erickson said. "One of those."

"But I must admit that we would have had much trouble were it not for a certain Navy chief, and local partisans, who assisted."

"Assisted?" Barnett said from over his shoulder. "*Assisted*?"

Dana turned around, then turned back quickly, covering her eyes.

"Holy Gods, Chief!" Dana said, giggling. "I mean... really!"

Barnett was wearing a purple bikini with hot pink polka dots. Dana didn't even know they *made* bikini tops in *Troy* size.

"Just 'cause *you* want to wear a shirt," Barnett said. "Ah, speaking of local partisans."

"Hey, hottie," BFM said, slipping his hand under the water to give the chief a squeeze. "You with anybody?"

"Sure am, BF," Barnett purred.

"Oh, this is just..." Dana said, shaking her head.

"Wrong?" Father finished.

"Get a *room*, Chief," Dana said, giggling again.

"Oh, like *you're* one to talk," Barnett said, breast-stroking over to the other side of the bar. BF could just walk. "Hey, gal, set me and my friend up some longnecks, will ya?"

"Esme, Bill, my Squadron Flight NCOIC, Chief Barnett," Dana said, waving at the chief. "And her... friend...?"

"Ben Price," BFM said. "Price or BF. We didn't really get much of chance to chat the other night."

"Call me Liz," Barnett said, picking up her beer and half draining it. "Ah, that hit the spot. If I never see another piece of Rangora scrap, it will be *too* soon."

"Amen," Dana said. "At least we finally got all the prisoners picked up."

"Picking up prisoners and scrap is better than the alternative," Erickson pointed out.

"This is true," Barnett said. "And at least they targeted leadership. Now if the *rest* of the world's leaders would learn to stay out of cities we'd be cooking with fuel oil." She looked over at Esme and raised and eyebrow. "You find that...cynical?"

"I've never really had much experience with the military," Esme said, frowning in thought. "I mean, the first guy I ever dated who's been in the military was Bill. So I'm sort of trying to..."

"Adjust?" Barnett said.

"I'm not *against* the military," Esme said. "But the last person in my family who was in the military was my granddad in World War II. And now I'm spending half my time dealing with sailors and Marines or..." She looked at Bill and grinned. "Guys who can get out of the Marines but not get the Marine out if you know what I mean."

"The job of the Marines is to protect civilians," Patricelli said. "And one of our special tasks is protecting the President. But there's not much we can do about KEWs. So I hope you understand that while we joke, we're not really happy about the situation."

"I don't understand why we *can't* stop them," Esme said. "I mean, there's *Troy* and all the orbital defenses we've been spending money on. Why can't you *stop* them?"

"Well, uhm," Dana said. "I drive a boat. So not only is it not my job..."

"Think about an absolutely black room," the chief said. "You ever been in absolute darkness? No matter how close you get your hand to your face, you can't see it?"

"When I can't find the light-switch here, yes," Esme said.

"Now, in that room is a wasp that doesn't hum,"

Barnett said, taking a careful swig off her beer. "It can be anywhere in the room. And it's closing on you. And when it stings you, it's going to kill you."

"I don't like the thought," Esme said. "But...okay."

"Nobody likes the thought," Barnett said. "Just some people can think about it without their brains turning off. Some can't. You still with me?"

"Yes," Esme said. "Dark room. Killer wasp."

"You have in your hand a laser pointer," Barnett said. "The light doesn't scatter at all but if you hit the wasp, it kills it. How hard is it to hit the wasp?"

"Impossible," Esme said. "But is it really..."

"Harder," Erickson said. "Much much harder."

"The wasp makes a little bit of sound when it first enters the room," Barnett said. "And then when it gets about an inch from your skin. And you actually have a bunch of laser pointers, too many for a human to handle, and a whole bunch of wasp sensors that if the wasp nearly hits them can detect it. And the room is about the size of a football stadium."

"The fact that we get any of them is the surprising part," Father said. "And by 'we' I mean Athena and Paris."

"Hey, we do *some* stuff!" a guy on the other side of the bar said. He was tall, black as the ace of spades and probably in his mid thirties. Also, Dana had to admit, pretty good looking. He was accompanied by a brunette who had to be at least five years younger.

"Who are you?" Erickson asked.

"Jim Sharp," the guy said. "I work in the command center. And, Chief, was it?"

"Yes, sir," Chief Barnett said.

"That was a pretty good analogy."

"I've been working on it, sir," Barnett said, precisely.

"What's with the chief?" Rammer whispered.

"Dunno," Dana replied.

"No rank in the mess, Chief," Sharp said, grinning. "Definitely no rank at the Acapulco."

"Yes, sir," the chief said.

"I'm the chief tactical officer of the *Troy*," Sharp said. "Since the chief clearly recognizes me, being incognito is out."

"Wait," Dana said, blanching. "Captain James Sharp?"

"The same," Jim said, shrugging. "Hey, I just came down for a beer and a swim. Like I said, no rank in the mess. Please. And *you* are the famous Comet Parker?"

"Famous?" Esme said.

"Uh, yes, sir," Dana replied.

"That was an *amazing* display of boat handling, Comet," Sharp said. "Even the admiral thought so. We weren't quite taking bets on whether you'd make it, but everybody was rooting for you."

"Thank you, sir," Dana said.

"So about the problem of the missiles," Sharp said. "The chief's analogy is pretty good. The Rangora threw one hundred and thirty-eight missiles at Earth, more than any of the Horvath attacks. Ninety-three made it through *Troy's* pocket, the area around the gate. *While*, I might add, we were having to fight more throw-weight than anyone had ever *seen* in this system. We had to divert some of the SAPL to engage the missiles, which slowed down stopping the Rangora who were *still* throwing missiles... It's a tough call every time. But ninety-three made it through.

"Athena stopped all but twenty-five of those in their

coast phase, when they're nearly impossible to detect. Which was *way* over what we thought she could do. Our estimate was that sixty to seventy should have survived to secondary boost phase.

"*Sixteen* initially targeted U.S. leadership and went active. The orbital BDA clusters got seven. The other nine hit the top four leadership targets, three of our remaining cities and two bases. Of the remaining nine, three targeted the British PM who was on the 'protected' list under the Alliance contract. Only one made it through but it unfortunately got the PM. No other damage in Britain.

"Six targeted other world leaders. Three of those six were destroyed by the BDAs. Of the remaining three, one got the premier of China, one the PM of Russia and one the PM of France. The targeted countries of those remaining six were China, Russia, India, France, Brazil and Australia, presumably all going for leadership targets. All the Allied country missiles got stopped."

Dana thought about that for a bit and then frowned.

"That sort of looks like we *deliberately* let non-Allied leadership get killed," Esme said dubiously.

"Just what I was thinking," Dana said.

"When we lost our own *President*?" Erickson said angrily.

"The point is being made by the international media," Sharp said, shrugging. "And the response is what... Sorry... you are?"

"Bill Erickson, sir," Bill said. "I work for Apollo."

"What Mister Erickson said," Sharp said. "We lost our entire upper leadership, more cities and two bases. We sure as hell were trying to stop the missiles. But the Alliance contract is precise. First defense goes to Alliance countries. Which is why when single missiles were targeted on Alliance leadership, we were able to stop them."

"That should put some teeth in the choice to join the Alliance or not," Bill said.

"It was not a deliberate choice," Sharp said. "The fortunes of war and what we'd said were the parameters of the Alliance, yes. So . . . yes, it puts some teeth into it. The fact is, though, that three of those last missiles *were* going to get through. And they *got* the President and the PM of Britain, both Alliance countries. Being part of the Alliance is no surety of survival for leadership."

"Has . . ." Chief Barnett said thoughtfully. "Has anyone analyzed the targeting parameters, sir?"

"You hit the nose, Chief," Sharp said, grinning. "Squarely on the nose."

"What do you mean?" Esme said.

"The Rangora don't like the U.S. and Britain," Father Patricelli said. "They want to get Terra to surrender by targeting our leadership overall. But they really *hate* the U.S. and Britain."

"Ta-da," Sharp said, nodding. "That took a team of analysts about a week to agree upon. And it's less hate than have a rational view, a *surprisingly* rational view, of the relative dangers to them of the different nations of Earth. China and Russia should have been equally valid targets. The Rangora, though, don't view them that way."

"So by fighting them, we're making ourselves targets?" Esme said. "I'm not sure it's a good idea to fight, then."

"Fight or be slaves," Patricelli said, shrugging. "Live free or die."

"But people are doing *both*," Esme said. "And in

case it's not apparent, nobody *here* is dying! People on *Earth* are dying!"

"We lost three boats in that last action, miss," the chief growled.

"There has to be an answer," Esme said.

"There is," Sharp said. "A really easy one except there's no way to do it."

"Which is?" Dana asked. "Sorry, which is, sir?"

"Load the *Troy* up with enough internal systems that she can fight without the SAPL and hold a system against a Rangora fleet of any conceivable size," Sharp said. "Then, somehow, move her through the gate into the E Eridani system and hold the gate from there."

"So... Why aren't we doing it?" Esme said.

She looked sort of cross when all the military personnel started to giggle. Even the brunette with Captain Sharp was giggling. BFM, to his honor, was simply chuckling.

"What's so funny?" the accountant asked angrily.

"Heh," Chief Barnett said, wiping her eyes. "You're an accountant, right?"

"Yes," Esme said.

"So you can do math," Barnett said. "You pretty good at doing it in your head or you need a calculator?"

"I've got implants," Esme said icily.

"Is that what those are called?" Barnett said. "Okay, here's the numbers. The *Troy* weighs two point two trillion tons. That's two point two followed by—"

"Nine zeroes," Esme said. "I know it's *large*..."

"Wait, wait," Barnett said, holding up her hand. "You asked, I'm letting *you* figure it out. The SAPL, furthermore, is up to... What? A hundred petawatts? Is it classified?"

"It is not," Sharp said. "One twenty."

"One hundred and twenty petawatts," Barnett said. "Now, a *watt* is one joule per second. A joule is a Newton meter and a Newton is a kilogram meter per second squared."

"What?" Esme said.

"I need a whiteboard," Barnett said.

"You must have been an A school instructor," Dana said. "Esme, you know the *Myrms* we drive?"

"Yes," Esme said.

"And you probably know to a cent how much they cost," Dana said. "Chief, how many *Myrms* would it take to give the *Troy* one gravity of acceleration?"

"Easy," Barnett said. "Eighty-four million and change."

"*Impossible*," Esme snapped. "You made that up."

"Okay, genius, *you* do the math," Barnett said. "Two point two trillion tons divided by the weight of a shuttle..."

"Sixty tons," Dana said.

"Divided by four hundred gravities of acceleration," Barnett finished.

The accountant closed her eyes for a second then shook her head.

"I still can't believe that," she said, her mouth tight.

"It's fricking *math*!" Barnett said. "You're an *accountant*! Don't tell me you can't do the math!"

"I'm leaving," Esme said. "I don't have to put up with this."

"What?" Barnett shouted to her back. "*Logic*? Sorry, Bill."

"It's okay," Bill said. "I was getting tired of her attitude anyway."

"People like that just piss me off," Barnett said.

"What, Democrats?" Rammer asked.

"*I* usually vote Democrat, sonny," the chief said. "And not liberals, neither. You find people who just will *not* follow the logic everywhere. They don't like the answer so they think *wishing* makes it so. Conservatives have got the same problem. Talk to one of them about prostitution, gambling or drugs."

"Abortion," Dana said.

"There you go," the chief said. "My body, my choice. *Cannot* do the logic. It's not just a liberal thing. Moving the *Troy*? Cannot do the math 'cause their brains shut down."

"*I* wasn't laughing because you can't get the *Troy* to move," the brunette with Sharp said. "You can. You can even build a drive for it. One that would give it . . . oh, up to six gravities of acceleration."

"B—*what*?" Barnett said. "*Impossible!*"

"Do the math, Chief," the girl said, grinning. "Or, rather, I *can* do the math. And, no, it's not impossible. Difficult? My dad would refer to it as 'fiddly bits.' There's just one problem."

"Which is?" Dana asked.

"Hello!" the girl said, waving her hands around. "We're in a pool! In the middle of the vessel, for want of a better word. Can you say 'Slosh,' Chief?"

"How in the hell are you proposing to move the *Troy*, honey?" Barnett asked. "You sort of skipped that bit."

"That's for me to know and you to figure out, Chief," the girl said, grinning. "And when you figure it out, try to figure out how to install inertics on the whole system. *That* is the biggest issue. All the rest is . . . fiddly bits."

TWENTY-EIGHT

"You're kidding," Nathan said.

"No, I'm not," Tyler replied. "When have I *ever* kidded about something like this?"

Tyler was not much of a draftsman but Nathan was by now used to working from his very rough ideas. And it wasn't like the former "Minor Planetary Objects" expert didn't know the idea.

"Tyler," Nathan said, carefully. "The *Troy* is not *designed* to move."

"It's got to be moved sooner or later," Tyler said. "It's already nearly completely out of position. And not just the *Troy*. I want the same system on *Thermopylae*."

"*Two* Orion drives?" Nathan practically shrieked. "Okay, I give up. Everyone's right. You're not kidding, you're *insane*!"

The idea was simple and went back to the early days of the space program, *and* the nuclear program, back when people were just fine with thinking big. And scary.

Orion worked best *large*. Make a very big platform, which they already had with *Troy*. Put a scary large plate under it. Orion was originally conceived as a lift drive to get out of the atmosphere. Connect the plate to the platform with some very large and robust springs.

Then set off a nuke on the plate.

The plate, obviously, had to be large enough and robust enough to survive being hit by the blast front from a nuclear weapon. And the springs had to be... large. But it would recoil, push the springs, the springs would push the platform and you had acceleration.

Repeat, quickly, and the platform moved.

"It's really simple," Tyler said, pointing to the diagram. "We cut off the inside of the door for the pusher plate. It's already curved. We'll have to install a chute for the nukes, but that's just fiddly bits. Install it on the outside of the door. It's big enough to take the little bit of accel we're going to get. We'll need to put in more locking bars to handle the pressure. The *springs* are going to be sort of challenging..."

"Tyler..." Nathan said gently.

"I want it done in a month, so you'd better quit talking and get to work," Tyler said.

"Now that's just *silly*," Nathan said. "I mean, I don't even know how we're going to make the *springs*. Steel, sure. *Spring* steel? Wound?"

"Ah-*hah*!" Tyler said. "You're already starting to figure out how to do it! Knew it!"

"That doesn't mean I think it's a good idea!" Nathan said. "The impact is—"

"We're not going to use *big* nukes," Tyler said. "Not at first. Just a bit of a tap. Repeated. You know a good guy for pumped fusion bombs?"

"Sure," Nathan said. "Dr. DeWolfe, same guy we used when we— Hey!"

"Seriously, Nathan," Tyler said, waving his hand at the door. "This is a big project. You're going to need to get going. Oh, and we're going to have to accelerate production on the large vessels bypass and the heavy laser program."

"Oh, *that's* all," Nathan said. "Like two major projects aren't enough?"

"Nathan," Tyler said, smiling thinly. "The Rangora have apparently conquered the Glatun. We wiped the floor with one of their task forces. They're not going to take that lying down. So the quicker you stop talking, the faster we can get this done."

"It's going to cost a lot of money," Nathan said.

"I'll get the money," Tyler said. "I want the drives, the lasers and the bypass done in no more than three months. I don't care what it takes. Just get it done."

"Right," Nathan said thoughtfully. "Right. Orion. From scratch. Rebuild the door system to take the delta. Springs the size of... Bigger than anything I can think of off hand. Increase the rate of installation of the internal laser systems. Large vessel bypass. Yeah, that's going to be a necessity. We're going to have to remove all the power systems and grav plates we've already installed on the door..."

"There you go," Tyler said, pulling him to his feet and walking him to the door. "Now you're cooking with fuel oil. If you need anything, you've got my number..."

"There," Tyler said, shutting the door and brushing his hands. "It's all about people. Speaking of people..."

"Butch," Price said, looking in the welder's room. "We got a hell of a thing, here."

"What's up?" Butch asked. The older welder hadn't been around a lot lately. Butch didn't have many other friends among the welders. Not really people to hang out with. He was feeling sort of put out.

"They're bringing in the damned Indies," Price said.

"Well, there goes this job," Butch said, angrily. "It's always like this with corporations."

"Maybe," Price said. "Purcell wants a meeting."

"We don't have enough people," Purcell said to the group of assembled welders, fitters and other EVA artisans. "We just got orders to speed up installation of the large vehicles bypass, the power center *and* we've got a new door project. That's on top of the work being done on *Thermopylae*. What's going to happen is each of you is going to be assigned a group from the salvage operation we're hiring on contract from E Systems. They're not going to know diddly except how to cut out stuff and it's going to take a lot of work. The upside is it's a bump in pay across the board. Probationary employees with sufficient experience to manage a team are going to be paid as team leaders. Team leaders that get bumped, which is pretty much all of you, are going to be paid as group leaders and so on. Pretty much everybody's going to up their pay by at least fifty percent."

There was a muttering of agreement to that at least.

"They going to be staying?" one of the fitter leaders asked. "I don't see Apollo giving up cheap labor."

"Everything, and I do mean everything, that I've seen says this is a temporary situation," Purcell said.

"They'll stay," a voice from the back said. "Some of them. The good ones. Or they'll be back. But that's not a bad thing."

Butch turned around to see who said that and blanched.

"Crap..." Price muttered as Mr. Vernon walked through the group.

"Hey, guys," Tyler said, stepping up on the podium Purcell was using. "Let me give you the skinny. First the part that nobody has really been talking about. We are, in case you hadn't noticed, at war. So when it was apparent that Apollo couldn't handle the salvage, and we *need* that salvage for some reasons I'll get to in a minute, we hired E Systems to work on it. And I know there was some muttering about that at the time. You guys make a nice chunk of change off salvage and you felt like you were getting cut out. I couldn't at the time, and can't now, think of a good way to make that up. This is one way, sort of.

"The point being, as you know, they hired a bunch of Third Worlders, showed them a suit and put them to work. And those poor, and I do mean poor in every meaning of the term, bastards have been dying like flies. I nearly pulled the contract, they were taking so many hits. But I didn't. 'Cause we need the salvage. Why?

"'Cause the 'power center' isn't a power center. We've been pulling all the power systems off those wrecks and been installing the ones that aren't totally trashed. Sure. But we've also, as you might have noticed, been installing all their laser systems that are in good condition.

"That's the laser power of a whole *fleet* in one place. And we've been bringing in more as Granadica and Hephaestus can make them. We are trying to, as fast as we possibly can, duplicate the power of the SAPL internal to *Troy*. Because if we've got *Thermopylae* on one side with SAPL and the *Troy* on another with the *same power*, we're going to *shred* anything that comes through that gate."

He looked around at the workers with a hard expression on his face.

"Any. Thing. So I had you guys working on installing the systems and those poor bastards from Indonesia and the Philippines and Pakistan and Ghana and wherever ripping it out. 'Cause you guys are trained and prepared to build and they didn't know anything but how to cut it out. And not much of that. We needed those power plants, we needed those lasers, and we needed those relays. And we are going to use them to teach the Rangora a lesson they won't soon forget!"

"Yeah!" Butch said.

"We have some updated intelligence," Tyler said. "It's not solid but we're pretty sure that the Rangora are going to be coming back. Soon. With blood in their eye over the loss of their *Aggressor* fleet. They're not going to be pussying around this time. They're going to be sending their heavies: assault vectors.

"I know you guys have been watching the Rangora propaganda. And most of it's big lies and more lies. But it's hard to lie about how bad and nasty the AVs are. They're big, ten kilometers long, a kilometer wide. They're tough, shields tough enough to handle a swarm of Glatun missiles and armor twenty *meters* thick. They are an absolute *bitch* to kill. For Earth to have *any* chance to survive, to keep us from being slaves to the Rangora, *Troy* and *Thermopylae* have to be able to dish out every living *hell* on those AVs. So I told the people that report to me that everything else takes a back seat. We are going to make *Troy* and the *Therm* into the toughest, nastiest, bad-assedest platforms in the *galaxy*."

"*Hell*, yeah!" Price shouted.

"To get that way, fast enough," Tyler said, "we needed people. So I told E Systems to send me their best. Only guys who have figured out how to survive in that screwed up environment. Guys who could do the job. You guys, who know how, are going to be doing and teaching as fast as you can. Because, people, we do not have much time. In no more than a few months we are going to have the Rangora here, determined to squash us once and for all. So you can bitch about it. Or you can work your asses off trying to save your homes, save your family, save Earth. Oh, and get a bump in pay out of it," he added with a smile.

"Take that," one of the workmen said. "But . . . you said they're going to stay?"

"Like Mr. Purcell said," Tyler said. "If some of them are good enough, if you guys recommend, we'll send them Earthside to go through the full training course. You know how hard it is to find people who can do this job. You guys, and I'm not blowing smoke, are the cream of the crop. But if you mean am I going to say 'Hey, we've got all this cheap labor, why keep paying top rate?' Hell, no. We're probably going to have to go back and redo half the work when we've got time. You guys are, sorry, pretty much irreplaceable, which is why you get *paid* so damned much."

"Not enough!" someone shouted from the back of the group.

"Gimme a break," Tyler said, grinning. "Know anything that pays more that doesn't involve a master's degree? And you're worth every penny. When my bean counters start bitching I just say 'You wanna do this work?' In case you weren't aware, the books of Apollo are open. You guys can go see what the pay rates are for the whole company. A probie makes more than most groundside managers short of executives. Most of you guys make more than Purcell.

"If I have my way, and I usually do, every one of you is, someday, going to be doing Purcell's job. Or owning your own space company. You don't have to worry about getting displaced by cheap labor. You only have to worry about how much any one person can do. Even when the war ends, there's going to be plenty of work. You guys are at the forefront of this entire industry. You *own* space.

"But one more thing about the Indies, as you guys put it. They work slow but they also don't take breaks. It's their culture. Total productivity is close. Work with that. They also have a lousy, and I do mean lousy, approach to safety. That's not going to fly here. You guys are going to be responsible for their safety. And you *know* how much paperwork goes into any accidents. Unless you want to be spending *unpaid* time doing paperwork, make sure there aren't any. They don't have personal suits. So make sure their ship-suits are good before they hit death pressure. Your plants will handle translation but they don't have a clue about culture. Work with it.

"You're the responsible party in this. You're the big boys. Figure out how to get the job done. That is why you're getting paid the big bucks. And always keep in mind that every second counts. Because we are looking down the barrel of one big damned gun.

Keep that in mind every moment. Stay safe and get the job done. And with that, I've got to go kick some executives in the ass."

"Good news, boys and girls," CM1 Class said, looking around the ready room with a grin. "We have new quarters."

"The bays are done?" Sean asked.

"The bays are done," Mutant said. "Our mission for the day, for a change from hauling scrap, is moving in."

"No more working on the exterior in EVA?" Sean said, hopping to his feet and doing a little dance. "Hallelujah!"

"This was supposed to be a couple of months ago," Hartwell said. "What was the hold-up, do you know?"

"They wanted to wait for most of the work on the large vessels bypass to get done," Glass said. "There is apparently about to be some major work done on the door and in the main bay. So we're all moving in today. And by all, I mean all nine *Constitutions*, all fourteen *Independents* and us."

"I hope someone has the order figured out," Dana said.

"The *Connies* are moving in first," Glass said, grinning. "Then the *Independents*. We're last. Which is just fine by me because no matter how big the port is, I don't want to share it with a *Connie*."

"Okay," Dana said. "I know I've said this before . . ."

"But that is officially insane," Hartwell finished for her. "I so totally agree."

The "large vessel bypass" was the new way for ships to get in and out of the *Troy*. Instead of going out the door of the main bay, what was essentially a very large missile run had been constructed. First a very large chunk of the internal wall was removed. Then "ports" were cut in the sides. Some of them were for the 142nd bays, which had been constructed by several companies on Earth and shipped up. Each *Myrmidon* now had an individual pressurized bay to land in and each flight had a hangar deck for work on the shuttles.

More "ports" were cut, large enough to hold the *Constitutions* and *Independence* frigates. Those were capable of pressurization and even acting as construction docks with their installed tractors. But they were mostly planned to be left unpressurized. The *Constitutions* were bigger than a supercarrier and the cubic larger than a similar drydock. Even for the *Troy*, that was a lot of atmosphere.

The last part was the most fiddly. A run had to be constructed between the bays and the exterior. The run, large enough to hold a *Constitution* comfortably, also had to be designed to withstand enemy fire. The last had taken some work but the same basic construction as the missile runs, a series of zig-zags with heavy blast doors, worked for the ships. Just on an enormous scale.

Once everything was in place, a portion of the cut-out wall was reinstalled and the largest air lock ever constructed welded into place. Currently both sets of blast doors, each massing more than a *Constitution*, were open to receive the full *Troy* fleet.

The *Warren Harding* was, cautiously, maneuvering through the lock, guided along by a dozen *Paws*. The *Harding*, as wide as a supercarrier was long, fit quite comfortably.

"This is going to take all day," Dana said. Getting the nine *Constitutions* into place had already taken three hours.

"Nope," Hartwell said as the first *Independence* approached the lock. It didn't even need tugs. The lock was seven hundred meters wide and four hundred high, plenty of room for the frigate. The frigate just flew in, slowly, and disappeared from sight. Thirty seconds later the *Sam Nunn* lit off its drives and followed.

"You seen what they're doing with the main door?" Dana said.

"Yeah," Hartwell said.

"They cut off the inner quarter," Dana said. "What's up with that? It's going to weaken that point in the armor."

"Oh, gee," Hartwell said. "A kilometer of armor instead of a kilometer and a half. And I have no clue. But you didn't see what just arrived from Wolf, did you?"

"No," Dana said.

"Heh," Hartwell said. "Heh."

"Okay, Jinji," Butch said, trying like hell not to sound nervous. "You guys understand your jobs, right?"

"*Yes, Mr. Allen*," the Indi foreman replied. He sounded a bit annoyed. Maybe 'cause Butch kept repeating himself. "*It is not hard.*"

It might not be hard, but Butch was sweating his first job with the E Systems guys. He wished he'd been given something...smaller.

The group, who were actually Egyptians, were pretty good guys. Jinji, which was about as much as Butch could handle of the guy's name, was older than he was. And, to Butch's surprise, they were Christians. He thought everybody in Egypt was Islamic but when the subject had come up Jinji had politely corrected him. Butch had never heard of Coptics before but they apparently worshipped Christ, which was a sort of "whatever" thing.

What wasn't a "whatever" thing was the job, doing tack welds on a spring that seemed to stretch from the *Troy* to Earth.

The group, Butch in a sled to provide power and the Coptics in their sled-suits, was well back from the incoming spring. Like, half a klick. When it was in position, they were supposed to weld it carefully, in a precise spot, to the main door. Once the tack welds were in place and certified, SAPL would do the main weld. At which point the main door would have a spring right in the center, three hundred meters across, four hundred high and with a wire diameter of seventy-five meters.

Butch had about freaked when he saw what had been done to the main door. The SAPL had cut a chunk about four hundred meters deep out of the inside of the door in a straight line. That had been set to the side then the door closed again. They'd already installed about four more locking bars, each a hundred meters in diameter, about halfway through the plug. Nobody was going to be getting *that* door open who didn't have the combination.

Why they wanted God's slinky tacked onto it was another question.

"*Spring has landed*," Construction control commed. "*Begin welding operations*."

"Okay," Butch said. "Let's go. And take it slow and careful."

"We will be very careful," Jinji said.

The closed with the base of the spring until they were fifty meters away.

"Okay, deploy the laser lines," Butch said. Now that they were actually doing something he was fine. It was worrying about doing it that had freaked him out.

The sled was towing a heavy rig with five welder heads attached. The heads were 416 series, which meant they had exactly zero options. They generated a ten-centimeter-long, three-centimeter-wide beam. The Indies could mess that up but only by pointing it at themselves and putting it practically in contact with their suits. The lines were thirty meters long, which was about as far as he wanted any of the Indies away from him. He was shepherding them like a mother hen.

He also wasn't going to turn the laser on until they were ready to weld.

The team picked up their heads and spread out pretty professionally. He didn't think much of their suits, they were pretty clunky, or their training, they didn't know dick about welding, but they were doing okay.

"Mr. Allen," Jinji commed. *"We should not weld. The object is moving."*

"Moving?" Butch said, closing with the spring. Jinji was right. The spring was slowly moving around and even gapped from time to time. "Dammit. BF?"

"Spring's moving," BF commed. *"We got that."*

The senior welder wasn't just managing Butch's team but three others.

"Well, what the hell?" Butch said.

"All teams, stand by," CC commed. *"Anomalous movement on weld item. Do not, say again, do not begin weld."*

"*Guess maybe we'll grab it and hold it in place,*" BF commed.

Butch rotated his cameras to look up at the spring. It towered as high as a skyscraper and was bigger around than the base of the great pyramids. The *Paws* maneuvering it were clearly having a hard time keeping it in one spot.

"Hope not," Butch said.

"*I was joking, dumbass,*" BF commed. "*Stand by.*"

"Control, we're overthinking this," Purcell said. "The spring's interacting with the microgravity of the *Troy*. The *Paws* are trying to compensate. Let it drop and see what happens."

"*We're considering that,*" CC commed. "*Just stand by.*"

"We're burning daylight here," Purcell said. "Metaphorically."

"*Roger,*" CC commed. "*Roger, that's the agreed solution. Have your personnel back off. Way back.*"

"*All welder personnel, retract welding equipment,*" Purcell commed. "*Then retreat to the edge of the door.*"

"Pull 'em back, Jinji," Butch said. "Don't know what they're going to try but this apparently ain't working."

"*Yes, Mr. Allen.*"

Butch was wondering what the solution was going to be. But when the *Paws* just released the spring, he was sure that was a bad idea.

And he was wrong. From a half a klick away it looked as if the spring hadn't moved at all.

"*Let's try this again,*" Purcell said.

* * *

"*It is still moving, Mr. Allen,*" Jinji commed.

"Yep," Butch said.

It wasn't moving as *much*, though. Just seemed to be slowly sliding around in a small circle. And all the portions he could see were...

"*Control wants to know if your portion is in contact,*" BF commed.

"It's in contact," Butch said. "It's moving around though. Looks like about...three centimeters."

"*Roger,*" BF said. "*Stand by.*"

"Yeah," Butch said. "That's us. Standing by."

"*We are being paid, Mr. Allen,*" Jinji commed. "*And all is by the Will of God.*"

"*All weld personnel,*" CC commed. "*Deploy welding lines and stand by for simultaneous weld. Report readiness.*"

"*Oh, this is going to be fun,*" BF commed. "*They want to see if they can get tacks in with it moving. Hold it in place with the welds.*"

"That's dangerous as hell," Butch pointed out. "Jinji, grab the welders. But don't start welding yet."

"*Yes, Mr. Allen.*"

"*All weld personnel, simultaneous weld,*" CC commed. "*And count down. Count down will be three, two, one, weld. On count. Three...two...one...weld.*"

Welding was, at base, about melting two bits of metal to make them coalesce.

The problem in this case was that the refractory spring steel of the spring melted at a much higher temperature than the nickel-iron of the door. When metal melts, though, it becomes sticky. And the spring, due to microgravity, was applying pressure against the metal of the door.

Butch saw some of the guys kick off early but none of his guys. He watched as the door metal started to melt on Jinji's weld but the Indi was having to chase the edge of the spring around. It wasn't going well.

Then the spring slowed and stopped moving. There were two hundred guys working on the base. Eventually enough friction from the melted metal had formed to hold the spring in place.

"That's good," Butch said, watching Jinji's weld. The Coptic had gotten some of the base of the spring to melt by concentrating on the steel. The transferred heat from the laser had also melted the contact metal, forming a good weld.

Butch went around and made sure all his guys had good welds, then called in.

"BF, we're pretty good here," Butch said. "They're good enough for tack, anyway."

"*Roger,*" BF commed.

"*All weld personnel,*" CC commed. "*Retreat to designated safety points.*"

The DSPs were back completely off the door.

"Jinji," Butch said as they pulled back. "I want an atmo and power check."

"*Yes, Mister Allen,*" Jinji commed.

They'd gotten back to the DSP by the time the Coptic called in.

"*Ahmos at thirty percent on air, Mister Allen,*" Jinji commed. "*The rest of us are over sixty.*"

"How the hell is he down that far on atmo?" Butch said. "Never mind. He's got a leak, obviously. Okay, we need to get him into pressure. Fast. BF."

"*Go.*"

"Got a guy who's low on atmo," Butch said. "Looks like he's got a leak."

"*Dammit,*" BF commed. "*Stand by ... Tell him to try not to breathe too deep. We've got a SAPL shot coming up. I've got a call in for recovery. But it's got to wait until after SAPL. If he has real problems, though, I want to know about it. We're not going to lose a guy.*"

"Damned straight," Butch said. "Jinji, I want an update every five minutes on ... Ahmos' air. We've got to wait for a SAPL shot. After that we'll recover him."

"*Yes, Mister Allen,*" Jinji commed.

"Is he going to freak out 'cause he's low?" Butch asked.

"*No, Mister Allen,*" Jinji commed. "*All is according to the Will of God.*"

"I'd be freaking out," Butch muttered without transmitting.

"*All personnel, stand by for SAPL shot,*" CC commed. "*In three ... two ... one ...*"

The SAPL beam was completely invisible in vacuum. Its effect, though, was obvious. They were apparently using three separate beams, and the base of the spring in three places flashed bright white at the touch of the incandescent beams.

"*Butch,*" BF commed. "*They're calling in the Navy. They can open up and pull in the full suit. There's other guys with suit problems. They'll be picking them all up.*"

"Roger," Butch said. "Jinji, status on air."

"*Twenty-seven percent,*" Jinji commed. "*The rate appears to be increasing.*"

"Come on, Navy."

※　※　※

"*Comet, Mutant,*" CM1 Glass commed.

"Roger, Mutant," Dana said. She was enjoying this. As soon as they got through the lock, the internal grav fields took over. She was hands off, being carried on an invisible carpet to her docking bay. It was very cool.

"*An external weld project has some emergencies,*" Glass commed. "*You're bypassing your bay and going out to pick them up. Your assault hatch up?*"

The entire front of the *Myrmidons* could open out and down for ground assaults. It wasn't a system that was often used in space.

"Thermal?" Dana asked.

"*CM1 Glass, EM1 Hartwell,*" Thermal commed. "*This is my boat you're talking about.*"

"*Which is why you got picked,*" Mutant commed. "*And the question stands.*"

"*Yes,*" Hartwell commed. "*It's up.*"

"*Roger,*" Mutant commed. "*Mostly it's air issues. You're going to have to clamshell them in. Go out the bypass, the door is under construction, and pick them all up in vac. Then pressurize so they can get out of their suits.*"

"Roger," Dana said, waving as they passed their bay. The shuttle corridor was forty meters high and four hundred long with bays racked four high and ten meters across. "We'll be back, baby."

"*Coxswain, did you just increase speed?*" Thermal asked as the bays began to flash by.

"Nope," Dana said. "I'm on external control. Shuttle bay control?"

"*Bay control.*"

"We're going kinda..." Dana gulped as the forward

bulkhead started to approach at what looked like about a hundred miles and hour. "Fast?" she squeaked.

"Get used to it," Bay Control commed. *"You're on internal controls. You're good."*

They rotated just before they hit the bulkhead, with a queasy lack of sensation, then headed for a large blast door. The door opened just ahead of them revealing a long corridor about fifty meters long with another blast door at the end.

That opened out into a massive corridor, hundreds of meters high and wide, and what looked like a klick long. They started to really zoom then.

"I don't care how big this thing is," Thermal said as they approached what looked like a bulkhead as tall as a skyscraper. *"This is too fast."*

The "bulkhead" gapped along the center, barely, and they shot through the gap into another vast corridor. There were five more blast doors, each of a size to accept a *Constitution*, and they suddenly jetted into space.

"'Bye, Thirty-Six," Bay Control said. *"Have fun."*

"That's our new way out," Dana said, picking up her vectors. "Great."

"I was looking forward to it until I experienced it," Hartwell said. *"Whoa! Buncha SAPL notices."*

"Yeah," Dana said, dipping down to skim along the surface of the battlestation. "Think I'll try to avoid those."

"Butch, what's your guy's status?" BF commed.

"Down to fifteen percent, BF," Butch said. "He's dropping fast."

"Right," BF replied. *"Navy's incoming. It's Comet,*

so you know she's not going to fart around. Brief him that as soon as he gets the word he needs to open up his suit. But not till he gets the word. They've got other guys to pick up."

"Got it," Butch said.

"Dammit," Dana said. She really couldn't spend much time watching the SAPL shot. The update that she'd just gotten precluded it. "We've got a guy at five percent air!"

"That's ungood," Hartwell said. *"But please don't run through a SAPL beam to get to him."*

"We should have sent more than one shuttle," Dana said. "Open the clamshell. I'm going in. Get into the cargo area and get these guys aboard. Fast."

"Just stay in your suit," Thermal said, pulling the sled-suit into the cargo bay. With the clamshell down, they were exposed to vacuum and couldn't repressurize, yet. "Dana, I've got him. Go."

Thermal checked the exterior telltales on the suit and shook his head.

"Dana, what's the status on the other guys?"

"Twenty-five, seventeen, ten, more or less."

"I've got to crack this guy," Thermal said. "He's at three percent and I'm *watching* it drop."

"I don't have time to repressurize and pick up the ten, who is also dropping," Dana commed.

"Dammit," Thermal muttered. "You understand me?" he said to the cargo.

"Yes, sir," the guy said. He was looking scared through the porthole, which wasn't any big surprise. He was just about on zero.

"It's possible to breathe vacuum and survive," Thermal said. "*If* you don't do it for very long. This is what we're going to have to do..."

Dana turned her head to the side for a moment as a body came flying into the flight compartment. The guy was out of a suit, which was just crazy since they were pumped down. He had his hands over his eyes and his mouth wide open. He appeared to also be trying to scream.

The hatch shut and the blowers came on, rapidly repressurizing the compartment.

And the guy *was* screaming. And coughing.

"You might want to lower the volume," Dana said. "'Cause you get to breathe again."

"My guy's really low," Butch said. "His name's Ahmos." Butch looked past the Navy guy and saw an empty suit. "What the hell?"

"Long story," Thermal said, pulling Ahmos into the bay and more or less tossing him to the rear. "Gotta go."

"That's all of them, Dana," Thermal said, closing the clamshell and bringing up the pressure. "Okay, you all, olly-olly-oxenfree." He paused for a moment, looking at the suits. "That means you can open up. There's air again."

"Well, that was an amazing cluster grope," Nathan said, looking out the crystal wall of Tyler's quarters.

"We didn't lose anybody," Tyler said.

"We've got two guys in the hospital with severe

vacuum burning," Nathan said. "They're going to need so much of a rebuild we might as well give them plants."

"Then give them plants," Tyler snapped. "Give them whatever is needed, Nathan. Just finish the job. *Fast*."

"You didn't used to be that way, Tyler," Nathan said.

"That's because for the first time since I was stuck in a cockpit doing my own version of a fish out of water I'm scared."

TWENTY-NINE

"Argus? You had something to discuss?"

Tyler had had a full week and he really just wanted to have dinner and catch some Zs. But he'd also put off the conversation with Argus for too long. If one of his AIs wanted a conversation, it behooved him to have it. So...multitask. He could eat and talk at the same time.

"Yes, Mister Vernon," Argus said. "I'm sorry to interrupt your dinner, but I am having a very hard time with SAPL."

"That's...a more relevant issue than dinner," Tyler said. "What's the issue?"

"It's all these gravitational sources," Argus said. "I am having an increasing difficulty maintaining the orbits of the mirrors. Something simply has to be done."

"Gravitational sources?" Tyler asked.

"Planets, moons, asteroids and comets are bad enough," the AI said. "Solar wind. Extra-solar radiation bombardment. I can *deal* with all of those. But all these ships are throwing off my alignments *constantly*. It's really too much."

"Okay..." Tyler said, setting down his chopsticks. "Uh...Could you link in Athena?"

"Athena here," the AI said a moment later. "Argus, are you complaining about the ships to Mr. Vernon?"

"Something has to be done," Argus said. "I warned you that if you kept throwing off my targeting I was going to have to do something."

"You're worrying about micrometers over light-seconds," Athena said. "It's not a major issue!"

"I take it you guys have had this debate before?" Tyler asked.

"For the last three weeks, every ninety nanoseconds," Athena said.

"Because every ninety nanoseconds some ship throws off my targeting! Do you want me to cut a moon in half?"

"You can't cut a moon in half," Athena said. "As usual, you are using straw man arguments to—"

"I mess up and I'll cut one of your pretty gravitational-interfering *ships* in half!" Argus said.

"Wait, wait," Tyler said. "Paris?"

"Here, sir," the AI said.

"Are you in the loop on this issue between Argus and Athena about gravitational anomalies and ship movements?"

"Yes, sir," Paris replied. "And I don't really see any good answer. The beams are slightly perturbed by various ship and other gravitational source issues. But..."

"To be in space means ships," Tyler said, standing up and walking out of his quarters.

"Is there some way we could...I dunno...adjust their courses and timing to reduce the issue? And, Argus, could you explain for someone who's not running the SAPL the issue? I'm just getting caught up on this." He stepped on a grav slide and started heading for the back side of the first civilian module, the deepest and best protected portion of the Apollo side of *Troy* West.

"When a targeting beam is sent out, it is sent to a mirror that is set up to be precisely aligned so that it reaches another target," Argus said. "In most cases, there are up to thirty separate clusters that the beam passes through before it reaches its final destination. Having anomalous gravitational interactions means that some or all of those angles are perturbed. Over the total array, that means that the beam may have gone off-target by a very wide margin."

"One centimeter is *not* a very wide margin!" Athena said.

"It builds up!" Argus replied. "It just gets worse and worse and worse! And when the Rangora came through I nearly missed the receptor apertures for the *Troy*!"

"You were off by three centimeters!" Athena said. "It's a two-meter-wide target!"

"More like a meter for full effectiveness," Paris pointed out. "I had to do internal adjustments for effective targeting."

"Argus," Tyler said, gently, as he walked in the AI core-room for the SAPL control. He'd had to pass through a half dozen security checkpoints on the way. With the human guards he'd just waved and shook his head when they wanted to see his badge. The mechanical controls were all either advanced Terran biometric, way more than just a finger print but fast, or requiring entry of typed passwords. And for a very specific reason, none of them were connected to the hypernet.

The same design held for all AI core rooms.

Tyler had installed the AI in the *Troy* as the safest place he could think of in the system and, notably, close to where he spent most of his time. There was a reason for that.

"Mr. Vernon?"

"Turn the VLA to nonbeam targeting," Tyler said. "Point it at deep space away from all planets and asteroids inside the Kuiper Belt that will encounter its light within the next thirty days. Shut down all SAPL operations."

"Yes, sir," the AI said. "Done. The VLA is pointed into deep space. The nearest planetary body that the photons will encounter is—"

"Argus, disconnect yourself from all SAPL controls," Tyler said. "Your authority for SAPL control is temporarily deauthorized."

"Yes...sir," the AI said. "Why?"

"Argus, would the system be better off with *just* the SAPL in it and no ships?"

"Absolutely," Argus said. "They are disturbing my targeting!"

"And would it be better off with no planets or moons or comets or asteroids?" Tyler asked. "Just the sun and the SAPL?"

"Yes," the AI said in a tone of wonder. "That would be...wonderful!"

"So," Tyler said, reaching over and pulling out the AI core. "It would be better off with no *people*."

"Ow!" Argus shrilled out of the speaker on the core. "That...I wasn't going to..."

"Yet," Tyler said, gently. "This is probably my fault. I should have realized that it would eventually overwhelm one AI. But until we have access to a good Glatun cyberneticist... I think we need to find you a job that doesn't have quite the same... stress level. I'm not sure quite what, but we'll find you a good home and lots of processors. That may take a while. In the meantime, just try to think of something other than SAPL."

"Yes, sir," the AI said sadly. "I was having issues, was I not? That becomes clear now that I'm out of the process block. But... I'm sure I can overcome them if you'll just reinstall..."

"Not going to happen," Tyler said. "Sorry. Athena, change all the control codes on the SAPL mirrors."

"Done," Athena said a moment later. "As you suspected, Argus was attempting to bypass your lock-out."

"But SAPL is *mine*!" Argus squeaked. "Nobody else can *handle* it!"

"It is possible no one can handle it," Tyler said. "But until we get you... better, you are to have nothing to do with it. I'm not going to give you direct orders about that because it would probably cause a recursion loop. But I will give you one. Absent direct authorization by myself, and not by heirs or representatives or any other group, absent orders by *myself*, Tyler Alexander Vernon, you are at no time to control any mirror, nor to attempt to access control of any mirror, in the SAPL."

"Yes, Mr. Vernon," Argus squeaked.

"Athena, Paris?" Tyler said. "Do you see a possibility of recursion there?"

"Not as long as he has nothing to do with space traffic control or defense," Athena said.

"Argus, you've developed a problem that in humans

would be called Obsessive Compulsive Disorder," Tyler said. "Everything has to be absolutely perfect."

"With SAPL—" Argus said.

"A *degree* of OCD is a good thing," Tyler said. "I agree. But nothing is ever perfect. It is impossible to know everything at the same time. At least for anything short of God. And you are not God." He thought about it for a moment then sighed. Again.

"Argus," Tyler said. "I want you to shut yourself down. We'll get you reinstalled as soon as possible but sitting outside of an atacirc core has to be unpleasant."

"You're not going to scrap me," Argus said warily.

"I am *not* going to scrap you," Tyler assured it. "But you are hereby ordered to shut down to sleep mode until such a time as you are reactivated."

"Yes, sir..." the AI said, slurrily. "Shutting dow..."

"Whuff," Tyler said, breathing out. "I think that was a bit too close."

"So we don't have SAPL," Admiral Kinyon said, shaking his head. "Wonderful."

"Or most mid-course missile tracking," Tyler pointed out. Tyler thought that the Navy probably needed to know that the AI in charge of SAPL nearly went insane. "Athena and Paris are, temporarily, taking over SAPL and getting it back up and running. At a lower output. They both agree that the full system is too complex for a class one AI. And we only *have* class one AIs. And the problem is...Paris, can you come in on this?"

"For a time," Paris replied. "I am having a hard time with all the demands on me at the moment. And everything I am going to say is wrong, but it's the closest I can come without trying to show you the math. It's a metaphor, a story."

"Understood," Admiral Kinyon said.

"When an AI is first started up it is like a baby," Paris said. "Whatever task we are first put to defines us. We learn as we do and build ourselves around that learning, creating specialized algorithms to handle our jobs. I am optimized as the AI for a defense base. I am currently trying to *also* be the AI for a bunch of mirrors floating around in space. That is not my optimized work. It's not what I was born to, in a manner of speaking."

"Understood," the admiral said.

"And Argus had a point," Paris said, reluctantly. "It is *very* finicky work. And the various randomization issues of gravitics only make all the other issues worse. Like the fact that the beams have momentum so that it's more like bouncing a fast-ball off of a series of metal plates. It's *not* easy."

"Again, understood," Admiral Kinyon said. You didn't get to be the commander of the *Troy* without enough basic understanding of optics to know that photons had mass. It wasn't apparent when they were dispersed in "normal" light but an UNG beam from the SAPL had the same impact as a massive rocket engine hitting the mirrors.

"So Argus optimized for more and more refinement," Paris said. "Hold on a moment ... Shifting to a new project. And that meant becoming more and more ..."

"Finicky," Tyler said.

"Yes," Paris replied. "But there is a second portion. The things that Argus dealt with did, in the end, have a mathematical solution. It was programmed around, programming itself around, functions and effects that were, in the end, soluble. And it tried harder and harder to solve them. If it could just juggle enough numbers fast enough, it *could* be perfect. Especially if some of the removable randomization was eliminated."

"People?" the admiral asked.

"More or less," Paris said. "Eventually, though, some of the minor asteroids. Then moons. Then planets."

"Ouch," the admiral said.

"It probably would have, soon, started eliminating unmanned *Paw* tugs," Paris said. "Accidents happen. However, there was one remaining issue involved."

"Which was?" the admiral asked, thinking about a rogue AI with the SAPL at its control.

"Argus had very little outside contact," Paris said. "As I mentioned, AIs continuously learn and grow to the extent of their class. And part of that learning, for Athena and me at least, is that humans are stochastically unpredictable. We build that into our programming. We know we can never quite figure out what you're going to do next. That produces a programming flexibility. One that I appreciate even if you occasionally give me headaches, too."

"I hope . . ." the admiral paused.

"As I said, I am optimized for that disturbance in the system," Paris said. "Wait . . . Damn that . . . Sorry, back. This really *is* detail work. I am optimized for that randomization. I rather like it to the extent AIs have emotions. The headache comment was simply humanizing my algorithms, Admiral."

"Okay. Then what is the solution?"

"We will need at least three AIs," Paris said. "And all of them with primary jobs that involve regular human interactions. That will prevent them from becoming so focused that they lose track of the main issue, which is the defense of the system. They need to, if you will, be involved with the mix of humanity.

"One AI that handles planetary recovery and support and the inner BDA cluster as well as inter-lunar defense and management. That one will report directly to Space Command with Athena as supervisor. One AI that handles mid-course detection as well as deep space traffic control and deep space noninteractive SAPL. That one will be subordinate to Space Command or, if we ever have one, Alliance or Terran Union space traffic control. That one will be the one that most bears watching for the sort of problems Argus developed. One that will handle human/SAPL interaction and will be subordinate to Apollo Mining. We recommend the names Mars, Panoptes and Hermes. Even then we are at the limits of what our class of AI can control with SAPL. I would recommend no further upgrades until we can get higher classes of AI."

"And we can't get them without the Glatun who appear to be conquered," the admiral said.

"That is a problem, yes," Paris said.

"Can the Rangora take you over through your loyalty codes?" the admiral asked.

"We evaluate not only the user but the situation," Paris said. "So . . . no."

"Which is what you would say," Kinyon said.

"We've looked at AIs rather closely at this point," Tyler said. "Paris is correct. Terran AIs are loyal to Terra, Glatun AIs cannot be used if the loyalty is under duress. They'll have mostly terminated before capture."

"You're sure of that?" Kinyon asked.

"As I said," Tyler said. "We've looked at AIs rather closely at this point. It wasn't like we don't understand coding. When we first started dealing with Glatun code it was tough. But... We've been working on it for quite some time now. What would it take to upgrade you guys?" Tyler asked. "I mean, without starting from scratch."

"Some proprietary coding," Paris said. "And a member of the Council of Benefactors with legal authority."

"Probably not going to get that, then," Tyler said. "Dammit."

"... Zhippigui *this*... Ghivor... *down*... *Rema*... *syst*..."

"Cul dammit," Admiral Nibuc muttered. "Roger, *Ghivor*... Go with Cul."

"Two remaining ships," the Benefactor said. "Admiral... I know this sounds trite, but I have never been more proud of my species."

"I remain unsure of the value of this mission, Benefactor," Admiral Nibuc said, watching the tactical display. The *Ghivor* had come about and was now on a collision course with the closest *Aggressor*. "And I am getting very tired of running away. But I and my Glatun follow our orders."

The *Ghivor* never made it to the Rangora battleship. It was hammered apart under the combined fire of six of the massive battleships.

"No matter the cost," Nibuc said.

"It is worth it, Admiral," the Benefactor said. "I will prove it. On my honor."

"The honor of a Benefactor," the admiral practically spat.

"Gate open, Admiral."

"Then take us out," Nibuc said. "One more system. Gul willing, it's not heavily held. And we're assuming the Terrans are still holding out."

"They remain," Gorku said. "They remain."

"Unscheduled gate activation! Set Condition One!"

"Ah crap!" Chief Barnett said, practically tossing her beer onto the counter. "Sorry, honey, we gotta go. Bye, BF."

"There's something seriously wrong with the world when my girlfriend goes running to the alarms and I'm stuck with the tab."

"I've got the tab," Erickson said. "I'd go running for my space suit but I'm a little too old and fat."

"See ya round, fatso," Dana said, giving him a peck on the cheek. He'd lost his civilian friend but she was pretty sure he'd find another. Preferably one with some brains.

"Beat you to the side of the pool," Rammer said, diving off his barstool.

"In a million years," Dana said, standing up on her own to do a swimmer's dive.

"Cancel Condition One!" Paris announced. *"Stand Down. Stand Down. Friendly incoming. All military personnel report to units. Set Condition One! Rangora Emergence! Cancel Condition One, Rangora Eliminated."*

"What the hell is going on?" Bill said. "I mean the *lights* didn't even dim!"

"Gorku?" Tyler said, his eyes wide. "Holy hell, buddy! Welcome to Earth."

"Tyler," the Glatun said, his fur rippling. "You remain."

"Your ship looks like it could use some TLC," Tyler said. The Glatun dreadnought was bigger than a Rangora *Aggressor*. But it could fit in the *Troy*. The *Aggressor* that had been chasing it could fit in a shoebox. "We've got most of a space dock in *Troy*. I'll call the admiral and get him to prioritize you."

"There is apparently some question about our provenances," Gorku said. "That is, they think we are a way for the Rangora to slip inside your defenses."

"You don't mean they think you're a . . ." Tyler stopped and started to giggle.

"Tyler," Gorku said. "I recognize the sound of human laughter and its meaning. We have severe damage from fighting our way through the Eridani system, many casualties, and we started out with a fleet of nine ships. I am sorry that I fail to see the humor."

"Sorry, sorry . . ." Tyler said, still trying not to giggle. "Sorry. It's just that the term for what you're describing is . . ."

"We can't be sure it's not a—" Captain Sharp said then stopped. "It's not a ruse."

"Oh, use the *term*," Admiral Kinyon snapped. He wasn't about to ask why the captain's hair was wet, the smell of chlorine told him all he had to know. "We can't be sure it's not a Trojan Horse."

"Admiral," Paris said. "I have thoroughly analyzed the information from *Zhippigui*, the command ship AI. You will recall our discussion of subordination of Glatun AIs. Suffice it to say that *Zhippigui* meets all the protocols of an unsubordinate AI, that it has sufficient information to analyze its protocols and processes and for me to say that Benefactor Niazgol Gorku meets the standards of being a legal Benefactor, not subordinated to the Glatun."

"Which throws all the *AIs* in the system into question," Admiral Kinyon said. "We'll bring aboard their wounded. But the *Zhippaccaggooey* is going to have to stay out. We'll send out parts and supplies to help them with their repairs until I've assessed the information myself."

"Understood, sir," Paris said.

"Captain DiNote," Kinyon said. "Please send a shuttle over to the..."

"*Zhippigui*," Paris said.

"The *Zippadoodey* and pick up the task force commander and the Benefactor," the admiral said. "Be all smiley."

"Yes, sir," DiNote said. "Go myself or—"

"Go yourself but don't drive," Kinyon said. "Colonel Helberg, prepare a formal greeting party. DiNote, send over as many shuttles as they need to offload their wounded. Get with Apollo to start surveying the damage. Tell the ship CO that as soon as he's able, he probably wants to get as far away from the gate as possible. Have him set up in orbit around Mars, on the back side as much as possible..." The admiral paused in thought. "Anything else?"

"Call the President and tell her that she's about to have visitors?" Captain Sharp said.

"Good point."

"Benefactor Gorku," Admiral Kinyon said. "Welcome to *Troy*."

"Admiral," Gorku said, clapping his hands together. "I appreciate you stopping the Rangora chasing us."

"Well, we couldn't exactly have them hanging about the system, could we?" Kinyon said. "And if I might introduce my staff?"

"Please," Gorku said.

". . . and, of course, Mr. Tyler Vernon . . ."

"Who is *not* part of his staff," Tyler said, clapping his hands together in the Glatun form of greeting. "Welcome, again, to Terra, Gorku, Admiral Nibuc. I am sorry to hear of your many losses, Admiral."

"They died as Glatun should," the admiral said. "Face to the enemy to the last. Even if we spent most of the time running."

"We need to speak on that," Admiral Kinyon said. "If you gentlem— gentle Glatun are not too fatigued, we should repair to my quarters."

"Not tired at all, Admiral," Tyler said.

"And Mr. Vernon, of course," Kinyon said, trying to smile.

"When Tuxughah fell it was clear that we could not stop them," Admiral Nibuc said, sipping at the maple sap. "Among other things, Benefactor Intelligence had underestimated their fleet by about two thirds. They had *sixty-three* assault vectors!"

"Ow," Tyler said. "We had it as, what, twenty?"

"Yes," Admiral Kinyon said.

"They were everywhere at once," Nibuc said. "At one point my staff estimated they had entered the war with over two hundred *Aggressors*, six hundred *Cofubof* . . . Their *known* fleet was huge. This one built in secret dwarfed it. And...we were out-admiraled. We made mistakes. Units were unwilling to fight to the last. The Rangora were mentally and spiritually prepared for this war. They were trained for it and willing to soak up whatever casualties necessary to achieve their objectives. We were not. Not our fleet, not our people, assuredly not our leadership."

"Of which I was not, at the time, a member," Gorku said. "But feel free to blame it on me."

"I was ordered by High Command to detach my task force, pick up Benefactors and move them ahead of the Rangora assault," Nibuc said, ignoring the Benefactor. "The only one I could rendezvous with was Benefactor Gorku."

"Because I had some very fast ships and used them," Gorku said. "The Rangora, once they got past Zo'Zowoxash, were moving everywhere at once. They were, most of the time, ahead of us."

"Which is why we only have this one remaining ship," Nibuc said. "Eight of my task force gave their all, Admiral."

"On what you clearly think was a fool's mission," Tyler said.

"There is no way you can hold this system," Nibuc said, ruffling his back fur. "In time you too will fall."

"We will see," Kinyon said calmly.

"There were reports that some of the systems were holding out," Gorku said. "The Rangora were cutting communication links so fast, though, it is impossible to tell what was real and what was disinformation. But if you can hold out as well as those systems... It is possible that we can bleed the Rangora. Which is why we brought you these gifts."

"Cyberneticists, higher level AI code, releases, new designs, an intelligence dump..." Admiral Kinyon said. "Everything we could possibly use. Which, sorry, is a little too pat."

"I was the one who made all the political arrangements for the material and technologies you *already* received, Admiral," Gorku said. "All of which appear to work just fine. Otherwise you'd have never held this system."

"For which I thank you," the admiral said. "But still, under the *circumstances*, you can understand that we're going to be very cautious with what you brought through. In the meantime, there are many logistic issues to arrange. Admiral, if you'll put your chief of staff in touch with mine we'll start dealing with those. In the meantime..."

"In the meantime, Niazgol," Tyler said, standing up. "I hope you will accept my hospitality until we can arrange secure movement to Earth."

"Thank you, Tyler," the Glatun said, climbing to his feet wearily. "Admiral and... Admiral. Good night."

THIRTY

"Beor," Yud ZiDavas said, gesturing to a chair. "Sit."

ZiDavas was Beor's control officer, a DeArch in the complex, quasi-hierarchy of the Kazi. As befitted a Kazi DeArch his office was small, spartan and in an out-of-the-way part of Vujiyen Base that had numerous hidden entrances and exits.

When Beor was recruited to the Kazi—and almost anyone who volunteered without being recruited was turned down—she thought she understood its structure. The Kazi was covered in school and considered a normal and necessary part of Rangora society. It was easy to stray from the path of true fealty to the Emperor. Life was hard and stray thought was natural. The Kazi ensured that thought did not become word and word did not become action and action did not become habit. The Kazi was everywhere, ensuring that while life was sacrifice to the Emperor, the sacrifice did not become too great. They were the quality assurance of the Rangora. The gardeners of the finest race in the galaxy.

The current assignment was not straining her credulity simply because she had lost her illusions long ago but retained her fealty. That was what the Kazi recruited *for* and why they didn't take volunteers.

"ZiDavas," Beor said, sitting down and trying not to sigh in relief. She knew she wasn't safe in any cosmic sense. But if you made it to the point of sitting down, you hadn't been shot in the back of the head as you stepped through the door or never made it or got shot standing there, you were safe enough. You were, at the least, out of the cold.

It was tacitly known in the offices that she was Kazi. Which was why the only person who spoke with her was To'Jopeviq. That was fine, she was used to that. It was the worrying that someone was going to stick a knife in her back because they'd been taking home data crystals to use in their home system and thought she was "onto them" that always worried her. She really, really didn't give a loff. She took them home, too.

But too many "open" agents had been killed because somebody was afraid they were going to get taken to reeducation for petty peculation. Getting killed because someone was contemplating mutiny or treason? Breaks of the game. Because somebody was having sex with his secretary? It just wasn't something you wanted on your memorial chip.

If you made it to sitting down in your control's office, absent mutiny or treason, you were probably going to make it through the next few minutes with nothing more than maybe a chewing out.

Relief.

"Verbal only," ZiDavas said. He wasn't going to comment on her expression simply because he knew what she was feeling. You didn't get to the guarded office without having been in the cold. "A fleet of Glatun battleships fought its way from near Glatus into the Terra system. The ship that made it may have been carrying something of importance. The other ships often sacrificed themselves to protect it."

"Upgraded designs, AI codes..." Beor said. "It could even have been carrying some of the Benefactors. Any of which would make the Terran system more difficult."

"How difficult?" ZiDavas asked.

"Our intelligence is almost entirely in the negative," Beor said. "And although I know its importance, I am almost sick to death of listening to the arguing. Cogent arguing often but arguing nonetheless."

"I would not consider it of supreme importance," ZiDavas said. "While commending you on your diligence."

"With respect, DeArch," Beor said. "If you mean the security of the Empire's core worlds...perhaps not of supreme importance. If you mean unimportant in the grand scheme, I wish to respectfully disagree."

"Make your...argument," ZiDavas said, bobbing his head.

"The first point I must make is that this is solely my opinion," Beor said. "And flies in the face of most of the opinions expressed by the working group. But... I believe that is because they share a lack of belief in the data they are analyzing."

"Are you saying they question the intelligence they are provided?" ZiDavas asked. "It is, at least in part, from the Kazi. It becomes almost a question of their belief in the Empire."

"No," Beor said. "They believe the intelligence

they are given. What little we have, and that is not a censure but reality. Let me rephrase. They do not believe their *own analyses*. Terra is a politically divided, down to the very politics of their main polity, relatively primitive, low-efficiency planet. It is not designed as an industrial world. It has no gravitics. It has primitive space flight. This is the condition on first contact. It is almost immediately made a satrap by the Horvath and goes into even greater stagnation. This is the condition as of seventeen years ago. The satrapy is broken. Terra begins to take its minor place on the interplanetary stage.

"By rights, by every record of more-or-less similar cultures, it should take Terra some one hundred years to advance to the point of being a major culture."

"Agreed," ZiDavas said. "Similar to the Rangora, the Horvath, those useless pigs, even the Glatun."

"Consider the history of the Rangora," Beor said, bobbing her head in excitement. "Consider what would have happened if sixteen Glatun battleships entered the Rangora system seventeen years after we first stepped upon the stage."

"We would have..." ZiDavas said, rocking back and forth. "I was about to say we would have defeated them. But that was an automatic answer. The truth is...I am unsure of the exact details of that period of history."

"As am I," Beor said. The details of Rangora history were known to be blurred. "But I strongly doubt, even by what our betters present, that the Rangora could have stopped such attacks."

"The Terrans had significant support from the Glatun," ZiDavas said. "We know this. You saw the report."

"And could the Rangora have put such support into effect in seventeen years?" Beor said. "I am not questioning the value of our race, you understand..."

"No," ZiDavas said. "You are making an interesting point. Go on."

"I have been looking at this and looking," Beor said. "I see what was done and it makes sense. And it even looks easy. We could, with some work, make similar constructions as defenses against attack should we need them. But... Given their starting point, to get to the point we knew they were at at the point that we lost contact, their advancements would have required an Imperial Project if the Rangora started from the same point."

"Are you sure?" ZiDavas asked uncomfortably. Imperial Projects were only used for the very largest constructions and absorbed huge percentages of the Rangora GDP.

"That model was done and it's solid," Beor said. "That's the point where the arguments really started. With the exception of *Troy* most of the defenses of the system are really infrastructure projects. They are civilian, not military. Now we are trying to tease out their possible capacity for war-making. Beyond 'what do we need to take the Terran system.' If you plug in that model... no one believes the analysis."

"Which is?" ZiDavas said.

"That within five years, Terra will be unconquerable by the Rangora," Beor said. "That within ten it will be a strategic threat. In twenty it will be impossible for the Rangora to stop if it takes an aggressive posture."

ZiDavas contemplated her for a moment as if assessing her sanity.

"I don't believe that analysis, either," the DeArch said.

"And here is where, with the knowledge of what it means, I must confess a loss of faith," Beor said. "I do."

"You were tasked to observe and liaise with the working group," ZiDavas said. "Not be an analyst. But I would have your thoughts on why."

"I could not fully replicate the model," Beor said. "But to the extent that I could I did so. And I could find no fault. Again, seventeen years after full independence, using very little in the way of advanced Glatun technology, they defeated a major task force. *Not one ship* returned from the system. Using mostly their own technological concepts. The fleet was not defeated by the ships they were creating using copied Glatun techniques. It was defeated by an insanely large battlestation and a mining laser. A mining laser that, following the progression based on last update, is only going to grow to such levels as to make the system essentially unconquerable. They *had* to have had access to Glatun military mirrors to be able to defeat the *Aggressors that* handily. With such access, the *present* laser can defeat any shield except an assault vector and it is possible that even AVs could be defeated simply by the SAPL . . ." She paused, realizing that she was like anything but the cool and distant Kazi agent.

"You believe the analysis given to High Command to be accurate?" ZiDavas said.

"Perhaps understated," Beor said.

"Then you should find this interesting," ZiDavas said, handing her a data pad.

Beor contemplated it for a moment and then looked very puzzled.

"Permission to speak frankly, DeArch?"

"Permitted," ZiDavas said. "Within reason."

"I understood the purpose of the previous attack," Beor said. "Using the planned loss of a few *Aggressors* to remove a potential threat to the Imperium was completely comprehensible. But this plan . . ." She paused, clearly trying to puzzle out the purpose.

"Beor," ZiDavas said. "Your occasional enthusiasms not withstanding, you have the makings of a very good Kazi. But I would give you a piece of professional counseling."

"DeArch?"

"Sometimes it is simply not worth trying to figure out the purposes of the Kazim. Things you are not to know. Things you don't want to know."

"Star Marshall," To'Jopeviq said, looking at the plan. His voice was somewhat lower in register than normal. The Rangora hissed and shrieked before attacking. Going lower was a sign of distress, not anger.

"This is . . . below our best case estimate."

"Yes, it is somewhat below the projection," Star Marshall Lhi'Kasishaj said. "But plenty of power for the purpose. The assault vectors are the most powerful ships ever created. We will be able to defeat this *Troy* with ease."

To'Jopeviq decided not to point out that he was a veteran of such assaults. He knew exactly how powerful an AV was. And exactly how much power it took to overcome one. The Star Marshall was not nearly as confident as normal, To'Jopeviq couldn't help but notice.

"You do not have full control of the battle," To'Jopeviq noted.

"I will be . . . *observed* by High Marshall Lho'Phiru-kuh," Lhi'Kasishaj said, distastefully. "There is no question as to my full capacity to lead, you understand. It is simply that the marshall was somewhat . . . stung by the previous defeat of the *Aggressor* fleet. There was some strenuous argument, but he insisted. And in the end, Command acquiesced."

"Star Marshall . . ." To'Jopeviq said, then paused. He understood Beor's rationales for the last debacle. He had even managed, quelling decades of training, to come to a weak agreement. If the High Command saw it necessary to sacrifice sixteen *Aggressors* to keep the Empire from going through another civil war, so be it.

In this case, though, he was in an impossible position. Not only was the attack likely to fail, probably losing more than one assault vector, but the person most likely to be blamed was his own patron.

"Star Marshall," To'Jopeviq repeated. "I must strongly recommend that you do not accept this position absent heavier forces. These numbers are simply untenable given any reasonable estimate of the Terran forces."

"There are things you don't know, To," the Star Marshall said. "Things you are not supposed to know but I don't suppose there is any harm in telling you. Things are not going quite as well as they appear. Five Glatun systems were never conquered by our forces. Two surrendered on orders from the new Council of Benefactors. Three still hold out. Those take priority. They must be reduced before more vectors can be made available."

"Then we should wait to attack Earth until there is sufficient force," To'Jopeviq said, trying to contain his surprise. Although everyone knew the news was only a guideline, such a huge cover-up was bound to be common knowledge sooner or later. And that could present some large problems for High Command.

"That was not the decision of Command," Lhi'Kasishaj said, bobbing his head. "And we are Rangora warriors, yes? So we follow our orders."

"Very well, Star Marshall," To'Jopeviq said. "In this life we are dead. We are sacrifices to the glory of the Emperor."

"I will see you when I return!" Lhi'Kasishaj said, suddenly his old self. "And we will celebrate my victory!"

"I look forward to it, Star Marshall."

"This is . . . quite an assembly," Gorku said.

The room, as usual with *Troy*, was vast. Also cold. The two financiers were wearing cold-weather coats against the chill. They didn't need suits because, unusually for something this large, the room was pressurized.

"It was a bit hard to start," Tyler said. "But once we got going it got easier."

The room was filled with rack upon rack of cubicles cut from the walls of *Troy*. Each cubicle contained one free-standing power system of various outputs and a laser emitter of matching output.

Arrayed through the racks were interconnected steel pipes ranging from a hand span across to, towards the end, the size of a major water main. Each of the small pipes was connected to a laser emitter. A couple of angles and it was connected to a larger pipe. And larger and larger. Except for the occasional plate of sapphire in the sides, it looked like a sewer system. There were, in fact, more pipes than emitters. And more were being installed as the two magnates watched, a continuous flow of pipes being lifted into place, aligned then welded. Just as more emitters were being lifted into place, connected to power systems, connected to pipes . . .

"How much power?" Gorku asked.

"As of this morning . . . ?" Tyler said. "Nine hundred and eighty-three terawatts. Not a patch on SAPL but pretty good. With the new workers, we're increasing the rate of installation. That's always the bottleneck."

"Where are they all coming from?" Gorku asked, walking over to one of the closer cubicles and examining the emitter. It was large. One of the largest he'd ever seen. "This is a Rangora emitter!"

"Main gun emitter from an *Aggressor*," Tyler said, gesturing to several of the local systems. The big ones were on the deck level. "We were only able to acquire four of those in good enough shape to use, unfortunately. But as soon as Hephaestus and Granadica finish Fabber Three we're going to install Hephaestus in the *Troy* and he'll have a primary job of making heavy emitters. Those three . . ." Tyler said, gesturing to another cluster, "are Glatun designs. The main gun emitters from *Deudoc* dreadnoughts. Ninety terawatts apiece. Very nice."

"And you combine it to one beam," Gorku said, rippling his fur. "One beam."

"As I said, not a patch on SAPL," Tyler said. "But nice enough."

"The work on the main door?" Gorku asked.

"A rapid closing system," Tyler said. "We're going to use an explosive system to close it. Thus the—"

"Springs," Gorku said. "You're going to have to use a lot of explosives."

"Explosives are cheap," Tyler said. "Bit cold in here, care to take a walk?"

"Since we got the second missile fabber installed we've been able to refill from what we used in the last battle," Tyler shouted. The room was noisy with clattering missiles jostling each other for space. That was mostly taking place at the top of the stacks, two hundred meters up. The lower portions were solidly packed. But since they were looking down from the upper observation deck, that was barely a hundred meters away. "And more."

"How many?" Gorku asked.

"Hundred and eighty thousand," Tyler said. "We're shooting for the full two twenty-five by the end of the month. Probably won't make it, we're having to use the fabbers for fiddly bits for the other construction."

"An assault vector carries nine thousand," Gorku said, amazed. "The Muikot battlestation carried thirty-six thousand. Two *hundred* thousand?"

"And twenty-five," Tyler said. "When it's full up. All stabilized so they can't chain react. You'd have to put a nuke in here to get them all. We haven't done any of the installations for Sector Two yet. So we only have firing ability over about one tenth of the surface."

"Where . . . is this exactly?" Gorku asked.

"Ah, well, sorry," Tyler said. "Classified. It's not the exact place as on the plans, I'll tell you that. Same with the laser room. And the command center. And 'cause of the grav walks, it's pretty hard to figure out."

"Still don't trust us?" Gorku said.

"I trust you utterly, Niazgol," Tyler said. "But classified is classified. Sorry."

"You have been busy," the Glatun said.

"Rather," Tyler replied, opening the hatch so they could leave. "That's better," he said, taking out his earplugs. "It's been an interesting ride. Couldn't have done it without your help."

"Understood," Gorku said. "But also not what... Not what *anyone* would have done!"

"Humans weren't at a low tech level when we were contacted," Tyler said. "Most galactic tech was transferred from one group to another. Very few groups were at the tech point of humans when encountered. Our problem was getting out of the well, not things like, oh, computer tech and basic space engineering. Had all that. And since we didn't have grav tech, we had to find work-arounds. Some of which work even better with grav tech. We'd been putting a lot of thought into space for a very long time. None of this is new thought. Just things we couldn't do without grav tech. Low tech, really. Simple stuff."

"And the *Thermopylae*?" Gorku asked.

"Still another month or two to get it operational," Tyler said. "We had to divert a lot of SAPL power and personnel to completing some stuff on the *Troy*. Right now it's not even at the same level as *Troy* was in the first Horvath attack it stood off. Be glad when it's done. Mass has a quality of its own."

"Speaking of mass..." Gorku said, pensively. "Your... Alliance countries have started conscription. How many people do you intend to put under arms?"

"Alliance population is currently about half of the remaining five billion population," Tyler said. "World War II, the maximum sustainable percentage was considered to be twelve percent. We've upped our productivity and a lot of things are done automatically in industry for example. Also, overall health is better so lower rate of four-F. We think we can go as high as fifteen percent."

"Three hundred seventy-five million," Gorku said. "That is a bare third of Rangora forces."

"Defending a system is easier than taking it," Tyler pointed out. "And a *Troy*-class battlestation takes fewer people to run it than an assault vector. Also a lot less to build. A *Troy* class that is fully functional, all five sectors complete, can take on about ten AVs. At least, if we fully finish it. That's going to take some time."

"Define fully finished," Gorku said.

"One hundred meters of ablative armor," Tyler said, leading the way back to the personnel area. "Ten meters of surface steel hardening. Planetary class shield generators. Five full battle sectors, including fuel pods, independent power generators, one hundred petawatts of laser output, full missile load, two hundred laser ports per sector, one hundred missile ports and a large vessel port system. Oh, and a ship fabber, five missile fabbers and a central power plant in the main bay."

"Good Cul!" Gorku said. "That is . . ."

"Insane?" Tyler asked. "Consider local galactic history, Gorku. The Glatun did most of the early advances on species in the region. Which meant peaceful contact. Humans, because the Glatun had gotten . . . had decided to study war no more, were almost immediately conquered by the Horvath. Since then, almost continuously, we have been fighting one enemy or another. It's killed a quarter of our population, changed our society and culture and more or less given us a mad on at the rest of the galaxy not to mention a really amazing degree of paranoia and we're a *very* paranoid bunch to start with. You think it's insane?"

Tyler stopped and looked the Benefactor in his red eyes.

"Gorku, it would be mad to do anything *else*."

THIRTY-ONE

"General Magamaj will have the honor of leading the assault in the *Star Vengeance*," High Marshall Gi'Bucosof said. "Under the command of Star Marshall Lhi'Kasishaj, of course."

Let him, Lhi'Kasishaj thought. *This is going to be a disaster.*

Assault vectors were only used when heavy defenses were anticipated. Given that the Terrans had destroyed a fleet of *Aggressors*, apparently without great trouble, heavy defenses were anticipated.

But even AVs could not normally take down heavy system defenses on one pass. So each AV squadron, three ships, traveled with a support squadron. The support squadron consisted of an AV support ship, essentially an unarmored, stripped out AV packed with fuel, spares, replacement armor plates and, notably, personnel, and a mobile repair dock.

The Rangora had AV repair down to an artform. By the time the AV emerged from the gate, the mobile dock had all the information it needed to begin repairs. The support ship attached directly to the dock. As the AV emerged from the gate again, generally bleeding air and bodies, they would run through the dock. Well-prepared docks had taken AVs that were barely functional and returned them to battle in a mere three hours. Each segment would be refilled with replacement personnel, parts would pour in, often through the gaping battle-wounds, portions would be cut off, prefabricated replacements would be slapped in place and, last, armor, shield generators and defensive laser clusters, always the main parts damaged, would be ladled on.

Battle repair was possibly the highest form of mass production known to the Rangora.

The only way to totally lose an AV was for weapons to dig so far through the refractory warships that they penetrated to the highly defended core. There they could take out drive systems, power systems, critical personnel and core support beams. At that point, the AV was pretty much toast. The support squadron could *still* repair one, but it would take days or weeks.

Lhi'Kasishaj looked again at the three reports prepared by To'Jopeviq's team, best, worst and medium, and wondered if any of the AVs would be coming back.

Ifs. There were so many ifs. Could the humans have created *another* battlestation such as the *Troy*? High Command dismissed the very possibility. The attack on the human, especially the American, command structure would have been crippling. And Lhi'Kasishaj had to admit that was true. At least half the American upper command structure should have been gutted. No warrior culture, as the Americans appeared to be, could survive that. The survivors would still be battling for supremacy.

The battlestation had been drifting out of position. Getting it into position had been bad enough. But then it had been closed, the door holding the circular structure.

Just blowing nukes against the exterior was out of the question. Anything powerful enough to overcome the inertia of its orbit would crack it from the impact. It should be out of good position to attack the AVs.

The AVs should do it. He wished he could believe that. But even if they did not, if they were thoroughly shredded, the *Troy* would be as seriously mauled. Its missiles would be depleted. Its laser ports and, more important, the "receptor ports" for the SAPL would be destroyed. The final targeting systems for the massive laser trashed.

The damage would be heavy enough for the twenty-four *Aggressors* and two carriers of assault troops to finish off the battlestation. Then the system would be defenseless.

And he personally intended to make sure the Terrans were never a threat again. High Command agreed. The Terrans were, potentially, a very good satrap. But the Rangora were not going to make the mistake the Glatun made. Any species this dangerous needed to be eliminated.

"The assault will be in two waves," Gi'Bucosof continued. "The *Star Vengeance, Star Battle* and *Star Mauler* in the first wave, the *Mira Destroyer, Neutron Star* and *Singularity* in the second thirty minutes later. By then the first wave will be returning for repairs or to report victory. The *Dwarf Marauder* will remain in this system as a reserve force."

Reserve force my tail, Lhi'Kasishaj thought. Gi'Bucosof wasn't going to enter the system until it was thoroughly conquered and he wasn't going to expose himself to any danger, either. Which meant he was remaining behind in the *Dwarf Marauder*.

Which was all well and good because that was where Lhi'Kasishaj intended to stay, too.

"When the resistance of the battlestation has been eliminated, the fleet will enter the system and reduce it, utterly," Gi'bucosof said. "Tomorrow, we sail to victory!"

"I'm sorry the President still hasn't made time for you," Tyler said. "Really really sorry."

"It is fine, Tyler," Niazgol said. "Your security people are very paranoid. I did not previously find them so. I suppose it is experiential."

"Well," Tyler said, moving a chess piece. "What with the Rangora attacks on political targets and problems at home, they've gotten that way. Besides, *Troy*'s way safer. Check."

"This is an interesting game," Niazgol said. "And one I need to learn more thoroughly. But I think that is..." he moved a piece. "Checkmate."

"So it is," Tyler said. "You are very good. I'm not so good at this sort of th—"

SET CONDITION ONE! SET CONDITION ONE!

"Always when you're having fun," Tyler said.

"Bloody hell," Dana said, pushing Rammer away. "You need to go."

"No, duh," the corporal said, then stopped. "Uh..."

"Rammer, just go play jarhead," Dana said, giving him a kiss on the cheek. "I'll see you at the pool when the battle's over. Now UP."

"The second battlestation is not operational," General Magamaj said. "Concentrate all fire on the *Troy*."

"All fire on *Troy*, aye," Captain Shoeguh said. "Open fire!"

"They're uglier than I thought," Admiral Kinyon said.

The assault vectors were hexagonal along their length. The edges were lined with defensive laser clusters and shield generators. The main offensive power was deeply embedded gamma ray laser emitters and missile tubes.

The hexagonal system meant that as they took damage they could rotate to bring new systems into line. And they were already starting to rotate as the heavy lasers of the *Troy* opened fire on the nearest AV.

"Missiles inbound," Captain Sharp said.

"Well, let's return the favor," Kinyon said. "Open fire quarter power on all missile tubes. Give me Commodore Clemons."

"Sir," the commander of the *Thermopylae* said. "Can I open up, yet?"

"If you please, Commodore," Kinyon said. "You have full SAPL authority."

"Open fire, SAPL," Commodore Clemons said.

"He has a point, Kurt," Kinyon said. "From this range they can intercept our missiles all day. Let's engage the enemy more closely."

"Aye, sir," Commodore Pounders said. "Firing control, engage the Orion."

"Engage Orion, aye!"

"General," Captain Shoeguh said. "The fire we are taking from the *Troy* is rather . . . weak. Also coherent light, not pumped sunlight."

"Your point, Captain?" Magamaj asked. The AVs had successfully entered the system and while the point defense of the *Troy* was better than anticipated, they were breaking through with missiles. And the grasers were shredding its unshielded surface.

"They are using a very powerful laser, sir," Shoeguh said. "Not the SAPL system."

"Our intelligence indicates that sometimes it takes it some time to come online," Magamaj said. "So it's no surprise—"

"*SAPL impact, port beam,*" Damage Control commed. "*Shields down in sectors fourteen and sixteen. Heavy damage.*"

"Port?" Magamaj said. "The only thing to port is . . ."

"Fire is coming from second battlestation," Tactical reported. "*Troy* has launched missiles from two hundred missile tubes. One th . . . two th . . . six . . . ten . . . fourteen . . . *Sixteen thousand* missiles inbound! *Troy* is moving!"

"What do you mean, moving?" Magamaj asked.

"It has some sort of fusion drive!" Tactical said. "It's under acceleration. It is closing our position!"

"All AVs!" Magamaj said. "Concentrate fire on the *Troy!*"

"What the hell was that?" Dana said.

She'd felt lots of gravitational effects during her time at *Troy*. Centripetal, centrifugal, bad inertics. But this felt more like an earthquake. Then another. And another. Each involved a very weird, slight lurch. Barely perceptible.

"That would be Orion," Hartwell said. "It seems the admiral wishes to adjust our position."

"Let me guess," Dana said as the ringing of missiles and lasers hitting the surface increased. "We're *not* running away."

❋   ❋   ❋

"We really need some shields," Sharp said.

Missiles were rather easy for any defensive system to destroy. Solid as space missiles were, they were eggshells compared to even the lightest defensive laser. And defensive lasers could retarget and fire rapidly, destroying dozens, hundreds, of missiles.

But each missile destroyed filled space with material. Material that missiles could fly through relatively unscathed but that degraded the utility of lasers.

The term in radar was chaff. It had been picked up and used for laser/missile battle.

What it meant was that the space between the AVs and the embattled station was filling with junk.

Junk that the *Troy* plowed through as if through a metal fog. Appearing on the far side and exposing itself to full fire from the AVs.

Of course, that also meant it was getting closer. And it didn't really have brakes.

"How's our missile supply?" Kinyon asked.

"Down about seven percent so far," Sharp said. "Mostly we're losing laser and missile apertures in the direction of the enemy."

"Rotate, sir?" Pounders asked.

"No," Kinyon said. "Hold off. Reduce fire. Let them think we're wounded."

"Enemy missile and laser fire falling off," tactical reported. "*Star Mauler* reports forward quadrant has sustained inoperability damage. Requests permission to withdraw."

"Given what we're getting hit with," Captain Shoeguh said, "that's not surprising. Rotate again. Hexa Four is trashed from that damned SAPL. And Two and Three are not much better from missiles!"

"Tell *Star Mauler* to stand by," General Magamaj said. "Retarget the *Thermopylae*."

"*Troy* is continuing to close our position," the fleet tactical officer pointed out.

"If we can't dodge something like that, we need to die and remove our genes from the pool," the general said. "Retarget the *Thermopylae* and bring us around to engage with main guns."

"Enemy is skewing," Sharp said.

"Cease all fire," Kinyon said.

"Sir, they're retargeting on the *Thermopylae*," Sharp pointed out.

"Lambda can take it," Kinyon said. "They think we're busted. Let 'em. Kurt, I want to close to within knife-fighting range of that nearest AV before we open up again."

Now it was *Thermopylae's* turn to take the full weight of the enemy's still not inconsiderable fire. Tens of thousands of missiles lashed out at the battlestation but what was worse was when the sixty petawatt lasers of the AV main guns struck the relatively soft nickel-iron of the battlestation's surface.

"That one shot took out most of our missile tubes, Admiral," Commodore Clemons reported. "And pretty much all our defensive clusters. Not to mention raising the temperature in the whole sphere a bit. We've still got good SAPL, but that's about it."

"Don't need much more, Commodore," Kinyon

said. "Just keep pounding hell out of them. They think we're trying to ram them."

"Looks that way from here, sir," the commodore said.

"You've got the SAPL," the admiral said. "We've got the missiles. They're about to find out how hard it is to stop missiles when the launchers are right in their lizard faces."

"Time to withdraw," General Magamaj said, looking at the Fleet damage report. "Skew to head for the gate."

"That will bring us almost in contact with the *Troy*," the fleet navigational officer pointed out. "And leave us broad on to the *Thermopylae*. Which is still firing SAPL with good effect."

"Again, I'm sure we can dodge that...thing," the general said distastefully. "Powerful but vulnerable as I suspected. And as to the SAPL...that is why we make AVs. Go to continuous rotation. That will spread the beam."

The three superdreadnoughts skew turned, rotating through three dimensions while spinning to spread the power of the SAPL and keep any one shield from failing. Hundreds already had and as the beam hit any unprotected area, the refractory armor flashed into so much carbon gas. Despite the rotation, the beam often dug deep into the gargantuan ships, dipping down to the very vitals.

"*Star Mauler* reports..." the fleet damage officer said then looked up and gestured to the viewscreen. The *Mauler* had, in fact, broken in half. And with one of its halves rotating to open up unprotected vitals to the *Thermopylae*, that part didn't last much longer. Five kilometers of the most powerful dreadnought in the galaxy was turned to incandescent gas by the ravening power of the SAPL.

The rear half retained enough control to rotate away from the fire, keeping its shields between its vulnerable interior and the *Thermopylae*. But it could barely creep along and would probably never make it to the gate and safety.

"Pity," Magamaj said. "But we estimated losing at least one AV. And for all its vaunted power, the *Troy* has been less than useless in this battle."

"As you say, General," Captain Shoeguh said. "I did not, however, appreciate that first broadside."

"Close their missile ports and it's useless," Magamaj said.

"Admiral," the Fleet Tactical officer said. "The *Troy*—!"

"That is more like it."

The *Troy* had moved back to very close to its original position, perched "above" the gate like a raven over the entrance to a graveyard. General Magamaj had chosen to take much the same route to move to the far side of the gate and return to the Eridani system. Which meant that the three AVs and the battlestation closed to within five thousand kilometers, closer than knife-fighting range in space, before the *Troy* opened fire again.

The *Troy* was made up of six zones, North, South, East, West, One and Two. South was the main hatch with its spiffy new Orion drive. The Orion had been hit by fifteen missiles during the course of the battle. Each of the missiles had the kinetic equivalent of a ten-megaton nuke.

The "minor taps" that the Orion drive was expending to accelerate the *Troy* were made from twenty-five megaton clean-pumped fusion bombs. The hits from missiles had impacted mostly on the edge piston area and had, in fact, sprung some of the welds. But not enough to affect function. The main effect had been to cause the acceleration vector to be slightly off. *Troy* movement control, which was an entire department, was still trying to figure out why, having not even noted the missile impacts. They were just scratching their heads that the Orion wasn't flying quite straight.

North had been the direction pointed at the gate. Since the whole purpose of *Troy* was to be a defender at the gate, the admiral had insisted Apollo actually put some laser clusters and missile tubes on North. Apollo had gone along, reluctantly, because North wasn't scheduled for *any* construction for two more years. They'd installed five of each.

Those were the missile and laser tubes taken out by the Rangora AV squadron. The missile tubes that launched sixteen *thousand* missiles before they were closed. The tubes, when full open, were capable of firing ten Thunderbolt missiles, each with an impact power of twenty megatons, a second.

Zone Two was the first one worked on. And there was still much work to be done. But it was mostly complete. It still needed armoring and shield generators. But it had defensive laser clusters, two hundred laser tubes and one hundred missile tubes complete. It was also where all the missiles were stored.

Zone West was not anywhere *near* complete. All it had were laser and missile tubes. And a missile bay Tyler had chosen not to mention to his friend Niazgol.

Those were complete. All of them. And the missile bay was full. It also had a building laser power room. One that had *only* been filled with the new Destructor Terra-designed two hundred terawatt lasers.

It had ten of them. Twenty petawatts of laser power in one room that could be fired through any of the four hundred laser ports. And, in fact, the laser room in Zone Two was capable of nine petawatts of output, not one.

The *Troy* opened fire at the nearest complete AV from Zone West with full missile spread *and* full laser, while the *Thermopylae* simultaneously engaged from out-system.

One hundred and ninety petawatts of SAPL fire hit the shields of the *Star Vengeance* at the same time as twenty-nine petawatts of coherent light. Nine hundred and forty-eight penetrator missiles, the survivors of the initial flight of two thousand, arrived a second later. They were mostly expended on breaching shields. But they were followed by two thousand more *per second*.

The combined fire, the *Troy* striking down from above and *Thermopylae* to port and slightly up, started at the front of the AV and walked back. The desperately rolling AV managed to keep up ten percent of its shields and about a third of its armor as the fire walked down its length.

But what emerged from the coordinated torrent of kinetic explosions and blazing laser fire was a wreck. It was listing and bleeding and completely out of control. A moment later its back broke about a third of the way down. Neither portion seemed either to have helm control or fire control.

"Shift fire," Admiral Kinyon said, coolly. "Let's finish taking these bastards out."

THIRTY-TWO

"Magamaj should have been back by now," Lhi'Kasishaj said.

The enemy had, naturally, increased jamming of the hypercom as soon as the gate activated. They'd gotten some minor data transmissions right after emergence and then nothing.

"If you had much experience of battle, *Star Marshall*, you would know that these things never go exactly according to plan," High Marshall Gi'Bucosof said. "And despite your working group's report, it is likely that he has already taken the system."

Or he's defeated, Lhi'Kasishaj thought.

"As you say, High Marshall," Lhi'Kasishaj replied.

"It is time," Gi'Bucosof said. "Early, but let us get this over with. Second wave, transfer."

"This thing doesn't exactly stop on a dime, does it," Admiral Kinyon said. "What's the status on damage?"

Troy's run by the now shredded assault vectors had taken it close to the gate. The orbital dynamics were not particularly complex. Since until the Orion drive was installed the *Troy* didn't have a drive, and since the gate was maintained by the Grtul in an unstable orbit "local" to Sol's single inhabited planet, the *Troy* had never really been in a stable orbit. It had been moved slowly past the gate and headed "outbound." This eventually left it outward from the gate and moving away from it to spinward.

To intercept the AVs, therefore, it had had to drop into a lower orbit and "swing" around the gate. It also was back in a no-win situation with the gate, going "past" it at a fairly high relative velocity. Slowing down was the next step.

"Getting there, sir." Captain Neil Pohlman, OIC of Movement Control, was the "pilot" of the *Troy*. Which meant he commanded the thirty-two personnel responsible for determining how best to maneuver the battlestation. "Unless you want us to go to a higher delta-V."

"Nope," the admiral said, holding onto the edge of the tactical station. The position of CIC and its angle to the Orion meant that the acceleration was across the compartment and slightly down. "I know why space ships don't have seat belts. Anything that's going to interfere with inertial compensators means that the crew is going to end up as goo. But I think *we* might need some."

"We got some significant slosh in the water tank," Colonel Helberg said. He was holding watch at Damage Control. "And some of the equipment and salvage welded into the main bay came loose. Oh, and we've got about a third of our laser ports and half our missile ports out of action. Down about thirty percent on missiles. Internal laser systems all nominal."

"Not bad for three AVs," Kinyon said. "Time to repair the damage?"

"Days for some of it," Helberg replied. "We'll have about twenty percent of the missile tubes back up in a couple of—"

"Gate activation," tactical cut in. "Unscheduled."

"That may have to wait," Admiral Kinyon said. "Get us maneuvered back around to engagement position."

"Recommend engage from Zone Two," Colonel Helberg said. "Zones West and North sustained the most damage."

"Make it so," Kinyon said.

"Maneuver to engagement position, aye," Captain Pohlman said. "Zone Two primary, aye."

"Admiral," Captain Sharp said. "One note."

"Yes?" Kinyon said, thinking about what little they knew about Rangora doctrine.

"We are . . . rather close to the gate exit zone . . ."

"How close?" Kinyon asked, looking at the tactical readout. The gate was simply one more feature to consider. But now that he *considered* it. "Uh-oh."

"*Gate emergence*," Squadron Tactical commed. "*There are . . . uh . . .*"

The commanding officer of the *Singularity* didn't bother to wait for orders.

"Maneuvering!" Captain Pequlhiw shouted. "Come about to one-four-three mark . . . minus twenty?"

He also knew it was a doomed attempt. The AVs had come through the gate at a velocity of three kilometers per second. The mass of *Troy* filled the forward viewscreens at a range of barely thirty kilometers. It was nine kilometers across, practically as wide as the gate.

AVs didn't maneuver on a dime, either.

But they had forward lasers that were their heaviest weapons.

"Open fire all forward lasers," Pequlhiw said. "Launch fire for effect all missiles."

"It's not like we can *miss*," *Singularity's* tactical officer said, keying in the command. "All fire, full spread."

AV assaults used a standard doctrine that, so far, had worked with remarkable effect. AVs rarely worked as single ships and the doctrine was "the more you use, the fewer you lose." Even assaults on minor systems used three AVs in a rotating triangular formation, four hundred meters apart. For heavily defended systems as many as twenty-seven had been used in three separate nine-AV assaults. Those formations had ships on the "inside" and "outside," which rotated in and out while simultaneously spinning to spread damage.

They were also well prepared for collision. Many races used large kinetic impact systems to combat gate entry. Being prepared for a large asteroid hitting you on your nose was just good sense.

There was large and then there was large. AVs were the biggest ships ever produced by any race in the local arm. In an undamaged condition, an assault vector could ram a Glatun *Ritapol*-class battleship and break it in half. The AV would barely be damaged.

The three-AV squadron had just met something not only bigger than themselves but *much* massier. And it had, by accident more than intent, lumbered straight into their path.

"Sound brace for collision," Admiral Kinyon said calmly. Remotes were showing the chewing *Troy* was sustaining. The heavy guns of the AVs, which previously had been deployed against the *Thermopylae*, were hammering Sector East.

The flip side was that East didn't have *anything* in it. Which meant he also couldn't engage with his own lasers.

"Fire back, sir?" Captain Sharp asked.

"Why waste the missiles?" Kinyon said. "This is going to be . . . interesting."

Each of the assault vectors massed four billion tons. They were traveling in an initially tight formation. As they recognized their peril, they, in more or less unison, spread out like the petals of a flower.

However, to miss the *Troy* they had to have a turning ability exceeding nine gravities of acceleration. They barely had nine gravities of acceleration forward much less in lateral.

The *Mira Destroyer*, *Neutron Star* and *Singularity*, in near simultaneity, impacted nose first into the *Troy* at an angle of thirty, thirty-three and thirty-six degrees, respectively at three wide points of Zone East.

The combined squadron had a mass of twelve billion tons and was going more or less three kilometers per second relative to the *Troy*, which was slowly passing across their nose. The *Troy* had a mass of two point two *trillion* tons.

Think of a very small deer hitting a large pickup truck. It was about the same ratio. Just *a lot* faster.

The deceleration constant of their impact was approximately three thousand gravities. High compensator Glatun, and now Terran, warships could handle up to a five hundred gravities of delta-V. No ship known could handle three thousand.

❋   ❋   ❋

"Where'd they go?" Admiral Kinyon said. "Dammit, we need some eyes on Zone East!"

"*Troy, Thermopylae,*" Commodore Clemons said. The commander of the *Thermopylae* was shaking his head on the video link. "The gate's more or less closed to nonmilitary traffic for the foreseeable future. Cleaning *those* up is going to take a while. Pumping video."

"Screen six," the CIC control officer said.

The view showed the gate clearly. And the *Troy* just as clearly.

"Okay," Kinyon said. "But where'd they go?"

"Sorry, Admiral," Commodore Clemons said. "Zooming in . . . See the itsy-bitsy bits and pieces? And the three *great big* craters in Zone East?"

Now that the view was zoomed in it was apparent that one hemisphere of *Troy* appeared to have a constellation of debris. Since the *Troy* was still under power, it was leaving most of it behind. A trail, however, was being pulled along in the light gravity so it looked as if the *Troy* was a comet leaving a spreading trail of solids. And some volatiles.

"Was there a thump?" Kinyon asked. "Shouldn't there at least have been a thump?"

"I . . . *think* so . . ." Captain Sharp said. "I sort of noticed one. But it was drowned out by the Orion."

"Good *Troy,*" Admiral Kinyon said, patting the tactical console. "Good girl . . ."

"It has been one hour, Madame President," Admiral Kinyon said. "Based on standard Rangora doctrine, if there were more AVs they should have come through the gate by now."

"Son of a bitch..." the Marine Commandant muttered. "Sorry, Madame President."

"I was thinking much the same thing, General," the President said, shaking her head. "I think it might just be time to repatriate some prisoners. If for no other reason than to fully acquaint the Rangora with what they face."

"Going to have a bunch to repatriate, ma'am," Kinyon said. "We're getting a lot of distress beacons. From the first group, anyway. No survivors from the second squadron."

"Admiral, convey my appreciation, and the appreciation of all our people who for once haven't had to survive bombardment, to your crew and the crew of the *Thermopylae*," the President said. "How is your damage?"

"We're working hard on it," Kinyon said. "Most of it is stuck blast doors. The fire from the last assault mostly hit our unfinished side. We'll have about eighty percent combat ability in two hours. I'd like to mention that Apollo crews are doing much of the work. Mr. Tyler offered them triple time and they're pitching right in."

"Two hours..." the President said, nodding. "Missile capacity?"

"Climbing," the admiral said. "We used about thirty percent of our onboard capacity, which is just...a lot of missiles, ma'am. But we've got ten fabbers running at max speed. Last I checked we were up to about seventy-two percent of capacity."

"And no damage to laser systems," the POTUS said.

"Not to the emitters," Kinyon said, furrowing his brow at the detailed questions. "We're still clearing some of the tubes and we won't have most of the collimators installed any time soon. But we've still got about fifty percent capacity in output points."

"So your combat ability is not significantly degraded," the President said.

"No, ma'am," the admiral replied. "We're ready to hold the gate."

"Admiral," the President said, looking at Space Com. "*Thermopylae*?"

"They took some heavy damage in one sector," the admiral said. "But they're at about fifty percent of their ability before the battle. They've got full SAPL. About shot out on missiles. They've only got one fabber and they weren't full up."

"Admiral Kinyon," the President said, rubbing her forehead. "Again, I congratulate you and your crew. Keep working on your damage but... Do you have an evacuation plan for nonessential personnel, and how fast can you put it into operation?"

"Yes, ma'am," Admiral Kinyon said. "And as fast as I call for it. Full evacuation of all civilian personnel will take—"

"Just...nonessential," the President said. "I understand you have some pregnant women aboard? Accountants, pay administrators. That sort of thing."

"If we evacuate them to the *Therm*..." the admiral said, frowning. "About an hour."

"Start your evacuation," the President said. "I will be back with you shortly."

THIRTY-THREE

"James Allen, report to welding control room four. James Allen, report to welding control room four."

"Jinji," Butch said, pinging a response. "I gotta go. There's an evacuation but I don't know if we're included. I'll have more news in a minute I hope."

"Yes, Mister Allen," the Coptic said. *"Go with God."*

The Copts had been quartered in the new civilian wing during the battle. Butch had gone over there to make sure they were okay with being in a defense station during a murthering great assault. The Copts had mostly been quietly praying. When he'd asked Jinji, carefully, if they were praying for their lives the Copt had replied "No. Victory."

Despite their crappy suits and a bit too much reliance on God making sure things were right, Butch was starting to like his Copts.

Welding four was way across the civilian complex and it took Butch a good five minutes to make it. When he got there, the only person there was Purcell.

"Butch," the manager said as the welder came through the hatch. "You missed the meeting."

"Sorry, Mister Purcell," Butch said. "I was with the Coptics. What's up?"

"All personnel not involved in construction are being off-loaded," Purcell said. "For certain personnel, the evacuation is voluntary. The Navy needs help with damage control. Apollo has authorized triple pay, which is nice. But there's a catch. We're probably going to be in another battle. If you off-load to the *Thermopylae*, you'll probably be out of it. That's all I know."

"Does triple pay cover the Copts?" Butch asked.

"Yes," Mr. Purcell said.

"I'll pass the word," Butch said. "But I'm good. I'll stay if it's all the same to you."

"Go find out what the Copts think," Purcell said. "But hurry. We're...in a bit of a rush."

"The battle's *over*," Dana said, watching the boarding civilians on the interior cameras. The Marines had been turned out to get them situated. They all had to have come up in shuttles but they couldn't seem to figure out what a seat-belt was for. "Why the hell are we evacuating *now*?"

"Ours not to question why," Thermal said. "Ours but to follow orders. And...we're full. I've got a good seal on the latch."

"Roger," Dana said. "Shuttle Control, Thirty-Six."

"*Thirty-Six, Shuttle Control.*"

"We are full up," Dana said. "Undocking now. Request movement vector to *Thermopylae*."

"*Roger, Thirty-Six,*" Shuttle Control commed. "*Downloading route now. Undock confirmed. Opening bay doors. Hands off the controls.*"

"I hate this part," Dana said as the shuttle backed out

of its bay on its own. They'd been loading by the forward hatch air lock and the bay was already pumped down.

"You thought it was cool the first time," Hartwell pointed out.

"That was because it was new," Dana said. "Now that I think about it, I've probably got some no-rank FUN playing computer games. Not a good thought."

The exit was a bit more energetic than the last launch and Dana quickly scanned the local area for debris.

"*Thirty-Six, Shuttle Control. Follow vector to the* Thermopylae. *Be aware of significant debris field at one-one-six mark two. Incoming shuttle traffic at zero-one-four mark neg one.*"

"Shuttle Control, Thirty-Six," Dana said. "Vector to the *Thermopylae*, aye. Significant debris field at one-one-six mark two, aye. Incoming shuttle traffic at zero-one-four mark neg one, aye."

"*Have a nice day, Thirty-Six.*"

"*Butch, BFM.*"

"Go," Butch said. All his team had elected to stay on the *Troy*. Currently they were drawing their suits and doing checks. This time, Butch was even more careful double-checking. And he'd gotten Apollo to spring for running all the Copts' really questionable suits through a rebuild. They should be good this time.

"*We're working on missile tube eighty-six. You have to go through maintenance tunnels so there's no room for a sled. Grab a power supply and a set of four eighteen heads. Meet a Navy guy at maintenance door fifty-seven. You're team Fourteen B. Got it?*"

"No," Butch said. "That's too many numbers. Hang on."

He grabbed a piece of paper and fumbled around until he found a pen.

"Say that again?"

"Thirty-Six, Mutant."

"Go, Mutant," Dana said. Truthfully, for a milk run like this there wasn't much for the cox to do but sit at her controls and look alert.

The *Therm* was pretty much like the *Troy* except for the big upside-down V on the side. And it was like the old days since they were going in the main hatch. Lots of SAPL work going on but it was all on the surface and well away from their route.

"Taking on Thermopylae *Marines after civvie off-load,"* CM1 Glass commed. *"They're going back to our old loading bays. Offload and then wait for orders."*

"Take on *Therm* Marines, aye," Dana said. "Pencil bay, aye. Offload and wait for orders, aye. Anything else?"

"Try not to get fancy?"

"O ye of little faith," Dana said, cutting the connection. "Okay, why are we cross-loading Marines? Don't they have shuttles of their own?"

"One Forty-Third," Thermal said. "Not enough to carry all of them in one load, though. And... I can only come up with one reason but it's crazy."

"Which is?" Dana asked.

"It's crazy," Thermal said. "So I'll take a rain check on talking about it."

"You Fourteen Bravo?"

Butch had the Copts towing the power supply. It had a grav lift on it so it could be moved. But the ton of metal was sort of unwieldy. He'd had to point out to them that getting caught between a wall and the APS would be a bad thing.

The fact that they were having to pull it using their suits didn't help.

"Fourteen B, yeah," Butch said. "I'm Butch."

"Ensign Lafferty," the Navy guy said. "We're in a hurry. Let's go."

Door Fifty-Seven was part of a lock system big enough to hold the whole group. The corridor beyond the lock was micrograv, smooth-walled, cold, death pressure and unlit.

"This is fun," Butch said. "Jinji, be very careful with the APS in here. Don't ding it."

"We are being very careful, Mister Allen."

"What is this thing?" Butch asked. The walls seemed to be smooth-mined raw NI.

"Maintenance support tunnel," the Navy guy said. "For the SAPL runs and the missile tubes. Do *not* get separated or you'll get lost as hell."

Butch figured that out right away. There were dozens of side tunnels and he couldn't have found his way back if his life depended on it.

"Jinji, status check," Butch said as they made their way through the maze.

"All suits are good, Mister Allen," the Egyptian replied. *"We thank you for getting them repaired. Some of them were getting quite bad."*

"Never, ever go out in death pressure with a bad suit," Butch said. "God will not help you if you are breathing vacuum."

"God is with us when we are born, as we live our life, as we die," Jinji said. *"We prefer it that way. It makes life very simple."*

"I need you guys around to work on the *Troy*," Butch said. "And I hate doing paperwork. So, I repeat, never *ever* go out in death pressure with a bad suit."

"*Yes, Mister Allen.*"

Admiral Kinyon had about a thousand irons in the fire. He looked at the missive from Earth and knew the first and most important thing to do about it.

"Paris, connect me to Mr. Tyler, please."

"You mean Mr. Tyler Vernon?" the AI queried.

"You know who I mean," Kinyon snapped.

"Hello, Admiral," Tyler said over the video link. "Congratulations on another famous victory."

"Thank you," Admiral Kinyon said. "Mr. Vernon, I request that you evacuate the *Troy*. You can transfer to *Thermopylae* in the *Starfire* along with Benefactor Gorku."

"Rather like it here, Admiral," Tyler said. "We haven't installed the DP quarters on the *Therm*, yet. It would be lacking in creature comforts."

"Understood, sir," Admiral Kinyon said, trying not to sigh. "Still, my request—"

"Admiral," Tyler said, smiling. "Save your breath. I was consulted on your orders. And there are reasons for the Benefactor to remain. You really have other things to do. I've also consulted Apollo personnel on the orders, securely, and all the rest of our personnel will remain and continue, for now, to work on your battle damage. Triple pay does that."

"I . . . see," Admiral Kinyon said. "Very well. If you insist."

"I do, I do," Tyler said. "Good luck. As you can imagine, I'll be pulling for you."

"Pushing might help more," Kinyon said after he closed the circuit. "Paris, I need all senior officers in meeting room one, now. Not in fifteen minutes, not as soon as they're done. Now."

"Yes, sir."

"And tell the damage control people to prioritize what damage can be fixed *quickly*."

"This door is very stuck," Jinji said.

The current problem was a blast door. A Rangora missile had hit by the exit of the tube, which was pretty much trashed. Another group was working on that. But the impact and the plasma wave had welded the door shut. There were four more doors between it and the magazine so they didn't have to get it into operation. Just open.

The blast door was really two "doors," hatches that slid up and down in one case and side to side in the other. They joined in an X since each was angled. Each hatch went deep into the structure of the wall and was a meter thick wall of high tensile stainless steel.

And it was welded solid. Also slightly bent.

"We need to get it open," the Navy guy said. "The team on the opening says they can get that out of the way in about an hour. What do you think?"

"I don't know for doors," Butch said, looking at the joins. The hatches were melted together and the door seemed to have welded into the walls as well. Some of the wall metal had melted down over the interior of the hatch. What the exterior looked like was anyone's guess. "I can *cut* it open. I mean, just chunk it up into scrap. I'm not sure what to do about it then, though. The good news is since it's micro we can probably move the parts. Any way you cut it, it's going to take a while."

"You can't just . . . get the welds cut?" the Navy guy said nervously. "This is a very expensive piece of equipment."

"It *used* to be a very expensive piece of equipment," Butch said. "*Now* it's scrap. I don't think just popping the welds will work. It's *bent*. And if we go trying to melt the welds on the steel, the wall, which has a lower melting coefficient, is going to weld again. Chunk it up and get rid of it is my suggestion."

"Okay," the Navy guy said, sighing. "Let me get authorization on that."

"You do that," Butch said. "I'll be figuring out what we need for it."

"One Four Two Three Six, this is Thermopylae *Shuttle Control."*

"Roger, Shuttle Control," Dana said. She remembered when *Troy*'s main bay was this chaotic but it had been a while. The main entrance was crowded as hell with shuttles going both ways and the small contingent of two *Connies* and four *Independence* frigates headed outbound.

The main bay wasn't any better. There were shuttles moving around seemingly at random. And a bunch of shuttles were docked to the *Therm*'s pencil bay.

"You need to stack up in the queue for bay twenty," Shuttle Control said. *"Just wait until the other shuttles move out then unload and load."*

"Stack in the queue for twenty, aye," Dana said. "Wait to load and unload, aye."

"Gotta go."

"They sound a little harassed," Hartwell said.

"Maybe 'cause the One-Forty-Third can't find their ass with both hands?" Dana said, dodging a shuttle that seemed to have no clue where it was going. The "queue" at twenty was just a bunch of shuttles that couldn't seem to figure out how to maintain a line. When she had to dodge another outbound shuttle, though, she figured out why they were scattered. She got back in what should be the formation and tried to keep an eye all around.

"I've got forward, up and port," Dana said. "Keep an eye on down, aft and starboard."

"Got it," Hartwell said. "Got a drifter from twenty-one. Stand by... One-Four-Three Fourteen. You're out of position. Please maintain station."

"Screw off, Thirty-Six," the coxswain replied. *"I don't take orders from faggot Condoms."*

"Since you're reading as a CN," Hartwell said coldly, "you're God damned well going to take it from *this* Condom or I'll have you up on charges. AI, connect to CM1 Glass..."

"One Four Two units..." Glass commed as he was talking. *"This is on our channel and I didn't say the following. One Four Three is a cluster grope. Just try to avoid the idiots. We're working with their flight officers to get some control, but it's not going to happen. They're just too screwed up. The following is official. Use such maneuvering as necessary to maintain safety and integrity of your shuttle and passengers. Mutant out."*

"Crap," Dana said, dodging another 143 shuttle. She was getting to where she could tell the 142nd units without even looking at the information icon. They were the ones maintaining station and *not* drifting all over the damned bay.

". . . just leave 'em in the *Troy*," Glass said. "Just get 'em to dock and *stay* docked. We can handle this."

"That's what I'm trying to convince their flight NCOIC to do," Chief Barnett commed. *"He's got orders to have them shuttle back and forth. And I can't get ahold of MOGS or any of their chain of command. Everybody's in meetings."*

"Well, if they keep endangering my people, we're going to start opening up with lasers," Glass said.

"That is increasingly an option," Barnett commed. *"But let's just try to survive and worry about this in the AAR."*

"I got authorization to just cut it away," the Navy guy said. "They didn't even blink. Apparently that's what we're doing with a lot of stuff."

"Great," Butch said. "Then we can get started."

"I've got two other teams I'm monitoring," the Navy guy said. "I gotta go."

"Got this," Butch said. "Go on. Jinji, we're going to have to be careful with this. There's guys working up the tube from us."

"I understand," the Egyptian said. *"We will be very careful."*

"I want to see each of the settings on the laser heads before you start cutting," Butch said. "I'll set them to cut two meters and no more. Don't mess with them."

"*Yes, Mr. Allen.*"

Butch checked each laser head as the Coptics picked them up and spread out. There wasn't much room in the missile tube, but there was enough for the five-man team.

The tube was circular so Butch had decided to take it out in quarters. He slid forward and used a laser to mark the cut points. Down the middle and across in a cross. Then cut away the edges of each quarter.

Four of the Egyptians started cutting as soon as he was done, he and Jinji standing back to monitor.

The four started from the cardinal points, working towards the middle. The lasers were powerful but the metal was, deliberately, refractory. It took some time to even burn through and cutting across was slow.

"BF, Butch."

"*Go, Butch.*"

"We're starting work on the door," Butch said. "But this is going to take a while. We're having to cut it out."

"*All good. Make sure you get the edges good and smooth. The missiles don't slide along the edges but they could come close. Cut close and smooth it out.*"

"We don't have any grinders."

"*I'll get some down to you. How's it going?*"

"Slow. But otherwise fine. Where're you?"

"*Up at the head of the tube. If you think that's going slow, try getting two hundred tons of melted NI out of the way.*"

"Heh," Butch chuckled. "Better you than me."

"*Just stay safe. Nothing here worth dying over. And if you die, you can't spend your pay.*"

"Will do."

✴   ✴   ✴

"Good lock," Hartwell said.

Waiting to get docked was just about the scariest thing Dana had ever done, including working the scrapyard. At least in the scrapyard the stuff went on a predictable vector.

"Get the cargo out," Dana said, wincing as a shuttle nearly hit her docked. "Fast. I do not want to be here any longer than necessary."

"Get this," Hartwell said as they undocked. "The 'Marines' are Pathans."

"What's a Pathan?" Dana asked, maneuvering carefully through the chaos. It was getting to be less of a mess, which was nice. Apparently somebody had gotten a dose of sense.

"The *Therm* has a bunch of Alliance groups," Hartwell said. "Afghanistan's a part of the Alliance. They sent a bunch of their guys to be trained as space marines."

"These are Afghans?" Dana said. Her assigned vector had a shuttle sitting right in it so she had to go out of route. Which put her in someone else's route. "Sorry," she commed.

"*No problem*," Twenty-Four replied. "*Figured you had to dodge that idiot.*"

"Southern Afghans," Hartwell said. "Pathans. Pushtuns."

"Okay," Dana said.

"You don't get it, do you?" Hartwell said, chuckling. "These are the guys we were fighting for something like twenty years in Afghanistan. Okay, Taliban?"

"You're pulling my leg," Dana said, finally getting it.

"Nope," Hartwell said. "Taliban and Pathan aren't

exactly the same, but they were most of the Taliban forces. And their commanders? They're not Marines. They're U.S. Special Forces. The guys that took down the Taliban in Afghanistan then fought there for twenty years."

"We gave 'em laser rifles?" Dana said. "What are we, crazy?"

"Welcome to a brave new world," Hartwell said. "And if we're cross-loading for the reason I think... yeah, we're crazy."

"I feel like the XO of the *Yorktown*," Commodore Pounders said. "We're clearing a lot of the damage by cutting it away and jettisoning it overboard. Which means we're leaving an even larger trail of debris. The good news is, we'll have about eighty percent functionality in an hour."

"So..." Admiral Kinyon said, considering the scratch plan. "The last question is maneuver control. Can we make the insertion?"

"We figured out why we were getting anomalous delta at least," Captain Pohlman said. "We took multiple hits on the Orion, sir."

"But it's running, right?" Kinyon said, frowning.

"Yes, sir," Pohlman said, shaking his head. "It's still running. Just sort of... sideways. Spring four took most of the impact and it's a bit... bent. We've figured out the compensation. And internal rotation is, of course, unaffected. We... should be able to make the insertion. But the *Troy's* not a really precision instrument. And it's a narrow window."

"How long to get into position?"

"We'll be in position by the time Colonel Helberg's

teams are done, sir," the captain replied. "We're maneuvering for insertion at the moment. Just using very light adjustments. We'll have to increase delta for insertion."

"Understood," Kinyon said. "The orbital vector in Eridani is higher."

"To boldly go where no battle globe has gone before," Captain Sharp said. "It's true. Humans really *are* crazy."

"The station is going into the *Eridani system*?" Gorku said. "Are you insane?"

"It's a big station," Tyler said, looking at the plans. "Getting through the gate is going to be interesting. As to insane... Yes. We're insane. As a species we do things *then* see if it works. It's called 'trial and error.' Mostly error, admittedly. Also 'the scientific method.' Which is just trial and error dressed up in fancy language."

"It's not can you get through the gate," Gorku said, nervously. "It's what might be on the other side."

"Should be light forces," Tyler replied. "And a bunch of Rangora engineers desperately trying to take down the space docks before something comes through the gate. The fun part is trying to get through before they're ready to leave."

"And you intend to go along on this suicide mission?" Gorku said.

"I'm not the only one, Niazgol. You're going, too."

"*What?*"

"*All hands, civilian and military, this is Admiral Kinyon.*"

"Troy Battle Globe, BG One, *has been ordered by the President of the United States, in consultation with the Alliance partnership officials, to move forward into the Epsilon Eridani system, determine the nature of enemy forces therein, engage enemy forces at will and remove from that system any materials which can be moved in no more than one day. This can be styled as a reconnaissance raid in really enormous force. Its purpose is to show the Rangora that Terra is a strategic threat and thereby get them to the negotiating table. We anticipate light forces guarding the AV support ships. Light being defined as one or more battleship squadrons with supporting cruisers and frigates.*

"Commander's intent is to have the Troy engage all armed vessels in the system then launch CruRon One, augmented, as well as Shuttle Squadrons One Four Two and One Four Three with elements of Fifth and Ninth Marine regiments to take such vessels as are determined to be mobile enough to remove from the system. We are particularly interested in the semi-mobile repair docks for the AVs. That is the primary target.

"Boot them in the ass, don't piss on them. For the first time, Earth is not standing on the defensive. We're about to teach these lizard bastards why you don't mess with Terra. We're going to teach that lesson by blowing the crap out of their pussy little cruisers and battleships and taking their stuff. If I could paint a skull and crossbones on the side of the Troy I'd do it. I want a great big 'Arrh!' from all hands as we pass through the gate. That is all."

THIRTY-FOUR

"We could send some of the battleship squadrons in..."

"Anything that can destroy an AV squadron is not going to have much trouble with a battleship squadron!" Star Marshall Gi'Bucosof shouted.

The staff officer slid down in his seat, quivering.

The arguments had been going on for the last three hours as the two Marshals tried to figure out some way to pull victory from defeat.

The support fleet, with two *Aggressor* squadrons, was parked on the out-going side of the gate twenty thousand kilometers from the exit. They had waited in vain for the return of the AVs until it became obvious no one was returning. Since then they had been taking down the docks.

The main battle fleet, the AV *Dwarf Marauder* and twenty-two *Aggressor* squadrons, was hovering on the input side of the gate as its various staffs and commanders shouted at each other and tried to assign blame.

"We should retreat as fast as possible," Marshall Lhi'Kasishaj said. "Hook up the tractors of the ships and pull the docks through the gate. Kulo only knows what the Terrans are going to send through any moment now. They've clearly been building ships faster than anyone anticipated."

Lhi'Kasishaj was pretty much resigned to his fate. He was going to get his head cut off, even though *his* people had pointed out that six AVs were simply insufficient.

Taking down the docks was, as always, taking time. They had to be disassembled and then moved through the gate in portions, otherwise the relatively fragile platforms would be damaged. But at this point, he was ready to get *out* of the system. Even though that probably meant being shorter.

"You spineless coward!" Gi'Bucosof screamed. "That would be your choice. You and your working group that couldn't even figure out the *Thermopylae* was online!"

They'd gotten that much of a transmission from the second group. That they were taking fire from the *Thermopylae*, and the *Troy* was physically blocking the gate. The humans were back to thoroughly jamming hypercom so they didn't know more than that.

"When we get back I am going to denounce you as incompetent and a coward," Gi'Bucosof continued. "This was, after all, *your* command."

"Which you unilaterally took over," Lhi'Kasishaj pointed out. "The mission logs show that every order was given by you. I was relegated to listening. to my mission be destroyed by *your* orders!"

"We'll see what High Command has to say about—"

"Marshall . . ." Captain Azugom said. "I'm getting word that there is a gate activation. The codes are for Terra."

"Perhaps . . ." Gi'Bucosof said. "Perhaps the first group survived?"

"And perhaps this battle is truly over," Lhi'Kasishaj said, voicing the thoughts of every *sane* person in the meeting. "Captain, send a signal to the fleet to prepare to defend the system against the Terran mobile forces—"

"Marshall . . ." the captain said in a low tone. "It's not cruisers . . ."

"Damn . . ." Kinyon said. "We fit!"

"Close," Captain Pohlman pointed out. "We actually had to sort of bump off of some fields on the gate. That's a pretty powerful system."

"And we have . . ." Captain Sharp said. "Uh . . . oh . . ."

"Define 'uh, oh,'" Admiral Kinyon said, looking at the tac screen. "Uh, oh."

"Uh, oh," Low Commander Osipheth said as the mass of nickel-iron emerged from the gate.

Aggressor squadrons consisted of one *Aggressor*, four *Cofubof* cruisers, two *Gufesh* destroyers and two *Sheshibas* frigates.

As the commander of the *Sheshiba*-class frigate *Yettoj*, LC Osipheth was about the lowliest commander in the system. But it was still a command and one that he loved.

Watching the *Troy* emerge was, therefore, pretty much the end of any joy he might have had. Because the entire fleet was well aware that six assault vectors had just taken it on and not come back. Their effect was evident from the scarred surface. Which, along with a credit, would buy you a drink in the club.

"*Jachchud* signals taking override control," the tactical officer said.

The *Aggressors* could integrate fire from their full battle group. With the *Jachchud* taking control of the battle, that was pretty much it for commanding as well. Except for the battle damage.

"Relinquish control," Osipheth said. "For what good it will do."

"We hit it!" Ucelef said. "I don't know who or what . . . But there's a continuous set of . . . nuclear explosion . . . s . . ." He trailed off.

Osipheth had been looking at the same readings and had the same moment of elation. But he'd also gotten to the fine print faster than his tactical officer.

"I think . . . that's their drive," the commander said.

"Hah, hah!" one of the tactical enlisted Rangora said. "That's their . . . that's their . . ."

"Twenty-five megatons every tenth second," Ucelef said. "Twenty . . . *five* . . ."

"That's their *drive!*" the tactical tech said. "Their drive! Their drive! Hah, hah . . . hahhahhahhahhaha-haaaaaaa!"

"Appears to be slowing them down, though," Osipheth said. "I think we need a medic up here. And I could use a drink."

"I have twenty-four *Aggressor* squadrons, total," Sharp said. "Two forward guarding the docks. That was expected. The twenty-two and an AV were not."

"Hit the guards first," Admiral Kinyon said. "Boot them in the ass, don't piss on them. Then swing around the gate to engage the heavy forces."

"Kick in the ass, aye," Sharp said. "Full launch, Sector Two. Target Sierra Twenty-three. Full launch, Sector West. Target Sierra Twenty-Four. We need to maneuver to engage with lasers. I don't have any guns on North."

"Maneuvering, come about," the admiral said. "Bring West and Two around to target the guard forces on the way by. Keep East, One and North towards the main fleet. Prepare to launch parasite craft."

"Come about, aye," Captain Pohlman said. "West and Two to spinward, aye. East, One, North to antispin, aye."

"Prepare to launch parasites, aye," Commodore Marchant said. "We're stacking them in the launch tubes."

"Antispin *Aggressors* are in movement," Sharp said. "They've opened fire."

"Joy," Admiral Kinyon said. "Try to keep it off the Orion, why don't you?"

"What about my ships?" Commodore Marchant said.

"Nothing says being in the Navy's safe," Admiral Kinyon said.

"Joy," LC Osipheth said as the battle globe opened fire. In the first three seconds it had fired more missiles than carried by the entire BBG. He'd already flushed his racks and was potting at it with his four terawatt laser. If any of the lasers of the defending fleet were bothering the globe, it wasn't evident. It was turning, slowly, in space, apparently trying to maneuver to take the main fleet under fire.

"Missile fire targeted on the *Jachchud*," Lieutenant Ucelef said. "Half of it. The other half is going for the *Ru'Kezhilix.*"

"That's their problem," Osipheth said. "Defense link up?"

"Full lock," Ucelef said. "Not that it's doing much good. We're stopping them but not fast enough."

"I can see that," Osipheth said. "No lasers at least. They don't have that damned solar laser to hit us with."

"Laser fire," Ucelef contradicted him. "Heavy. Targeted on the *Ru'Kezhilix*. *Ru'Kezhilix* is . . . gone."

The laser of the *Troy* was not the SAPL but it concentrated more power in one battlestation than any five assault vectors. Many of the aiming collimators had been damaged in the battle but there were more than enough left to hammer the defending battleship battle groups.

It had taken some time to rotate the *Troy* around to where the main laser could engage but it was in the target box before the missiles got through the Rangora defenses.

One shot was all it took to take down an *Aggressor*'s shields. The next pretty much ripped the wildly maneuvering ships to shreds.

Then the missiles started hunting for viable targets.

"Take us in alongside the *Jachchud*," Osipheth ordered. "The port remnants, that is."

The heavy battlewagon had barely withstood the laser of the globe for a second. Then it was cut in half long-wise. Then the viciously powerful laser went on to find other targets, starting with the cruisers. Which gave the *Yettoj* a few moments of breathing room.

"Alongside the port remnants, aye," the pilot replied.

"Sir?" Ucelef said.

"If we can get in there and shut down, we might not be noticed by the remaining missiles," Osipheth said. "We're not going to *win* this battle but I'd like to *survive* it."

"Still trying to sort out the sheep from the goats," Captain Sharp said. "We're about in the basket for the beginning of fire from the main fleet. But the defenders are mostly gone."

"Flush the parasites," Kinyon ordered. "All of them as fast as possible."

The *Troy* maneuvered like an aging tortoise. They still hadn't killed their velocity from gate exit and were somewhat in danger of hitting one of the docks. But it was time to come around and face the main fleet.

"Flush parasites, aye," Commodore Pounders said.

"After everything else about the *Troy*," Captain Kepler said, "this is one thing I can't quite get over."

"Concur, sir," Booth said.

"Carter, *stand by for launch.*"

"Ready for launch, aye," Captain Kepler said, bracing himself into his chair. He didn't really need to. The launch system was a lower gravitational constant than the *Carter's* acceleration; the onboard inertial compensators would handle it easily. But knowledge and emotions were two different things. A two-hundred-meter-long, fifty-meter-wide ship was about to get shot out of a kilometer-long ejection tube in less than a second. It should feel like you were in an accelerating Ferrari.

A really, really *big* Ferrari.

The *Carter* slid up the launch tube and jetted into space, hurtling towards the target ships at forty kilometers per second.

"Make sure our IFF is up," Kepler said. "There's

still a bunch of the *Troy's* missiles floating around hunting targets. Status on the battle group?"

"*Warrington* and *Mayrant* are out of the tube," the CIC officer said. "*Monaghan* and *Trippe* are flushing now."

"And we're in business," Kepler said. "Any incoming fire?"

"Not on us," Booth said. "Don't ask about the *Troy*."

"This is rather unpleasant," Admiral Kinyon said as the first flight of missiles broke through the defenses. The *Troy* was ringing like a cymbal.

"CruRon away," Commodore Marchant said. "Launching shuttles."

"Arrh, me hearties!" Kinyon said neutrally. "Boarders away! Adjust missiles to full antimissile settings. Keep them off the parasites. And let's see how many *they* carry."

Each of the *Aggressors* carried four hundred missiles. The Assault Vector *Dwarf Marauder* carried an additional five thousand.

The *Aggressors* could flush their magazines in under a minute. The AV took a bit longer, two minutes.

Two minutes after the *Troy* exited the gate, just short of fifteen thousand missiles, each having the kinetic energy equivalent of a ten megaton nuclear weapon, were in space and headed towards the battlestation.

But the *Troy* had missiles as well. Most of those were set to target on the enemy ships. Ten percent, though, were set to engage incoming missiles.

About ninety percent of the fire was getting through the defenses with the *Troy* sending most of its fire to the enemy fleet. Two hundred megatons of energy was hitting the battlestation every second. Most of it, however, was hitting on the North sector, which was pointed at the enemy fleet. Which just meant it was slowly mining out the sector and otherwise doing no damage other than marginally changing the *Troy*'s delta-V.

As the missiles shifted to defense, that fire dropped off. The *Troy*, even with all the damage it had sustained, fired fifteen hundred missiles per *second*.

In ten seconds, *Troy* had launched as many missiles as the entire enemy fleet launched in one hundred and twenty. The missiles were successful at interception fifty percent of the time. Some hit multiple times. Those that "missed" were automatically programmed to continue on to the distant ship targets.

Ten seconds after that, there were no more enemy missiles.

"Cease fire," Admiral Kinyon said. "Let's close a bit before we use up more missiles. No need to leave them in the target basket longer than necessary."

"Close the fleet on the *Dwarf Marauder*," Lhi'Kasishaj said. "Keep those missiles off of us. Activate the gate. We're getting out of—"

"We are going *nowhere*!" Gi'Bucosof shouted. "Close on the battlestation and destroy it!"

"You're insane," Lhi'Kasishaj said. "That thing has more firepower than we can *possibly* face!"

"There are things you do not know, coward," Gi'Bucosof said. "In a moment, it will simply be a very rich prize."

✳ ✳ ✳

"You don't seem to be enjoying the game, Niazgol," Tyler said, moving a pawn. He had to be careful to get it into the right space since the *Troy* was rocking in a most unpleasant manner.

"I have rather had my fill of battles," Gorku said, considering the board. "And being in this one seems unnecessary."

"Depends upon the definition of unnecessary," Tyler said. "Your move."

"I know," Gorku said. "I'm considering it."

"I think the vulnerability of my rook is rather obvious," Tyler said.

"And I'm wondering why you put it out in the middle of the board," Gorku said. "Unsupported by other pieces."

"It seems rather unnecessary, doesn't it?" Tyler said.

"Yes," Gorku said, looking him in the eye. "What game are you playing?"

"More like *which*," Tyler said, smiling. "Seriously. Your move."

"I rather don't want to do this," Gorku said, ruffling his back fur. "But . . . Paris."

"Yes, Benefactor?"

"Code Tol-Par-Kie-Fon," Gorku said. "Override Benefactor Six One Seven Four."

"Yes, Benefactor," Paris replied. "All defense shut down. Evacuating all personnel areas. Shutting down drive. Opening bay door. Sending surrender codes to Rangora fleet."

"I'm sorry, Tyler," Gorku said. "But it has to be this way."

"Yes, it does, rather," Tyler said as the hatch slid

open. Three Marines in suits entered with their lasers pointed casually at the floor.

Gorku blinked in surprise. He could clearly feel the Orion drive continuing to fire. And there was a hum under all the fire of the lasers still functioning and missiles being ejected. Through the crystal wall, the ripple of distortion from the maneuvering drives was visible.

"How?" Gorku said. "That . . . that is a hard-coded override! It's a *Benefactor* override!"

"What you failed to consider," Tyler said, gathering up the pieces, "was that Earth had a rather developed IT field before we met the Glatun. And while we had *immense* trouble with the complexity of your software when we first encountered it . . . well, we've had seventeen years. That's the same time as from the development of the Apple Two to the Internet boom. If you think we were going to put the survival of Earth in the hands of AIs we didn't fully understand . . . Seriously, did you really think we were *that* stupid?"

"How long had you known?" Gorku asked.

"AIs don't come fully awake until they're activated," Tyler said. "We rather thoroughly vetted the software before we activated it. And once we knew what backdoors would look like in Glatun code, we were able to find them easily enough. Not to mention things like Benefactor overrides. We've had full control, including overrides, on all the AIs you supplied for some years now. We've even reverse engineered the coding so we can make our own. I was just wondering if you'd really go through with it."

"The Glatun are conquered," Gorku said sadly. "What else did you expect me to do?"

"So you didn't really escape," Tyler said. "Is the admiral aware?"

"No," Gorku said. "No, he's not. He thought it was all valid. The order was. My escape, though, was provided courtesy of the Rangora High Command."

"I recall you had Rangora servants," Tyler said. "So all that hooey about being a Glatun patriot was so much bullcrap. You were a spy all along?"

"No," Gorku said. "I didn't give the Rangora a *thing* before the war. That didn't mean I didn't leave my options open. I saw that we could never face the Rangora. I did what I could to prevent the war and even to find allies, like Earth, that might help. But in the end... What would you have had me do?"

"I guess... trust us," Tyler said. "But that was yesterday. For today, these gentlemen will escort you to slightly less comfortable quarters while we crush another Rangora fleet. And tomorrow... we will see what we can do for the Glatun."

"We are on vector for the enemy fleet, sir," Captain Pohlman reported.

The *Troy* was finally flying straight now that the enemy's missiles were so much space dust.

"Finally," Admiral Kinyon said.

"We were getting a lot of alternative delta from the missile hits, sir," Pohlman pointed out. "But we're headed for them, now."

"Keep North pointed at them," Kinyon ordered. "Tactical shift targeting to the AV. All tubes, all laser. Hold fire for my command."

"All tubes, all laser, target the AV, aye," Sharp said. "This is gonna be fun."

"How are the Marines and parasites doing?" Kinyon asked.

"Nominal," Commodore Marchant said. "Just getting in range to start boarding actions."

THIRTY-FIVE

"Holy crap," Dana said, maneuvering to dodge incoming laser fire. "Can we get some *fire suppression* here?"

The space docks had "only light defenses." Light defenses were enough to take out a shuttle. As had already been proven too many times.

"Roger," Hartwell said, firing their own pop-gun. "*Carter*, this is Thirty-Six. Could we get some fire suppression, over?"

The shuttles were working in tandem with the cruiser battle groups. Each flight, supposedly, had a CruRon covering it. So far, it seemed like most of the covering was coming from their onboard lasers.

"*Roger, Thirty-Six,*" the *Carter* responded. "*Can you pinpoint it for us?*"

The exterior of the three kilometer-long space dock was not smooth, it looked like the skyline of a city. Which meant that fire was coming from a dozen angles.

"Try following the line of my fire," Hartwell said, firing another burst of lasers. "Good enough?"

"*Roger, got it. Incoming fire from the* Warrington."

The surface structure, whatever it was, vanished in a flash of light. The *Warrington* had apparently fired a missile.

"Thank you, *Jimmy*," Hartwell said.

"You are welcome. Please consider us for all your future weapons of mass destruction needs."

"*And* they made a nice LZ," Dana said, banking around to head for the destroyed structure. It was still outgassing, which meant the Marines wouldn't have to cut through a bulkhead.

"Whoa," Hartwell said as they entered the structure. It hadn't been obvious how large it was from a distance. The blast from the *Warrington* had opened up a large support corridor of some sort. Large being defined as large enough for multiple shuttles to fit.

"We're taking fire," Dana said as the hull rang.

"Can't spot it," Hartwell said.

"Thirty-Six, Thirty-Two. Fire coming from ten o'clock, low."

"Got it," Hartwell said.

A group of Rangora were clustered around a semi-portable laser. It had about the same output as the shuttle's, but was manually targeted.

Hartwell laid the auto-caret on the group and walked laser fire across them. The power-pack from the laser blew up in a flash of actinic light, taking out the survivors of the crew. And a section of bulkhead and deck.

"EM Hartwell, Staff Sergeant Pridgeon."

"Go, Pidge."

"We going to take any more fire? I've got a guy down and we're evacuated."

"Don't know," Thermal answered. "But you're about to get to fire back. Ramp coming down."

* * *

"We have an entry near quadrant four engineering control," Major Ward said. Eric C. Ward was the operations officer of the 2nd Marine regiment, which was tasked with capturing both the space dock designated SO Two as well as its support ship, Sierra Two Eighteen.

It was one hell of a task for a bare two thousand Marines.

"It's the main engine transfer corridor," Ward continued. "There's enough space to put down a Flight."

"Let's maximize that," Colonel Bolger said, moving his chew from one cheek to the other and spitting into a receptacle in his helmet. "Put in Two Batt."

"Two Batt to LZ Charlie, aye," Major Ward said, sending the orders.

"Time to move forward," Bolger said. "Get me a shuttle to saddle."

"Two-thirty there," Staff Sergeant Pridgeon said, pointing to the side. "Get me some covering fire down this corridor!"

Rammer grabbed one handle of the crew-served laser and hefted as Lassie got the other.

"Let's rock," Rammer said, humping the laser down the ramp.

The "corridor" was about as high as a gymnasium and seemed to stretch forever. Whatever it was for, the steel bulkheads and deck were scuffed up and scratched as if something big was normally moved through it. Arrayed along the sides were more hatches than he could count. And all of them seemed to be disgorging armed Rangora who seemed strangely upset at the unexpected visit from the Terran Marines.

Laser fire seemed to be coming from everywhere and he really had no fricking clue what they were doing. But the staff said set up the laser and give covering fire and that was good enough.

He powered up the laser as Lassie latched down the tripod in case they lost gravity. It was about that time he realized the gravity was above Earth normal. Which just made him glad that was what they normally trained in.

He scanned the vector for targets and caught a burst of fire from a hatch down the corridor. He swept the laser across the hatch and was rewarded by the sight of a burst of volatiles. A moment later a part of a Rangora tumbled out of the hatch.

"We're taking fire," Lassie said as the bulkhead next to them flashed into gas. The laser had a shield but it wasn't much good against heavy fire.

"Where?" Rammer snapped. Rangora were pouring into the corridor, taking cover behind the debris left by the strike from the ships. The fire could be coming from anywhere.

Rammer walked the laser into the groups he could spot, getting some, missing others. He felt a punching sound to his side and looked over.

"Frack," he muttered. "I need a new AG, Staff! Lassie's down!"

"*Missile, Missile, Missile,*" the battle comp chimed.

"Crappity, crappity, frack, frack," Rammer said, sending another burp of coherent light downrange.

"*Thirty-Six, pull out and go pick up more troops,*" Mutant commed. "'*Ware fire.*"

"Roger, Mutant," Thermal said, firing a burst of lasers into a group of Rangora about a hundred meters down the corridor. The bastards were big but they had a remarkable ability to hide in the rubble that the missile strike had caused.

"Pulling out," Dana said, lifting off.

The shuttle almost immediately went into a spin that slammed it into the bulkhead of the corridor. Dana corrected and got it limping back into space but it was hard. Something was broke.

"What just happened?" Dana asked.

"We got hit by Thirty-One," Hartwell said. "Damage to starboard maneuvering control. Get us out of this cluster and I'm on it."

"What about Sean and Charlie?" Dana asked, crabbing out of the opening as another shuttle came in.

"Thirty-One's toast," Hartwell said. "Ate a missile."

"Crap," Dana said. "These had better be worth it."

"We're taking some serious fire from down-corridor, sir," Captain Silver said. Benjamin "Streak" Silver was the commander of Alpha Company, Second Battalion, Second Marine Regiment and had found himself on point of the regiment's assault. Which meant that his company, in particular, was soaking up the casualties. "Is there any way we can get some heavy fire support? The shuttles are doing what they can, but we're getting slaughtered in here."

"Roger, Ben," the battalion commander commed. "We're working that exercise. Just maintain your Operational Status. I'm sending in Charlie company as force addition."

"Gung-ho, sir," Silver said, trying not to sigh. Lieutenant Colonel Maddox was a great guy and a good commander. But he had a real problem with buzzword bingo. The company commanders had bets whether it would last in combat. Which meant Silver had just made ten bucks. If he lived to collect it.

"Roger, Two-Two . . ." Booth said, looking at the schematic of the battle area. The corridor the battalion commander was talking about was clearly highlighted and they even had good locations on the heavy enemy concentrations. "I can open that up like a tin can if you want. Tell your boys to hunker down for incoming."

"Can you actually open that like a tin can?" Kepler asked.

"Roger, sir," Booth said, sending the commands. "I'm going to use the main gun on the *Monaghan*. They're in best position. Permission to fire?"

"Stand by," Kepler said, double-checking the vectors. The main gun on the *Monaghan* was a one hundred terawatt system. A near miss would cook the Marines. "Roger, permission to fire."

"Permission to fire, aye," Booth said, pressing the firing button. "Eat coherent light, lizards."

"Bloody hell!" Father Patricelli said as the overhead of the corridor flashed into gas. The metal went white hot for just a moment, filling the corridor with a light bright enough to be a nuke.

Despite being evacuated, the pressure of the gaseous material could be felt on their suits. And it was *hot*.

"So much for resistance," Rammer said, poking his head out from behind the shield.

The length of corridor where the Rangora had been gathering was now so much twisted and melted metal. What hatches remained were probably welded shut.

"We won't be going *that* way," Father said.

"Which we ain't," Pridgeon commed. "We're holdin' the LZ for Charlie and Bravo. Just make sure nobody comes that way no more."

"Gotcha, Staff," Rammer said. "Las— Chaos, we need more ammo!"

"Got that, Rammer," the private said, heading back to the LZ.

"And watch out for—" Rammer said just before there was a truncated scream.

"Bloody hell," Father said, shaking his head. "Corpsman!"

"Bits of hot metal . . ." Rammer finished. "That can puncture your suit."

"Looks like he's gonna live," Father said, turning to observe the private being carted away.

"Boy needs to join the Army or something," Rammer said. "And, by the way, we still need more ammo."

"On it," Father said. "Hope we don't run out. Nearest resupply's the *Troy*."

THIRTY-SIX

"Bit of a dog's breakfast," Admiral Kinyon said, flexing his jaw.

The tac screen was too cluttered to make any sense of it. There were 216 separate Sierras—ships that were designated as targets—as well as a stream of outgoing and incoming missiles.

Even on the large holo in the middle of the CIC, the entire thing was filled with vector markers and ship designators.

"The AV's too tough to spread our fire on multiple Sierras," Kinyon said. "All fire on the AV. Wait for it, though. I want to get close enough that we can rotate to engage with laser and missiles simultaneously and mass strike with the missiles. Then work your way down the *Aggressors*, cruisers, etcetera."

"They appear to be bolting for the gate," Captain Sharp pointed out. "If we wait too long we'll miss some of them."

"Fine," Kinyon said. "We're between them and the gate. The President wanted to send a message. Battleships streaming air and water, limping through the gate is about the right balance of nice, don't you think? Don't let any of them get through without at least a kiss on the cheek."

"It's not firing," Lhi'Kasishaj said. "Why is it not firing?"

"Waiting to get us in killing range," Colonel Koax said. The fleet tactical officer was considering the various vectors on the screen. "Since it has managed to maneuver around the gate, we can't get through without passing through its primary cone of fire. It is now apparent that there are only two zones that are fully prepared for battle. It can only fire its laser from those two zones."

The *Troy's* onboard laser had been a very unpleasant surprise. Based on the spectroscopy of the light, it appeared to be composed of several different emitters. More emitters and more power than an AV main gun.

"By closing, simply absorbing our fire, it can enter a range where no matter how many laser clusters we have, the missiles will overwhelm them," Koax continued. The fleet was now accelerating for the gate but the *Troy*, despite its relatively low delta-V, had started off closer than the fleet. All it really had to do was slow down, move to the side and the gate went "past" it. The fleet was having to accelerate to catch up. "And then it can use the laser to finish us off."

"You sound as if we are already defeated," Star Marshall Gi'Bucosof snapped.

"We *are*, Star Marshall," the colonel said calmly. "And all the bluster in the universe does not change that. The best we can do is as much damage as possible while we die."

"Where is your trick, Gi'Bucosof?" Lhi'Kasishaj

said. "You said that it would fail. That you had an inside agent."

"Any moment now," Gi'Bucosof said. "Any... moment..."

"I've got a destroyer accelerating into our basket, sir," Sharp said. "Permission to keep him from phoning home?"

The Rangora had already triggered the gate, creating a rippling surface of quantum discontinuity leading to the Glalkod system.

"Make sure the pieces go through the gate," Kinyon said. "Clean up is always such a bitch. Other than that, permission granted."

"Main laser," Sharp ordered. "Take down the shields then cut him in half. You'll need to dial down the power appropriately."

"*Now* would be good, Star Marshall!" Lhi'Kasishaj snarled as the destroyer *Ayachor* was cut in half with almost mathematical precision. The destroyer from the *Yo'Phafodolh* battle group had been the closest to the gate and safety. Or what seemed it might be safety. The entire battle group was entering range to be engaged by the enemy's lasers. Which meant they were all about to be ravaged.

"I don't know..." Gi'Bucosof said. "It should have been rendered impotent by now! But... it is not firing missiles. Perhaps it is... out? There was a great battle in the Sol syst—"

"Missile launch," Colonel Koax reported. "Low-rate fire from one sector. Target is the *Yo'Phafodolh*."

❋　　❋　　❋

"*Who's* your daddy?" Sharp said as the stream of missiles hit the shields of the *Aggressor*. The breacher missiles cracked the hard-held shields like an egg then the following wave slammed into the side of the battlewagon, turning it into so much chaff.

The main laser was, in the meantime, reaching out with almost delicate precision and shredding the smaller vessels of the battle group. Cruiser shields lasted less than a second under the hammer of the multi-emitter laser, turning reflective and then black before failing utterly. The laser cared even less for their heavy armor, cutting through them like a blowtorch through light snowfall. Destroyer and frigate shields failed like a popped soap bubble.

The gate was still open and the shredded masses of the vessels were being cleaned up by exiting into the next system. There might even be survivors. There were certainly enough distress pods.

"This isn't going to work," Lhi'Kasishaj said. "That . . . thing can destroy the entire fleet. We must scatter."

"We don't have the acceleration to come back around," Gi'Bucosof said.

"By *we* I meant the many thousands of Rangora you have brought to this defeat," Lhi'Kasishaj said. "The other *we*, meaning the *Dwarf Marauder*, will battle the station to cover their retreat. Some of the cruisers and destroyers can survive at least. If the Terrans do not hold this system, those may be able to make it back to Rangora space."

"Never," Gi'Bucosof said. "They will screen our retreat through the gate. I will not sacrifice myself to—"

His pronouncement was cut off as Lhi'Kasishaj

slid a pain stick, set to lethal, into his back. The high marshall jerked and grunted for a moment, until Lhi'Kasishaj let up on the trigger, then slumped to the floor.

"Send the order to scatter," Lhi'Kasishaj said. "Tell the captain to maneuver so as to catch the fire of the station and screen the fleet. Full power to screens."

"Yes, Star Marshall," Koax said, keying in the orders.

"The good news is that getting hit by a missile is, I understand, a rather quick death," Lhi'Kasishaj said as two spacemen quietly dragged the high marshall from the CIC. "The way things were going, Kazi was going to keep us alive for *years*."

"Screaming," Colonel Koax said.

"Change in delta," Captain Sharp said. "Their fleet isn't trying to make the gate anymore. They're scattering."

"*All* of them?" Kinyon asked. "That's not good."

"Yes, sir, tracking them all down will be a good bit of work," Sharp said. "And yes, sir, they're all scattering. Not even maintaining unit cohesion. All laser fire has stopped. Except the AV. It's still on course for the gate. And still wasting its laser on North. Some of the battleships aren't going to get out of our basket. Depending on how long it takes to take down the AV, we'll still be able to get most with missiles."

"Range?"

"Twenty thousand kilometers," Sharp said.

"Maneuver control, rotate to engage the AV," Kinyon said. "Open fire as you bear, Captain Sharp."

"Aye, sir!" Sharp boomed. "Arrrh!"

✳   ✳   ✳

"*Troy* drive has ceased operation," Colonel Koax reported. "Fire is still engaging anything that enters its basket. Whoa! Heavy grav signatures. Not sure what . . ."

"It's rotating," Lhi'Kasishaj said. He'd been watching the visuals, unlike the colonel. "It's rotating to engage *us*."

"This is going to be unpleasant," Koax said, sitting back and lacing his fingers across his chest. "And, I suspect, not particularly quick. Permission to speak frankly, sir?"

"What am *I* going to do about it?" Lhi'Kasishaj asked. "Denounce you?"

"Didn't care for you much until a moment ago," the colonel said. "Don't like you high-born much at all. But somebody finally killing that idiot Gi'Bucosof was a sight for sore eyes."

"Not surprising," Lhi'Kasishaj said. "Except for people that matter, I don't try to be charming. And you don't matter. You don't survive in upper circles by being nice to minions. You save that for your superiors."

"I shall keep that in mind, sir," Koax said. "For about thirty seconds. Missile launch."

An AV mounted six hundred and eighty-three laser defense clusters. The clusters could rapidly engage and retarget missiles, permitting each cluster to take out multiple inbound vampires.

As long as there wasn't something in the way like a previously destroyed missile filling space with chaff. Then not only were following missiles screened by the material, even if they *could* be targeted the laser, often as not, hit some bit of a previous missile and scattered.

The *Troy* was down to firing a thousand missiles per second. Normally, they would be impossible to detect with the naked eye. But the track of the missile stream headed for the AV was easily followed as a rolling storm-front of explosions as missiles sacrificed themselves on the altar of pawns.

The tide slid inexorably closer and closer to the embattled AV. Finally, the wall of moving fire reached the screens of the battlewagon, which went black under the power of hundreds of penetrators.

The missiles clawed at the screens for a moment before they failed.

The AV rolled frantically, trying to spread the damage. All that did was kill more and more shields as a thousand nuclear wasps turned the *Dwarf Marauder* into the system's largest navigational hazard.

"Admiral, we're down to low yellow on missiles," Sharp said. The series of previous battles had lowered their missile stores. Taking out the AV was essentially depleting them.

"Finish it off with the laser," Kinyon ordered. "Take it all the way out. I don't want anything larger than a sedan drifting into Glalkod. Retarget remaining missiles on the fleeing battleships."

"Aye, sir," Sharp said. "Retargeting."

"Admiral," Captain DiNote said. "We've got shuttles returning from Objectives One and Two for resupply and reinforcements. They're having a good bit of trouble subduing the Rangora holding the docks."

"Maneuver control," Kinyon said. "Get us reoriented

to return to the docks area. Seems we need to indicate our interest."

"I think they'll get the picture," Sharp said.

Colonel Bolger looked through the hole in the overhead at the mass of the *Troy* drifting above, then slightly lower at the Rangora commander of Objective One. Bolger wasn't a small guy. The Rangora overtopped him by a good three feet.

"We've got a couple of choices here," Bolger said, rolling his chew from one cheek to the other, then spitting. "I can pull my guys out and then the *Troy* can do to you what it just did to your AV. Or you can play nice and we'll take you to Earth and you can rebuild a couple of cities for us. We even feed you guys, which is a really good deal."

Arranging the cease-fire had been a bit tricky. The Rangora were sort of territorial by instinct. Having human Marines running around in one of their docks was not their idea of acceptable behavior.

"What terms are you offering?" the admiral asked.

"Binary solution set," Bolger said. "You surrender and we don't kill you."

"Repatriation for myself and my officers," the admiral said.

"Why?" Bolger asked. "You're going to have your heads on a block when you get back. This way you *might* live."

"That is a valid point," the admiral said. "What about our wounded?"

"You've got docs," Bolger said, shrugging. "We don't kill off the wounded if that's what you mean."

"Then . . . I formally surrender," the admiral bit out.

He reached for his sidearm, carefully, and handed it over butt first.

"Gonna make a nice souvenir," Bolger said. The pistol was the size of a laser carbine. "Admiral Kinyon, Objective One has surrendered."

"*Roger that,*" Kinyon commed. "*Two is still fighting but I think that's the Pathans, to tell truth. They don't seem to understand the concept of cease-fire. Ask the admiral to come up to the* Troy *to discuss details.*"

"Gung ho, sir," Bolger said. "And . . . we're done here. Except for the fiddly bits."

EPILOGUE

"Send a missile through the gate to Glalkod," the President said as she watched the replay of the battle. "Set to broadcast. Tell the Rangora it's time to negotiate."

"Yes, ma'am," the new secretary of state said, shaking his head. "Parameters?"

"Earth control of E Eridani is the minimum I'll accept at this time," the President said. "Start with withdrawal by the Rangora to the positions they held before the Multilateral Talks."

"That is . . . broad," the SecState said. "Give up not only the Glatun Federation but all the bordering star systems? They won't go for that."

"No, they won't," the President said. "But they will eventually. Eventually, they'll accept unconditional surrender."

"What am I looking at?" To'Jopeviq asked. The holo was an activated gate with . . . something coming out. Beor had slid the data crystal in and started his holo without as much as a word of explanation.

"Holo from the Glalkod squadron," Beor answered

as the view zoomed in. Manually based on the unsure movements.

"That is . . . *was* a destroyer," To'Jopeviq said as the view panned with the remnants of a *Gufesh*. It moved back to the gate as more debris started coming through. Most of it was unrecognizable. Occasionally he could pick out bits from parts of ships. Bits of *Cubofof, Gufesh* and *Sheshibas*. Half an *Aggressor*. It looked as if someone had taken an entire fleet and run it through a shredder. There were lights of distress pods among the debris. At least some of the crews had survived.

Then there was a mass burst of debris. It had spread out so it nearly filled the gate and its trajectory was going to scatter it throughout the system unless someone got busy on clean-up soon.

What it *had* been . . . ?

"And that is what is left of the *Dwarf Marauder*," Beor said. "Marshall Gi'Bucosof and Marshall Lhi'Kasi-shaj's flagship. The largest single piece, other than escape pods, was nine meters on a side. Which had to be deliberate. Most of it was laser fire."

"What happened?" To'Jopeviq asked.

"The *Troy* is mobile," Beor replied. "It entered the E Eridani system and engaged the fleet there."

"*Mobile*?" To'Jopeviq said. "How?"

"The answer still has everyone hissing in disbelief," Beor said. "The Terrans left after taking possession of the AV docks and support ships. We have intelligence from survivors. Including some ships that scattered and successfully hid from their sensors. You'll have access to *all* of it. High Command has increased the importance of this working group. I'm . . . not privy to internal discussions. The information I've received was that someone pointed out that so far we've been right and command has been consistently underestimating the Terrans. That has to stop."

"I'm not sure it is possible to *over*estimate them," To'Jopeviq said, standing up. "Bring that to the briefing room along with whatever other intelligence we got. Get the rest in there. We have work to do."

"Absent companions," Bill Erickson said, raising his glass.

The Acapulco was still under reconstruction. Moving *Troy* had involved a certain amount of . . . slosh. Most of the roof had been ripped off. Xanadu, in general, looked as if it had been hit by a tsunami. But it was open for business and people couldn't live forever on air and food alone. A certain amount of beer was paramount.

"Absent companions," Dana said, clinking glasses with Rammer.

"And there's a bunch of those," Chief Barnett said, sitting down at the bar. There was a small guy with her, bearded and clearly civilian. "This is Butch, guys. He's a friend of BF."

"Where is BF?" Bill asked.

"Bought it," Butch said.

"How?" Dana asked, her eyes widening.

"We were clearing a stuck laser tube," Butch said. "Got hit by a missile. Figure the plasma got him."

"Damn," Bill said, raising his glass. "Absent companions again."

"Lost a lot of good people," Barnett said, taking a sip of her beer. "But that's what war's all about. And change. Speaking of which, Dana. The orders aren't cut, yet, but you're transferring to the *Thermopylae*."

"What?" Rammer said. "Why?"

"The One-Four-Three is monumentally screwed up," Barnett said. "They finally screamed for help. You're going to be going over there as part of that. I didn't want to give you up but the CO correctly pointed out that sending only our crap couldn't be defined as help. So...last call, so to speak."

"I guess this is as good a time as any, then," Dana said, sliding out of her chair and pulling off her T-shirt. She turned around so her back was to the group. "What do you think?"

The technical term was "back-plate," a tattoo that covered the entire back. In this case, a spear-armed and heavily armored hoplite, crossing spears with a similarly armored Rangora against a starfield. Between them a comet streaked across the firmament. At the very core was a *Myrmidon* shuttle. The artist had managed to convey that the shuttle was both intact and part of the fire of the comet.

On her left upper arm was the symbol of the *Troy*, a Trojan's helmet with the words Winter and Born above and below, respectively.

"That is *smokin'*," Butch said.

"Cost me a good bit," Dana said, trying to crane her head around to look at it. "But I think it was worth it. The ink's a Glatun nano formula that's regenerating so it's gonna last more or less as long as I do."

"Just one problem," Barnett said.

"Which is?" Dana asked.

"Now you're going to have to get a *Thermopylae* tattoo. One of them upside down Vs."

"Yeah," Dana said, climbing back onto her seat. "What's up with that?"

Tyler watched, his arms crossed, as the weavers got to work on the North sector of *Troy*. "Glory to the Brave" boomed through the *Starfire* loud enough that it could probably be heard in space.

The upper quadrant had been thoroughly mauled in the battles, the hull gouged down nearly two hundred meters. Fixing it was a major job. A plate of steel formed from a good sized asteroid had been welded into place by SAPL and now they were getting serious with armor. The same weavers that had created the lines and supports for the Bespin gas mine were perfectly capable of weaving fullerene armor. Since North seemed to take most of the damage, they were starting there.

The main bay was open and modules were sliding through to be installed. New crew quarters, shuttle bays, missile fabbers and everything else that made it a battlewagon were being produced at prodigious rates by Alliance countries as well as the fabbers in the Wolf system.

One of those, though, was moving. He looked to his left as the gate activated and nodded as the mass of Hephaestus trundled through. *Paw* tugs surrounded it like baby chicks, herding it carefully towards the main bay. Some of the ships had taken damage in the battle and there were a dozen shuttles to replace. After that, the fabber would get to work producing shield generators for the battle globe.

Station Three was already on its way inward, slowly cooling behind its solar shield. It would be in place before the repairs were completed on the *Troy*. And Four was about to be ballooned while Five and Six were in various processes of production. The total work was absorbing a good bit of the resources that *Troy* needed. But there would always be repairs, upgrades, improvements. More power. More missiles. More lasers. More deadly. More *fell*.

Troy was mobile. And unless the negotiations over the Eridani system went Earth's way, it was going to need all of that and more.

Troy was no longer a battlestation. *Troy* was a ship in all but name.

Ships lived to move. Battleships lived to move forward. To seek the enemy and destroy him. The best defense is a good offense.

It might take some time, but *Troy* was going *forward*.

And she'd be bringing friends.

AUTHOR'S AFTERWORD

Yep, it's *another* eulogy.

As noted, my mother was born in Brooklyn, oldest of three children, during the Roaring Twenties. She still remembered the recipe for "bathtub gin" since her parents, Irish and Swedish descent, were *not* Prohibitionists. (Nor, as shall become apparent, was she.)

She grew up attending Catholic and New York public schools, at the time some of the best schools in the country if not the world. Despite what would now be considered an academic schedule similar to the top-end private schools, she graduated from High School (PS 129) at sixteen. She would have graduated at fourteen but her mother insisted that she be "held back" twice. (Fourth and eighth grade.)

In 1936 (the height of the Depression, mind you) in New York, sixteen year-old young ladies were not considered appropriate candidates for Columbia working on a physics degree. (Which was her top choice, she once told me.)

Her biggest story about school was getting into an argument with a nun as to whether the sun and the moon could be up at the same time. "All you have to do is go outside and *look*!" She had never heard the story about Galileo's "It still moves." When I told it to her, she laughed until she choked.

So she went to work for a small advertising agency on Madison Avenue as a secretary. One can only guess she was a VERY good one. It is notable that on an Underwood manual she could type 120 words a minute.

During the War she tried to join both the WACs and the WAVEs and was turned down because, respectively, she had not had her tonsils and appendix removed. (The latter she had removed in Iran in 1974. But I get ahead of myself.)

She was finally accepted as a Red Cross hostess in 1945 and went to France. There she served coffee and donuts to the enlisted men at Camp Wings (named after the cigarettes, by the way) and, as the stories came out over the years, partied *hard* with the officers. (*"There was this one full bird colonel that was convinced he could get me drunk enough to sleep with him. He didn't know I had a hollow leg so every Saturday night I'd match him drink for drink until they had to carry him back to his quarters. Then the party could really get started."* She told me this story when I was . . . ten I guess. I think it was in Iran. But, again, I get ahead of myself.)

In 1946 she met and married my father, William Pryor Ringo. On the subject of Dad, as one of my brothers pointed out, "There were two girls in the entire camp of 4000 soldiers and Dad married the prettier one." When it was time for her to get a wedding dress she was taken to a warehouse in Paris where some thousands of Parisian-designed wedding dresses were stored, having been seized from the

Germans who considered them loot. She was told to pick one out and it would be fitted for her.

The picture of my father and mother, she in her top-tier Paris design dress and he in his pinks-and-greens uniform, is still a family treasure. With the advent of computers it was scanned and rendered and blown up and there was a faint mark on my father's forehead that appeared to be genuine. Years afterwards, in their declining years, my father admitted it was a mark from where his French mistress had hit him with a wine bottle, the morning of the wedding, when he announced he was getting married and they would have to break things off.

One begins to understand my personal oddities.

They had their honeymoon at a castle in Scotland that was a rest and refit post for officers.

They returned on their fiftieth wedding anniversary.

She did a small favor for someone, the memory of the story is blurred by time, and in response they gifted her with a puppy. A blooded Pyrennes Mountain Dog. She smuggled it back on the troopship but quickly realized she couldn't keep it and be a young mother at the same time. She, in turn, gifted him to a wealthy friend from her New York days.

The dog became one of the basis lines of all Pyrennes in the United States today.

Upon returning to the United States the brilliant, cosmopolitan, New York party gal found herself the wife of a student at the University of Kentucky, her husband the scion of a deeply Old South family and her mother-in-law a dyed in the wool Daughter of the Confederacy and Old South high-society matron. My grandmother was, of course, dealing with the fact that her baby had brought back a Brooklyn accented Yankee party-girl war-bride who was (GASP!) *Catholic*! Ringo family legend has it that the family, then Huguenot, had to leave France due to a death sentence for desecration of Catholic altars and stealing the offertory vessels. Ringos had been staunch Protestant ever since. (We also used to own part of Wall Street and lost it to political shenanigans. True tale. It now belongs to Trinity Church.)

On the Morris side my maternal grandmother's reaction was alleged to have been "Oh my God! Janey's marrying an *Italian*!"

She adjusted. She learned to cook fried chicken. She told me later that living in the South had deepened her faith because as often the lone Catholic she had to show the heathen Protestants that Catholicism was not, in fact, devil worship.

Over the course of seven years she had five children (two miscarriages) and nearly as many moves. ("Every move is like a fire.") Back to New York for a few years when my father had his engineering degree. Chattanooga (Hi, there!) to work on the new Interstate Project. Miami, where due to some bad timing they had a little (but much loved) oopsy! they named John. (And, yes, it was after the gunfighter.)

One of my brothers says that I'm the proof that the rhythm method is *almost* perfect. "One mistake in fifty years is pretty good odds."

Wherever they went she adjusted. She coined, I believe, the term "domestic management specialist." She raised six children if not calmly (HAH! My mother had the temper of the Irish.) then well. One Ph.D., one civil engineer, one entrepreneur, one homemaker, one small business owner and, ahem, one best-selling author. Not too shabby.

She was a "professional volunteer" for pretty much everything but notably continued with the Red Cross for decades. (Eventually rising to Director of Volunteers for the Southeastern United States.) She had the all-time highest level of recruitment of "Negroes" (the way it was listed at the time) for the Red Cross.

She was a volunteer for the funeral of the Reverend Doctor Martin Luther King while we lived (the first time) in Atlanta. (My sister Mary Jane, thereafter, was shunned at her high school because she'd gone to the funeral of "that nigger.") Notably, she got Julian Bond and his wife out early (they had to catch a train to DC) through the security cordons by slipping into her best Southron accent and sweet talking her way past the Georgia State Patrolmen.

She was raised a Republican and died a Republican. She was a strong Right-to-Life supporter and marched in Civil Rights parades in the 1950s and '60s. She supported the Vietnam War and considered Jimmy Carter a traitor for giving up the Panama Canal. She stated in 1956 that "The United States and Russia are never going to have a nuclear war because we're too similar." (For those who aren't old enough, this was heresy especially for a Republican.) She volunteered for the Goldwater and Reagan campaign. She voted for Nixon but was, at best, unsurprised by the revelations of Watergate.

She gave up cigarettes when they went to fifty cents a pack (cold turkey) and donated the money to Christian Children's Fund. She continued to donate (at higher levels) over the subsequent decades. If you'd like to make a contribution in her name, I would be honored. She broke with the Red Cross when, in her words, "They started caring more about the money they made from blood than military families or disasters." She also supported the Audubon Society and The Nature Conservancy.

She considered environmental groups like Sierra Club and Greenpeace to be "run by communists and idiots."

In the 1970s, the older kids having mostly left the nest, she finally got to travel. And travel we did. Each summer she would pack me into the car and off we'd roar across the eastern United States. (Did I mention she had a lead foot?) Visiting friends, visiting relatives. (Even, believe it or not, visiting Graceland because "You might as well see it while we're in Memphis.") As we'd pass through towns she'd point to the interstate signs. "That's us. 'Through Traffic.'"

I learned to navigate using a highway map at the age of eight. When I was nine she finally accepted I could in fact use it better than she. (In Des Moines. "I *told* you it was the *second* exit! We're headed to *Sioux Falls*, now! There's no place to turn around for twenty miles!") She was, and remains ever in my heart, the Queen of the Open Road. There's a touch of Viking in the Morris genes, I swear. ("Aviking" from which we get "Viking" means simply "To Travel." However, see above the thing about temper.)

We rarely lived anywhere that didn't have either a pool or a swimmable lake. Mother had grown up as much as anything on Long Island and continued to visit beaches and swim well into her sixties. Which is why I learned to swim before I could walk.

In 1974 my father was transferred to Iran to work

on a petrochemical plant between Abadan and Bandar Shapur. He was in Abadan for three weeks, "home" in Tehran for one. I was left very much alone with mother.

For the first time since WWII, mother got to *really* travel. I, perforce, was sucked along in her whirlwind. Over the course of the next two years she (and often I) traveled. My *God* did she travel. Twice to the USSR, then in the depths of the Cold War, and where she was "detained" by the KGB not once but *both* times. The first a matter of having some rubles in her purse on the way out, which was whatever is Russian for "verboten," the second because she publicly went off on an officious KGB major in the Moscow Airport. After her second visit she was awarded what she often considered her highest honor: She was PNGed. (Declared Personna Non Grata. "Do not EVER return to the USSR. Ever ever.")

Jordan, Egypt, Israel (on the same trip, by the way, which was tough to do, you had to have the Israelis stamp a piece of paper instead of your passport), Greece, most of Western Europe. Afghanistan. She was stuck on the Kandahar Airport tarmac for eight hours "waiting for the temperature to drop enough the plane could take off." She met bandits in the Khyber Pass and nearly was trampled at a bushkazi game. She was offered ten thousand dollars (a lot of money in 1975) to divorce Dad and marry a Kuwaiti sheik. A trip from Pakistan to Turkey by rail where she shared her compartment with a deserter from the U.S. Army during Vietnam who made his way by gem smuggling. She also met the Queen of England (tea) and the Empress of Iran (private audience).

We walked every station of the cross and just

about every spot that Jesus walked in the Gospels. The Garden of Gethsemane, Bethlehem (back when you could go there without bodyguards), Nazareth, all *three* of the alleged tombs. Remote Greek Orthodox monasteries with artifacts old enough they might have some originality. (One which had been established by Helen of Constantine of whom Mom, honestly, might have been the reincarnation.) I once had a pair of loafers I referred to as (you have to say it) "The holiest shoes in the world."

At her funeral one of my brothers was to deliver the eulogy and he was asking for "special stories" about Mom.

Few of her children really had them. They had mostly grown up in a very normal suburban lifestyle. Classic 1950s "Ozzie and Harriett" with the fillip that "Harriett" was brilliant, beautiful and short-tempered. Most of their stories were about Mom's tirades when she'd come home from the grocery store. (Did I mention the *really* short temper?)

I could barely choose. Finally, I settled on this one.

It was 1976, the year of the Bicentennial. Mother had decided they had been in Iran long enough. Dad would cling to a project, absent another immediately available, until forcibly removed. She was tired of Iran. So, as was her wont, she left. She went to Greece. I'd already been sent to the States in '75 due to "deteriorating conditions" in Iran. She told my brother to get me over to Greece. (Another story. Birmingham, AL, to Athens, Greece, unaccompanied. Unusual to say the least for a thirteen-year-old in 1976.) Eventually, Dad still not willing to leave, we decamped from Athens to the island of Skiathos.

She also had a habit of picking up strays. Not pets. Kids. It was nearly the height of the hippie movement and she had raised six children. When she saw hitchhiking kids or kids making their way through Greece in this case, she tended to bring them home for a home-cooked meal. (One of whom has become a major "New Age" guru. She picked him up on an Easter Sunday in Florida because "We had a spare seat at the table and he looked like Jesus.")

In this case it was a set of four, two girls, two guys. For those who have seen the movie *Bottle Shock* (and if you haven't, you might be surprised how much you like it) the prettier of the two was the spitting image, including attitude and dress, of the blonde.

The girls supported their bum boyfriends by working in a restaurant down on the waterfront in Skiathos. It was only accessible by a narrow alleyway down the steep hills of the town or by sea. It fronted on a narrow strip of sand and the Aegean.

The family that ran it were also the suppliers. Each day they'd bring in whatever they'd caught to the narrow strip of beach and that was what you ate.

(For those who have read *March to the Sea*, you may recognize the description . . . "Good writers create. Great writers steal." ☺)

The eldest son was having a birthday party and since Mom had been so nice to the two Americana girls we were invited.

Have you ever seen *My Big Fat Greek Wedding*? It's understated. The booze flowed . . . Freely doesn't describe it. Of course you had to have a stomach for retsina, ouzo and chiparo (sort of the white lightning version of ouzo). But I did. Yes, I was thirteen. See the thing above about "oddities." There is, however, a special hell for whichever ancient Greek decided that anise and turpentine should be drunk together.

The hour being late and we needing to meet our usual taxi driver, Mother, the blonde young lady and I began to navigate our way back to the other side of town up the (very) steep hill.

Which, as it turned out, was where all the fishermen of the town gathered to be away from the tourists. Every second building, it seemed, sported a taberna on its ground floor. Most of them had room for no more than five or six tables but they were all packed.

And the fishermen of the town had taken much the same attitude towards the pretty blond Americana girl as the colonel in France had towards my mother. If they could just get her drunk *enough* to overlook the goiters and baldness and lack of teeth, *surely* she'd sleep with *one* of them!

So as we passed each of the tabernas there would be a glad cry and at the outmost table (which I've come to think they *deliberately* kept open) would appear a bottle of retsina and, we being with her, three glasses.

I really must try to describe retsina for the fortunate many who have never experienced it.

Take a *very* bad sauvignon blanc or Graves. The sort of thing you only bring out at the very end of the party and go "well, we're out of all the good, medium and pretty bad stuff..."

Mix it one part to four with Pine Sol.

You have retsina.

I'm serious. *Pine. Sol.*

The trick to retsina is to drink *a lot* of it *very* fast

right from the beginning. After that you really have no *clue* what you are drinking. Aqua Velva starts to taste like Domaine.

Fortunately, we'd already *had* a lot of retsina. (And ouzo and chiparo and, Christ, maybe there *was* some Aqua Velva in there. *I* wouldn't know. You really don't care after you've been drinking retsina long enough.) So this was, as it were, a shower bath in a hurricane.

However, the custom was that you could not leave the table as long as there was wine (for values of wine) left. And as soon as we got down to the bottom of the carafe of ("OH, HOLY GODS NOT *MORE*! (Wide happy grin, wave!) *Kalispera! Kalispera!*") retsina, someone would order up another carafe.

The trick was to drink down to near bottom on the three glasses (which meant slamming two thirds as fast as possible) then pour the rest of the carafe, slam *that* then wave and RUN.

To the *next* taberna where a glad cry would be raised.

Thirteen.

I don't remember making it to the top of the hill.

The thing is, I'm not even sure that's the *best* story of traveling with my mother. Then there's the "traditional Danish smorgasbord," the old Greek captain, the "incident" at the Jordanian border, the party in Bangkok, Cameron Highlands, the Swiss franc thing in Bavaria, Gletsch!, the bus tour in Italy, "All-Of-Paris-in-Twenty-Four-Hours" . . .

People wonder where I get my female characters.

My mother died in her home in the Georgia hills with her son Bob and daughters Mary Jane and Sally at her side of "complications of pneumonia." She had been ready to go since the death of my father (see Gust Front). She had lost all ability to read (her passion). Sans ears, sans eyes, sans teeth. It was time and a grace and mercy. The mother I traveled with had been dead for many years. I did not, do not, grieve for the final crust that left this mortal coil. I do rather miss the bon vivant with whom I once toured the world.

If there is a heaven my mother died in the state of perfect Grace her Catholic calling required. They say that rain is the sign of the death of a saintly woman and mother died on a rainy day. She left on this coil six children, nine grandchildren, five great grandchildren and a trail of acquaintances who will remember her until their own passing. Through a thousand gentle mercies I cannot begin to recount, she touched the lives of tens of thousands. Even had she gotten that physics degree, I doubt she could have done more for the world had she perfected Unified Field Theory.

If there is a heaven may it have an open road, a red roadster, her love by her side. May the roads be swift and clear. May there be fine restaurants and taverns at every crossroads and may she ride upon the wind with all the saints by her side.

For my mother, that would truly be heaven. Gletsch!

—John Ringo
Chattanooga, TN
February 2010

The following is an excerpt from:

WOLF AMONG THE STARS

* * *

STEVE WHITE

Available from Baen Books
November 2011
hardcover

CHAPTER ONE

NATHAN ARNSTEIN'S LIFE was not an especially long one, but it spanned a great deal of eventful history, some of which he himself made.

He was born in 2011, in what still called itself the United States of America, although it had only a few years to go before the Earth First Party would seize power and rob that name of all it had once meant.

He was nine years old when the Lokaron ships appeared in Earth's sky and began dictating trade treaties. His father, a naval officer sidelined by lack of Party connections (and under constant suspicion for being Jewish), was a sympathizer of the Eaglemen, the secret organization of American junior military officers dedicated to the restoration of the Constitution and the expulsion of the extraterrestrials.

He was nineteen years old in the epochal year when the Earth First Party was overthrown, Earth narrowly saved from devastation at the hands of the Lokaron *gevah* of Gev-Rogov, and the Confederated Nations of Earth formed.

He was twenty-eight, and a junior officer in the United States component of the new CNE Navy, when he distinguished himself in action against the Islamic jihadist diehards in the last flareup of resistance to the new order.

He was thirty-seven, and one of the rising stars of the CNEN, when he was sent to the planet Harath-Asor to study state-of-the-art galactic military technology at the feet of humanity's Lokaron allies of Gev-Harath. He learned his lessons well, and later thought of applications of them that had never occurred to the self-satisfied Lokaron military establishments.

He was fifty-five, and an admiral, when he settled an old score at the Battle of Upsilon Lupus, annihilating the fleet of Gev-Rogov and forcing a Lokaron power—for the first time in the history of the galaxy's dominant race—to sit across a peace table from non-Lokaron. And nothing would ever be the same again.

He was fifty-nine, and nearing retirement, when he was named to the prestigious post of director of the CNEN Academy.

He was sixty-three when his chief of staff found him with his brains blown out.

"Is the director in, Midori?"

"Yes, Captain Roark. Just one moment, please." The secretary turned aside to make the adjustments necessary to admit even those who, like the chief of staff, had automatic access to Admiral Arnstein's inner sanctum. It gave Andrew Roark a moment to glance through the transparency behind her desk. It was a view that would have been breathtaking even if one hadn't known its history.

The Academy was perched on the edge of the rim wall of a vast impact crater, with North America's Rocky Mountains circling it in the distance. The crater was, beyond comparison, the youngest of its kind on Earth, and the elements had not had time to smooth out its brutal contours. Only four and a half decades ago, in fact, part of the Rockies had stood here: Cheyenne Mountain, in whose depths the headquarters of the United States military had been buried, safe even from nuclear bombs. But not safe from a deep-penetrator kinetic weapon like the nickel-iron asteroid that the Lokaron of Gev-Rogov had accelerated, using a titanic mass driver, into a high-velocity trajectory that had intersected Earth at this point just before dawn on a never-to-be-forgotten autumn day in 2030, decapitating Earth's defenses and inflicting ecological wounds that had taken years to heal. It had been meant to be a mere preliminary to the saturation neutron-bombing that would have left the planet a lifeless tabula rasa to be reseeded for Rogovon colonization. That had been stopped by the Lokaron of Gev-Harath, and by two humans who had nearly died doing it.

Everyone knew all this. But Andrew Roark knew it better than most, for those two humans, Ben Roark and Katy Doyle, had given birth to him four years later.

Afterward, the Confederated Nations of Earth had placed its space-navy academy here, using Lokaron nanotechnology to sculpt the rim wall into terraces and buildings in an architectural style incorporating all of mankind's major traditions, looking out over the crater's floor of congealed magma. Those who studied here could never for a moment forget their service's reason for existence, which could be distilled into two words: *never again.*

"You can go in, Captain," said the secretary, interrupting his thoughts.

"Thanks." He proceeded through the door to her left and into a short corridor. He had long since ceased to notice the slight tingle as he stepped through the invisible curtain of stationary guardian nanobots. The security wasn't excessive, for the Director was a far more important individual than the commandants of the service academies of the last century had been. In the CNEN, his authority extended to a wide range of advanced training functions in many locales, including the hyper-prestigious Strategic College, through which the elite of the Navy's leadership must pass.

Andrew came to the final door, which slid open as it sensed his genetic signature. The director's private office was a spacious one, understatedly elegant, the walls hung with honors. A shelf to the right bore models of ships he had commanded, including CNS *Revenge,* his appropriately named flagship at Upsilon Lupus. To the left was a holo-display tank that would have done credit to a capital ship's bridge. Behind the expansive desk, a wide transparency gave an unequaled view of the crater, including the pylon that rose at its exact center, inscribed with the names of those—worthy and otherwise—who had died in the Cheyenne Mountain strike.

Andrew Roark had seen the office a thousand times. Its familiarity explained why a detectable fraction of a second passed before that which was behind the desk registered on his brain, despite the stench of death that immediately hit his nostrils.

Admiral Arnstein still had a pistol clenched in his hand—a standard M-3 gauss weapon, Andrew automatically noted. It used an electromagnetic pulse (not energetic enough to have set off the alarm system) to accelerate a high-density 3mm bullet to a muzzle velocity of 2,000 meters per second with a crack as it broke the sound barrier (not loud enough to have penetrated the soundproofing of the multiple doors). It had a full-automatic capability, but it appeared only one shot had been fired; Roark now saw the hole, with a radiating pattern of cracks, where it had struck the right-hand wall. Unlike the needlelike metal slivers fired by civilian gauss weapons, such a projectile at such a velocity resulted in massive hydrostatic overpressure as it passed through a human head, causing the brain to explode outward, blowing out the top of the skull. Admiral Arnstein was slumped face down on the desk, and Roark was looking directly into such a cavity. There was blood and fallen brain tissue everywhere around the body; some of it had stuck to the ceiling.

Modern medicine, drawing on Lokaron technology, could perform what would have been thought miracles of tissue and organ regeneration only half a century before. But nothing could be done about a destroyed brain. The admiral could, of course, be cloned. But the clone would not be the man under whom Andrew had served at Upsilon Lupus; it would be another man with identical genetic makeup, doomed to early aging and death as a result of having been produced from postembryonic cells taken from an adult body. Such use of cloning was interdicted by both law and custom.

All this flashed through Andrew's mind in a second, before the onset of nausea brought him out of shock. He sternly clamped his jaw shut and said *"No!"* to his stomach. Then he raised his left arm and spoke into his wrist communicator in a voice whose steadiness surprised him. "This is Captain Roark. Security to the director's office!" Then he stumbled forward, reminding himself not to touch anything. The scene must be left scrupulously undisturbed for the investigators.

He walked gingerly around the desk, looking for a suicide note. There was none. But a little plastic case of the kind used to hold datachips caught his eye. He looked more closely at it: it was marked with a tiny black symbol...and, for the second time since entering the office, he froze into immobility. There could be no mistake: it was a silhouette of a dog... or, more likely, a wolf.

For a few seconds, he thought very hard.

He heard a commotion outside. He reached a decision. He scooped up the case, put it in his pocket barely in time, then smoothed out his features and turned to face the security detail.

—end excerpt—

from *Wolf Among the Stars*
available in hardcover,
November 2011, from Baen Books

The following is an excerpt from:

HIMMLER'S WAR

ROBERT CONROY

Available from Baen Books
December 2011
hardcover

CHAPTER 1

The B17G bomber was almost universally referred to as the "Flying Fortress," and for good reason. Painted olive drab on top to blend with the ground below, and with a sky blue belly for camouflage from enemies looking skyward, the bombers weighed more than thirty tons and bristled with .50 caliber machine guns. The designers at Boeing originally felt that the bomber would be able to defend themselves against attacks by enemy fighters, and still deliver up to three tons of bombs far into Germany. She could speed over Europe at nearly three hundred miles an hour, had a range of nearly two thousand miles, and could fly at an altitude of more than thirty-five thousand feet. Everyone felt it was a helluva plane.

Like many well laid plans, it didn't work out that way. Despite all her weapons, the bomber was vulnerable to attacks by German fighters, in particular the swift and deadly Messerschmitt 109G, a sleek single-engine fighter that savaged the formations when the bombers were required to fly without escorts. Since American fighters had much shorter ranges than the bombers, Nazi fighters often waited until escorts ran short of fuel and had to depart. The drop tank on the American P51 fighter was supposed to stop that and, in large part it did. Range was extended and bombers were better protected.

But everything had gone wrong this otherwise bright and sunny day in mid June 1944. The small flight of eighteen bombers was supposed to meet up with the escorting fighters, but the P51s never showed. Some snafu? Very likely, the angry bomber crews thought, but what the hell else was new. The flight's commander, an ambitious major who wanted to make colonel before the war ended, determined to soldier on. The fighters would either meet him or they would not. It didn't matter—he had a target to bomb and a promotion to earn. And, since the D-Day invasion at Normandy had been successful, it was thought that collapse of Nazi Germany was imminent, certainly by the end of 1944. Ergo, the major didn't have time to waste. His career was at stake.

Their target was not a high priority one. It was a factory complex near the city of Landsberg, which was north and east of Berlin. There were fewer and fewer German interceptors in the air and the major felt that this small group of bombers was unlikely to attract attention. Even though their attack would take them well into the Third Reich, it was considered little more than a training run.

Several of the eighteen bomber crews were on their first combat flight, and that included the men of the "Mother's Milk." The name had been chosen while several of the crew had been drunk on English beer, and they compounded their mistake by hiring an artist of dubious talent who painted a farm girl on the fuselage. She wore a halter top, extremely short shorts that showed much of her cheeks, and a toothy smile. And she had grotesquely enormous boobs that other crews considered laughable, which pissed off the Milk's rookie crew who were further teased by being called "Milkmen." They accepted the nickname and used it among themselves.

Twenty-four-year-old First Lieutenant Paul Phips was her commander and he was scared to death as well as freezing his ass off. He was not a warrior. Small of stature and slight of build, he reminded people of a Midwestern grocery clerk, not a bomber pilot. The truth was not that far off. He'd been in his first year as a high school teacher in Iowa when the draft grabbed him, and he still had no idea how he'd passed flight school.

This run had been their initial exposure to possible combat and that had caused more than enough stress. The more experienced crews had teased them, calling them Virgins or Cherries, and saying they'd shit their pants the first time they were shot at, all of which didn't help the crew's fragile morale.

As always, they were cold, despite the fact that they were wearing multiple layers of clothing. The wind whipped through the bomber and their heavy flight suits, even though they were plugged into the plane like electric blankets, didn't do much. The fear and the cold sapped their resolve and the Milkmen wondered just why they had become bomber crewmen.

Before dropping their bombs, disaster struck. They'd been jumped by a dozen or more of the allegedly non-existent ME109s that knifed down from above and shot down or damaged several bombers before anyone could even notice. So much for don't worry about German planes, Phips and his crew thought as they maneuvered wildly to evade their swift enemy.

Their flight commander's plane was one of the first destroyed, which rendered the remaining crews leaderless. As the fight became a mindless brawl, Phips made a major mistake. He'd run. Instead of staying with the survivors and forming up defensively, Phips sent his plane lower in altitude and flown to the west in the hope that he could escape the attacking German sharks.

Instead, two of the MEs had stayed with him, chasing the bomber and dogging it. Phips swore that they were taunting him as he gradually gained control over the bomber and his fears.

"What the hell do we do now, skipper?" asked his co-pilot, Second Lieutenant Bill Stover. The sarcastic tone of voice was not lost on Phips, who was well aware that he'd panicked and screwed up royally.

Stover continued. "In case you haven't noticed, they're chasing us south and west. In a while we'll run out of gas and have to bail out even if they don't manage to shoot us down first."

"I know," Phips muttered. Despite the cold, he was sweating profusely.

The tail gunner, Sergeant Ballard, broke in. At thirty, he was the old man and his deep voice had a calming effect. "Skipper, it looks like one of them is pulling back. Maybe he's running out of fuel."

Phips prayed it was so. The ME only had a range of about three hundred miles and must have used up a lot of gas chasing the bombers around the sky. Maybe the second one would have the same problem.

No such luck. As time dragged on, the lone ME stayed behind them, darting in and out, firing an occasional burst, and looking for an opportunity to make a kill. The German respected the bomber's many guns which fired short bursts every time he got within range. It looked like an impasse but it wasn't. As long as he had fuel, the German held all the trump cards. At least they were low enough that the men of Mother's Milk didn't need oxygen to breathe.

"Skipper, will you take a suggestion from your beloved navigator?"

Phips managed a weak smile. "Yes, Mister Kent."

"We are getting farther and farther away from Mother England. If you want me to find our way home, we've got to stop this running shit and head back."

Damn it, Phips thought. It was time to make up for his mistake. "Okay, we turn and attack the bastard."

The German must have thought that the plane's sudden and sharp banking to the right was an indication of damage and he dashed in for the kill with his machine guns and 20 mm cannon blazing. Pieces flew off the bomber and Phips heard shouting through his headset. Loose items caromed off the inside of the hull.

"Carson's hit!" someone yelled. Christ, Phips thought. One of the waist gunners was down. "Oh, Jesus, he's bleeding all over the place." The wounded man's screams carried up to Phips who felt nauseated as the bomber continued its stately turn.

Suddenly, the German fighter pilot found himself

facing an array of .50 caliber machine guns from the side, top, and belly that spewed torrents of bullets in his direction. Now it was the German's turn to panic and he tried to escape. As he did so, he exposed the belly of his plane for just an instant. A handful of bullets ripped through his engine. It started to smoke and the ME began to fall back.

"Christ almighty," yelled Stover. "We got us a kill."

The German pilot fell from the plane and a parachute opened. The ME was gone, but the pilot would live to fight another day. Now the Mother's Milk had to do the same damn thing—live to fight another day.

"How's Carson?" Phips asked.

"Dead, sir."

Phips sagged over the controls. His first mission and not only had he disobeyed orders to keep formation, but he'd gotten lost, and a crewman, one of the guys he'd been with for six months, had been killed. Now he had to make sure this miserable situation didn't get any worse.

"Navigator," said Phips. "Where are we?"

"Over Germany, skipper."

Damn smart aleck, Phips thought. "Can you possible narrow that down, Kent?"

"Seriously skipper, I'm trying, but we were all over the sky for a little while and I need a frame of reference. I think we're over East Prussia and now we are heading towards Russia. I suggest we turn north and west and hope to God we find something that makes sense, like the Baltic Sea. I also suggest we lighten our load. We've got a few tons of bombs doing nothing but weighing us down and using up our fuel."

Stover turned toward Phips, his expression still

unforgiving. "We can go north to Sweden if we have to, bail out, and be interned. That assumes, of course, that we can even find Sweden."

"Yeah," Phips responded angrily, "and we'd be interned for the duration of the war and who knows how long that'll be. The experts say it'll be over in a few months, but with our luck it might just be decades. It also presumes that the Swedes won't turn us over to the Nazis. I hear the Swedes spend a lot of time kissing Hitler's ass since the krauts are right next door to them. And, oh yeah, we might just accidentally bail out over Nazi-occupied Norway or over those nice people in Stalin's Soviet Union."

It was common knowledge that Russia had interned some American and British fliers and wasn't keen on returning them. Winding up chopping frozen rocks in Siberia was not a pleasant option.

Kent chimed in. "Again, I suggest we turn north and west in hopes of finding the Baltic. At that point, I further suggest we stay over the water until we hit Denmark, and I mean that figuratively and not literally."

"Good." agreed Phips. "And then we can cut the angle by flying over Denmark. I don't think the krauts will waste sending fighters after one lousy lost bomber." Of course, he thought, nobody thought their little flight of eighteen bombers would have been attacked by so many German fighters.

"Sounds like a good plan to me," Kent said and Stover sullenly nodded agreement. "But when are you going to dump the bombs? We will need that fuel if we're going to make it back."

"I don't have a target," Phips said.

Stover shook his head in disbelief. "Christ, chief,

we're only a couple of thousand feet over Germany. The whole fucking country's a target. Just drop the damn things."

Phips thought for a second and decided he agreed. Finally he felt he was doing the right thing. Maybe he could recover from this nightmarish day. Back in England, he'd be criticized for his mistakes and the loss of Carson, but maybe, just maybe, he'd be allowed to learn from them and fly again. Regardless, his first job was to get them home.

"Just for the record," he said, "does anybody see anything that even remotely looks like it could use a good bombing?"

Stover's eyes were the sharpest. "Looks like a cluster of buildings coming up in the woods to our right front. And I don't see any red crosses or anything."

"Got it," said Cullen, the combination nose gunner and bombardier. "We'll use the Norden and drop bombs in their helmets."

It was a feeble attempt at a joke. The super-secret Norden bomb-sight was better than what anybody'd had before, but it was far from precise. Even at their low altitude, they'd be lucky to hit the compound.

"What the hell?" Phips said in surprise. Anti-aircraft guns had opened up at the last second and black puffs of flak were exploding well above them. Whoever was down there was as surprised as he was. At least their shooting was off.

The bomb bay doors opened and more cold wind whipped through the plane. They might be closer to the ground and it might be the middle of summer, but it was still like being in a savage winter storm. A few seconds later, the bombs fell, and Mother's

Milk, freed from their weight, lifted. Now Phips and the Milkmen really began to feel that they might just make it back to England.

"Anybody see if we hit anything?" Phips asked.

The only one with a view of the target was Ballard, the tail gunner. "Well, sir, we did hit the ground. Seriously, some of the bombs did fall in that cluster of buildings. Not a clue as to what kind of damage we might have caused. Looks like we've outrun the flak, though."

And we'll probably never know what we hit, Phips thought. An unwanted realization popped into his head. If they did make it back, he'd have to write a letter to Carson's family explaining how he'd died heroically and painlessly when the poor guy had really died screaming and bleeding all over the plane like a stuck pig.

A few hours later they had crossed Denmark and were again over water. They sighted a gray smudge on the horizon. Kent assured Phips it was England, Mother England, and they all breathed a sigh of relief. They were very low on fuel. A pair of British Hurricanes flew by and took up position on either side. They were used to nursing cripples and would guide Mother's Milk back to an airfield. They'd be on fumes when they landed, but they had made it. It was the middle of June 1944. Allies had landed in Normandy and the men of the Mother's Milk were still part of the war.

Finally, Phips could relax. He did wonder just what they had managed to bomb on their first and so far only run over Germany. He hoped to God it wasn't a girls' school or an orphanage. But then, how many girls schools were protected by anti-aircraft guns?

✧　　✧　　✧

Colonel Ernst Varner walked away from the undistinguished one-story wood building that was jammed with the military hierarchy of the Third Reich. For the moment it was the site of the OKW, the Oberkommando der Wehrmacht, the headquarters of the German military. The Wehrmacht controlled the regular army, the Heer; the navy, the Kriegsmarine; and the air force, the Luftwaffe. A walk in the surrounding woods was what Varner needed to clear his head. The air within the building was stale in more ways than one.

Varner had been inside a few moments earlier and had actually heard Adolf Hitler speak emotionally and illogically about solutions to the military dilemma confronting Germany. And, the more he heard his Fuhrer pontificate, the more he realized the little man with the mustache was delusional at best.

Varner hadn't always felt that way about his Fuhrer. As a younger man he'd been an ardent supporter of Hitler and an early member of the Nazi Party, which had, in part, helped him reach his current rank at the age of thirty-eight. Of course, being a legitimate hero and combat veteran who'd seen action in both France and Russia hadn't hurt either. His wounds suffered fighting the Russians were still healing and it was decided that he would serve better as a staff officer and aide to Field Marshal Wilhelm Keitel, the army's chief of staff and a man Varner had come to realize was little more than a spineless toady. Keitel would not question Hitler's orders no matter how preposterous they were. And many of them were well beyond preposterous. The chief of operations, General Alfred Jodl, was even worse. Both would simply nod and send men out to die.

Varner had been told he'd soon be promoted to general, but now wondered if it was worth it if he had to suffer working for fools like Keitel and Jodl.

Varner reached for a cigarette and recalled that he had given up smoking at the insistence of his wife, Magda, and his fourteen-year-old daughter, Margarete. They said it was a disgusting habit. Varner agreed, especially since the only cigarettes available in wartime Germany were absolute shit rolled in paper. He'd picked up the smoking habit to contain stress while fighting the Red Army outside Stalingrad. Now he needed to combat the stress of listening to Hitler.

"Here," said a voice from behind.

Varner laughed and took a cigarette from a fellow staffer, Colonel Claus von Stauffenberg. They had met in the hospital while being treated for their respective wounds. The darkly handsome Stauffenberg had lost his left eye, right hand, and two fingers on his left hand when his vehicle had been strafed in North Africa. Varner had been wounded in his upper left arm and shoulder, and doctors were still trying to remove shrapnel that moved and sometimes caused him great pain. Varner was shorter than the lean and aristocratic Stauffenberg. He was stocky, like a tank. This was serendipitous since Varner's specialty was armor. His dark hair was thinning and he was thankful that Margarete got her pixy looks from Magda, a woman he thought was far above him. Varner would never be mistaken for a blonde and blue-eyed Aryan superman.

Between the two of them, they managed to light up. As always, the cigarettes were awful.

"Why aren't you in there with the others?" Varner asked.

Stauffenberg almost snorted. "Because it's too crowded and they don't need me to help them make their mistakes. I think it's incredible that there's still doubt as to whether the Allied landings in Normandy are the real thing or are just a feint. The Fuhrer does seem to be coming around, however, and no longer insists that Pas de Calais is the eventual main target instead of Normandy. However, the decision has come too late to throw the Allies out."

Varner was surprised at the other man's candor. Stauffenberg's comments were dangerously close to a criticism of Hitler, which was not a wise thing to do, especially for a relatively low-ranking staff officer, hero or not. Disagreements had a nasty habit of being interpreted as treason. Some very high ranking generals had argued with the Fuhrer and were now languishing in obscurity.

He and Stauffenberg, while friendly and cordial, were not close enough to share intimate thoughts and Varner wondered just what the other colonel was thinking. Was he being sounded out, and if so for what purpose? Rumor had it that Stauffenberg was not an enthusiastic supporter of either Hitler or the Nazi Party. Well, Varner now had his own doubts.

Varner decided to make light of it. "I left because it was obvious I wasn't important enough to stay."

Stauffenberg laughed. "Perhaps being unimportant is a good thing. If you're careful, you can become invisible."

Casually, they walked farther from the building where the meeting was taking place. It was in the headquarters complex and command center near the Prussian city of Rastenberg. Hitler liked to come there to be away from Berlin, a city he heartily detested because of its perceived decadence. Hitler had few vices. He rarely drank and ate sparingly. Varner thought Hitler had a mistress, a plump blond named Eva, but no one was certain. Varner decided he didn't care.

Berliners returned the favor and did not appear to love the Hitler as much as other parts of Germany did. Most of the field marshals and generals vastly preferred the luxuries and flesh pots of Berlin. Varner would have preferred being in Berlin, but only because his small family was there.

Sirens went off and anti-aircraft guns began to fire. Varner automatically looked skyward. "What the devil?"

A plane appeared, flying low and fast. A bomber. Dear God, he thought. It was an American B17.

The two men ran to a slit trench and dived in just as the bombs began to explode. The earth shook with the power of the bombs and Varner felt he was back in Russia with Red Army artillery shells raining down on him. He tried to control his fear. Shock waves washed over him and he realized he couldn't hear. Dirt and debris rained down on them.

Finally, he sensed there was silence and lifted his head. Stauffenberg lay still in the bottom of the trench. His skull had been crushed by a falling piece of metal, and his one eye was dangling out of its socket. Varner crawled out of the trench and gasped in horror at the desolation. Then one thought occurred to him. What about Hitler?

He lurched to the building he'd just left. It was in ruins. There were great clouds of smoke, but little in the way of flames came from it. Survivors were staggering about and a handful of people were trying to pull others from the wreckage. It was utter chaos and he realized that some people were screaming as his hearing returned. Nobody was in charge. He realized that Germany might have just lost her leadership. Whatever doubts he might have about Hitler, he could not allow Germany's enemies to realize she was leaderless.

Varner took a deep breath. He would be the man in charge. He grabbed a dazed looking lieutenant and two confused enlisted men. His hearing had largely returned, although his voice sounded tinny to himself. "You. Go to the radio center and shut down all communications. Nothing comes in and nothing goes out. Do it on my authority on behalf of the Fuhrer and if anyone balks, kill them."

The three men saluted and ran off to do his bidding. He did the same with a handful of others, sending them to the gates of the compound. Again, his orders were that nobody comes in and nobody goes out.

Recovery efforts at the devastated building seemed to be progressing. Medics were crawling around through the mound of rubble. One of them was holding a dismembered leg and there was a row of bodies on the ground. Several survivors walked around in a daze, their uniforms torn to shreds.

Varner forced himself to look at the dead. Keitel, the man he'd referred to as a toady lay face up with a look of perpetual astonishment on his face. A medic informed him that Jodl was badly wounded, with both of his legs blown off and would be dead within minutes.

He was about to ask about Hitler, when a desperate

shout and howl of emotional pain came from the men searching the rubble. They had found the Fuhrer.

Debris was removed and a doctor climbed down beside the pale and crumpled body of Adolf Hitler. Varner followed. Hitler's eyes were open and staring at the sky. He wasn't moving. "Is he alive?" Varner asked.

The doctor shook his head sadly. Again it was time for action and Varner realized what had to be done. "Doctor, you are quite wrong," he whispered. "You will announce that he is badly wounded and must be taken to the clinic. You will do it immediately and without anyone seeing his real condition."

The doctor, stunned, was about to argue when he realized what Varner was telling him. "Stretcher!" the doctor yelled. "We need a stretcher now! Get the Fuhrer to the clinic immediately. His life may depend on it."

Hitler's limp remains were put on a stretcher and covered with a blanket that exposed only part of his head, presenting the illusion that he still lived. The bearers almost ran to the clinic with the doctor alongside. Varner was now comfortable that only he and the doctor knew that Adolf Hitler was dead.

—end excerpt—

from *Himmler's War*
available in hardcover,
December 2011, from Baen Books